*season
of
desire*

Also by Sadie Matthews

The After Dark Series
Fire After Dark
Secrets After Dark
Promises After Dark

Sadie Matthews is the author of six novels of contemporary women's fiction published under other names. In her own work, she has described decadent worlds of heady escapism and high drama. The After Dark series was her first provocative romantic trilogy, exploring a more intimate and intense side of life and relationships. She is married and lives in London.

Find Sadie Matthews on Twitter
@sadie_matthews.

season
of
desire

SADIE MATTHEWS

HODDER

First published in Great Britain in 2014 by Hodder & Stoughton
An Hachette UK company

First published in paperback in 2014

1

A CIP catalogue record for this title is available from the British Library

Paperback ISBN 978 1 444 78110 6
Ebook ISBN 978 1 444 78111 3

Typeset by Hewer Text UK Ltd, Edinburgh
Printed and bound by Clays Ltd, St Ives plc

Hodder & Stoughton policy is to use papers that are natural, renewable
and recyclable products and made from wood grown in sustainable
forests. The logging and manufacturing processes are expected to
conform to the environmental regulations of the country of origin.

Hodder & Stoughton Ltd
338 Euston Road
London NW1 3BH

www.hodder.co.uk

To T.G.

CHAPTER ONE

I storm out of the study, slamming the door behind me. My father's voice follows me – 'Freya, stop it, come back!' – before the heavy oak door cuts off the sound.

'Goddammit!' I exclaim, frustration and anger bubbling around inside me. I would say something a lot worse if it wasn't for the maid who is dusting the enormous gold lamps that sit on the console tables in the hall. She looks up at me, apprehensive, as though she's worried I'm going to throw something in my fury. I look her straight in the eye and say loudly, 'I'm not a baby!'

'No, miss,' she agrees swiftly, and goes back to polishing the lamp.

'I refuse to be treated like one!'

'Yes, miss.'

I feel momentarily ashamed for involving her in my family troubles – she's not paid enough to put up with that – and try to calm down a little. I sigh and head down the dimly lit corridor to my suite of rooms. I don't like this place. My father had it built a couple of years ago – he has a ceaseless passion for creating and acquiring homes – and I've never warmed to it. We used to have a cosy chalet on the outskirts of St Moritz, an old-fashioned, charming place that I adored. But my father decided that it wasn't new or different enough, and soon there were six different architects working on plans for something really

1

special. It took years to complete but at last my father has what he's always wanted: a super high-tech and ultra-modern mountain eyrie, like something out of a Bond movie – except, of course, it's exactly the sort of place where the villain would live, though I've never pointed this out to him.

In fact, in some ways I'm as frightened of my father as I used to be of those sneering bald evil-doers who always decided to kill Bond in a slow, inventive way, giving him plenty of time to escape. My father is, after all, known all over the world, having built his fortune in airport construction, and then branched out into shipping to create a vast empire that means our family name – Hammond – has become synonymous with buckets of cash. And you don't become a success like that without being ruthless. Then there's my father's controlling streak. He has no intention of letting me or my sisters grow up and he keeps a beady eye on me wherever I am in the world. I might seem to have an enviable life, but the truth is that I'm never really free, even when I'm away from him.

I open the door of my rooms, stalk inside and slam it shut behind me. My bags are sitting in the middle of the room, packed as per my instructions. I know that inside each layer of clothes has been separated by sheets of fine, acid-free tissue paper. My shoes have been stuffed with more tissue and placed reverently in their soft cotton bags. Jewellery – I only travel with a few simple pieces unless there's a really big party in the offing – is locked into my Asprey's case, and the key is kept cunningly hanging from my charm bracelet.

I gaze at my bags and say loudly, 'Damn it all to hell!'

'What's the problem?' says a cool voice behind me.

I turn to see my sister Summer standing in the doorway. She's technically the youngest of us because even though she and Flora are twins, she arrived second, and I think she's the prettiest too, with her fair hair, willowy figure and the winsome gap between her front teeth. But, in my opinion, she's also the most spoiled, a daddy's girl if ever there was one.

'Nothing,' I say, turning back. 'I'm on my way to the airport.'

'Oh right.' Summer saunters into the room. She is the epitome of mountain chic in a cream cashmere polo neck and dark ski leggings worn with leopard print ballet flats, her glossy blonde hair spilling over her shoulders. 'Going somewhere nice?'

I grit my teeth. I'm not in the mood for Summer right now. And why the hell is she in my rooms? Isn't there enough space in this crazy glass and steel construction for her to steer clear of me? 'LA,' I say briefly. 'To stay with Jimmy.'

'Uh huh.' She nods. She gets this. We all love Jimmy. He was our polo coach when we were in the States and one of the most beautiful men we'd ever seen, knocking spots off movie stars and models. Just remembering how he looked as he played a chukka makes me happy: he was tanned, his dark hair windswept, a pony between his muscled thighs, a mallet swinging as his biceps bulged, and beads of sweat on his perfect nose. We all loved him madly but Flora, the older of my twin sisters, loved him most. She truly believed they would get married. When Jimmy announced he was gay and moved to LA to become an actor, no one was surprised, apart from Flora. When she heard the news, she dropped to the ground in a dead faint. It was all very dramatic, which is par for the course with Flora.

'Give Jimmy my love,' Summer says, approaching my luggage. A scarlet wool shawl embroidered with black skulls is draped over the largest case. She picks it up. 'This is nice.'

'Put it down. It's going with me.'

'McQueen?'

'What do you care? It's mine.'

She throws me a look. 'Keep your hair on, I'm only asking. Honestly, Freya, what's with you? You're so touchy!' She narrows those blue eyes of hers. 'Have you had a row with Dad?'

'What do you think?' I snap back. Rows between Dad and me are pretty much the norm these days.

'What about this time?' I can practically hear the eye roll, even though Summer has turned back to inspect my luggage again. It's all right for her. She and Dad are still in perfect harmony, just like I used to be – before I dared to want some independence for myself.

'None of your business.'

'Something to do with Estella?'

'None of your business!' I repeat. I am seriously annoyed now. Just the mention of Estella's name is enough to ratchet my anger levels up a few notches. 'Now, I'm leaving, okay? So get out of my room, go back to your own.'

Summer shrugs and heads slowly back towards the door. I feel bad suddenly. She's pretty young after all, only twenty-one. And maybe she's lonely, just like I am, locked away up here on the side of a mountain. We have everything we could possibly want in this place – as long as what we want can be bought.

I swoop up my scarlet scarf and wrap it around my shoulders as I stride over to catch up with her. 'Wait – you can walk with me to the elevator if you want.'

4

She flashes me a smile and I get a glimpse of that cute gap between her teeth. Dad always wanted her to wear braces and she refused, and now I can see why. It gives her good looks a special something. Character, I suppose.

'How long will you be gone?' she asks, as we head out of my suite and start walking along the quiet, grey-carpeted corridor towards the lift. This place is always quiet and dark – because it's built into rock, I guess. Half the house is concealed deep in the mountain. The other half defies gravity as it juts out over the mountainside, with spectacular views of the Alpine valleys and peaks, the glass walls and floors giving a dizzying perspective. I always feel a little safer in the back of the house, knowing that I can't possibly plummet through the solid rock around me.

'Not long,' I reply. 'But I don't think I'll come back here. The weather is seriously depressing.'

Summer nods. 'It snowed all night. They say it's getting worse.' She frowns. 'Are you sure you'll be able to fly today?'

'Of course. It's not that bad. It has to be pretty deep before they ground the flights, and it's not even snowing now. I'm sure they'll have cleared the runway.'

'Where will you go after LA?'

I shrug. 'Somewhere warm!'

'I might go to London,' Summer says tentatively. 'Do you think you might go there too?'

I look at her sympathetically. She's only a kid, really. She needs me, I remind myself. Ever since Mother died, she's looked to me for guidance, which I never felt qualified to give, considering how lost and helpless I felt myself, but I guess it's my duty now. Despite her closeness to Flora, Summer still seems to need the support of someone

5

older, perhaps because she and Flora are often apart. At least she's not looking to Estella – I have to be grateful for small mercies. 'Maybe I will. Keep in touch. Tell me where you're going. Send me an email when you know.'

That's the way our family operates. Any of us could be anywhere in the world at any given time. Maybe if our mother were around, we'd have more of a sense of home, but as it is we're constantly on the move, bags always waiting to be packed or unpacked, heading off to one of the many places Dad has acquired around the world, bumping into each other half by chance, unless we're summoned to a particular place at a particular time. Then we all know better than to disobey orders.

'Who's taking you to the airport?' Summer asks, as the elevator light flashes and a tiny bell pings to let us know that it's arrived. The doors slide open.

I scowl, my good humour evaporating. 'The new guy.'

'Miles?' Summer's china-blue eyes open wide.

'I guess so . . .' I step into the plushly carpeted, mirrored interior of the elevator, and jab the basement button with my finger.

'What's wrong with him? Don't you like him?' she demands, but before I can reply, the doors slide closed and she disappears from sight, replaced by the brushed aluminium of the elevator door.

'No, I don't like him!' I declare to my reflection in the mirror opposite. My brown eyes glare fiercely back at me and I can see how cross I look. There's a creased furrow between my brows and my mouth looks set and tight-lipped. I'm not wearing much make-up beyond a little mascara and a slick of lip gloss, and I'm dressed for travel in jeans and long black boots with heels that are a little too high to be practical, a red woven tunic under a puffy black coat, and a glossy black leather handbag slung over one shoulder. My brown hair is cut in a sharp bob, with a fringe that skims my eyebrows and a pair of sunglasses nestles on the top of my head. They're not for the sunshine – after all, there are steel grey skies outside – but in case I get photographed at the airport. The press and airport photographers are always about and if they spot me, you can bet that within minutes, I'll pop up on some website. I'll be praised for my chic outfit or admired for my figure, or else attacked for having a sulky expression (as if I'm going to grin happily at people taking my picture without asking) or slated for my expensive jet-set lifestyle. I never know what line they'll take, and neither do they, I suspect. I can see the headline now: *Hammond heiress takes her eighth holiday of the year! Lucky little rich girl has no idea how the rest of us live . . .*

The truth is that they have no idea of what really goes on in my life. Lately they've all been wondering about my break-up with Jacob. They want to know all the gory details but so far it's a secret that hasn't been leaked. Maybe it's too hot to handle, even for the tabloid press. They know that lawyers and injunctions would slam down on them and there would be big legal bills involved.

But if they knew what was on the tape locked in my father's safe, they would probably pay any amount to get hold of it.

The image flashes into my mind. It was a terrible day when I was forced to watch that film, sitting there with my father and the lawyer on either side of me as it played on the computer screen. I was horrified at what I was seeing and deeply embarrassed.

'Is it him?' my father asked.

I'd nodded, half paralysed and unable to drag my eyes away from what Jacob was doing, even if I was revolted by it.

'You're sure?' pressed the lawyer. 'How can you be certain? His face isn't visible.'

'The tattoo,' I whispered, my heart breaking as I watched the man I'd thought I would marry thrusting his erection into the mouth of a willing girl. 'On his thigh.'

You'd never have noticed it if you didn't already know it was there: a letter F in a curling script inside a tiny padlock.

'You see?' my father had said triumphantly. 'I told you! All along, I told you but you wouldn't listen. He's a gold-digger. A gigolo. Now do you believe me?'

'Yes,' I'd whispered, and stood up on shaking legs. 'But I loved him!' and then I burst into tears.

I know my father was acting in my best interests but I can't help hating him for interfering in my life, for exposing the truth to me and for causing me such pain. Perhaps it would have been better if I'd never known about Jacob's predilections for call girls and all the things he liked them to do to him. But I suppose I would have found out one day: after all, we'd received the tape with a blackmail demand that the lawyers swiftly dealt with. It's just a fact that the Hammond fortune attracts a lot of low-lifes hoping to get a piece of it for themselves. I learned that lesson once before, and now I've had to learn it again with Jacob.

My reflection in the elevator mirror shows the pain in my face. My eyes are no longer cross but full of wretched-ness as I think of the painful break-up. It's only been a few months and I'm not over it. Not at all.

'That's why I'm going to LA,' I say to myself firmly. 'A few days with Jimmy and I'll be fine again. Anything to get away from here.'

I look up at the elevator ceiling, wondering if it's wired for sound. I know there's a camera in here. They're everywhere, their little red lights flashing as they record people coming and going inside the house. Security, Dad says. We can never be too careful, we all know that. There are, apparently, none in the bedrooms or bathrooms, but I wouldn't put it past him to secret those beady little glass eyes behind mirrors and into the fittings so that he can be absolutely sure what's going on. Big Brother has nothing on my dad. As a result, I have to behave like everyone is watching, and it makes for a stiff, furtive kind of a life.

The elevator has glided swiftly down the six floors to the basement level. I've never even been out on to the first and second floors. They're the engine rooms of the house, where the boilers, electrics, heating and air-conditioning systems are to be found. There are also storage rooms, the security centre, and a control hub that monitors the use of the elevators, garages, and even the doors and lights. I know one floor houses the laundry because sometimes I catch a sniff of freshly cleaned hot cotton as the elevator passes it. And there are staff bedrooms and an industrial kitchen. But like I say, I've never been there.

The doors open onto the dimly lit foyer that leads to the basement and garages. A man is sitting on the black leather sofa, checking his phone. He's frowning, a crease between his dark eyebrows, and I can see the fine line of his very straight nose. As I stride out into the foyer, he stands up, sliding his phone into his jacket pocket. Then he fixes me with a stare, that half-challenging look he has. It's irritated me since the moment I met him two weeks ago, and that irritation is getting more intense, not less. He says nothing but waits for me to speak.

'Is my luggage on its way?' I demand.

He raises his eyebrows quizzically and then shakes his head. 'I've no idea. Have you asked for it to be sent down?' He has an accent that I haven't quite identified yet.

I draw in a breath huffily. 'I would have thought it was obvious! Has it not occurred to anyone that I'm going to need my things?'

He goes over to a small table where one of the internal phones sits, sleek and black, and picks up the handset. 'It's always more effective to tell people what you want rather than expect them to read your mind.' Before I can frame a retort, he presses a number and a second later says, 'Yes, can you bring Miss Freya's luggage to the garage immediately, please? It's in her room, I assume. Thanks.' Glancing back at me as he replaces the phone, he says, 'Would you like to wait in the car?'

I stare at him, irritation crackling over my skin. Why does everything he says annoy me so much? It has to be his attitude. It stinks. Everyone else treats me with respect. They can't do enough for me. But this man . . . something about him gives the impression that, deep down, he thinks I'm ridiculous. I hate that. How dare he? My father pays his wages and he ought to remember it. It's why I hardly ever call him by his name. What is it? Summer said it just a few minutes ago. Oh, that's right. It's Miles. Well, until he learns his place, I won't be calling him anything.

I decide to remain in the foyer as it's the opposite of what he's just suggested I do, but there's no reading anything into his impassive expression. He simply stares back at me and waits for me to speak.

'I'll wait here,' I say airily, and go over to the black sofa.

'Very well,' he says. His accent is Scottish, I think.

Who cares? I sit down. He can come from Cloud Cuckoo Land, it makes no difference to me. He might be a little more good-looking than most – it's impossible not to notice that he's got those remarkable blue eyes, chiselled cheekbones and a strong square jaw, and that his dark jacket sits well across his broad shoulders – but he's just another in the long line of bodyguards who've been a part of my life for almost as long as I can remember. He'll be around for a while, and then he'll leave, like all the rest. Only Pierre, the grizzled head of my father's security, has stayed.

I check my phone for messages. Another dozen or so have hit my inbox in the last twenty minutes, organising the complex social life that binds me and my friends together. Our playgrounds are all over the world and when we pop out for a girly night, it might be that we'll need a plane to take us to our venue, and a yacht to stay on when we get there. We sisters used to have an assistant – Estella – to help us with our complicated lives. But since Estella became my father's girlfriend, we've roped in Dad's PA, Jane-Elizabeth, to help. We love Jane-Elizabeth, with her jokes and her adoration of very expensive shoes, and even though she complains about us like crazy, she loves us too.

If only Dad could have fallen in love with Jane-Elizabeth, I think wistfully. It was secretly what we all hoped for, and it's plain that she adores him. But once Estella arrived on the scene and made her play for Dad, Jane-Elizabeth didn't stand a chance. He was entranced by the wide green Bambi eyes, scarlet pout and the pneumatic figure she showed off in tight dresses and high heels. *Estella.* I hate her. We all do.

The elevator doors open and a man comes out carrying my luggage. I stand up, one eye still on my messages. We all move in silence towards the garage doors, then we are in the vast dark room, full of powerful gleaming machines and smelling of rubber and oil. Our footsteps echo on the concrete floor as the bodyguard leads me to the black Mercedes, the model that we are usually driven in. Dad has explained the security benefits: it's bomb- and fire-proof, apparently, and heavily reinforced. Super safe.

The door is opened for me and I slide onto the back seat, tapping out a message as I go. The interior smells of polish and new leather. My luggage is placed in the boot and then the bodyguard climbs into the driver's seat and starts up the engine. I'm vaguely aware we're moving, the powerful car purring its way out of the garage, then we're outside.

Great, I think, blinking in the grey light. In just a few hours I'll be in sunny California. *Free at last.*

Or as free as I ever am.

CHAPTER TWO

I hear a noise. The bodyguard is talking to me. I look up from my phone.

'What?'

His blue eyes fix on me in the rear-view mirror. 'I said, the weather is terrible.'

'Is it?' I look out of the window. He's right, the world is completely white outside, the snow piled up in huge drifts. Something has been through to clear the mountain road but it's still thick with ice and studded with grit. I gaze out with a kind of detached curiosity. Things like the weather rarely affect me. If I want sun or snow or whatever, I just go wherever it can be found. I'm well insulated from events like floods or tornados, the things that happen to other people. My world is so protected that the weather is just the occasional mild irritant when it interferes with my plans. Like today.

'Why are we going so slowly?' I demand, looking at my watch. I don't bother arriving for the usual check-in time. I fly so frequently and have so many VIP memberships, that I'm usually ushered straight from the car to the plane. If I'm late, it's been known for planes to wait for me.

Those blue eyes land on me again, as cold as the weather outside, before they return to the road. 'We're going slowly because it's bloody dangerous out there. The road's like an ice rink.'

'It's what you're trained for, isn't it?' I retort. 'Put your foot down. I'll be seriously annoyed if I miss this plane.'

'Your plane might not be going anywhere. There's obviously more snow to come any minute now. The sky's heavy with it.'

I feel a surge of panic at the idea that I might not be basking in Californian sun later today. The thought of returning to the mountain house makes my hands clammy. 'No. You've got to get me there. Go faster. I can't be late, just in case they don't hold the flight for me.'

I hadn't realised until now how much I want to see Jimmy. He's one of the few friends I really trust, and I can confide in him about Jacob and all that awful stuff, and he'll understand. I need that right now. I really need a friend.

'Listen,' the bodyguard says gruffly. His accent is definitely Scottish and it seems to be getting stronger. 'Maybe you haven't heard me correctly. The weather is bad and the conditions are treacherous. I can't magic up a way for you to get to the airport or guarantee your plane will take off when you get there. Sorry and all that, but that's how it is. Not even *you* can buy good weather.'

He hasn't bothered to meet my eye in the rear-view mirror this time. Fury surges over my neck and shoulders and I can feel my hands trembling a little. *How the hell dare he?*

'*Don't* speak to me like that!' I say, anger making my voice slightly quavery instead of strong and authoritative, like I'd hoped.

There's a long pause and then his blue eyes flicker up to meet mine. 'I apologise if I've been rude,' he says in a slow, deliberate way. 'I'm simply trying to explain to you that there's not much we can do about whatever Nature has in mind for us.'

'I realise that!' I exclaim. 'I'm not an idiot. But you're supposedly trained for all weathers! Your expertise is what you're paid for, but maybe you're not up to it . . .?'

There's no response from him except for a small quiver of the head as though he's making some kind of expression of anger, but of course I can't see from the back seat. The road descends tight against the side of the mountain in long snaking curves. At its edge is a small railing, all that stands between us and the huge drop down the mountain-side. The view is usually spectacular, of the valley below and the range of mountains stretching away for miles. I'm never afraid. The bodyguards are all ex-SAS and highly trained in advanced driving techniques. I know that they're not fazed by the mountain roads, and after the first few times, the drive loses its power to frighten.

Today, though, there's nothing to see. The cold steely light already seems to be fading and a freezing fog is swirling up from the valley below. It's white and grey everywhere, and we can only make out what is immediately around us.

Oh God, this is awful! We must be travelling at a third of our usual pace. I'll never make the plane if we carry on like this. And I have to get there!

I'm clinging on desperately to the hope that if we can just get to the airport, everything will be fine. Anything rather than go back to that house. Even if I can't get to LA, maybe I'll be able to track down some friends some-where else and try and forget everything in parties and dancing and bottles of champagne and all the usual indulgences.

15

I lean forward towards the driver and now I can see the side of his face. He's not like most of our guards, who are usually big beefy men, bursting out of their jackets like Incredible Hulks. This man has sculpted features, and he carries himself with a kind of elegance I don't usually associate with strength – but he's certainly strong. I can see from the set of his shoulders and the way he's holding the steering wheel that he's tough and muscled. His hair is cropped close to his skull, dappled with silver at the temples and dark brown otherwise.

I try not to sound as if I'm giving him orders. 'Listen, I understand that the weather is not something we can control. But please – if you can – please can you try to get to me to the airport?' I wait. He keeps his eyes fixed on the road and I can see now that he's holding the wheel very tightly as he steers us around the endless hairpin bends of the mountain path. I notice a muscle twitching in his cheek and for the first time I feel a flicker of anxiety. He's clearly working hard to keep this car under control. And, I realise, he can't see the edge of the road with its little barrier, or easily make out the mountainside that usually rears up on the other side. It's been whited out by snow and fog. All he can do is edge forwards, following the icy tracks directly in front.

'Oh, God,' I say, as I begin to take in the reality of the conditions out there. Protected in the Mercedes' warm interior, I've been slow to understand what's actually going on.

Then he speaks. 'I'm doing my best, believe me. One thing's for sure: we won't be going back up this way again, not for a while at least.'

He's right. I feel a little happier. If we can just get down, I can check in at the hotel by the airport until the weather improves. If I'm a day late to LA, it doesn't matter so much. Jimmy will understand.

I begin to ask another question, even though I can sense his irritation. 'How long do you think—'

Then it happens. I don't know exactly what starts it. One moment we are moving forward, keeping in the furrows ploughed out ahead of us. The next, everything has changed. It is as though the road below us has turned into glass, and instead of gripping its surface, the tyres begin to slide. The sensation of movement changes completely, as if we've just driven onto a frozen lake and are gliding out over it. As we skim over the surface of the road, the car begins to turn of its own accord, apparently unaffected by what the bodyguard is doing with the steering wheel. His knuckles are white with effort, and everything about him shows he's using all of his strength to attempt to regain control but we're turning now, the back of the car inexorably wheeling round so that we'll soon be reversing down the mountain.

'Oh God, what's happening?' I shriek, terrified. 'Turn it back, turn it back!'

He says nothing but is wrenching the wheel hard into the direction we're spinning. What good will that do?

'Turn it the other way!' I cry, adrenalin coursing through me, making my hands tingle and shake while my insides whirl with fear. The car is still turning: we're spinning slowly down the road. How long can he control it? Surely we'll hit the mountainside or the barrier before too long.

'I know what I'm doing,' he says through clenched teeth. 'For God's sake, sit back in your seat and get your belt on.'

He's right, of course he's right. I'm feeling sick and dizzy, as we begin to enter a second cycle of a spin. I sit back in the seat as he directed and fumble for the seat belt. It seems to take forever to push it into place, my hands are shaking so badly, but just as it clicks into the socket, everything changes again. I feel the wheels grip the road, gaining traction as they hit a seam of bare tarmac, but it's only for a second and then we're not sliding but skidding over a layer of stones and grit, and a kind of chaotic force seems to take possession of the car. The loose skimming turns have become bumping, jerking, teeth-clattering madness. The white world outside the window judders past.

I hear him shout something out – it sounds like a curse.

The car rocks violently as he applies the brakes, the machine struggling to obey him against the powerful forces dragging it out of his control. Then, as panic fills my chest and throat so badly I can hardly breathe, I sense that we've entered another element altogether. With a sickening crunch, the barrier crumples, the road beneath us vanishes, and we're out into the white void.

It happens so slowly, every instant dragged out to ten times its usual length, as I gasp, suck in a terrified breath and scream. I know it's coming: an impact. I can almost anticipate the hugeness of it. I know it will crush me into my very core. My body is already straining against the belt as the car tips forward and begins to plummet. It veers wildly to one side, hits something and flips back the other way. I can see the blurry vision of the man in the driver's seat still wrestling with the steering wheel. I wonder what the point is, and at the same time I wonder what it will be like when this long tumble is over and we're smashed to oblivion at the bottom of the mountain.

I'm still screaming and yet inside, a quiet, scared voice is saying, 'Will it hurt when I die? Will it be quick? I don't want to be hurt, just let it be fast . . .'

And then another voice screams back in panic, 'I don't want to die! This can't be happening to me, it can't, I want to GET OUT!'

'Let me out!' I'm shouting. 'Oh my God, please! No, no no!'

Then it comes: a huge, elemental jolt that sends me tearing into the seatbelt. A pain fills my chest and then I'm thrown upwards and into a blessed blackness.

When I come to, I have no idea where I am, or why. It's as though a section of my memory has been discarded. I can remember being in the elevator in the house and here I am, lying somewhere strange, cold and uncomfortable. Where am I? And this is more than uncomfortable. *It hurts.*

A voice is speaking to me urgently, its insistent tone piercing the fog that's clouding my mind.

'Come on, Freya,' it's saying, 'come on, sweetheart. You need to move for me. We need to get away.'

I let out a long sigh and a burning pain clamps my chest. My face contorts.

'Are you okay?' the voice asks, a note of anxiety in its measured tones. 'Where does it hurt?'

I feel too tired and confused to speak. I lift one hand towards my chest instead, trying to indicate that I'm in pain there. Every breath is sharply excruciating.

'All right, all right,' the voice says. It's deep and masculine with something comforting in its timbre. 'Take it easy. Shallow breaths, if you can.'

I can smell a strange and powerful scent. It has a metallic quality with notes of burnt rubber and I realise it's fuel.

I try to open my eyes. The world outside is a sharp jumble of black and white. It hurts to try and understand it, so I shut my eyes again. *Oh, I'm so tired. I want it all to go away. I want to sleep and I will too, even though it's so cold . . .*

'Wake up, sweetheart!' It's that voice again, close to my ear this time. 'Don't go to sleep, do you hear me? You've got to put your arm around my neck.'

A strong hand grips my left wrist and lifts up my arm. The pain in my chest bolts through me again and I cry out, but he ignores it, pulling my arm around his neck despite my sob of agony. Then his arm is underneath me, another around my back, and I'm being lifted up. My head lolls onto a broad shoulder as he stands up, taking my weight with ease. Then we are moving with difficulty, jolting and swaying with every unsteady step. He's carrying me through a deep snowdrift, the white blanket masking the rocky, uneven ground beneath. I shudder with cold. In fact, I'm freezing. Why have I not felt this cold before now?

We're moving faster now, we must be out of the deepest drift. I'm being jolted in his arms as he strides through the snow, holding me tightly as he goes. The pain in my chest is agonising, each step stabbing me. There's a sound behind me, a creaking, sliding, crunching noise, and I open my eyes and blink, looking back to where we've come, straining to focus. He stops and turns so that we can both watch. I can see the car now, a concertina'd, broken wreck of bent metal that makes me gasp. The black, twisted body is moving, slowly at first, grinding over the snow-covered stony ridge like a dark glacier, and then gathering pace until it slides over the edge of the plateau and crashes down a hundred feet in a shower of falling snow, hitting the white carpeted valley below. The impact sends up a flurry of snow as the car vanishes into the whiteness.

I can feel the bodyguard's chest rise and fall in sharp breaths, and almost hear his heart thumping.

'That was a close one,' he murmurs, more to himself than to me.

Now I begin to understand our situation. The wild panic of those last few minutes before the car left the road starts to come back to me. I don't know how long it has been since I felt that fiery pain in my chest and lost consciousness, but here we are now, in the freezing wintry afternoon, without our car. I'm rapidly losing body heat. One side of me is warm from the proximity of the guard's body, but the other is chilled and I'm shaking with cold despite my puffy jacket.

He feels my body trembling and with one arm tries to wrap my scarf a little more tightly around me. 'Is that better?'

I can't feel any difference at all, except for a scrap of comfort from the softness of the scarlet cashmere, but I nod anyway.

He looks at me seriously. His face is so close to mine, and I can see right into the depths of his eyes. They are a bright blue with dark rims around the iris, and steely with determination. 'Do you have your phone on you?'

I shake my head. 'It was in my purse,' I manage to say, drawing in enough breath to speak but not so much that it triggers the pain in my chest. 'In the car.'

We both look down again to the place where the car landed. Only a few dark flecks on the snow show its resting place; to anyone ignorant of what it happened, it looks more like a couple of jagged dark rocks emerging from the whiteness than a buried Mercedes.

'Right.' He gives nothing away in his voice but I can guess that this not the answer he hoped to hear.

'Where's your phone?' I ask in a husky whisper.

There's a pause before he replies, then he says, 'Charging on the front seat.'

'Oh.'

'Aye. Not ideal.'

Until now I've been too dazed by my situation to feel much more than relief that I'm somehow still alive after the car left the road. It's amazing that we're both out of the twisted body I saw fall into the valley. But as the reality of our predicament begins to sink in, I start to feel fear gripping me once more.

'What are we going to do?' I ask, staring up at him anxiously. I'm more awake now and more able to process what's going on.

'Don't worry,' he replies swiftly. 'They'll soon realise we're not at the airport. Any moment now we'll be missed and they'll start looking for us. Your father is the kind of man who will move heaven and earth to find you, don't worry about that.'

I wonder how well he knows my father but quickly push that thought out of my mind. Of course Dad will be frantic when he realises what's happened.

'Can we climb up to the road?' I ask, and crane my neck to look over his shoulder at the mountain towering above us.

He glances back as well and says dryly, 'I don't think so. Unless you're hiding some crampons and a few ropes in that jacket of yours.'

I see what he means: there's a steep wall of rock behind us that disappears into the white fog that shrouds everything more than a few feet away. There's no clue of where the road might be.

'Then what do we do? Stay here?'

He doesn't answer at once. Then he says, 'That would be sensible. The car will be warm for a while yet. If they come out with heat-seeking equipment, that's what they'll find. It might be more visible from the air than it is to us in any case.'

'Visible?' I look around at the white, misty world we're lost in. The idea of being seen seems entirely hopeless. I whisper, 'Oh my God.'

'Listen,' he says brusquely, 'we've been lucky so far. We hit the plateau instead of falling bang slap into that valley – that was just a matter of a few feet. And I got us out of the car before it fell. There's no reason why we can't go on being lucky. If we can't go up, then maybe it makes more sense to go down.'

'Down?' The idea is horrifying. 'You can't be serious!' The only way I know of getting down a mountain is skiing.

He glances down at me again, and I'm suddenly aware that I'm in the arms of a total stranger, and even though he's employed to ensure my safety, I am relying on him more than I ever could have anticipated. He blinks at me, his expression impassive. His lips tighten as he thinks. Then, without warning, he turns and carries me swiftly over the snowy ground to the wall of mountain. In the comparative shelter of the sheer mountainside, he puts me down. I'm worried that I have no strength to support myself but as I'm lowered I find that my feet can take my weight, though a cramping pain seizes my chest as I stand on the ground. I can't help whimpering with it.

'Here,' he says, 'let's build you some shelter so you can sit down.'

He starts to hollow out a space in the snowdrift at the foot of the rocky wall, scraping out snow with his bare hands until he has made an oval shape. As he goes about it, he starts to talk in his deep Scottish burr, speaking in a curiously sing-song way that I guess must be to keep me calm. 'So, we're going to be found, don't you worry about that . . . but just in case it takes longer than we want, I have to get you a little warmer. I'm going to tuck you in here and then I'm going to scout about a bit so I can assess our situation. I want to find out where we've fallen and if there are any easy routes out, and if there's a wee bit of shelter in case we have to wait a while—'

He goes on but I've stopped listening, as soon as I grasped the fact that he's going to leave me here in this little snow cave he's made for me.

'Wait!' I cry, putting one hand on his arm. 'You can't leave me here!'

He glances at me and a smile curves his mouth. It's a handsome mouth, I realise, with well-shaped lips above a strong square chin. 'You can't exactly come with me. You're hurt – not badly, I think, but enough to mean you're in no state to walk.'

'I can walk!' I say, panicked. I take a few steps but quickly stumble, gasping with pain. He reaches out and steadies me, one strong hand on each of my arms.

'I don't think so,' he says softly. 'I'll be quicker without you, do you understand? Just wait here and rest, and I'll be back in a jiffy. Don't be afraid. I won't leave you alone.'

'I'm not afraid,' I retort. It's not strictly true but I resent the idea that I'm helpless, a pathetic scaredy cat. 'But if you get into trouble, you might need me to help you.'

A smile flickers momentarily on his lips but to his credit he doesn't allow it to stay there. 'Good point,' he says gravely. 'You'll just have to trust me on this one. Believe me, I've been trained for exactly this kind of situation.'

I look at what he's wearing: jeans, a black jumper over a shirt and a dark well-cut suit jacket over that, a just discernible grey stripe in the black wool. On his feet are well-polished leather shoes, already caked with snow. 'In that get-up?' I say sardonically.

He flashes me a steely look. 'In any get-up. Now sit down and let me get on with sorting out this less-than-desirable situation. God, look at you.'

I'm shaking with cold, and my teeth are chattering. My fingers are numb and yet simultaneously burning with the icy cold. My toes are the same inside my ridiculously thin high-heeled black boots. He steers me back to the snow cave he's made and lowers me down until I'm sitting. Then he tucks my hands inside the sleeves of my puffy jacket – thank God I put it on instead of the sparkly white tweed I was considering – and rewraps my scarlet scarf around me tightly. I let him. I suddenly don't have the strength to resist.

He comes down to my level, his face opposite mine. He's serious now. Very serious. So serious that real fear swoops through me. 'I'm going to leave you, but not for long, I promise. If you hear any helicopters, come out into the open and wave that scarlet scarf of yours as hard as you bloody can, understand?'

I nod, trying to stop myself shaking.

25

'Good. You're brave. I won't be long.'

Then he's gone, his dark form striding out over the snow before it's quickly lost in the fog. I'm all on my own, on a freezing mountainside. And no one knows where the hell I am.

I wait, shivering, trying to recall anything I've learned about survival in cold conditions. I mustn't sleep, I remember. Instantly I feel desperately tired and long only to close my eyes and surrender to my deep fatigue.

No – no! I mustn't. Stay awake, Freya, for God's sake.

I remember that I mustn't drink alcohol because the sensation of warmth it gives is an illusion.

Well, that's very useful, I tell myself sarcastically. *Hold the gin and tonic, barman! I mustn't get tipsy before I freeze to death.*

What else? Stay warm. Stay alert. Try and give a clue of your whereabouts to potential rescuers. All I have is my scarlet McQueen cashmere scarf with its motif of black skulls. If this doesn't stand out against the snow, nothing will. It'll be more use as a flag than keeping me warm.

I struggle to my feet, fighting against the awful clenching pain that grips me when I try to move. What have I done to my chest? Have I cracked a rib? Pierced a lung? Displaced my heart, torn an artery . . .? Cold fear rips through me at the thought that I'm dying from whatever injury I sustained in the car's ricocheting plummet down the mountainside. Every minute that ticks by is taking me closer to my body shutting down completely. Without medical attention, I may be finished . . .

Shut up, I tell myself firmly. *Being afraid is not going to help. Even if I'm dying, I've got to use what strength I have left to help myself as much as I can. Otherwise I might as well curl up here and give up.*

Breathing in short, shallow breaths to keep the pain to a minimum, I pull myself up out of the seat and begin to hobble through the snow into the open. I'm nervous. I've skied enough to know that there could be treacherous hidden ridges, invisible to the eye because of the effect of white on white. I might stride out onto what I think is flat ground, to find that I've walked over the edge. I can understand now that the bodyguard was right – we've been amazingly lucky. This small plateau broke the car's fall down the mountain. The protection of the vehicle's heavy reinforced frame meant that while its outer body crumpled around us, we were kept relatively safe as it bounced from outcrop to outcrop and landed here briefly before sliding on to land in the valley below.

As the slenderness of our escape comes home to me, I'm shaking even harder, and not just from the cold.

Oh my God. I should be dead.

But I'm not. Not yet, at least. And until I am, I'm damn well going to keep trying.

I take the scarlet shawl off my shoulders and lie it down on the snow. It takes a long time to get around it, pulling it out to its full extent. It's about a metre square, the bright red and black vivid against the white. I've nothing to anchor it with, and even though the cashmere seems to stick to the snow, I worry that it will be blown away by the strong wind that comes in freezing buffeting gusts, so I gather up scoops of snow and make small mountains at each corner that I hope will hold it down. My hands are so frozen that I can hardly feel the cold, let alone force my fingers to do what I want, but somehow I manage. When the scarf is weighted down as much as possible, I stumble back to the small snow cave and collapse down, exhausted by the effort and in agony from my chest.

How long has he been gone?

It must be at least twenty minutes, maybe longer. I blink out into the fog, looking hopefully for a dark shape emerging from it, but there's nothing. I wrap my arms tightly around myself, tucking my icy hands back into the sleeves of my jacket. For the first time, I begin to imagine the reality of freezing to death. The heat will leach gradually from my body until there will be no warmth to be had from my skin. My body will begin to close down, cutting off the blood supply to my hands and feet, and my heart will slow. Then, perhaps, delirium will come as my brain begins to lose oxygen, or perhaps I'll simply fall into a blessed sleep that will end in nothingness.

But I don't want to die! I'm too young!

My existence might seem futile to many people but, like everyone, I want to live. I want love, to have a relationship, to have children, to grow old.

Is that not going to happen?

I yearn to be home – even in that awful mountain retreat – with all my heart. I close my eyes and think of my mother.

'Hey! There you are!'

My eyes flick open. I've never been so happy to hear another voice in my life. 'You're back!'

He's there, right in front me, his face grey with cold but his blue eyes bright. He reaches out and puts an arm round me. 'Of course I am,' he says with a laugh. 'Didn't I say I'd come back? And I've got some good news!'

'They've found us!' I cry, relief drenching me like a wonderful warm shower.

'Not quite,' he says quickly, but he's still cheerful. 'I've got us the next best thing. If we have to stay out here, then I've discovered exactly what we need. And I've got to be honest with you – they're not going to find us for a little while yet.'

'They're not?' My spirits swoop downwards and I feel bleaker than I can ever remember.

'Not till this is over.' He gestures behind him into the white air, and I can see that a swirl of snowflakes is falling from the low sky. 'The storm is here. That's why we have to get moving. Right now. Do you hear me, Freya? We've got to go. Now.'

CHAPTER THREE

The journey seems to last forever, but I can only register it as icy stumbling through the cutting, blinding snow. I'm feeling cold now – properly cold, right into my bones – in a way I've never experienced before. It's as though I can never be warm again. The whirling snow is flung into our faces by the searing wind and all I can be sure of is the hand holding mine and leading me onwards.

At least I won't die alone.

It seems impossible that we can survive this storm. It's growing in strength with every second, the wind howling around us and the snow thickening until it's like walking through stinging white water. I don't know where we're going and I don't care. Then we are descending, climbing downwards somehow, and I'm up to my waist in snow, then out again, then plunging into its depths. The body-guard pulls me out and impels me onwards, even though I'm moving in a kind of frozen trance, hardly even noticing my pain. All I want is for it to stop.

Then, after what has felt like hours, he does stop. I am still stumbling forwards and I crash into him, coming up hard against his body. I groan with agony. He shouts something but the wind whips away his words before I have a chance to make out what he has said. A shape looms up before us, but I can't discern what it is. Then he pulls me forward and to my astonishment, I'm sudden out of the howling torrent of the snowstorm and in quiet darkness.

I'm shivering so hard I can hardly speak. I blink, looking about me, my eyes gradually becoming accustomed to the dark. 'Wh– wh– where are we?'

He's shaking snow from his jacket, brushing it out of his face and eyes. 'We're lucky again,' he declares. 'That's three times in a row. We might be at the end of our lucky streak but it may be all we needed.'

I'm gazing at my feet and the rough dirt floor I'm standing on. We're inside, I've grasped that. But where?

He's saying, 'Come on, we have to get you a little bit warmer.'

'What is this place?' I manage to say and this time, he turns back to me with a glowing smile that almost, for a moment, warms me with its happy optimism.

'It's a shepherd's hut,' he explains. 'It was used in the old days for summer lodgings. The shepherds would come up with their flocks for the grazing and stay with them the entire season, before taking them back down to the villages for the winter. It's not been properly occupied for years, though. Now it's used by mountaineers and walkers who need a place to shelter if the weather changes. I've seen a few places like this in the Alps: little stone – we'd call them bothys in Scotland – one-room cottages.' He starts to move around, looking in every corner of the small room. There's a large fireplace on one side just by the door we came in at, and I can see the remains of a fire in it. Along the other three walls are beds or couches, roughly made from crates and planks. A small glazed window is built into one wall on the side that looks out over the mountain, but there is nothing but white to be seen beyond it. The walls are thick

– the windowsill is over two feet deep – and the wind doesn't seem to penetrate them, even though they are bare stone. On the sill are some boxes and the bodyguard is already looking through one of them. 'Aha!' he cries, lifting out a box of matches and a large silver torch. 'Just what I'd hoped for. And look.' He pulls out a laminated card with writing on it. He begins to read out loud. 'Welcome. This hut is for the use of all who need it. Please leave it as you would hope to find it. If you can leave replacements for what you use, or money in lieu, please do. Otherwise, take what you need. This is not a place for holidaymakers but for those in genuine need of shelter, so do not abuse it. It is regularly checked. You are kindly asked to sign the visitors' book to record your presence here. Thank you.'

My eyes are more accustomed to the gloom now. Still shaking violently with cold, I gaze at him. He looks over at me, and his cheerfulness fades a little.

'Right,' he says with determination, 'let's get going.'

He leads me to one of the roughly made beds and I can see that there are sleeping bags on each one. He helps me to sit down, grabs one – a greasy-looking blue bag – and starts to unzip it.

'What are you doing?' I ask.

'I told you, we've got to get you warm. This will help until I can get a fire going.'

'No!' I push the bag away as he tries to wrap it round my shoulders. 'How disgusting! How many people have slept in that? It looks filthy! I don't want it.'

His eyes turn flinty. 'Don't be so ridiculous. What does it matter? You need it.'

'No, I don't, it's horrible. I'll be fine,' I say. I don't know why it matters to me, but the thought of that sleeping bag around me makes me feel ill. I'm sure I can smell it – sweaty, dirty, fuggy with the scent of unwashed bodies. He tuts impatiently and tries to push the thing around me. 'No!' I shout, flailing out with an arm. 'Stop it!'

He pulls back and we stare angrily at each other. I wrap my arms tightly around myself and drop my head. 'I don't want it,' I mumble.

'For God's sake, you stupid—' He breaks off, glares at me, then tosses the sleeping bag aside. 'Have it your way. You'll change your tune.'

He moves away from me, his good mood entirely gone. I sit there, helpless with fatigue and pain, as he gets to work in the hut.

Things are looking up, I tell myself. *We're out of the storm. We're somewhere dry. I'm not alone. Maybe we won't die.*

But depression is engulfing me. I ought to be happy that we've found this place but I'm wretched. I hate this. I want it to stop. I can't understand the powerful angry frustration that's building up inside me, but there's nothing I can do about it. The thought of Jimmy waiting for me at LAX, ready for the two of us to zoom into town in his convertible and hit the bars of downtown LA together, so we can laugh and tell stories and he can help me get that shit Jacob out of my system . . . The thought of not being there and not being able to do anything about it is almost more than I can stand. I watch the bodyguard as he lifts down the second box and begins going through it and instead of feeling glad that he is there, taking charge, I'm filled with furious resentment towards him.

It's his fault we're here. If he hadn't lost control of the car, we'd have got to the airport before the storm hit us.

33

He's supposed to be a hard-ass SAS guy and he can't even drive down a mountain!

The bodyguard works quickly. I watch, alternately miserable and angry, as he clears some of the ash from the middle of the fireplace. He finds a stash of old newspapers next to it and screws sheets into balls, placing them together in the hearth like a nest of little crinkly grey eggs. Then he takes some slim bits of wood from an old crate and lays them carefully across the paper. He lays larger bits on top of them, making a criss-cross pattern. When it's all arranged, he takes the matchbox and strikes a match. The little yellow and purple flame on the end of the match is the prettiest thing I've seen all day. I watch as he holds it to the edge of one of the paper balls; the flame strokes at the old newspaper, then bites into it, flickering along the paper's edge as it takes hold. He lights the paper in a couple of other places, before the match gives out. Now the flames are growing as the fire consumes the paper and becomes large enough to start on the kindling.

'That should do it,' the bodyguard says, 'as long as we look after it. A fire is a delicate thing. You have to feed it just what it needs at the right time, or you can stifle it. We've got to create a hot heart. That's the only way you'll get a decent fire.'

I stare over at him, still shaking with cold, wondering if he can sense that I'm seething with fury at him.

Who cares about your stupid fire? It's your fault we're here!

I know in my head that we need the fire and that he's doing exactly the right things, and he's doing it to help me. But my heart is racing with ire at our situation.

He doesn't seem to expect an answer. Instead, he looks beneath the other plank bed and pulls out a large chest. He opens it easily and whistles. A little of his good humour seems restored as he glances over at me and says, 'Supplies.'

As soon as he says it, I realise that I feel empty. I haven't eaten since breakfast and that was little more than a bowl of a muesli with yoghurt and coffee. It must be hours ago now. I haven't been thinking at all about how we are going to eat. I feel a vague relief that this problem seems to have been solved – though I've no idea what supplies he's found.

I doubt it's sushi, I think bitterly. I'd been planning to go to the sushi bar at the airport, to have a light lunch with a glass of champagne. *Now look where I am.*

'You know what, this place is actually pretty good,' he says conversationally. 'We've got a fire going—' he looks over at where the fire is beginning to crackle now as it takes hold of the wood '—we have some food and some water and there's a pot and a kettle too.' He gestures at a couple of black items at the side of the hearth.

I don't know why but his attempts at optimism only make me feel worse.

'They look disgusting too,' I snap. 'You can't seriously expect me to eat or drink anything out of those. When were they last cleaned? There could have been rats or mice in here!' I shudder. 'This is all just too vile for words.'

He stares over at me, and I can see barely repressed irritation in his face. He's sitting on the floor, seeming not to care about the dirt there, the wooden chest open in front of him. The snow is gone from his jacket but he looks damp and very cold, though he hasn't said a word about it. His dark hair is wet from the storm and he's run his fingers through it, leaving it in black spikes: the effect is almost boyish. But his mouth is tight with disapproval and the blue eyes are glaring at me, slightly hooded with the force of his annoyance, and the way he's holding himself seems to hint at a great effort to rein it in.

At last he speaks, his one word dripping with scorn. '*What?*'

'You heard me!' I shoot back. 'They're a health hazard! I refuse to touch anything that comes out of them.'

He gives a short cold laugh and says in an almost drawling voice, the Scottish accent getting more pronounced with every word, 'A *health* hazard? That's priceless, it really is. Shall I tell you what a real health hazard is? Exposure, for one. And there's hypothermia, thirst and starvation. They tend to do for you a bit quicker than a well-used saucepan, you know? Lucky for you, your risk of succumbing to the first four dangers has just been reduced very significantly. If I were you, I'd take my chances with the risk of an upset tummy. Unless you'd prefer to be out in the storm, alone, freezing to death where at least there's no risk of *food poisoning*?'

His last words are full of contempt and my spirit flares up as if he's just poured oil on a dying fire.

'How dare you speak to me like that?' I shout.

'Are you crazy?' His eyes crackle with anger now. 'I would have thought that in this situation you might – just might – start letting go of that spoilt princess act of yours! I've always wondered if the way you swan about looking down your nose at everyone is really you, and until now I've given you the benefit of the doubt. I've heard that things haven't always been that easy for you, and you're young. But this . . . this is really taking the piss.' He's on his feet, then in one stride he's next to me, bending down, his lips set. Then he says in an ominously quiet voice, 'Listen, honey. You don't have to take anything from me. You don't have to drink water, eat food, or sleep in a sleeping bag. You can walk out of here, if that's what you want. It'll be suicide, but that's up to you. I've done my best for you but I can't force you to accept it. I'm going to tend to this fire, make some dinner and then think about what to do when this storm is over. You're welcome to join me.'

I stare back at him, furious. 'If you carry on talking to me like that,' I say in as menacing a voice as I can muster, 'I'm going to fire you.'

He raises his eyebrows and, despite himself, laughs. 'What?'

'You heard me. I'll fire you. Right here.'

'Oh, okay.' He nods as though he's in agreement with me. 'Yeah, sure. You fire me, and I'll just head off into the night, and leave you here. Then you can get on with the important business of being a spoilt little girl in peace.'

'I'm your boss!' I yell. I feel powerless. I want to exert some control in this situation. 'If my father isn't here, then you take orders from me. Do you understand?'

'Right,' he says, his deep voice half sarcastic, half amused. 'You're the captain, are you? All right, then. What are your orders? And please don't ask for chilled champagne, I'm not sure I can stretch to that right now.'

I cast about for something I can make him do, something to impose my authority. He needs to know that I'm in charge. My family pays his wages. He's standing up, and I don't like the way he's looming over me like some kind of parent over a crouching child. Then it comes to me. I lift my chin up high and say loftily, 'Fetch my scarf.'

He frowns, his blue eyes puzzled. I notice that there's a dark shadow of stubble over his jaw. 'What?'

'I'm cold and I want my scarf. I'll need it as a pillow if nothing else. I can hardly put my head down on bare boards.' I wave a hand at the plank bed I'm sitting on. 'I want my cashmere scarf.'

'Well, where the hell is it?'

'I left it in the snow as a signal. You remember where you left me when you found this place? It's there.'

He stares at me in silence and then says at last, 'You're joking, aren't you? It's snowing out there. It's getting dark. The scarf will be buried by now. And even if it isn't, it's a crazy risk to take.'

'I want it,' I say obstinately. For some reason, it's become a matter of great importance to me that he does what I say. I'm the boss. He needs to understand that.

'It's a crazy stupid bloody risk,' he says softly. 'I'd be mad to do it. The thing will be sopping wet now anyway.'

I jump to my feet, and shout, 'Do as I say, dammit!' Then I crunch over in agony as my chest feels like it's being squeezed by a huge and relentless hand.

He has me by the arm in a moment, holding me so I don't fall. 'Are you okay? Where does it hurt?'

I manage to get the words out despite the pain. 'My . . . my chest.' He puts his arm round me to support me, while I pull my own arms close to my chest, trying to relieve the pain. I look up into his eyes beseechingly. My rage has vanished in a fresh wave of fear. 'Do you think I'm dying?'

The fact that he doesn't answer at once makes me even more afraid. Then he says in a grave voice, 'It's possible that you could have a cracked rib.'

'That's what I thought,' I say through short, shallow, panting breaths. 'Do you think I've punctured a lung?'

'I don't know. I'll need to look at you.'

'What do you mean?'

'You'll have to let me examine where it hurts. I've had some basic medical training. It might help.'

I blink, taking this in. The pain is right in the centre of my chest, and that would mean taking off my top. 'I . . . I'm not sure . . .' I stammer.

'It's okay,' he says. 'I'll be very gentle. I won't hurt you.'

I turn my face away so he can't see that I'm reddening with the thought of undressing in front of him. 'I . . . don't think so.'

He's quiet for a moment, then he takes his hand away from my arm and says quietly, 'All right. I understand. I'm going to get some food on. We'll get the scarf tomorrow when it's light.' He nods his head to the small window. The white outside has darkened to almost black. The little room is lit by the orange glow of the fire. 'The sun's gone already.'

'What time is it?' I say. I feel so tired, I can barely continue to stand.

'It's nearly four thirty.'

We left the house only a few hours ago. That's all it's taken for my life to spin entirely out of control. I sink back down onto the bare planks of the bed. My puffy jacket is the only comfort I have now and I retreat down into it as much as I can. The fire is burning well and the bodyguard goes over and feeds it with more wood from the crate by the hearth. He looks round at me.

'By the way, if you need to pee, there's a bucket over there in the corner.'

39

I follow where he's pointing and see the gleam of a grubby aluminium bucket tucked between the plank beds. I'm horrified. 'What? With you here?' As soon as I think about it, I realise that I do need to pee, and that I have for some time without acknowledging it.

'Yes, with me here. I don't mind. I won't look.'

I bite my lip anxiously. *I can't use that bucket!* I can just imagine the racket I'll make squatting over it, peeing against the metal. It would be too humiliating. *I'll just have to hold it in.*

He's watching me, his eyes a little softer than they've been for a while now. 'Listen,' he says, prodding one of the small logs so that it turns into the flames, 'I'm going to see if there's a wood pile outside, okay? If you need to use the bucket, you can do it then.'

'And leave it full of pee?' I shudder.

'We'll cover it up with something.' He looks at me with something like sympathy for the first time. 'I know. It's not what you're used to. But believe me, it'll be fine. We all have to do it. I won't think any the less of you for needing to pee.'

My defiance flares up again. 'That's not what I'm afraid of,' I retort. 'I'm just used to living like a human being, that's all. Maybe you're happy to perform your private bodily functions in public, but I'm not!'

He holds up his hands, laughing softly. 'Okay, okay! I know – you're far better than all of this. I'm a peasant and you're a lady. But even ladies need to answer the call of nature. So I'm going to look for that woodpile now, all right?'

He stands up, picks up the torch and heads for the door. As he opens it, the howl of the storm outside ratchets up several decibels. I feel suddenly deeply relieved that he hasn't obeyed my orders to go looking for the scarf. My anxiety levels are rocketing just watching him step out into the freezing darkness. He looks back over his shoulder, and his expression is playful as he says, 'I'm just going out. I may be some time.'

'What?' I say, fearful. 'How long? How long will you be?'

'It's a quote . . . Captain Oates. You know, on Captain Scott's expedition?' He smiles and shakes his head at my baffled expression. 'Never mind. I'll tell you all about it one day. I won't be long. But you've got plenty of time to use the ladies' room.'

I frown at him, wishing he hadn't brought that up again. But as soon as he's shut the door behind him, I get up, slowly because of my chest, and reach into my pocket. My fingers curl around a fresh packet of tissues. Good. Nothing worse than drip-drying. Suddenly, now that relieving myself is a possibility, I'm desperate. I almost hop to the bucket, pull it out into the open and start to undo my jacket. I'm not so cold now, I realise. I've stopped shaking quite so violently. The little room has filled with warmth from the fire and it's been gradually seeping into my bones without my noticing. I revel in the sensation of being liberated from that teeth-chattering cold. My fingers and toes are still numb but I'm warming up gradually and I can imagine being warm again at some point in the future.

I undo my jeans and shove them down to the tops of my boots, then I try and sit over the bucket. It's difficult to balance and hold my coat out of the way, but somehow I manage and at last I'm able to let go but at once I'm mortified because the noise is truly astounding, like a rainstorm

41

pelting on a tin roof. *Surely he can hear, even outside?* Even though I know rationally that he can't, I'm scarlet with embarrassment but there's no way I can stop, I have to let everything out and it clatters away until I'm finished. I sort myself out with the tissues and pull up my jeans again.

I literally cannot believe I've just peed into a bucket that's sitting on a dirt floor in a terrible hovel. My life isn't like this. It's full of luxury and indulgence and absolute comfort. I've never suffered like this in my life. But what choice do I have?

By the time the door of the cottage opens some minutes later, the bucket is back in the corner, covered with a piece of old newspaper, and I'm sitting back on the planks, watching the fire dance and feeling simultaneously sleepy and incredibly hungry. The bodyguard comes in, carrying some wet, snow-covered logs under his arms, the torch beaming in one hand. His hair is dotted with snow, as though someone has thrown handfuls of white confetti over him.

'Success!' he says, smiling at me. 'There's a pile in the area at the side. It's hard to spot it but I had a feeling it would be there. It'll need to dry out, of course.' He looks at me. 'Everything okay?'

'Yes, thank you,' I say a touch primly, embarrassed again. I'm horribly aware of the bucket in the corner, but I try to brazen it out. 'I'm glad you've found some more fuel.'

He walks over to the fire and puts the logs close by on the hearth so that they can begin to dry out. The flames are well established now, and he throws on some more of the dry wood.

'Time to eat,' he says. 'I don't know about you, but I'm ravenous.'

My stomach rumbles painfully in response but I don't know if he's heard it or not. I watch as he takes two tins from the food supply box and empties them into the blackened saucepan. I'm so hungry now that I really don't care what state the pan is in, and while the brown slop that pours from the tin doesn't look in the least appealing, the smell of stew that begins to float upwards as the heat hits the bottom of the pan is simply delicious. My mouth is watering hard. I really am hungry.

I am hardly ever this ravenous, I realise. My life is about having every need answered almost before I really feel it. Meals are served without my lifting a finger, and if I'm hungry I give an order and a moment later, whatever I want arrives. It might only be a salad or a dish of fruit, but whatever it is, it's mine at the merest wish: a tray of oysters, caviar, a plate of smoked salmon, truffle-infused scrambled eggs, *salade niçoise* . . .

Now I'm slavering over a pan of cheap beef stew! I know that I would turn my nose up at this stuff in horror if I saw it prepared for me at home. But I'm so anxious for the meal now that I can hardly think of anything else.

'It's ready,' the bodyguard says cheerfully. He pours some of the stew back into the tin and passes it to me. 'Be careful, it's hot. But it'll be an excellent way to warm your hands.'

I take the tin, staring into the dark depths. I need my jacket sleeves over my palms to be able to hold it. 'How will I eat it?' I ask. 'Where's the cutlery?'

He shrugs. 'No cutlery. You'll have to use your fingers.'

43

I'm silent, aware that I haven't washed my hands since using the bucket.

'It's not perfect, I know.' He pauses, evidently in thought, and then passes me the lid of the tin. 'Use this. Watch out for the sharp edges.'

I take it, and start to scoop out the stew, sucking it carefully off the tin lid. It's gloopy and far too salty but it's also delicious, the thick meatiness filling my empty stomach and warming me inside. As it cools a little, I begin to wolf it down and it's gone all too quickly.

The bodyguard is eating too, scooping up the stew from the pan and swallowing it down almost without chewing. He grins over at me. 'It's good, isn't it?'

Maybe it's the food that has lifted my mood but I feel suddenly full of utter contentment. The bodyguard . . . *Oh what is his name? Yes, that's it . . . Miles . . .* Miles is sitting in front of the fire and I can see a hint of steam rising off his jacket where it's drying out. He's illuminated by the firelight, his form outlined in gold and an orange glow lighting his straight profile and strong chin with cinematic effect. He is utterly unconscious of it, which makes it all the more beguiling. I can't help being entranced by the way his features are lit, with the dark shadows beneath his cheeks and over the hoods of his eyes. His eyes glow and when he smiles, his teeth look astonishingly white.

He's not just good-looking. He's handsome. Very handsome.

He's talking now, unaware of what I'm thinking, not realising that every movement of his head is showing off the fine shape of his face and the strong line of his shoulders against the glowing heart of the fire. He seems to fill the small room with the bulk of his body and his strength.

'I guess that you're not really accustomed to tinned food but let me tell you, when you get to the end of a long hard day in the open, you're grateful for anything hot and tasty. Fuck all that organic, yogic, macrobiotic shit.' He stops, looks at me, and laughs again. 'Sorry. For all I know, you're addicted to free-range avocado with a helping of yurt fries and active yoghurt. But trust me, all the body really knows is hunger and satisfaction.'

I stare at him, saying nothing. In the silence we can hear the storm yowling outside. There is a constant patter against the glass of the small window as the wind flings the snow against it. A sudden awkwardness fills the room.

'Are you all right?' he asks, frowning. The way the light falls means that I can see the shadows deep in every crease of his skin.

'Yes,' I reply. I put down the empty tin. 'This has been the weirdest day ever.' I lean back, suddenly aware that when I got dressed this morning, I could not possibly have envisaged where I would be that evening. Now that I'm warm again and I've eaten, my fierce anger and resentment is dying down. It's being replaced by a kind of disbelief at where I am. I feel as though I've stepped out of everything I've ever known, out of my usual life, and into something utterly different. All the norms have been swiped away, just like that. Here I am with a man who saved my life. And I've been little more than a bitch to him. I look over at him. 'Do you think they're going to find us?'

He pushes away the saucepan and looks at me, his expression serious. 'Yes. I do.'

'Are you just saying that to make me feel better?'

'I believe it. This storm will blow itself out. We'll both be missed. I was expected back at the house by mid-afternoon; you didn't make your flight. It will be noticed. They'll guess what happened. I bet they're out looking for us right now.'

'Really?' I ask longingly.

'Of course.' His voice is firm, comforting. 'We just need to get through tonight, that's all. Come on. You must be tired.'

It can't be six o'clock yet. Not even cocktail hour. And yet, I am tired. Very. I sigh a long, exhausted sigh.

'You need to sleep.' His voice is low, buzzing, almost hypnotic. 'You've had a shock. It'll help if you can get some of your strength back.'

'Yes.'

'Come on. Let me help you.'

He gets up and comes towards me. I tense. I can't help it. 'Hey . . . hey . . .' he says. 'What's wrong?'

I look up. His shape is silhouetted against the firelight, blocking out most of the light. A shudder of fear convulses me and I can't hide it.

'What's wrong?' he asks again.

'Nothing,' I say wretchedly. 'Nothing.'

'Are you sure?'

'Yes.'

'Let's get you comfortable then.'

It's hard to imagine that I could ever be comfortable on this assemblage of planks, with nothing much to provide softness but I need to sleep so badly now that anything will do. He's next to me, taking up another of the sleeping bags – I hope vaguely that it's less greasy than the blue one but I'm beyond caring now – unzips it and lays it on the planks. Then he gently lowers me down so that I'm lying on its fleecy interior, and lifts my legs up on to the bed. I can smell the well-used scent of the bag, but now it doesn't call to my mind other people's filth, but seems to symbolise the human need for warmth, sleep and comfort. I'm like other lost travellers now, finding some shelter through the good-will of others.

'There,' Miles says. He sits down on the edge of the planks, like a grown-up checking on a child before turning out the light. 'That should be okay, shouldn't it? Will you be able to sleep all right?'

I nod. Then I manage a smile and say, 'This isn't my usual bedtime routine. I haven't even washed my face. And I usually have a herbal tea before I sleep.'

'You'll be all right, just this once,' he says, smiling back. 'Pretend you've given the maid the night off.'

I blink up at him. 'Do you need to use the bucket?'

He laughs softly. 'That's very kind, sweetheart, but I took care of that outside. We men are lucky that way.'

There's a tiny shimmer of something in the air as it strikes me that he is a man, and I'm a woman, and here we are alone together, about to go to sleep.

Don't be ridiculous! I scold myself. *He's a bodyguard! I'm his employer. It's completely unthinkable.*

His nearness though is causing all sorts of strange sensations to flutter around my body. It's as if the experience of being virtually frozen and then warmed again has left my nerves in a heightened state, because my skin feels suddenly alive, tingling electricity sweeping over it in response to the extremely attractive male body radiating warmth and power right beside me.

'Freya,' he murmurs almost thoughtfully, and my nerves jump again at the sound of his deep voice saying my name. 'That's pretty. It's Scandinavian, isn't it?'

I nod. 'She's a Norse goddess. The one they named "Friday" after. And she's the goddess of winter.'

He raises an eyebrow at me. 'Really? Appropriate today, huh? Well, maybe your goddess was looking out for you in her season.'

'Maybe she was.' I smile back.

'Well . . .' We gaze at one another, awkward again at this intimate moment. We're virtual strangers, after all, but here we are. Suddenly, we only have each other. 'Goodnight, goddess Freya.'

'Goodnight, Miles.'

He looks astonished. 'That's the first time you've ever said my name.'

'Is it?' I'm embarrassed he's noticed.

'Yes. You've never called me anything before. Just "you".'

'I've called you by your name now, haven't I?' I retort. 'Is it really a big deal?'

'Put your fur down, kitten, I don't want a fight. I'm just glad you feel you can use my name, that's all. It's progress.'

My touchiness dies down as quickly as it flared up. 'I'm . . . sorry. And . . . thank you for today. For what you've done for me. I do appreciate it. Really.'

'That's okay,' he replies softly. His blue eyes look black in the shadows, the firelight burns a line of gold around his cheekbone. 'It's my job after all.' He gives me a sideways look. 'Unless I've been fired?'

'No . . . no.' I laugh, despite myself. 'I'd like you to keep the job – if you want to.'

'I've got a three-month notice period anyway,' he says with a smile. 'I'm stuck with you for a while longer, and you're stuck with me.' He leans in to tuck the sleeping bag around me. 'Sleep tight, sweetheart. See you in the morning.'

The touch of his hands sends all sorts of curious feelings zipping over my skin, and a strange excitement curls in my belly.

Stop it, I tell myself firmly. I murmur, 'Goodnight.'

He gets up and walks over to the fire, where he sits down and starts reading something he's taken from one of the windowsill boxes. I watch him for as long as I can, his dark form stark against the orange light, but within minutes my eyes have slid closed, and I'm asleep.

CHAPTER FOUR

I wake in the night, not knowing where I am. I'm in pitch blackness, my body is stiff on the hard wooden planks, and I'm freezing despite my jacket and the pungent sleeping bag tightly wrapped around me. I'm moaning with the pain in my chest, a throbbing ache that feels as though someone is continually squeezing me tight, homing in on the tender area with unerring aim.

Panic sweeps over me with the confusion. *What's happening? Where am I?*

I'm accustomed to different beds, moving the way I do across the world from hotel to apartment, to villa and mansion. But no matter where the beds are, they are always the same: luxurious with soft mattresses and crisp clean sheets, cool in summer and warm in winter. This experience is entirely different – the unforgiving boards, the cold and the dark. In fact, I've only known this once before in my life and the memory of that rears up in my head like a black ogre.

I'm there, I think, agonised with fear. *I'm back there.* I cry out, 'Mama! Are you there? Mama?' I sit up suddenly, wild with panic and slump under the pain that washes over me.

The next instant, Miles is beside me, hushing me, wrapping strong arms around me and rocking me gently. His cheek is against my head, and I let myself fall into his embrace, sobbing a little as the terror subsides.

'Hey, it's okay, sweetheart, it's fine,' he says. 'You're all right. I'm here.'

'I thought—' I choke on the words. I can't begin to explain what I felt.

'I know. You're afraid. But you're safe, I promise.'

It's not just that. I want to tell him that I'm not simply frightened of our situation, to explain about the fear, but I can't begin to find the words. For one thing, I've never talked about it with anyone, not even the shrinks they sent me to.

I can't see him but that somehow makes it easier to accept the comfort of his body in a way that might not be possible if I could. I press up against the warm strength of his chest, inhale a comfortingly masculine scent, and feel the roughness of his stubble against the side of my head. He murmurs in his soft Scottish accent, 'You called for your mother. She died when you were young, didn't she?'

I can't speak. My throat feels as though it's closed up and there's a pressure in my skull that will be released as tears if I try to talk, so I nod, feeling the soft wool of his jumper on my face.

'You poor wee girl. I'm sorry. That's tough for anyone.'

I take a deep breath and manage to say, 'Please don't be nice to me.'

He laughs and I feel the rumble in his chest. 'Freya, you're a one. Don't be nice to you?'

'It will make me . . . lose it,' I say, my voice coming out thickly. I really don't want to cry.

'I understand. You're strong. But it's all right to be scared. This isn't a great situation, I'm not pretending it is. But our chances are good, I promise.'

51

'How long do you think it will be before they find us?'

He's quiet for a moment and I sense him turn his head towards the window although there's only blackness outside. 'It depends on the storm. It's quietened down for now. Maybe that means they can start looking for us. There's no point otherwise, they'll never see a thing with the visibility at almost zero. Hey now . . .' I feel him turn back to me '. . . you're cold.'

I realise I'm shaking lightly. The fire has died and the bitter cold is returning as the heat fades away.

'Come on,' he says, 'we can't have that. I'm going to sleep here with you so we can share body warmth. I'll get the other sleeping bag.' He gets up, moves cautiously in the direction of the fireplace and finds his sleeping bag.

I feel comforted. A body close to me is what I want most right now. I move to make room for him on the narrow planks and gasp.

'What is it?' Miles asks, returning with his bag.

'My chest. It's still hurting.'

'Okay.' His voice is serious again. 'I'm going to take a look now.'

'But—'

'No buts. Come on, it won't take a minute.'

Maybe it will be easier in the dark. He won't be able to see my face.

He goes back to the fireplace where he's obviously left the torch in easy reach, and comes back. He helps me sit up straight and I don't bother to protest any more. I'm worried about this pain and I want to know what's wrong with me. He switches on the torch and the cold white beam lasers through the darkness. It blinds me momentarily, then the light swings away from my eyes and onto my body. He sits down next to me and puts the torch on the bench so that its beam illuminates me.

'That's right, let's get this coat off you. Not for long . . .' He's unzipping my puffy jacket and gently pushing it off my shoulders. My sweater is underneath. 'Do you want to lift this up for me?'

I nod and roll the soft cashmere upwards, exposing first my stomach and then my chest. I'm wearing a plain white cotton bra, the straps embellished with small cotton daisies. My skin prickles into goosebumps as the cold air hits it. Miles lifts the torch and focuses the beam on my breasts. I look down and see the icy light playing over my flesh; it looks white in the cold beam, the soft mounds of my breasts rising from the bra cups, but there's something else.

'I thought so,' Miles says. He's focused the torchlight on a livid purple mark that crosses my chest from the top of my left breast and straight down the centre of my chest in a long diagonal line. 'You've been badly bruised by the seatbelt. You must have been thrown very hard against it.'

Relief flows through me. 'Is that all?'

'That's my hunch. I think we would know if you had a punctured lung – you'd have an accelerated pulse, wheezing and probably a good deal more pain. It's possible you have a broken rib but the pain would be intense at all times. My guess is you've got some severe bruising and it will go down after a while. We could put an ice pack on it . . .'

I shiver at the thought. 'No thanks.'

'Well . . . you need to take it easy, that's all. And we'll get you properly checked by a doctor as soon as we can.' He drops the beam of light away from my chest and I pull

53

my sweater back down. 'Let's get some more sleep. There's nothing else we can do right now.' Miles helps me put my coat back on and zips it up. I'm glad of the warmth.

He shifts on the bed so that he is between me and the stone wall and lies down. 'Come in here,' he says. 'Get up right against me.'

I lie down so that my back is turned to him and shuffle back into the curve of his body. The warmth and strength that comes from him is intensely comforting. He wraps his sleeping bag around the two of us, and puts his arm around me. My heart, for some reason, is racing and I remember his words about an accelerated pulse. Is my lung punctured after all?

Or maybe it's something else entirely . . .

A strange lightness fills my body, a sort of heady excitement. For the first time, I feel comfortable, almost luxurious.

'Are you all right?' he murmurs and I feel his breath against my neck. It sends waves of almost unbearable tingling over my flesh. I start to tremble lightly.

Surely he's going to notice what he's doing to me!

'Yes,' I say in a small voice. 'I'm fine.' But I have a fierce urge to turn over so that we are face to face, to press my body into his and offer him my mouth.

What the hell are you thinking? I'm filled with mortification at the way my body is taking my thoughts in this direction. It would be wrong to cross that line with him. It's bad enough that he's witnessed me lose my dignity entirely in the last twelve or so hours. Now I want to humiliate myself entirely by trying to kiss him?

His words from earlier play through my mind. *He thinks I'm a spoilt princess. He thinks I'm stuck up and rude.* He laughed at me when I tried to tell him what to do. He refused to go out for my scarf.

A kind of turmoil rises up in me. On the one hand, I want to reinforce the difference between us: he's the hired hand, I'm the lady of the house who ought be given respect and deference. It doesn't matter what our situation is, he still has to show me that I'm the boss. And yet . . . I need him. Right now, I need strength and comfort and the way that he's reducing me to a quivering jelly is discomforting and deliciously pleasurable at the same time. My body is lighting up like an electric bulb, delighted at the way this man's closeness is firing up the snapping synapses of pleasure. It wants to respond. It felt that torchlight over my breasts as acutely as if he was running his fingertips over me. Now it's hungry for skin, for touching and caressing and sucking and kissing . . .

Oh God! Stop it! I can't help twitching with the force of what I'm feeling, as a treacherous warmth spreads out from my groin.

'Everything okay?' he asks, his voice triggering more of those rippling tremors over my skin. 'Are you in pain?'

'No,' I say. *Not in the way you think.* 'I'm all right. Really.'

He mustn't know. He obviously isn't affected by me at all. I can't give him the satisfaction of turning me down.

I remember the last time I had sex. It was with Jacob, a night spent romping in a bed after an evening dancing at a club in St Tropez. That was before I knew he had a habit of paying for sex with prostitutes and call girls. I'd had to have the full range of tests afterwards, once it had all come to light. Thank goodness I'd been clear. I hadn't been able to stomach seeing him again, not after the things I'd witnessed on that film. But I had loved him, and sex with him had been enjoyable. I have a flashback to Jacob, naked, his cock rearing up, as he parts my legs and gets ready to enter me . . .

I shiver again, and Miles's arm tightens around me in response. *He thinks I'm cold.*

I command myself to stop thinking about sex. It isn't helping. I have to put it out of my mind, and make myself sleep. The sooner I can sleep, the sooner I'll be able to wake up and move away from Miles's disturbing proximity. And then he won't guess my guilty secret, which is that I'm being eaten up with desire.

I don't know how long I lie awake but at some point I drift into sleep and the next thing I know, I'm awake, blinking into greyish light that's coming in through the tiny window. I'm warm, properly warm for the first time in a long while. Miles's body is still pressed against mine, and I can't resist snuggling into it, relishing its muscled firmness. He's asleep, I can tell by his deep and regular breathing, and I wriggle slightly backwards, pressing my bottom against his groin. A hardness there presses against my buttock, and I frown, wondering if he has something in his pocket, before my face turns hot as I realise what it is. I'm wiggling up against his morning erection.

I freeze, not knowing what to do. The hardness is unmistakable, a steel rod up against me. And it's impressive too, solid and long. I can't help imagining how I could release it, free it so that it can do whatever it wants . . . All the feelings of the night before come racing back and a needy wetness instantly appears between my legs. We're so close. His erection is only inches from where I can feel longing buzzing and calling.

Miles groans softly in his sleep and the arm around me tightens, pulling me closer to him so that his erection is now pressed against the cleft in my buttocks. He's moving against me, his hips shifting so that the hardness rubs against me.

Is he awake or asleep? He must be asleep! It must be unconscious . . .

I let myself revel in the sensation of his hard cock pressing so close to where I want it. Then he moans again and moves away slightly, so that the pressure between us is reduced. I'm disappointed, still hungry for it, my desire now well stoked. But he's obviously asleep and unaware of what's happening between us.

This is going to drive me mad.

Impulsively, I move, twisting round. 'Miles?'

His eyes flick open at once and he's wide awake. 'Yes? Everything all right?'

I was right. He was asleep. He hasn't got a clue.

'I . . . I need to . . .' I stumble over the words. 'Could you go outside for a moment?'

His puzzled expression clears as he grasps my meaning. 'Sure. Sure. Of course.' He seems to become aware of his own morning arousal, as he looks suddenly uncertain of himself, and the merest hint of embarrassment crosses his face. Moving quickly, he climbs nimbly over me and is standing up, stretching, keeping his back to me. Then he goes to the cottage door and lets himself out, a gust of freezing wind entering as he leaves. I sit up and feel the familiar ache in my chest but it's definitely lessened since yesterday. He was right – it's a bruise. I've been incredibly lucky.

While he's outside, I do what I need to into the bucket.

God, this is revolting. I could manage here so much better if it weren't for this awful, humiliating excuse for a toilet. Lucky Miles only has to go outside.

I imagine him waiting for that huge erection to subside. I picture the cold air doing its work and close my eyes against the image in my mind. Just thinking about his cock is sending my breath crazy, and my sex is tingling hard.

What's wrong with me? I wonder if it's the brush with death yesterday that has fired up my desires so strongly. After all, they say that a normal response to a funeral is to want sex, to prove that you're still alive in the presence of death . . .

I think I've got control of myself by the time Miles comes back in, his cheeks flushed with the icy wind outside.

'The storm's over,' he says cheerfully. 'That's the good news. But I think there's more in the offing. And you can be pretty certain that all traces of our crash have completely disappeared.'

'What are we going to do?' I bite my lip anxiously. 'I just don't know how long I can stand this.'

'I know.' He looks sympathetic. 'It's tough. But we're alive and they'll be looking for us by now. So here's the plan. I'm going to get the fire going again, make us some coffee and something to eat, then I'm going to put a marker out so that they can find us.'

'How? What kind of marker?'

He nods over at the fireplace. 'We've got some burnt wood there. I'm going to use it to make a mark on the roof of the cottage – it'll be like pen on white paper. They're bound to spot it if they fly over.'

I cheer up. This seems like a good idea. Then I'm bleak again. 'It would be so much simpler if we just had our phones with us.'

'I know. Of course it would. But sadly, they're buried in the snow with the remains of the car. So we'll need to think of some old-fashioned solutions, that's all.' He gives me a knowing look. 'When you start getting gloomy, it's usually a sign that you need something to eat. I'll get on with breakfast.'

'Amazing how well you know me after less than twenty-four hours,' I say sardonically but I don't have the usual bite in my tone.

Miles ignores me, and starts work on the fire. I can see now that it hasn't entirely died, but that he carefully damped it down with logs the night before so that the glowing heart would be kept alive and it could be easily rekindled in the morning. In only a few minutes, the fire is up and crackling hard around fresh wood. He pours half a litre of water into the kettle and hangs it over the flames on a hook that I hadn't noticed before now. There are no cups, so he swishes out the tins from the night before, tossing the dirty water out of the cottage door, and spoons some freeze-dried coffee granules into the tins. Within quarter of an hour, we are holding hot tins of black coffee, and beans are bubbling in the saucepan, mixing with the remains of the previous night's stew to create a temptingly savoury aroma.

'Don't say I don't treat you to life's little luxuries,' Miles says cheerfully, and I laugh. Anyone who knows me would be amazed at the sight of me sipping black coffee from an empty tin and waiting eagerly for a breakfast of a mess of beans, to be scooped up on a tin lid.

After we've eaten, Miles goes outside armed with hand-fuls of black charcoal and the beans tin full of ash in his pocket. I hear him moving about, finding a way to scale the cottage wall and get onto the roof. I only hope it can bear his weight. A hole in the roof would be an unpleasant addition to the cottage's amenities. Meanwhile, I look through one of the boxes and find the visitors' book, just a plain school exercise book with scrawls in many different hands, some long and detailed, some just recording a date and a name. There have been plenty of travellers who've passed by here, some evidently extremely grateful for this little piece of community shelter and the provisions left here for those who need them. Thanks are expressed in French, Italian, German, English and other languages. The most recent stay was a few months ago, a trio of climbers who used this place when one of them was injured and they needed to wait for help.

Easy enough when you just phone the rescue centre and explain where you are. Not so easy when you can't do that.

There is a little cash box for donations. It's locked but there's a slot in the top to insert notes and coins. I decide to leave a large amount before I realise that I've got no money on me at all. I'll have to remember this place, make sure someone comes back to leave some money. Or maybe I'll have mattresses, duvets and pillows sent down, so that no one else has to suffer those gruesome sleeping bags. I'll provide pots, pans, plates, cups and cutlery. Perhaps I'll even have running water put in, a proper bathroom with a loo and a shower . . .

I'm lost in fantasies about how I can transform this place into a luxurious little chalet where weary travellers can enjoy a spa bath and perhaps a sauna before opening a hamper from Fortnum and Mason for a delicious feast and a bottle of good wine, when the door opens and Miles comes back in.

'All done,' he says. But his expression is grim.

'What's wrong?' I ask nervously.

He makes a face, evidently reluctant to say too much in case it worries me.

'Come on. I'm a big girl. I can take it. Don't treat me like a baby.'

He nods. 'You're right. I'm sorry. It's just the weather out there doesn't look good. Not at all. There's another storm coming and visibility is extremely low. I doubt they would see the mark on the roof unless they were right overhead and I can't see any signs of helicopters.'

I gaze at him, stricken. 'You mean – they're not out looking for us?'

'To be honest, I've no idea. The way things are, they could be close and we'd neither see nor hear them.'

'Oh, God.' I sink down on to the nearest plank bench. 'How much have we got in the way of supplies?'

'There's enough for a few more days, as long as we ration ourselves.'

I gaze up at him. 'What if we're stuck here for weeks? What if it's like this for the rest of the winter?'

He stares back, his expression grave. His lips have tightened in that way I've already learnt means he's serious. We both know it's not impossible for us to be stranded for a long time. If bad weather really sets in, we could be snowed in for weeks. People around here are usually prepared for such occasions, with well-stocked larders, snow chains for their car tyres, and snow ploughs for the roads. But this place isn't designed for that. Miles comes over to me and crouches down in front of me, taking my hands. 'I'll get us out of here, I promise. We're not going to die here. I won't let that happen.'

I stare back, my anxiety turning to frustration. 'Really?' I say icily. 'You weren't able to stop the crash from happening. You didn't prevent us falling off the damn mountain. Why should I trust that you're able to stop us starving and freezing to death in this bloody hovel?'

He flinches as though I've slapped him. His blue eyes turn flinty and he lets go of my hands. 'You know that the accident was out of my control. I like to think that I actually prevented us suffering a much worse outcome. I got you out of the car before it fell.'

'Remind me to arrange a medal,' I say sarcastically. I can hear myself and I don't want to be like this, but my panic is coming out as anger and vindictiveness. I need Miles, desperately. I want him to like me. This morning I was curdled with desire for him, and now I'm treating him with cold contempt. *What the hell is wrong with me? Why do I do this?*

'Listen,' he says, his voice furious. 'I didn't want to take the damn car out at all in those conditions. I advised against it. But my orders were clear. Freya Hammond wants to get to the airport and what Freya Hammond wants, she *always* gets. No one is going to tell that pampered madam to take her head out of the fucking Gucci-styled clouds and see the world as it really is.' He looks at me with scorn. 'Did you really think that you can make the weather obey you? That your money can buy control of the elements? Well, it can't. You're going to learn it the hard way, and unfortunately, so am I. Your stupidity could get both of us killed – and God knows what will happen to the poor saps they send out to look for us. You've put plenty of other lives at risk, besides your own pointless, cosseted existence. I hope you're happy.

You've got your own way. If it kills you, it'll be your own goddamned fault.'

I gasp. No one – *no one* – speaks to me like this. I can't stand his expression of contempt or the vile things he's just said to me. I draw back my hand and go to slap his face but as I fling my palm towards his cheek, he grabs my wrist and twists it away.

'How dare you?' I shriek, trying to wrench my wrist out of his grasp. 'You can't speak to me like that!'

'Who's going to stop me, you little vixen?'

I go to scratch him with my other hand and he grabs that wrist too, twisting his face out of the way of my nails. He stands up, yanking me up on my feet as well. I'm vaguely aware of the pain in my chest but my fury has grown into a full-blown attack of hysteria. I'm losing control and I don't care. I need to express all the fear and anxiety and helplessness I've experienced over the last day and Miles is the only thing I can turn my emotions on. I begin to struggle, trying to bite his hand to make him release my wrists so that I can pound my fists on his chest and punish him for everything I'm feeling, but he easily evades me. He's immensely strong and with only a small amount of exertion, he holds me away from him while I shriek and flail, helpless against his superior strength. I'm simultaneously frustrated and excited by my vulnerability. I know he won't hurt me. I can express my pent-up emotion and, I realise somewhere in the back of my mind, I'm getting a little taste of the physical contact I've been long-ing for since the dark hours of the night. His presence is driving me wild and I have to let it out. I'm enjoying the tight clasp of his large hands around my wrists, and the way he's controlling my struggle with ease.

'What the hell is up with you?' he demands through clenched teeth. 'You're going crazy! Calm down, for God's sake!'

I stop struggling, and stare up at him, panting. He's frowning at me in bewilderment.

'That's better,' he says, releasing his grip on my wrists. 'What's the matter, Freya? One minute we were fine, and the next—'

I ambush him, taking advantage of his being off guard, and run at him. He grabs me and shouts, 'That's enough!'

The next moment, he's wrestled me down onto the plank bed, holding me down there with my wrists above my head. Our faces are close, and we glare at each other, his blue eyes staring into mine, and we're both panting with the fury of the last few minutes. Suddenly, the atmosphere is highly charged and my stomach whirls over in an intense somersault of excitement. I can't stop my gaze dropping to his mouth – those handsome lips that are so close to mine– and my own lips fall open in an unconscious invitation. I look back into his eyes and his expression is changing. The baffled anger is becoming a kind of wonderment and a startled realisation is coming into his eyes.

Does he feel it? Surely he must. I can't be the only one sensing this extraordinary electricity.

His gaze is raking my face. He's staring at my eyes, my lips, and then at my prone body, the rise and fall of my chest as I pant. I'm defiant but also signalling what I want from him, and he must understand that now.

We're poised there, occupying that space between desire and action for what feels like a long, beautifully agonising minute. My body is alive with need, delicious sensations firing everywhere as I revel in the touch of his hands, the closeness of his body, the fluttering feel of his warm breath on my face and the overwhelming effect of his masculinity. I can remember the promise of that long hard shaft pressed against my back this morning, and I'm hungry for it. I need it like I've don't think I've ever needed sex before. Everything about this man is fuelling my desire: the complexities of our relationship and the mad situation we've found ourselves in have acted like petrol on the flames of lust. I'm more desperate for his touch than I've ever been in my life for anyone. My desire for Jacob now seems like a childish and pointless infatuation compared to this elemental need. It doesn't matter that Miles is my bodyguard, an employee, a person whose past I know nothing about, and who is a stranger to my world of wealth and idleness. All that matters is that he is a man, hard and muscled and utterly masculine, and I want him.

He knows. I can see that. We are both still panting but our breathlessness is less from our recent struggle than from our growing excitement.

'Miles,' I whisper, gazing into his eyes.

'Christ, Freya . . . I don't know . . . I . . .' His expression is becoming fierce, not with anger but with his desire for me. But I can see the struggle there. Should he give in to it? What about his duty to me? Could this backfire on him? Am I in a state to know what I'm doing?

'I'm not crazy,' I say, and I smile. 'I know you'd think that from the way I've just acted but it's only because you've been driving me wild.'

He looks startled. 'Me? Driving you wild?'

I nod. 'Yes,' I whisper, looking longingly at his mouth. Suddenly I can't resist a moment longer. I raise my head and press my lips on his, feeling a sort of fevered relief that at last I've been able to answer my overwhelming need. His lips are soft and cool and for a moment he doesn't respond, and then his own desires take possession of him and he begins to kiss me back, hard. I let my head fall back on the wooden bench, opening my mouth to him, wanting to drink him in. His tongue presses into my mouth and we're kissing furiously, all the emotions we've felt in the last twenty-four hours focused into this desperate passionate kiss. We want to devour one another, it's as if we can't get enough. My hands are still pinioned over my head as we surrender to the ferocious needs possessing us. He tastes divine, a sweet but masculine taste that makes everything in me burst with need. I can feel myself swelling between my legs as the blood courses through me, engorging me and setting all my nerve ends on fire. There's only one way I want this to end. I need him now – hard and strong. I have to have him or I'll explode with longing.

The fevered kissing is too gorgeous for us to let it end, but we also want more. He pulls away from me, his lips wet. His eyes are hard with lust but questioning.

'Freya,' he says, panting. 'Is this what you want? I mean it, I have to know for sure.'

'How can you ask that?' I say huskily. 'Of course I do. Don't you?'

'Yes . . . God, yes.' He closes his eyes for a moment, as though he's fighting some kind of internal struggle. 'You're a mystery but you're also irresistible.' He gazes down at me again and says throatily, 'Now I've had a taste of you, I don't want to go back.'

'So don't.' I pull one of my wrists free from his grasp, put my hand behind his head and pull his face to me, so that I can feel his lips again. I push my tongue into his mouth, and we consume each other with a hunger that seems to grow stronger the more we feed it. I want everything: his hands, his skin. I want to run my nails over the flesh on his broad back, I want to feel his hard thighs and the muscled bulges of his biceps as he pulls me to him. I want to release that stiff shaft I felt this morning and feel it hot and hard in my hand. Even more than that, I want him to taste me, feel me, caress me and drive me wild with his lips and tongue before he gives me what I really want.

'But what will happen after this?' he asks, pulling away from me again. 'I don't want you to regret it.'

'I won't regret it,' I insist. I'm dizzy with lust now, all I can think about is answering the call of my body for his.

'It will change things between us.'

'Who cares? I want them changed.'

His mouth is on mine again. He drops his weight onto me, and my hands snake around his back to pull him tightly upon me. My legs open to let him lie between them, and for the first time I feel that electrifying hardness right on the heart of my sex. He's as fevered with longing as I am. I'm swelling and wet with sweet juices and I moan. This is almost too much to bear, and we're still fully clothed. He drops his mouth to the tender junction of my neck and shoulder and bites there, driving me wild so that I can't help arching my back, pressing myself against his hard body. I run my hands through his hair, as one of his reaches for the bottom of my sweater and finds the soft flesh of my belly beneath. The feel of his fingers on my skin is electric, taking my excitement to yet another level. I want him to touch my breasts, squeeze them, suck the nipples, kiss me again, press his fingers into my depths . . .

I groan with the intensity of my desire.

He lifts his head to me and says, 'No turning back, Freya . . .'

'No turning back,' I reply, my eyes burning into his. 'Please . . . no turning back.'

CHAPTER FIVE

We are possessed by our passion, kissing each other wildly, desperate to touch one another. I lift Miles's jumper and he quickly shuffles it off. I help him unbutton his shirt, our fingers meeting in delightfully charged clashes as we fumble with the buttons, and then he pulls it hastily from his shoulders so that I can see the impressive sight of his naked chest. His upper torso is magnificent, tanned and bulging with muscles. I moan lightly at the sight, while he tugs at my top, lifting it up and yanking it over my head to reveal my white cotton bra. My nipples are already stiff and erect with the force of my need for him. I wriggle out from under him, get to my feet, undo my jeans and slide them off. I don't want to waste too long in preliminaries – I want to get down to action and satisfy the longing that's burning inside me. More than anything, I want to enjoy the prom-ise of the erection I've felt pressed against me. Just in my underwear, I get back onto the bench, squeezing on beside him, and wrap my arms around his neck.

'Let's get going,' I urge him, my eyes sparkling, and I start to kiss his lips while my hand goes to the fastening on his jeans. 'Come on, I really need this.'

A strange expression fills his eyes – a kind of doubt.

'What is it?' I ask impatiently. 'Come on, Miles, let's do it . . .!' I go to kiss him again, but he frowns, turns his head to avoid me, and pulls away.

'What is it?' I say, panting. I reach for his arms, trying to turn him back to me, but the strength of his muscled body is far too much. I'm utterly ineffectual.

'I don't know if this is right,' he mutters. 'This is too fast. You're in my care. I can't . . . I can't—'

'Fuck me?' I whisper. I'm throbbing with lust. I want to be dirty – think dirty, talk dirty, do dirty things and release the pent-up need inside me. I'm sure we both want it to happen . . .

But my words don't inflame him. If anything, they seem to create a chill in the atmosphere.

'If you want to put it as crudely as that.' He turns his face back to me and I can see that his eyes have lost that look of glassy desire that's been turning me on so acutely.

'Please?' I say, my voice full of yearning. I'm staring at his mouth. How have I only just noticed how perfect it is? An exquisitely formed pair of lips that promises so much and, I know now, can deliver that promise. 'Please, Miles, don't stop.'

He gazes downwards. 'But if that's what it is . . . if I'm simply fucking you . . . That's all wrong, can't you see that?'

I let go of his arms and prop myself up on my elbows. I feel my inflamed passions begin to subside. He's ruining this moment. I was so deeply into it, so desperate for him, so fired up that I knew whatever happened would be explosive for us both. How can he pull back now? My sex is practically whimpering with need and I shift a little with the insistent ache that's still throbbing there.

'What's wrong with fucking?' I ask. The force of my thwarted desire makes it come out more sharply than I meant it to.

'You know what I'm talking about.'

I shrug, trying to pretend insouciance, hoping that if I can convince him that there's nothing to worry about, he'll stop fretting and get back to what our bodies are begging of us. He can't be immune to what's just raged between us, can he? I know that I didn't imagine that glorious steel-hard cock.

The image makes a hot shiver course over me and my stomach does a huge flip.

I groan inwardly. *Oh my God. Stop it. I can't stand it . . .*

'People fuck all the time,' I say, trying to sound airy and sophisticated. 'What's the problem?'

It's true that in my world there's a lot of casual sex. Something about money seems to make everyone who comes into contact with it incredibly horny. Perhaps it's because when you have plenty of it, the only thing you need to think about is how to enjoy yourself. Money buys indulgences, like booze and drugs and hot nights by the sea in beautiful places. When you're young, rich and care-free, the thrills of sex are sometimes the only real thrills left . . . I've known boys who've grown up with too much cash, who discover that dozens of girls want to sleep with them. Lots of those girls are on the make and the result is that the guys expect sex not too long after the first hello. The problem for me was that casual encounters just weren't my scene. I hide it well, but I'm a romantic. I had my first experiences – the kissing and petting and explora-tions – with guys I really liked and who I hoped liked me in return. Some were jerks, and some were wonderful but I didn't want my first real lover to be a one-night stand or just a casual fling. I needed to feel that I was in a couple situation before I had sex with someone. Feeling emotion for the other person, and feeling cherished by him, was everything for me. That's why I waited until it was no-holds-barred love before I slept with Jacob, my first real boyfriend and only sexual partner. At least, that was what I thought it was.

That's what makes this situation with Miles so strange. I can't explain this fierce desire I have for this man who is a virtual stranger to me. He doesn't know that I'm not usually like this. He doesn't know that he would only be my second lover.

'What's the problem?' he echoes. He frowns, that crease appearing between his black brows. I've seen him frown a lot since yesterday.

'Don't you want to?' I say almost helplessly. I'm bewildered. This man seemed to be possessed with desire for me, and now he's put on the brakes and the whole thing has skidded to a halt. I don't understand. I thought men were hungry, unstoppable beasts as far as sex was concerned. Jacob was like that: always eager for it, persistent, determined to slake his desires with me. If I kept up, well and good; if I didn't, that was my problem. Is this man different?

His lips tighten again in that way I've realised expresses his inner agitation. 'Of course I want to – I think you can tell that, Freya.'

God, I love the way he says my name.

His Scottish accent seems to curl softly around it, giving it a beauty I'm not used to hearing. My father only uses my name when he's angry, so it sounds like a swear word when he says it – I'm usually 'honey' or 'sweetie' to him. My American friend Lola gives it a tinny twang. My posh

English friends leave half of it out so that it sounds like 'Frere'. But Miles's 'r' rolls slightly, lengthening it and making it almost poetic. For the first time I understand how it might be the name of a goddess.

'Then why stop?' I whisper huskily.

He gets up and begins to stride around the small room as best he can, considering that one step takes him almost across it.

'Christ!' he says through clenched teeth. 'You know why! I'm in a position of trust as far as your father is concerned. You might believe you want this, but think about how it would look to someone on the outside. A bodyguard in sole charge of a beautiful young girl ends up bedding her less than twenty-four hours after a distressing car accident in which she sustains serious bruises. It would look as though I'm taking advantage of you, at the very least.' He stops and looks down at me with almost a pleading expression. 'Can't you see? I could lose my job and maybe my career if there's any hint of me crossing the line.'

I gaze back at him. 'But I *want* you to! I'm the one who's crossing the line.' I sit up and then get to my feet. I'm wearing only my underwear and the heat of our exertions is wearing off. The chill in the hut is making my skin goosebump and my nipples stand up stiffly against my bra. I can see his eyes drop to my breasts but he looks away quickly. I glance down and see that yesterday's bruise is still livid across my chest, a sharp diagonal that's turning a bluish purple. I haven't even felt it in the fervour of my desire but no doubt the sight of it has reminded Miles of my vulnerability and the fact that he's charged with my wellbeing.

I put one arm over the bruise to cover it, hoping he'll forget it if it's out of sight, and tip my head winsomely on one side. 'Please, Miles . . .' I say beseechingly.

His voice when he speaks is cracked slightly as though he's fighting some inner turmoil. 'It makes no difference. It might be what you want but it's up to me to hold back. No matter what you say, people will always assume I coerced you. Or they'll think I should have refused. And they'd be right.'

I stare at him, desire flowing over my skin again. He's standing just a few feet away, his torso naked, and it's all I can do to stop myself reaching out to touch him. That tanned skin looks warm and inviting and I can't help admiring his well-muscled physique. He clearly keeps himself in peak condition – I suppose being fit and strong is a requirement of his job. I can see the bulge of his biceps, the definition of his pectoral muscles, and the ripple of hard abs down his belly. Muscle men have never turned me on – Jacob was slim and boyish – but the beautiful shape of Miles's body and the strength it contains is making my throat go dry with longing. I notice the trail of dark hair emerging from his jeans and circling his belly button, and soft scatter over his chest and round the dark red bullets of his nipples, and I can't help biting my lip. He's so gorgeously male, so different to Jacob's smooth skinniness, and my body thrills at the sight of him.

He'll show me a world I've never known.

The words come unbidden into my mind and instantly I'm certain of it.

But how am I going to break through his stubborn resistance?

74

I've only ever really known one way to get what I want. I lift my chin haughtily and stare him straight in the eye.

'I don't care what people might think, especially if they're wrong. I'm not a helpless child,' I reply in lofty tones. 'Anyway – I order you to do it.'

He gazes back at me, disbelief growing in his eyes.

'I'm your boss – we've established that. You're supposed to do whatever I tell you. That's what my father would expect. So I want you to . . .' I falter just a little. 'To . . .'

'To what?' Miles's sardonic tone matches the expression in his cool blue eyes.

'To . . .' I want to command him to fuck me, but now that the heat has gone out of the moment, I can't summon up the brazenness I need. *To make love to me? No, that sounds too romantic, too emotional – it'll scare him off even more* . . . I rack my brains for the right words and then say firmly, 'To pleasure me.'

My words hang there in the chilly air for a moment. He registers them and then, to my horror, his expression changes to one of amusement, his lips curling up into a broad smile, showing his straight teeth, and then he laughs loudly.

A blush of mortification spreads over me. My cheeks are burning and the heat of embarrassment crawls over my chest and arms. 'What are you laughing at?' I say frostily, trying to hide my discomfort.

'I've had a lot of strange requests in my time,' he says, still laughing. 'But this is the first time one of my clients has asked that. And your turn of phrase is priceless. *Pleasure me.*'

Humiliation stings me at the way he says it. I'm suddenly aware that I'm standing in front of him, practically naked, demanding that he have sex with me. *Oh God, that's what I should have said – just plain 'have sex'. Too late now.* I deal with the embarrassment in the only way I know: I toss my head and say imperiously, 'I'm glad you're so entertained by me but it makes no difference. I've told you what I want. Now do it.'

He raises one dark eyebrow at me. *God, I love it when he does that. It does very curious things to my insides.* 'I thought we were past this kind of behaviour, Freya.'

'Well, we're not.' I gather my dignity as well as I can, standing there in my bra and knickers. 'Nothing has really changed between us. I'm still your boss and you still have to do as I say.'

As the words come out, I instantly regret them. Part of me wonders why I act like this but it's so ingrained in me, I can't seem to prevent myself using my status to control things and people, even if I know it doesn't really get me what I want. The amusement fades from his eyes and his smile disappears. Now there's something more like anger. Or is it disappointment? To my dismay, he reaches for his shirt and begins to put it on. 'No, you're right,' he says tersely, buttoning it up in short, sharp movements. 'Nothing has really changed, has it? I thought for a moment there that I'd misjudged you but maybe I was on the right track all along.' He stops buttoning long enough to fix me with a stony look and says quietly, 'Employing people is not the same as owning them, Freya. It seems to me that you don't understand that. You are not some Roman empress surrounded by her obedient slaves, as much as you might like to think you are.'

I lift my chin and my hands go to my hips. 'Of course I don't think that. I know the difference. I know how to be a good employer.'

'Really?' He goes back to his buttons.

The way he says it provokes me. 'What do you mean – *really*?'

He shrugs. 'Some of the staff at your mountain retreat might beg to differ. Not that you would care.'

'What do you mean? Who would differ?' I demand, outraged by the suggestion that anyone could be anything other than delighted to be working for the Hammond family.

'I'm not going to name names, I don't intend to get anyone into trouble. But if you think people don't mind being treated like faceless, nameless servants, kept up late on a whim, sent on stupid errands that you're too lazy to do yourself, or made to tidy up after you because you can't be bothered to lift a finger yourself – well, you'd better think again, that's all. People aren't fools. They have thoughts and feelings and opinions, and they certainly have an opinion about *you*.'

I draw in a shocked breath. I'm appalled and offended. 'What rubbish! How dare you make such nasty accusations? Withdraw them right now!'

He sighs. 'Are you ever going to stop issuing your ridiculous commands? You're a little nursery dictator, a spoiled child who only knows one way to get what she wants. Maybe if you opened your eyes, you'd see how your behaviour affects other people.'

This is too close to the bone for me. I snatch up my top and start putting it on, managing to get my arms twisted up in the sleeves in my fury. My desire for Miles is dampened down very effectively by his attitude. 'I won't listen to this. You just want to make me feel bad! I can't believe I actually wanted you to sleep with me! I must be an idiot.'

I wrestle myself into my top and emerge just in time to see that sardonic eyebrow shooting upwards again. A few minutes ago it made me shivery with lust. Now I'm infuriated by it.

'Do I understand that her ladyship is rescinding her previous orders?' he drawls, his Scottish accent lengthening every word and loading each one with something that seems to me like insolence. 'Are my pleasuring services no longer required?'

'Don't talk to me like that!' I stamp my foot angrily. I realise that I've been standing on the cold dirt floor for some time.

Miles laughs again as he picks up his jumper and puts it on, sliding it over his head in one easy movement. Then he reaches for his jacket. 'You know what? I feel like a fool. For a moment I thought I'd got you wrong. I thought something had changed between us. But you've made it very clear that's not the case.' As he puts his jacket on, he gives me a look that brings me up short suddenly: it's full of a power I've never seen before and it almost makes me gasp. I feel a kind of fear shimmer through me, as though I've been playing with a tame tiger that has just turned round and shown me its bared teeth. The atmosphere becomes charged with something I can't identify. It's not fevered lust now but a sense that we're preparing ourselves for combat and he's letting me know that he'll be a challenging adversary.

He turns and goes to the door. As he reaches it, he turns again to face me and stands very still. Those bright blue eyes, hard as granite, are fixed on me again.

'Let me make something clear to you, Freya Hammond. I'm not your slave, for sex or anything else, and I'm not here to service you, like some pathetic gigolo. No one can

ever order me to sleep with them, and certainly not you.'
He lets those words hang in the air for a moment before
adding, 'I'm going out now to assess the weather and scout
out the area while it's clear. You'd better get dressed.
You'll freeze your arse off dressed like that.'

With that parting shot, he opens the hut door, letting in
a gust of freezing air, and is gone in a moment, leaving me
standing open-mouthed, staring after him, speechless with
impotent fury.

At first, I'm glad Miles has gone. I pull on my jeans, buttoning them up furiously.

*He drives me crazy! I knew from the moment I met him
he had attitude and I was right! Well, as soon as we get out
of here, I'm going take great pleasure in sacking his ass.*

I imagine the scene. I'm standing at my father's side as
he sits behind that huge desk of his – a desk that shows
who really wields the power round here. Together we
watch as a thoroughly cowed Miles comes in and stands
before us. He glances meekly at me. I know that he can see
in my eyes that he's about to get what's coming to him.

'Daddy,' I say coolly. 'This is the one. You must sack
him at once.'

'Anything you say, honey,' responds my father. 'If that's
what you want, that's what you get. He's toast.'

I smile at my father. 'Thank you, Daddy.'

Miles stares down at his hands, his shoulders bowed.
He's utterly beaten.

My father looks up at me, frowning a little. 'Just one
thing, honey. Why am I sacking him?'

'Because . . .' I falter a little. 'Because . . .' Then I say
firmly, 'He disobeyed my orders.'

'Did he?' My father looks grave. 'Why, that's awful. He must certainly be dismissed in that case. And what were your orders?'

I blink hurriedly and say, 'Well . . .'

'Yes?'

'I . . .' Even in my fantasy, I have no idea how to tell my father that I want this bodyguard sacked because he refused to have sex with me when I demanded it. It just isn't the kind of father–daughter conversation I can envisage. My imagination fails and the picture in my mind disappears.

I know what's more likely to happen. Now I can see Miles sauntering in, his right eyebrow lifted in that arrogant way, a sardonic look in his eyes. He's totally in control and completely self-confident. My father is asking him why he wants to quit, and Miles looks at me with a piercing gaze and says quietly, 'Why don't you ask Freya, Mr Hammond?'

'Oh, damn it all!' I say loudly, pulling on my boots. I can't even successfully *imagine* a triumph over him. 'And damn Miles to hell!'

For a while, I let my anger stew, taking pleasure in thinking up ways that I might be able to bring him down and give him a little taste of the humiliation he's given me. Once I'm dressed, I begin to warm up again and the little room is becoming quite cosy with the blaze from the fire. I pick up a log and throw it on, noticing that there're only a few dry ones left. Miles will need to bring some more in from outside so that they can start steaming out their moisture in the warmth of the fire. I wonder where he is. He's been gone a while. I lie down and try to imagine all the things I'll do when I'm out of here, dozing and dreaming while I wait for Miles to come back. I spend a while trying to remember what was in my diary for next week, what my plans were. It's strange how distant and unlikely they all seem now. Was there ever a time when I could do exactly what I wanted – walk out any door, go any place, please myself entirely? There's a different reality now. What will it be like when I get back to my old life? I picture myself telling all my friends about this crazy adventure, all the drama of the crash and the luck of finding the hut, and the way we were rescued.

Rescue? says a little voice in my head. *What rescue?*

I jump up and look out of the little glazed window. Earlier the view was of complete glistening whiteness, pure in the morning light. Now, the window is filled with a yellowish-grey colour that seems to be moving. I realise that the snow has started falling again. The wind is picking up too – I can hear it battering about in the chimney. The storm is back. There won't be any rescue while it's raging outside and I have the distinct sense that it's just getting started. It could last all day. We'll be here another night at least.

I sigh. A night. Memories of being close to Miles in the darkness flood back into my mind and set loose that powerful longing again.

What the hell is *that feeling?*

I've never known anything like it: this intense yearning for Miles's physical presence. I thought I felt that way about Jacob, but what I felt for him was nothing like this desperate desire to be close to Miles. I could happily spend days away from Jacob, as long as we texted and emailed. But the magnetic pull towards Miles is something else:

only being close to him will do. I want the nearness of his body so much.

If only he weren't so incredibly annoying . . . if only he didn't take so much pleasure in pissing me off!

Just thinking about him feeds my hunger for him but I suspect that whatever we had last night is unlikely to be repeated. After what just happened between us, is he likely to want to get close to me again? We had that amazing, delicious encounter and then he had to go and spoil it. I remember the taste of his mouth, the sensation of his lips on mine and those strong arms around me, and I realise that I'm moaning gently at the thought. One hand is rubbing at my shoulder, over my neck, down over my breasts. My sex gives a little judder to remind me that I've teased it horribly today. I'm on the edge of instant arousal. My hand plays over my thigh and I wonder if it would make things easier if I got rid of this troublesome need for Miles by unbuttoning my jeans and letting my hand slip inside to my white knickers. I could let my fingers play over their soft surface, tantalise myself a little, feel my bud swell up to meet my fingertips. It's already tingling in anticipation, I can feel it. I imagine how I would caress it lightly, swirling my fingertips over it so that it buzzes with pleasurable vibrations. I'd feel the honeyed juices rise to meet me, taking a little on my fingertip to allow me to circle the bud all the more easily. I'd increase the pressure slowly, letting it harden under my teasing, and feeling the pulses of pleasure it sends out grow in power . . .

Oh God, I want to do it . . . I need some relief from this hunger . . .

But it wouldn't be enough. He'd only have to walk through the door and I'd be enslaved by need again instantly.

Then my lust dies away in a sudden sensation of unease. How long has he been gone? I've had such complete faith in him, and such trust that he's indestructible, that I haven't been worried. Now, though, I realise that he's been gone for a long time, over an hour. Long enough for my rage against him to die down a little and for my desire to rekindle.

I gaze out of the window again.

It's snowing hard out there. He said that there was almost no visibility when he went out this morning, and that was before it started snowing again. He can't be scouting in this weather, he won't be able to see a thing.

Anxiety flickers in the pit of my stomach.

What else did he say he was going to do?

I can't remember anything else. He's been gone much longer than it would take to look around. My anxiety flares up into fear. What if something's happened to him? Perhaps he tripped and fell, maybe he's broken a leg. He could be lying out there alone in the snow . . .

A mental image presents itself: Miles, pulling himself through a snow drift, in agony from an injured leg, his clothes no match for the fearsome power of the elements. He's fighting it but it's no good – he's gradually freezing to death.

Oh my God – what shall I do?

I stand up, agitated, and begin to pace around the small room. If he's out there, I'll have to go out and find him. There's nothing else for it.

What good will it do if you both freeze to death outside? asks the voice in my head. *Besides, even if you find him, you won't be able to carry him. He's much heavier than you. You should wait here.*

But the image of Miles alone, in danger, in the snow, is too much for me. I pull on my jacket and zip it up with one determined movement. I'm going to go out there, just to take a look. I can't stay here imagining the worst. Besides, what are my chances of surviving without him? I might get through another day or two but without Miles's expertise, I'm not likely to make it.

As I prepare to go outside, it strikes me what a fool I've been.

What the hell was I thinking, talking to him like that?

I know suddenly that if Miles had given in to my commands – if he'd ever obeyed me in the way I insisted that he did – my desire for him would have fallen away. The antagonism between us, the way it keeps flaring up – it's important. I think I understand that now. We're working each other out. Or maybe I'm testing him.

And I'm giving him every excuse he could possibly want to hate me.

I shudder inside suddenly at the memory of how I spoke to him earlier, how I must have looked, the way I used my empty threats to try and manipulate him.

I don't know if I'm ever going to learn to conquer my tendency to act like a spoiled brat when I feel at my most vulnerable but, maybe, if I can persuade Miles to give me another chance, I can make things right again.

That's if I can find him.

There's no way I can go far, but I need to check he's not somewhere nearby. If he were just a metre or two from the hut, unable to make it back alone, how could I live with myself? I'll do a circuit of the hut, I decide, and see what I can find. If there's no sign of him, I'll come back inside.

Taking a deep breath, I walk to the door. I'm ridiculously ill equipped for this. My clothes are laughably inadequate – I look down at my high-heeled boots, the black leather marked with grey ripples from yesterday's snowy walk, and look quickly away again. I've never considered myself a heroine, but I'm about to venture outside anyway.

I open the door to a howling gale of snow and wind, and gasp at the intensity of the cold that instantly engulfs me.

These conditions are deadly. Only an idiot would go out into this weather.

I won't get lost, I tell myself. *It'll be okay if I stay close to the hut. I just have to make sure he's not nearby.*

Then I press my hands into my pockets, lower my chin into the puffy collar, and head out into the white maelstrom.

CHAPTER SIX

I haven't gone very far before I know beyond all doubt that this is the stupidest thing I've ever done. Forget trusting Jacob, this wins first prize in the numbskull stakes. Going out into the storm is sheer foolhardy madness. Almost instantly I'm blinded by snow, stumbling forward into a wind that cuts into my face like hundreds of tiny knives. How will I ever see Miles in this? He could be anywhere.

I have to try. I can't just abandon him.

I keep going, forcing myself forward against the grim strength of the wind that buffets and batters at me. It almost floors me with its punching gusts, but I manage to stay upright and stagger on for a few more minutes before I come to a halt. I try to shout for Miles but my voice is a tiny reed-like sound that is lost instantly in the squalling wind and my mouth fills with snow the moment I open it.

It's no good! I'll have to go back. I won't be able to do a circuit in this.

Fighting to stay on my feet, I turn back the way I've come – and then realise to my horror that I can't see the hut. I can't have walked more than a few metres from it, but I can see nothing in the whirling snowy air. I wonder if I've turned exactly 180 degrees to face the way I came, so that if I go straight on I'll just get there somehow – and immediately lose all sense of direction. I have no idea how far I've turned.

A cold, clammy realisation comes over me. If I'm facing the wrong way and begin to walk, I'll be walking to my death. Without a doubt.

I feel desperately afraid. Everything hinges on what I do next. A surge of anger at myself washes through me before I banish it resolutely. I can't waste time on regretting things. I'm here now and I have to deal with it. I take a step forward into the storm, with the sure certainty that my fate is now decided, and there's no way of knowing yet if I've made the right choice or not. I take another step and then another. I'm committed now. I can only go on.

I begin to pray. *Are you there, Goddess Freya? If you are, I'm in a sticky situation and I need your help. Please, please guide me to where I need to go. Please . . .*

My arms are stretched out in front of me, my fingers, ice-cold, reaching for the stone of the hut wall that could be mere metres away – or in another direction entirely. I blink away the blinding snowflakes, trying desperately to see something, anything, that isn't whirling and white.

Then I see it. My prayers have been answered. A dark shape is emerging from the storm. It must be the hut. I stagger forward to meet it, and it resolves not into the stone wall of the hut but into a figure and I'm falling into a pair of strong arms.

Miles!

Deep gratitude and relief rise up inside me and I send up a heartfelt thank you to the goddess. *He's here. It's going to be all right.*

He's shouting something in my ear, but I can't make out what it is. Then he wraps one arm around me and turns me slightly to the right. We begin to stumble forward together, only able to concentrate on pressing into the force of the buffeting wind. It's only a few minutes before the dark bulk of the hut shows through the storm but it feels like much longer, and another age seems to pass before Miles is yanking open the door and we are falling into the blissful quiet and relative warmth of its interior.

'What the hell were you thinking?' Miles yells, his angry voice ripping through the silence.

I jump, startled. I'm so happy and relieved to be back that his fury shocks me. 'What?'

'You fucking stupid child! Why the hell did you go out into that? Are you suicidal or something?' His dark hair looks white, it's so thick with snowflakes. They hang on his eyelashes and frost his cheeks. His shoulders are coated with a layer of snow and he begins to brush himself off, while still berating me. 'You have to have a brain like a peanut to take such a crazy risk. How on earth am I supposed to protect you if you indulge in such stupidity? Christ!' He looks seriously angry.

I'm indignant at the injustice and try to shout back but my chattering teeth and violent shakes mean I can only say in a quavering voice, 'I'm not stupid, I was c-c-coming to look . . . f-f-for *you*.'

He stops brushing off snow and stares at me in contemptuous disbelief. 'You were trying to look for me in *that*?'

'B-b-because . . . I thought you were . . . *hurt*!'

He frowns, bewildered now.

'I was . . . trying to help you.' I sink down on to the planks nearest the fire. It's died down to a glowing heart, but there is a good heat coming from it.

When Miles speaks again, his voice is softer. 'Well . . . all right. I appreciate your concern. But it was sheer madness. Don't do it again! You were heading off course. You'd have missed the hut and could have plummeted down the mountain.'

'Where were you? You were gone for so long, I didn't know what to think!'

He looks a little sheepish. 'Okay – maybe I did take longer than I should have. The storm hadn't started in earnest when I set out, and I went further than I intended. The conditions changed so fast, I could only get back slowly.'

My shakes are subsiding a little. 'But how did you get back?' I ask. 'It was impossible to see anything.'

He makes an impatient expression at me as he takes off his jacket and lies it on the planks to dry. 'I'm trained for this kind of survival. I've got ways of orienting myself. And, more importantly, I've got this.' He rolls back his jumper sleeve and I can see a black chunky watch on his wrist. I noticed it earlier, I realise, when he took off his shirt: a particularly masculine kind of watch, multi-faced with dials and gadgets. 'It's got a compass,' he explains, and smiles suddenly. 'I wouldn't really think about venturing out in dodgy conditions without one.'

'I'll ask for one for Christmas,' I return.

He laughs. 'You should. Maybe I should teach you a bit about survival. Then you'll think twice before going out into a storm like that with no equipment.'

I say softly, 'I'm sure there's lots you could teach me.'

The atmosphere is instantly charged and he goes very still. He looks away and says in a terse voice, 'I'm not sure you'd like me teaching you anything. You prefer giving the orders, from what I've seen.'

I gaze at him, willing him to look at me. The snow is gone from his dark hair now but it's left it damp and I have a wild desire to run my fingers through it. The expression in his eyes is hidden from me by the hoods of his eyelids and the shadow cast by his strong brow. He sits down opposite me, planting his feet firmly down, and clasping his hands. His mouth has turned into a straight serious line and he's looking anywhere else but at my face.

I feel nervous and shaky inside. I'm about to do something that doesn't come naturally to me. 'Miles . . .'

'Mmm?' He's still not looking at me, gazing instead at the dirt floor of the hut, frowning.

'I . . . I want to say something—'

He begins to talk briskly. 'You know what, we ought to be thinking about lunch. And I'll need to get some more wood in. We can safely say that there won't be a rescue today so we're going to be here until tomorrow at least. If the weather doesn't improve after that, we may have to think again about our options. Now – I'll get the wood if you look through that chest and see what's on the menu.' He stands up, still not meeting my eye.

'Miles – please look at me,' I say beseechingly, stretching out a hand towards him. 'I have to say something, please let me . . .'

Miles turns his head slowly and looks down at me. I can't read the expression in the blue eyes but they look darker somehow, the iris and the rim almost the same shade of navy. His lids are more hooded than ever as though he's determined to keep his innermost thoughts hidden from me. 'What is it?' His voice is low, his tone short.

I realise that there's a huge distance between us. All the intimacy we shared yesterday, the relationship we built up, is all gone. And that's my fault. I wish so much I didn't sabotage everything that matters to me. But I have a chance to put it right. In this situation, no one can jump on a plane and fly across the world because they're offended. There's no huge mansion to keep the warring factions apart. We're together with nowhere else to go. We can't hide from what's gone wrong and we have to put it right, or coexist in miserable enmity.

'Miles, I want . . .' There's that nervous fluttering in my stomach. I've said sorry before but this is a little different. 'I want to apologise for the way I spoke to you earlier. It was awful and you must despise me for it. I know I shouldn't throw my weight around and give orders, and behave so childishly, most of all to you when I owe you for saving my life. So . . . I'm sorry. I won't do it again. Can you forgive me?'

He takes all this in impassively.

I watch him, anxious. Is he going to accept my apology or not? He probably doesn't realise how rare it is for me to humble myself in front of someone else – especially not an employee.

'Of course I forgive you,' he says at last, his voice gruff. 'Thank you, Freya. I appreciate it.'

'Are we okay again then?' I say, venturing a smile at him.

He lets the corners of his mouth turn upwards a little, and something in the set line of his shoulders relaxes a little. 'Yeah. Sure. Of course we are. Now – will it be stew again or do you fancy minestrone instead?'

Despite my apology, the atmosphere is still a little awkward and we busy ourselves with activity to get over it. Miles brings in the logs he left near the door and sets them to dry, and we heat up an unidentifiable casserole for our midday meal, following it with a cup of instant black coffee. Miles talks a lot, telling me what he discovered on his recce earlier and what conclusions he's drawn about how our rescue might be effected.

I listen, taking comfort from the soft burr of his voice and the pleasure of having him near to me. His solid masculinity is reassuring, and the way my body constantly responds to his presence, my skin prickling and tingling whenever he gets close, is something I can't help enjoying. I won't be so stupid as to command him to give me pleasure again, but I can still take it even if he's unaware that he's giving it.

When Miles speculates about the rescue attempts, I wonder what's happening back at home. It's a full day since I walked into that garage with Miles, and the car purred out to head down the mountain. The two of us have disappeared without trace as far as the outside world is concerned. Has anyone noticed? Does anyone care? I imagine Summer sending me a message and wondering why she hasn't heard back. She'll be looking at my networking feeds, to see what I'm saying about LA, and there'll be nothing. Maybe Flora has sent emails and is surprised I haven't replied.

I imagine everyone going about their daily lives without worrying about me, oblivious to my plight. Then I catch myself up. It's just self-pity talking. I know very well that my father will have been told within a very short time that I didn't make the plane. The fact that Miles didn't return will have alerted the house to something out of the ordinary, if nothing else. I can picture my father now, in a fury of panicked activity as he tries to find out where I am. The thought is comforting. I want him to care about me.

I look over at Miles, who is drinking his coffee and leafing through the visitors' book, trying to read in the glow from the fire.

I wonder if someone is frantic with worry about him. He's lost too, after all.

I picture a beautiful woman with two young children. She's walking around a kitchen, a phone clutched to one ear as she tries to feed a baby in a highchair and a toddler. She looks frightened, in utter turmoil because Miles hasn't come home and she's been told that he was last seen heading off down the mountain into an oncoming blizzard.

I glance at his hand. His ring finger is bare. And, from his scruples in denying me this morning, I don't think that he's the kind of man to get as intimate with someone as he did with me if he were married. The picture of the beautiful wife disappears, and I feel obscurely relieved that she doesn't exist. Instead, I see Pierre, our head of security, cursing Miles for obeying my orders and taking one of the boss's expensive cars and his beloved daughter on a fool's errand to almost certain death.

Maybe he has even fewer people who care for him than I do.

I think of my sisters, my family and my friends. In the long hours of the afternoon I wrap myself up in the sleeping bag, and lie down so that I can see the fire dancing, and let my mind wander. It's ages since I've done this. I'm so frightened of being bored that life is a ceaseless round of travel. If I'm not on the move or out with friends, I'm on my phone or tablet or laptop, or I'm at the movies, or watching TV, or at the gym. Relaxing for me usually means lying on the deck of a yacht chatting with friends as we bake a golden tan into our skins, but it's just a chance to plan more activity – more parties, more trips, more of everything.

Here, there is nowhere I can possibly go. There's nothing to do. I'm reliant entirely on myself – and on Miles. I look over at him. He's finished reading the guest book and examining the creased old map he found in the bottom of the box. He's leaning back against the hut wall, a sleeping bag draped around his shoulders, gazing moodily into the fire.

What's he thinking about?

I want to ask, but I fear being too intrusive. I've made my apology but I can't presume too much on it.

It's getting dark outside, I can tell, and I check my watch. It's only three o'clock but the storm is vanquishing what light there is left on this winter afternoon. It'll be black as night soon.

From my prone position on the planks, I glance over at Miles and find his eyes upon me. His dark-blue gaze sends a thrill rippling through me, and I wonder how I'm going to survive being near him and not being able to touch him. I give an involuntary sigh and a tiny shiver.

'Are you all right?' he asks.

I nod.

'Anything troubling you?'

I shake my head slowly but he's not convinced because he says firmly, 'It's going to be all right. I promise. I've had a good scout outside and I've studied that old map. I think I can get us out of here once the weather improves. Even if we can't rely on a rescue.'

The mention of rescue makes me think of my father again, and instead of feeling comforted, I swoop down into a kind of bleakness. I wriggle deeper into my sleeping bag and stare into the flames that are licking around the charred remains of a log.

Miles leans towards me. 'Really, Freya – are you okay? You don't seem full of your usual fire and spice.'

'I'm fine,' I reply in a low voice. I turn my head to face him. 'Is your family going to notice that you're missing?'

'No doubt they'll be informed. They live a long way from here, so my mother won't have been expecting me back for dinner or anything like that.' He laughs lightly. 'It's a long time since those days.'

'So your mother is still alive?'

'Aye. She's in her sixties now but she's in good health, as far as I know. Still running around after my pa and my brother, and looking after her grandkids. She's never thought she should take some time for herself after all these years.'

'Don't you see her then?'

'Not as much as I should. She'd like to see more of me, I know.' He looks thoughtful. 'I suppose she'll be worried about me, if they've told her what's happened. I'll have to call her when we get out of here, make sure she knows I'm all right.'

I can feel my emotions being dragged down into the darkness. This is partly why I keep so busy, why I keep on the move so much. So that I don't have to think about the things that hurt me. I say in a low voice, 'Sometimes I wonder what my life would be like if my mother hadn't died. If I had someone who really cared about me.'

When Miles speaks again, his voice is softer. 'Hey, your father cares about you. I'm sure he's frantic with worry about you.'

'You don't understand how we live,' I say, my tone bleaker than ever. 'There seems to be so little holding us together since we lost my mother. It's as though an explosion blew us all apart and we've never been able to get back together again. My father was always so busy and now he's got a girlfriend, he's got even less time for us.'

'Wait a moment,' Miles says, sitting up straighter. 'I've not been working for your family for long, but I've noticed one thing: your father is obsessed with your security. He keeps tabs on you girls, all the time. Wherever you are. He's going to be moving heaven and earth to get you back home safely, I guarantee it. I can only guess at what it's like to lose your mother so young, but you've got to believe that your father cares about you.'

I sigh again. 'I'm not sure if all the watching and monitoring is because he cares – or because he's afraid.'

'Afraid of what?'

I say nothing. I can't talk about it.

'He's afraid of losing you,' Miles says gently. He watches me for a moment and then says, 'We'll be all right. I'm going to get us out of here. I don't intend ending my days in this hut, glad though I am to have found it. I've still got things I want to do.'

I turn to look at him. 'I don't know much about you at all.'

'Why should you?'

'I'm interested.'

His eyes flicker with dark amusement. 'Really?'

'Yes. I want to know about you. And we can't sit here in silence for the entire time, can we?' I sit up so I'm facing him. 'Tell me about yourself.'

'There isn't all that much to tell,' he says, but I sense that what he means is that there isn't all that much he wants to reveal.

'Well, where are you from?'

'You can't tell from the accent?' He raises that right eyebrow at me again.

'Scotland, obviously – but where in Scotland?' I'm going to persist, damn it. I'm going to get him to tell me something.

'I had no idea you were familiar with the geography of Scotland.'

'There's lots you don't know about me,' I return pertly. 'As it happens, I've been to Scotland once or twice. I stayed near Inverness.'

'Well, I'm not from there. I'm from a small village about ten miles from Edinburgh.'

'I've been to Edinburgh too,' I say quickly. 'It's beautiful.'

'Aye. It's fine.' His accent strengthens the moment he mentions Scotland. 'But I've not been back to Edinburgh for a long time. It's probably quite different now.'

'When did you leave?'

He gives me a bemused look. 'Are you seriously interested?'

'Yes! Of course I am. Tell me. I want to know.' I shuffle forward in my sleeping bag, leaning towards him and fixing him with an earnest look. 'Please.'

Miles looks almost suspicious, as though I'm playing some kind of trick on him but he says, 'Okay then. If you

97

must know, I left when I was a lad to go into the army. I was about nineteen and pretty desperate to escape. Home was all right, don't get me wrong, but I needed to see the world. I was never going to be happy staying where I was and living a life like the one my pals were happy with. The army was my ticket out. I joined as a private and worked my way up to sergeant. It was tough but I loved it, and flourished too. Then my superior officer gave me an interesting talk – a word in my ear, if you like – and when the opportunity came to volunteer for the Special Forces, I took it. The recruitment process was the hardest thing I'd ever done but I was determined that they were going to select me. I did all the physical stuff even though it was gruelling – the runs weighted down with equipment, the river swims, the night missions – but the hardest thing was the interrogation. Thirty-six hours of it, to see if I had the mental toughness to survive being in enemy hands.' A distant look comes into his eyes and I guess that he must be back in whatever place it was that they handed out the treatment he can't forget. He shakes his head slightly and looks back to me. 'But I survived it and I got in. And there I was in 22 Special Air Services Regiment.' He smiles. 'And lucky for us, I was assigned to the Mountain Troop, which meant I was trained in mountaineering, arctic survival and altitude techniques. I've been put through the toughest possible training in Germany and Norway, and climbed the most dangerous mountains in the world.'

'Very handy,' I say, smiling back. 'And what happened then? After you'd joined the regiment?'

He looks almost dreamy for a moment. 'I loved it. I loved my mates, the camaraderie, the bond we all shared. I relished the challenges and pushing myself to the limit.

The work was almost like a game to me, like a boys' own comic, full of mad adventure and strange locations. Yeah . . . it was great . . .'

'So why did you leave?' I ask.

His expression grows darker suddenly. 'I got tired of it. Burnt out. I lost the joy in it, and once you do that, you risk getting scared and you can't ever be scared. I didn't want to go that way, so I left.'

'Just like that? You simply got tired of it?' I can't help thinking there's more to the story than he's telling me. It's obvious that he loved the SAS. Why did he give it all up?

Miles sighs shortly. 'If you must know, it was after a stint in Afghanistan. We were sent out there to deal with Taliban resistance in the mountains. I spent two years out there and by the end of that, I was finished. I'd had enough, simple as that.'

'Why did you decide to become a bodyguard?' I'm looking at him in a new light now. I knew he was strong but I had no idea how skilled and highly trained he actually is. This man has been in situations I can't even imagine. It seems ridiculous that someone with his abilities spends his time looking after pampered girls like me and my sisters. My high-handed attitude towards him now seems even more unforgiveable than ever.

Miles shrugs. 'It seemed like a good stop-gap while I decide what I want from life. One of my mates did it and recommended it – easy work for very good money, with some travel and comfortable lodgings thrown in. Plenty of ex-servicemen go into security. We've been trained to be the best in the world, and people like your father need us for their protection. So . . . here I am.'

'That's it?'

'Aye.'

'Your entire life told in about ten minutes?' I make a face. 'I don't believe it. What about a wife or a girlfriend? What about family?'

His face takes on a closed expression. 'No wife, no girlfriend either right now. My family consists of my old ma and pa, still happily married after forty years, my brother and his wife and kids, a few cousins I used to see if I went back for Christmas, which wasn't often. That's plenty enough for me, thanks. I like to travel light.'

There's more to it, I know there is, but I can't press him any longer. I've have a feeling I've gone far enough already and, as my new resolution is not to throw my weight around, I don't think I can insist on it. Besides, he's already told me how much he hates interrogation. So I decide on an unaccustomed path for me: I'll bide my time. I'll just have to be patient.

After all, we've got all night.

A delicious shiver judders over me at the thought of a night with Miles. I feel that certainty again, the sense that there's a lot that Miles could show me . . . *He knows what he's doing, that's for sure.* I wonder about the women in his past – who they are, how many there are. I imagine him caressing a woman, driving himself hard inside her, kissing her mouth, breasts and shoulders. *God, I wish it were me.*

Miles stands up suddenly and his form towers over me, appearing to fill the room. 'That's enough about me. I'm sure your stories are better than mine. Why don't you tell me a bit about your life while I make us some coffee? Would you like some?'

I nod and he fills the kettle and sets it over the fire to boil. He asks me a few questions about my life but I'm not in the mood for talking about myself. I'm interested in him but whenever I try to turn the subject back towards him, he dodges it. It feels as though we're playing a subtle and complicated word game where the aim is to give away as little information as possible. In the end, over tins of black coffee, we chat about our favourite films instead. I expect Miles to like gory violent thrillers and martial arts pictures, but instead it turns out he loves film noir of the thirties and forties.

'Barbara Stanwyck in *Double Indemnity*,' he says, wrapping his hands around his tin of coffee. 'Now there was a dame. And anything with Jimmy Cagney. His charisma just leaps off the screen.'

I'm impressed. 'I don't know much about early film. I love comedies – anything to make me laugh. But that's more modern stuff.'

He gives me a look of mock outrage. 'Some of the funniest films ever were made in the thirties and forties!'

'Really?'

'Yes!' He laughs. 'Cary Grant was one of the most gifted comic actors in film. As for Claudette Colbert, Carole Lombard . . .'

'I've heard of Cary Grant, of course,' I say tentatively.

He slaps his forehead in pretend despair. 'Oh my God, girl. There is a lot to teach you!'

I gaze at him with wide eyes, hoping he can see my desire to be taught. He catches my expression and quickly turns back to his coffee.

'Well, the good thing is how much you've got waiting for you to enjoy. I'll make you a list of my favourites if you like.'

'I would like that, very much,' I say.

101

'All right. It's a deal. All I ask in return is that you tell me what you make of them. Okay?'

'Okay.' I smile at him.

He tells me about some of his favourite directors while we eat our soup; he rates John Houston and Preston Sturges, neither of whom I've heard of, but I make a note to look them up when I have access to Google again. It's strange to think that unless circumstances had thrown us together, I would never know this stuff about Miles. I'd have no idea that he's tracked down the Taliban in the mountains of Afghanistan or that he's a nut for classic film. I'd still be treating him with haughty disdain, expecting him to obey my orders as though that's what he was born to do, as though he had no other purpose in life. This situation has changed everything around. Now I'm hanging on what he's telling me, trying to learn a bit about life outside my own orbit of privilege and instant gratification.

After a while, he suggests we have something to eat.

'Is it supper time already?' I ask, surprised. 'It feels like we've only just had lunch.'

'It's getting close to six o'clock, we've been talking for a while.'

I hadn't noticed. For the first time, the hours have slid by almost pleasurably. 'I'm not very hungry.'

'We should eat something just to keep our strength up. There're some soup sachets. Let's have one of those each.'

He goes about refilling the kettle, prodding the fire back to life with a fresh log and making us each a tin of soup, chicken flavour with bits of reconstituted sweetcorn floating in it. It's surprisingly comforting, and while we eat it, I tell him stories about my days as the naughtiest girl at my St Moritz boarding school, and how I used to escape late at night and head out to nightclubs in the town. He laughs when I tell him some of my most daring exploits, and I feel my mood lifting. I like to hear his laugh when it's not mocking me. The way he throws back his head and roars heartily at the stories of my bad behaviour makes me feel warm and happy.

'What did they do to you in the end?' he asks, after I tell him of Mademoiselle D'Anton's shock when I skied in my underwear for a dare.

'Oh, they expelled me, of course.' I shrug. 'But it didn't matter. There were always places that would take me in. My father just paid for me to go to the next on the list.'

'Didn't he give you a good telling off?'

I shake my head. 'No. His assistant, Jane-Elizabeth, told me off – then she arranged a new school for me. I don't know if she even told Dad what had happened.'

Miles gives me a sideways look and just says 'Hmm' in reply. I get the feeling he's understood more about me than I meant to give away.

When we've finished, it's properly dark outside and the only light comes from the fire. Miles has decided that the torch has to be kept for emergencies. I don't mind; I like the way the little hut descends into velvety blackness illuminated by the orange glow from the hearth. The crackling, flickering flames are comforting. They seem to be our allies: something warm and alive to help us combat the freezing cold elements outside. I wonder if the storm has abated at all, but the wind is still howling.

I look over at Miles. He's gazing into the fire too, lost in his own thoughts. I wonder what they are: if he's thinking about the past, or about how we're going to get out of here, or maybe . . .

He turns suddenly to me and says, 'You've been different this afternoon, Freya. I didn't really expect it but ever since you've apologised – it's like the anger has gone out of you.'

'Do I seem very angry?'

'You're quick to feel persecuted, quick to square up for a fight, that's all. I never know what's going to set you off.'

'I guess . . . I'm not used to not having my own way. Now I'm in a place where I've got no control at all . . . maybe that made me want to try and control you instead.' I shrug lightly. 'I've been in therapy. My father made me go. I've seen loads of shrinks and more than one of them said my need to control comes from a fear of loss or something like that. I don't know if there's anything in it.'

'Shrinks . . .' he echoes. 'How old are you?'

'Twenty-three.'

'That's young to be in therapy, isn't it?'

'Depends what has happened to you, doesn't it?' I gaze back at the fire. 'Things happened to me when I was younger. That was why I needed therapy, apparently.'

He doesn't press me to find out more. Instead he says, 'You've got so much time to enjoy, Freya. You're young. Life is on your side right now. Grasp it with both hands, make something of it.'

'How old are *you*?' I ask, turning to look at him. He doesn't look old but the silver speckles in his short hair and the lines on his brow show that he's lived a little.

'Thirty-five,' he says. 'Older than you by a considerable margin.'

'Not that much older,' I say quickly. 'Twelve years. That's nothing.'

He gives me a quizzical look. 'How old was your last boyfriend?'

'Well, he was twenty-five but—'

'And I bet you thought he was the height of adult sophistication!' Miles laughs.

'No I didn't!' I reply hotly. 'He was a stupid, immature kid who'd never learned anything worth knowing in his life! All he cared about was partying and getting laid – not always with me, as I discovered. I can't tell you how humiliating it was to have to get myself checked up for STDs. Luckily, all the tests came back clear, so that's something.' I unwrap myself from my sleeping bag and lean even closer towards Miles. 'I was hurt at the time because I'd really loved him. But now I'm beginning to realise that he had nothing real to teach me about life.'

I feel a strange quivering excitement in my belly. All day, at the back of my mind, I've been thinking about the moment when I will make it clear to Miles what I want. I've thought of it with nervous anticipation and a kind of giddy thrill, wondering how it will happen. Now, I'm sure that the moment is here. I'm going to put all my cards on the table. I take my sleeping bag and spread it out on the dirt floor, the fleece lining uppermost, and then I kneel on it so that I'm at Miles's feet as he sits on the bench opposite me. I look up at him, admiring the way the orange firelight falls on his face, giving him romantically hollowed cheeks and emphasising the shadowed depth of his eye sockets. He's frowning slightly, puzzled, watching me, waiting to see what I'll do next.

'Miles,' I say in a quiet voice. 'You remember what happened between us this morning, don't you?'

He's suddenly awkward. 'Of course,' he says gruffly.

'I tried to seduce you. I made a mess of it.'

'Please . . . don't worry about it.' He looks away, not able to meet my gaze. 'Consider it forgotten about. We don't need to mention it again.'

'But I want to talk about it. The things you said about me, about the way I treat people. It was hard to hear, but you were right. I've realised now that I'm going about so much in the wrong way.'

He looks back at me, intrigued by what I'm saying. 'Am I hearing right? Is Miss Freya Hammond being humble?'

'For once,' I say, with a short laugh. 'You've made me take a look at myself and I'm not sure I like it.'

'You shouldn't be too hard on yourself,' he replies. 'You're young. And the way you've been brought up – well, it's hardly surprising that you have a well-defined sense of your own importance. But you're a decent kid, you really are. You'll get there in the end.'

I lift my chin to look him right in the eye. 'But I can't get there on my own. I need help. I need . . . a teacher.'

He gives me a sideways look. 'What do you mean – a teacher?'

'Someone who understands the world, who knows something about life. You know so much – about how to survive out here, how to look after yourself . . .'

'That's my job,' he interjects.

'Yes, but it still means you have knowledge that I'm lacking. I want some of the wisdom you've got.'

'Freya, you can't just be given wisdom. It isn't that easy,' he says gravely. 'We all have to make our own mistakes, you know that.'

'But everyone needs a teacher, someone to show them the way.'

'You want me to teach you mountain survival?' He frowns.

'No. Not that. I mean something else. I . . . I . . .' I look away, lost suddenly. It all seemed so clear in my own head but I'm not articulating it very well. *What do I really want? What am I actually asking for?* Then it comes to me. 'I want you to teach me about what men and women do.'

There's a loaded pause and then he says softly, his accent more rolling and caressing than ever, 'It seems to me that you know very well what men and woman do, if this morning was anything to go by.'

I smile up at him, his tone relaxing me. 'I'm not a virgin but I have the feeling that there's much, much more to know. More than my boyfriend was ever able to show me.'

'Wait.' His eyes glitter with amusement. 'You are a cunning little kitten, I will give you that. You've lulled me into a sense of false security but actually, we're back where we started, aren't we? When you asked me to . . . *pleasure you.*'

I lower my head so that I'm not looking directly at him. 'Yes – nothing has changed. I'm still desperate for you. But then I was ordering you. Now . . . I'm asking, humbly.'

I stay very still, looking at the floor again, feeling as though everything is balanced on this moment. I don't know if I've persuaded him, but the way I've asked feels right to me. I want him to be my teacher, my instructor in a world I'm eager to explore. I know that the condition will be surrendering my power over him – the power I have in the outside world. I wait, desperate to know his answer, my fingertips trembling lightly.

He speaks at last, his voice strangely rough. 'But something hasn't changed. I would still be abusing my position of trust if I sleep with you, no matter how much you beg me.'

I lift my head slightly to look at him, hoping that my sincerity will be evident in my eyes.

'You have my word that whatever happens here will remain a secret. I will never divulge to anyone anything that takes place inside this hut. I give you my solemn promise.'

He is staring back at me, his lips tight and his eyes grave beneath their hooded lids. 'Can I really trust your promise?'

'Yes,' I say in a heartfelt voice. 'I might be many things, but I'm not a liar or a traitor. I'll never go back on my word.'

'You know what, Freya Hammond? I think I believe you.'

'Then . . .' I turn my gaze to him. 'Will you? Will you be my teacher?'

There's a long pause. I know he's thinking it over. He desires me, I felt it this morning, but he needs more than that to agree to this. At last he speaks, his voice low, its roughness gone. 'There would be . . . conditions.'

My breathing quickens and the shaking in my fingers gets stronger. A throb of desire swells between my legs.

'Yes,' I whisper. I lift my top and remove it in one swift movement, so that I'm sitting there, my skin touched by the orange firelight, the light falling on my breasts as they rise from the cups of my bra. My bruise is still there, dark against my white skin but I hope that this time it doesn't put him off. 'I'm ready for my first lesson.'

CHAPTER SEVEN

Miles is staring at me, his gaze raking my body as I sit in front of him, offering myself to him. The atmosphere between us has become highly charged. I can feel electrical currents of desire zipping over me, flicking out to the zones of my body that most long for Miles's touch: my lips, my nipples and my sex. My breath is coming fast now and my chest is rising and falling quickly as I try to control my growing excitement. I've been deadly serious in everything I've said to Miles: I want to be taught. I don't want some mindless quick fuck, the kind he thought I wanted this morning: I want something beautiful, something meaning-ful. I have a feeling that Miles is going to change my life and it is about to start right now.

'You look very beautiful,' he says. 'Do you know how hard it was to pull away from you this morning? I've never had to fight so hard to control myself.'

'It was the same for me,' I say softly. 'I've been desper-ate for you since last night in a way I've never felt for anyone.'

His gaze is intense and feels as though it is burning right into my skin.

Oh my goodness, if this is what his eyes do to me, what will happen when he actually touches me?

My skin prickles with delicious anticipation at the thought of it. My desire moves up another notch and I can feel the answering throb between my legs. I know I'm already wet and ready.

'Freya . . .' His voice caresses my name. I love it on his lips. 'I'm flattered you feel this way about me. I'd be a madman not to want you – but I'm not going to take advantage of you. You're young. We're in a strange situation. Emotions are riding very high. So let's discuss my conditions.'

'Yes?' I'm intrigued as to what they are.

'First: health and safety. You said your last boyfriend slept around and you had yourself tested afterwards, so I'm assuming you have a clean bill of health.'

I nod. 'I haven't slept with anyone since the tests.'

'Okay. I have an annual health check, the latest was a few months ago. I only have protected sex until my partners are tested and we're exclusive. I'm single at the moment.'

I'm curious and I want to ask more but I say nothing. I want to know the conditions.

Miles's gaze becomes a little more intense as he says, 'So, if we're going to have sex there's another issue. Contraception. I don't have any condoms with me. I assume if you're single, you're not on the Pill?'

I look up at him a little coquettishly. 'Actually, I am. I don't intend to have kids for a while, so I had a three-year contraceptive implant put in.' I hold out my arm, showing him the soft underside. 'It's under the skin here.'

He nods. 'I see. Sensible. As long as it doesn't stop you having safe sex as well.'

'Don't worry about that. I'm very safety conscious.' I smile.

'It's just right now that you want to throw caution to the winds,' he says with a kind of half smile.

'Well, we might be going to die anyway,' I throw back. 'We may as well have fun while we wait for the end. Safe sex doesn't seem so important when you might not be alive by the end of the week.'

'I'm going to get us out of here,' he says firmly, 'don't worry about that.'

'So what are your other conditions?' I'm being driven to pleasurable distraction by his nearness and my own semi-nakedness. I want him to touch me so badly it's all I can do not to leap up and take possession of his mouth.

He leans towards me, his blue eyes serious but crackling with something that excites me almost unbearably. 'Here are the rules. In this hut you're not going to be Freya Hammond, heiress, daughter of my boss, and I'm not going to be your bodyguard, someone you can order around. Things are going to be very different between us. When we get out, normal relations will be re-established and everything that has happened here will be forgotten. Do you agree?'

My heart is racing now. My imagination is titillated by this idea. 'I won't be . . . me?'

'That's right.' His lips curl up into a smile. 'If you really want me to teach you, you have to be a willing and obedient pupil. You have to do what I say without challenging my authority. You may ask questions as long as it is part of your education, but you can't gainsay me or question my decisions. Do you understand?'

A curling snake of thrilling pleasure is unwinding in my belly. 'Yes,' I say.

111

'Do you agree?'

I nod.

'You need to answer me when I speak to you.'

'Yes, I agree.'

'Good,' he says with evident satisfaction. 'To help you learn everything I can teach, you have to be prepared to do exactly as I say. But there may be things you do not wish to do, or that you fear will push you to the limit. If you feel that, you may stop the tutorial by requesting *study time*. Okay?'

I nod again, and then say quickly, 'Yes, I understand.'

'I want a willing student. You will not regret my instruction. If you are wilful, disruptive, rude or disobedient, I may have to punish you.'

My belly flips and my sex gives a violent judder. '*Punish me?*' I whisper.

'Of course,' he says in a low voice, 'but only if you merit it. Good behaviour will be rewarded, believe me . . .'

A tiny moan escapes me and I moisten my lips, panting a little as I wonder exactly what my rewards will be. *I have a feeling I'm going to like them.*

'Are you in agreement with all of this?'

'Yes, I agree.'

'Excellent. But to show that we're not who we are in the outside world, that my rules are the ones we follow in here, I'm going to give you a different name, one that you'll go by while you're my student.' He stares at me intently for a moment.

This is the most exciting foreplay I've ever known – and he hasn't even touched me yet.

Finally he says, 'I'm going to call you after your goddess's season. You're going to be Winter.'

I nod. 'Winter. Yes, I understand. Shall I call you Teacher?'

'No. This isn't a classroom: you're too old for school. This is more like private instruction. You may call me . . . Tutor. Yes, I think that's appropriate. Now, Winter . . . are you ready for your first lesson?'

I lick my lips again. I've been ready for a while but I've enjoyed this introduction to my new role as Miles's student. It's been stimulating. My bud has been inflamed by his induction talk and I feel as though he'll only have to touch me with a fingertip to set me off into shuddering ecstasy. 'Yes, Tutor,' I say.

'Good. Then we'll begin. First, I need to know what you've already learned.' He eyes me gravely, his gaze moving over me. 'Stand up, Winter.'

I get slowly up from my knees and say, 'I'm afraid my last instructor was not . . . very well qualified.'

There's a flash of amusement in his eyes. 'I'm sorry to hear that, Winter. I'll have to give my attention to undoing his clumsy technique and showing you a more polished way of doing things. I hate to see a woman of your calibre being given a second-rate education. I think you should take off your jeans now. I need to see you.'

Oh boy. I think we're going to enjoy this game. My education is about to begin.

I unbutton my jeans and slide them down, stepping out of them so that I'm standing in just my bra and knickers, wishing I wasn't wearing yesterday's underwear. But I have a delightful feeling that I won't be wearing them for much longer.

'You're very beautiful, Winter,' he says appreciatively. 'I always knew you were a fine-looking woman but I didn't realise what treasures you were hiding from me.'

I look down at my own body. I'm tall with long legs and my frame is slender with a decent helping of curves in the right places. I'm lucky to have inherited my mother's figure, rather than my father's stockiness. The sight of my own semi-nakedness is arousing. I feel a wash of excitement at Miles's evident approval, almost glad that I can make him happy with my body. I'm certain that he can take me to heights of bliss with his. 'Thank you, Tutor.'

He raises his right eyebrow. 'Your tone is excellent, Winter. You're evidently learning to be humble.' Miles stands up and the way he towers over me makes a thrill of excitement course through me. He's huge, so masculine. I can't wait to be possessed by him: I'm ravenous for him. He walks around me, inspecting me carefully as though I'm a prize exhibit or a specimen he's evaluating for quality. I'm buzzing with the anticipation of his touch but he stays at a distance. When he has circled me, he sits down again on the bench.

'Winter – come towards me and turn your back to me.'

I step forward so that my legs are almost touching his knees and turn around so that I'm facing the opposite wall and the tiny window, glittering black in the firelight. His hands land lightly on my back and swiftly undo my bra. It drops away from my chest and Miles takes it away. My breasts are free now, each pink nipple already hard with my arousal. I try to control my rapid breathing and the way my chest is rising so fast but it's difficult.

'Turn around and let me see you.' His voice is low but commanding and I obey, turning slowly to face him. His expression is impassive but as his eyes light on my breasts, I see a flicker of desire there. He examines them without speaking for a few moments and then says, 'You're beautiful, Winter. I'm going to enjoy your instruction a very great deal.'

Miles stands up again. He's tall and my head comes only to the top of his chest. My lips part at the impact of his nearness and the warm masculine smell of his body. He looks down at me: in the intensity of his blue eyes I can see desire and tenderness, and they are a potent mix, stoking my need for him to an even greater height.

'Winter . . . I'm going to kiss you. Let me lead you. Do not move your tongue until I say so.'

I nod.

Slowly he lowers his face to mine. My heart is juddering now, racing with the thrill his proximity is sending through me. My lips are tingling with the desire to feel his pressed upon them. He draws out the moment as he approaches, looking first deep into my eyes and then at my mouth, as though it's the thing he wants most in the world. His nose brushes my cheek and I sigh with longing and lick my lips again. His skin, raspy with the stubble that's grown since yesterday, grazes against mine.

Please, I beg silently, *I can't stand this. Please kiss me!*

But still he takes his time, pressing his face to mine, inhaling the scent of my skin. Then his hand goes to the back of my head – his hand is so broad that he can easily cup my skull in it – and he tilts my face upwards so that he can, at last, put his mouth on mine.

The sensation is blissful and I can't stop my mouth opening at once under his but he pulls away immediately. 'No. No – closed for now. Let me open you.'

I obey, closing my mouth so that he can press his beautiful lips on it as he kisses me softly and delicately. My eyes close so that I can concentrate solely on the light, bird's wing touch of his mouth as he kisses me, not just on my lips but on my face, my cheeks, my chin and even on at the junction of my jaw just below my ear. The kisses are burning hot trails wherever they touch me. I'm trembling with excitement and still he goes on with his soft, entrancing kisses. They're like nothing I've ever known, raising me to a new level of arousal. Then, when I don't think I can take any more, the kisses change: his mouth becomes more insistent, pressing harder on me, wanting more. He moves his focus to my mouth and lips, and now the tip of his tongues emerges to touch my lips.

Trying to obey his instructions, I keep my mouth closed, letting his tongue run along my lips. He licks me gently, the hand that's cupping my skull pulling me closer to him. I'm desperate to open my mouth but I use all my willpower to keep my lips sealed as his tongue begins to probe between them.

Then he moves his mouth to my ear and whispers, 'Now you can open your mouth – but keep your tongue still.'

The whisper reverberates along my nerve ends, sending powerful shivers out all over me. Then his lips are back on mine, his probing tongue pushing between them and at last I can open to him – but I must keep my tongue still, even though I long to respond to his as it enters my mouth. He tastes sweetly delicious, musky and masculine, and he takes his time, exploring me, tasting me back, while I wrestle with the urge to move my own tongue. Then he murmurs into my mouth: 'You can move now' and at last I can obey my impulse to meet his tongue with mine. The kiss is dizzying as I lose myself utterly in the delight of his mouth. The hand behind my head keeps me firmly pressed to him, but

Miles's other hand is running over my back, along the curve of my waist and on my hips, smoothing over my skin and making it burn where he touches it.

I've never known a thrill like this: the simple kiss and one hand on my bare skin is sending me wild, maddening me with desire. We kiss on, irresistibly hungry for one another, each moment heightening our passion further. I want to press my whole body against his, but he's keeping a space between us. I can guess that we won't be moving this lesson on too fast – not yet, at least – but I don't care. We could kiss like this for hours, as far as I'm concerned. I don't think I could ever tire of it, as his insistent mouth sends waves of pleasure coursing through me. It occurs to me that the effect on me is so strong, I could even come like this, brought to a shuddering climax by his kiss alone.

Miles pulls away from me for a moment, taking his mouth from mine with the consolation of more hot little kisses along my face. I open my eyes. I feel dazed, as though I've been in another world. He's smiling at me, tender and sweet.

'You have to know how to kiss,' he murmurs. 'These kisses are to warm your passion and fire you up. Later, we'll learn many different kisses, ones designed for when you are in the heights of ecstasy. Winter, you are definitely made for kissing.'

'I love it,' I say, while I think *made for kissing* you. *It wasn't like this with Jacob.*

'Good. You are a very enthusiastic learner so far.'

'What's my reward?' I ask huskily.

His eyes become stern. 'Don't get ahead of yourself, Winter. You've only just begun. There's a long way to go yet.'

I draw in a shivery breath of anticipation.

'Rewards will come in time. Get them too easily, and they won't mean anything. You will need to know the value of them before you receive them.'

'Yes, Tutor. I understand.'

He looks down at my breasts. 'These are very beautiful. You're deliciously made. Made for pleasure.'

I lift my chin and push my chest forward, so that my breasts almost touch his jumper. I'm desperate for him to caress them. The pink nipples have darkened to a dark rose, each one hard and ready to be toyed with.

'Slowly, slowly . . .' he says reprovingly. 'You want everything at once. You want to rush. I think you've never learned to savour your pleasures, and to engage the senses bit by bit so that you heighten your eventual enjoyment.'

'I can't help it,' I say longingly. I want to see and feel him, to undress him, run my hands over every bit of him, kiss each inch of his warm skin. I've never felt so possessed by lust for a man.

'You must help it. You must control yourself. Those are my terms, remember?'

I nod.

'What?'

'Yes, Tutor.'

'Good. Don't be impatient. You'll get all you want and more.'

More! I want the more right now! insists a voice in my head but I damp it down.

Miles drops kisses on my shoulders and then runs a finger across my sternum, trailing along it from right to left. 'You mustn't be greedy, Winter. Don't wolf it down – enjoy the meal.'

'Yes, Tutor.' My voice is cracked with desire.

'Now. Where were we? Ah yes, kissing.' He lands his lips on mine again and at once we're lost in that beautiful place where our mouths are joined together. I can't help myself – I reach up and put my arms around his neck. Instantly, he pulls away from me, frowning.

'Did I say you could do that?' he says, his voice stern.

'No, but—'

'No buts. You do as you're told, and you don't take the initiative. Those are our terms, remember?'

'All right – I'm sorry . . .' I say quickly, wanting to get back to the delicious kissing.

'You don't sound very sorry, Winter.'

'Of course I am.' I smile at him, expecting his expression to soften and his eyes to grow tender again but he seems as stern as ever, his lips just a little tight.

'Perhaps you haven't really understood what I want from you. I think that a small punishment is in order.'

'Punishment? What punishment?'

'I think that you'll have to wait a little longer before you get what it is that you want.'

'Oh!' My heart sinks.

Miles looks at me and purses his lips, then says, 'If you can't accept the terms, then our agreement is at an end. I'm the master here, that is the way it has to be.'

That thought fills me with horror. I couldn't bear to be deprived now. 'I'm sorry,' I say quickly. 'I understand – I've been too impulsive, too forward. I know that the way I'm going to learn is by following your instructions, not by doing things my own way. I promise I'll obey from now on.'

Finally, Miles's expression softens. 'All right,' he says. 'I'm glad to hear that. But I still have to make my point. Sit over there, and wait.'

119

I can't bear it. I don't want to be parted from him. But I can see that I have to show my acquiescence, demonstrate that I'm going to be obedient, so I go to the bench opposite and sit down. Miles sits down too, leans back against the wall and closes his eyes. There's nothing else I can do but wait until he decides to open them again.

I watch him, admiring the lines of his face, his straight nose and the way his mouth looks chiselled, as beautiful as a Grecian statue's. His thick dark brows with their slightly pointed arches give him that sardonic look.

He's so gorgeous. I can't believe I didn't notice it when I first met him.

I paid him hardly any attention, I just let his masterful aura rile me. Now here I am, willing to beg him just to open his eyes and look at me, let alone touch me. The frustration of wanting him, having him so near and yet so distant, is almost too much to bear. And then, after what feels like an age, he opens his eyes and stares straight at me, the blue almost black in the firelight.

'Ready, Winter?'

'Oh, yes, I am. I won't disobey again.'

'This has been a mild punishment to show you that I'm serious about obedience. You understand that now, don't you?'

'Yes.' My voice is freighted with longing for him.

He stands up. 'Come here.'

I stand too and walk the two steps that take me to him.

'Now.' He looks down at me, raising that right eyebrow just a little. It sends a thrill through me and I feel everything in me begin to warm again. 'The mouth is used to play the other person's body, to wake sensation in it. You've already discovered a little of the mouth's ability to tantalise and tease, and then awaken deeper desires. Now I'm going to show you how my mouth will bring you pleasure.'

I sigh lightly, thinking of what his mouth might be going to do to me. He lifts a hand and brushes it over my upper arms and shoulders, then gently cups my left breast, rubbing a thumb over my pert nipple. His other hand cups my right breast and does the same as he lowers his head to kiss me. Our tongues play lovingly with each other for a while and then he leaves my mouth and trails kisses over my neck and shoulders, nipping lightly at my skin, or sucking and licking with delicate feathery touches of his tongue lips. When he reaches the mound of my breasts, he slows down and approaches my left breast with exquisite tiny kisses that set my nipple tingling with anticipation. I'm desperate for him to take it in his mouth but he makes me wait as he caresses the soft skin and in tiny steps gets closer to the prize.

I'm panting and needy as he finally reaches the aureole and licks around my hard nipple. When Jacob sucked my breasts, it felt as though it was because it gave him pleasure. I've never realised what pleasure my breasts can give me, until now. My nipple seems to have an electrical connection to my deepest, secret parts and it's sending euphoric messages along the line, stimulating a delightful need. I feel almost faint as he at last takes my whole nipple in his mouth and begins to pull on it lightly, his tongue caressing it and drawing it out to an even harder peak. I gasp softly and watch his dark head bent over my breast as he cups me gently and sucks with increasing pressure. I'm so turned on, I'm shaking all over and my knees are trembling. After slow, delicious minutes, Miles turns his attention to my other breast, and once he has nipped and sucked the other nipple with the same loving ministration, I'm in a frenzy of desire, my sex hot now, burning with wet and almost unbearable need.

At last he pulls away from my soft mounds and looks at me with a smile. 'You're delicious, Winter. I think you're learning now about the power of the mouth, aren't you?'

I nod, not able to speak, just wanting him to use his mouth on me until I melt away into bliss. I can see from the intensity in his eyes that what he's been doing has stimulated his own lust.

I wish he'd let me touch him!

I'm desperate to feel his skin, to taste him, to feel the proof of his arousal. It's almost cruel to stop me following my desire like this.

He takes a step back and sits down on the bench again.

A rush of disappointment swirls through me. *What? What's happening now? Is he going to ignore me?* Panic flares in me: I've done nothing wrong. I've been obedient. Why am I going to be punished?

But then he murmurs in that sexy accent, 'Come closer.'

I move towards him and stand just before him so that my breasts are tantalisingly close to his mouth again. He kisses each nipple quickly, flicking his tongue over them and pulling his teeth over the sensitive buds so that I draw in sharp breaths as a bolt of pleasure hits my sex. Then, his large hands on my back, he draws my body close to his mouth and begins to anoint my skin with his tongue, taking in the curve of my breasts and moving slowly downwards, not missing any inch, even tenderly following the path of my bruise, taking care not to press upon it. He's driving me wild, but I stay as still as I can. I long to clasp his head in my hands and pull him to me even tighter but I keep my arms at side, my fists clenched with the effort not to seize him. All the time I'm aware that he's getting to closer to the core of me, where all the torrents of desire are gushing hard and strong.

I groan as he reaches my belly button and runs his tongue around it, causing exquisite trembling pangs. He pushes his tongue in, and I sigh at the sensation and at the sudden idea that his tongue is like a tiny cock and he's fucking me with it. My bud is swollen and stiff, eager for its share of Mile's attention. I can myself swelling against the fabric of my knickers, even the light cotton stimulating me where it touches and rubs against me. I can feel my wetness too, it's an all-too-obvious sign of the effects of what Miles is doing to me.

Now his mouth is burning a hot trail from my belly button downwards to the edge of my knickers. I can't stop my breath coming in excited pants as he runs one finger around the scalloped edging and lightly pulls the elastic away from my skin. I know the scent of my arousal must be as unmistakeable as the way my clitoris thrusts eagerly outwards.

Is he going to make me stand through this? I'm not going to have the strength!

His powerful arm supports me as I shake, while his other hand gently pulls down my knickers to reveal my sex below. I've never been shy but I feel suddenly more exposed than I ever have in my life. He says nothing and doubts race through me: am I beautiful to him? Does he like what he sees?

He inhales my scent and, as if reading my mind, he says, 'You're amazing, Winter. You're making it hard for me to concentrate on your lesson, do you know that? I'm working very hard here to stay in control.'

I imagine the hardness in his jeans, that strong shaft I've felt but never seen. I want it very badly but any chance of possessing it seems a long way off. I concentrate instead on what Miles's mouth is about to do. My knickers are at my feet, and he helps me step out of them and then parts my legs very gently with his hand. I'm standing right in front of him, my sex before him. He looks at me and now there's dark excitement in his eyes. His nostrils are flared and his breath is coming short now. He draws a finger gently over the lips of my sex, touching my swollen bud with a feathery touch that sends a bolt of excitement coursing through me. I stagger slightly and his arm instantly tightens, holding me up.

'I think you might be done standing,' he murmurs. 'We'd better change this arrangement.'

He stands up and takes me in his arms, and I relax into them. We look deep into one another's eyes and then our mouths meet and we kiss, more passionately than before. I sense that his lust is inflamed now, and that the lesson may take a different turn. As he pulls me to him, my nipples brushing the wool of his jumper with an almost painful sensitivity, I feel that his hardness against my belly. I want him so badly now.

He pulls away from me and says, 'Let's make this as comfortable as we can.'

My sleeping bag is still lying on the floor and he quickly takes the other two and unzips them, lying them down on top and creating as much of a mattress as he can.

'It's not exactly five-star accommodation,' he says with a grin, crouching on the makeshift bed.

'I don't care,' I say. I just want to be entwined with him, possessed by him. I want to open myself to him. He beckons me and I go him. Taking me by the hand, he pulls me down to the floor. I lie down, my skin white against the fleece linings. He reaches up to the bench for my puffy jacket which he quickly folds up and places under my head as a pillow, then lies next to me, dropping hot kisses on my shoulders and caressing my breasts.

'Now,' he says softly. 'Where was I? Oh yes, that's right . . .'

He pushes my thighs apart gently with his hand and moves so that he is between them. I groan a little, wanting him to release his magnificent cock and thrust it in to me so that he can calm this urgent desire he's been stoking for so long – but he's not going to do that. Instead, his mouth goes back to its work, kissing, licking and sucking. He revisits my breasts but his path from them to my belly is quicker now. I'm already so hot and fired up that he has no need to spend longer exciting me. I'm desperate for his tongue to find my secret places and for it to incite fresh pleasure there. He's at my mound now, his breath hot on my lips. His strong hands grasp me at the hips as he nuzzles at me, not quite touching, letting his breath fall onto the swollen tip of my clitoris.

I gasp. *Oh my God, that's gorgeous. Touch me with your tongue, Miles,* please!

I think I may scream if he doesn't do it soon. I open my legs wider, so that my sex yields itself to him like a flower. His face is so close, his lips move across me and he inhales my scent with evident pleasure. Then his tongue at last touches my bud and I moan with delight. It's delicious, the light probings that begin to grow in pressure. I can think of nothing else but the liquid pleasure bubbling up in my depths as he starts to lap and nip at my clitoris, his tongue pressing down harder as he finds the tiny seed-pearl hardness within the soft skin. My juices are flowing hard now and he licks them up with evident relish, pressing his face deeper into my sex. He leaves my clit to visit the slickness of my lips and slit, before returning back to my hard swelling to stroke me to more pleasure with his tongue.

I'm panting, each breath coming out with a high moan. *I'm going to come* . . . it's inevitable after the long approach to this moment, from the tussle we had this morning with its anti-climax and the frustration it left its wake, to the seductive parley that put our arrangement into place, and then to the inflaming work Miles has done with his mouth.

How can I hold out against that?

Even if without the long ignition of my desire, the tormenting delight of Miles's tongue would soon whip me up into a frenzy. He's dipped to my slit and is pressing his tongue deep in the hole, then returning to my clit to tickle and tease. I want to seize his head, hold that maverick tongue to its work and make it release me from this building fury inside, but I daren't act on my own initiative. The idea of his stopping now is beyond what I could take.

I've stopped thinking about his cock, or about his fingers, and can do nothing but concentrate on that insistent, lapping, nipping mouth, the nimble tongue that can find the apex of my clitoris and then anoint my lips with broad delicious strokes, before fucking me with it so it feels almost like a cock.

I'm in a fever of excitement and I know my climax is not far off. It's building like a tornado inside me and any second now I will be taken up into its whirling heart.

Is Miles going to let me come? He must! I can't stand this!

I know he is in complete control of me. He could be intending to play a tormenting game of bringing me to the brink and then holding me back. In a way, I want that too. I don't want this to end. I want this rapture to go on for ever – or, at least, for hours.

But I can't fight the sensations building inside. I'm beyond control now, I can think of nothing but the intensity of the passion rising within me.

His tongue engulfs my clitoris, he's biting me gently, the tip of his tongue flutters hard on the peak of pleasure. I can't do anything now but let the pleasure expand and possess me, taking me wherever it wants.

'I'm coming . . .' I gasp, as his mouth continues its divine work. He doesn't let up but sucks harder and tickles me more fiercely and then at last, the great convulsion comes and I'm shuddering with the force of my orgasm, my head twisting back and forth, my eyes squeezed shut as I concentrate on the explosion of dark, starry pleasure that rocks my body. I've never known an orgasm so electrically fierce – my whole body shakes with it, my thighs tensing as I buck and thrash in its power while still that insistent tongue licks and licks me.

It seems to go on for minutes before the spasms begin to subside, leaving me spent and panting. I forgot everything in the force of my climax, and I'm almost surprised to find I'm still in the hut, on the floor, lying on a heap of sleeping bags, my head on my jacket. Miles raises himself from the place between my thighs and lies down beside me, taking my hand in his. He smiles as I blink slowly and luxuriously at him, my breathing slowing as my heart rate returns to normal.

'Well, Winter,' he says, 'here endeth the lesson.'

CHAPTER EIGHT

I sigh with that languorous post-orgasmic satisfaction and nestle into his chest.

Gazing up at him, I say, 'That was incredible.'

'Just a beginner's guide to the mouth. There's much more to learn, believe me.' He smiles down at me.

'I can't wait for you to teach me everything you know. But . . .' I brush my hand over the fine wool of his jumper. 'What about you? Don't you have needs you want fulfilled? I feel that I'm the one getting all the attention.'

He strokes a finger over my cheek. 'You're very generous but at the moment, I'm the tutor, remember? I can hold back my own needs in favour of your education.'

'But still . . .' I want to reach out to that hardness at his groin. I want to caress and kiss him, give him back a little of the pleasure he's given me. But I daren't do it without permission. 'Tutor,' I venture shyly, 'I don't know what you have in mind for the next lesson . . .'

'Eager to begin again already? I salute your desire for knowledge,' he murmurs.

'I am,' I reply quickly. 'I want to carry on learning as soon as I can.'

'Very admirable,' he says, and kisses my lips softly. 'Perhaps you're right – there's a way to continue your education and allow some natural relief on my part. Giving you so much enjoyment has caused some tension. The delightful orgasm you just enjoyed was very stimulating for me. Very stimulating indeed . . .' He kisses me harder and as his tongue probes my mouth, I can taste a honeyed saltiness on his lips. *My juices*.

The orgasm has taken some of the fever out of my body but my desire is stirring again, this time without the unbearable drawn-out frenzy of our first encounter. Nevertheless I'm hungry to taste his body properly.

'May I be allowed to touch you?' I whisper. 'You haven't let me see your body yet.'

'A good point.' He thinks for a moment. 'Perhaps it will be an important part of the syllabus to examine me. Yes, Winter, you've hit on an excellent idea. Our next lesson will be a simple biology one.' He sits up and takes off his jumper, revealing his incredible body. I gasp to see it so close to me: his muscled strength is almost overwhelming. His shoulders are broad and powerful and the curves of his biceps are deceptively gentle but I know that they are iron-hard. His skin is smooth and tanned, sprinkled with dark hair that also curls alluringly in his armpits and is scattered over his well-defined pecs with their small, dark red nipples. His torso narrows into a rippling abdomen and that trail of hair around his belly button leads downwards as if promising a path to pleasure. He's aware of me drinking in the sight of him. 'The male body,' he says with a smile.

'I don't think you're exactly a typical example,' I breathe, awed by the sight of his physical perfection.

'I'll do for study purposes. Note the differences between us, Winter, but also our similarities. The male nipple, for example, is also a pleasure spot like your own. The male scent is trapped in the hair that we allow to grow on our body – unless you're the chest-waxing type, which I am not – and the female responds to it. It contributes to her own arousal, and the release of her own sexual aromas. Smell is very important . . .' His voice is low, hypnotic. 'Try it.'

I move my face towards his naked skin, and when I'm close to him, the heat radiating from him, I inhaled deeply. He's right – his scent is dark, cedary, with a top note of sweetness. My nostrils flare slightly as I take in the aroma. Arousal is there, and tang of something bitter and yet alluring. I move my face across his chest, inhaling, taking in long breaths that are delicious and darkly exciting, ripe with musk and sharp with a tang of something else. I think of how much has happened – his efforts to save the car from crashing, my rescue from it before it plunged over the edge of the cliff, the walks through the storm where every step was a battle through the fierce wind. The story of everything that's happened to us is in the smell of his body and it's exhilarating. Usually I would be repelled by anything less than absolute freshness but circumstances have forced me to accept standards that in normal life would horrify me. The idea of a man who hadn't just showered would usually be repugnant but there's nothing offensive about Miles: everything about him is exciting and alluring.

'You smell amazing,' I murmur. He's right, my body is responding to the effect of his scent. I can feel a buzz in my depths that replies to it as it enters my nostrils. I want to lick him and taste him, but I restrain myself. The lesson is not over yet.

'Now, run your hands over me and feel the difference between us.'

At last, I can touch him. I've been dying for this. Having him so close and yet being forbidden to touch him has been torture. I reach out to his tanned skin. It's smooth and warm and my fingertips tingle as I feel him beneath them. But where my flesh is soft and yielding, his is firm, the muscles that lie beneath worked into a state of iron hardness. He moves slightly and I feel the flexing strength in his chest and arms. I pull in a sharp breath – that movement sends a thrill of desire rushing through me. I move my hand over the undulations of his chest, circling each dark nipple and then running my fingertip down the narrow seam that runs down between his abs to the trail of dark hair. He's watching me all the time, his eyes hooded slightly so I can't see the effect I'm having on him, but even though he's lying still and breathing in a controlled, measured way, I think that my touch is having the desired effect. I can see now that there is a fearsome bulge in the groin of his jeans, a sight that provokes a shiver of intoxicating anticipation.

'May I kiss you, Tutor?' I ask breathily. 'I want to touch your skin.'

'You may,' he replies and I press my lips to his firm chest, then run my tongue to his left nipple, circling it carefully for a while before drawing the little nugget into my mouth. I pull on it, grazing it lightly with my teeth while sucking, and it hardens gratifyingly under my ministrations. His chest is rising and falling a little quicker now and I move my face across it, inhaling the scent that clings to the dark hairs there, before tending to his right nipple in the same way, running my hands over him as I suck. When

I look at him, his eyes have darkened even further, the lust in them impossible to mistake. Perhaps my tutor might not be as controlled and restrained as he likes to think . . .

There's only one thing I want now, and that's to see what lies beneath his jeans. I'm eager to give his cock my attention.

'Are you ready for the next part of your biology lesson, Winter?' His voice is lazy but below its insouciance I can hear a throb of passion.

'Yes,' I say happily.

'Excellent. Then you may undo my jeans and release me.'

This is what I've been waiting for. Eagerly, I undo the button and slowly slide down the zip. Something twitches and moves beneath the denim. He's wearing blue boxer shorts and I can see now that he's bulging against them. The waistband of his jeans has been holding down his monstrous erection but as I open them, the great shaft is free and juts out, making a tent-shape in the boxers. I still can't see it but I can feel the heat emanating from his stiff rod. I long to touch it and kiss it, set it free to be caressed, but I don't know yet if I dare. I look up at Miles again. I know my face is flushed and my lips are moist where I've been licking my lips with desire to taste him in my mouth.

'May I?' I ask humbly.

'Follow your desires,' he says.

I slip my hand into the gap in his shorts and take his cock in my hand, pulling it out into the open. It's smooth and hot and the girth makes me take in a sharp breath and my sex twitches in response to the promise Mile's shaft holds for me. Like his muscled arms and chest, the velvety smoothness conceals a rock-like hardness and at the top the round head is swollen and flushed, ready for my attentions. This evidence of his desire for me is exciting and rouses my passions further. I'm growing wet and ready again, my bud swelling once more, keen for further pleasure. I dip down and take the hot head of his cock into my mouth, stretching my lips wide to accommodate it, while I play my hand along the shaft, moving the skin beneath my fingertips. At its root I can feel a nest of coarse hair and the tight sack of his balls and I slip a finger down to touch them. As I do, I hear him breathe hard, and when I roll my tongue around the tip of his erection, he moans appreciatively. My stomach tingles with excitement to know that I'm pleasuring him, even if I'm no expert. But this is pleasuring me as much as him: I revel in the feel and taste of his cock in my mouth, and the sense of power in the huge erection I'm toying with. I kiss and suck the head for longer, not able to get much more of it into my mouth in the position I'm in, while rubbing the shaft and tickling his balls.

When he speaks, his voice is thickened by lust. 'Take off my jeans and shorts,' he commands.

I leave his cock for long enough to do as he says, pulling his jeans and boxers down over hard muscled thighs and off him, discarding them in a heap while I return to his jutting erection. He is a truly magnificent sight, his cock rising thickly from the curling dark hair at its base, looking almost too large ever to be accommodated by me, but I'm longing to try. First I dip my head to kiss it again, this time running my tongue over the soft veined surface and breathing in the exhilarating scent of his maleness.

'Play like that for a while,' he says. 'See if you can show me what you've learned about the mouth.'

I happily obey, sucking on him, rolling my tongue over the top of his cock, probing the tiny slit on the top, taking the smooth surface into my mouth and grazing my teeth across it. I rub at the shaft while I suck on his delicious knob, using more and more pressure as my own passions grow. I don't know how long I can do this now without demanding that he fuck me properly, but luckily our thoughts are in unison, because when his cock is standing more stiffly than ever and throbbing hard under my hand, he moves suddenly. He takes me in his arms and kisses me, and I open my mouth to him so our tongues can meet. We are more close than ever, taking our pleasure in the long open kisses, our tongues darting in and out, playing on lips, running over teeth. My heart is racing as I feel him press his great hard thing against my belly. He turns me onto my back, presses my legs apart with his thigh and moves between them.

We're staring deep into each other's eyes now, reading our fevered lust there, and in our open mouths and panting breaths. I want him so badly, everything in me yearning for the feel of that splendid cock in me. I know this will be unlike anything I've ever experienced before but I'm more than ready for it.

We kiss again, our mouths hot, and I open my thighs wider to him, hoping to urge him on. Now I can feel him, that glorious stiffness hard against my mound, my little bud eager to cling to it and feel it rub across it. I moan.

'Oh, please . . . I want it . . .'

His eyes glitter dangerously. He's holding his shaft in one hand, getting ready to direct it where I want it so badly. 'You want it, do you?'

'Yes, yes,' I cry, reckless in the desire he's kindled in me. 'Please, give it to me.'

His eyes are glassy with want as he pushes the tip of his cock to my slit. I rise to meet him, pushing my hips towards him. I can feel him pressing at my entrance. I'm so wet and slippery that the way is well lubricated but even so, the size of his cock and its girth means that he doesn't simply slip into me. The great head pushes against my lips and I feel myself stretching deliciously to encompass him.

'Ohhh,' I sigh with rapture as he moves a centimetre deeper. He's advancing slowly, holding back his considerable power to allow his cock to inch inside me in tiny but utterly divine progression. The sensation as he fills me makes me almost dizzy with delight. I open myself as wide as I can to him, eager for him to drive his whole cock home. I put one arm round his broad back, though I can hardly reach to its centre and with the other I grasp the arm that's supporting him, the muscles bulging out.

'Winter, you're exquisite,' he breathes. 'Your body is beautiful inside as well as out. You feel amazing.'

I can't speak, I can only register the intoxicating feelings he's rousing in me as he pushes his huge shaft deeper and deeper inside me, until it feels as though he's making his way into my very core. I thrill to the sensation of my belly being filled up as he buries himself inside me. Then he's in to the hilt, and I sigh joyously as I feel his balls against my bottom.

The pleasure is unbelievable.

'Are you enjoying your basic biology lesson?' he asks breathlessly.

'Very much,' I manage to say.

'You're showing a marked talent for this. I shall have to see how we can progress your studies further.'

'Please don't stop teaching me,' I beg.

'I won't, don't worry about that.' He begins to move his cock inside me and I groan with delight. It feels as though he could be no deeper within me as he begins to work away, thrusting in and out.

'Oh ... my God, that's unbelievably delicious ... it's heaven ... Oh ...' I am carried away by the beautiful feelings he's stimulating in me with his movements. I never thought I could feel so utterly filled up, but his great shaft stretches me more delectably than I imagined possible. He begins to thrust harder, my hips rising to meet his. I can feel the grinding of his pubic bone on my clitoris, the slap of his balls on my bottom, the power of his thrusts which almost move me off our makeshift bed.

If I never have another lesson with Miles, I've learned so much about what pleasures there are to be enjoyed – and I know I've barely begun to comprehend what he can teach me. I can feel his cock throbbing and swelling inside me as he pumps it in and out. I clutch at his back and arm as the passion in me begins to become more than I can bear. His jaw is set and his eyes are burning with the force of his passion, and he grunts as he pushes himself home deep within me. We are two animals become one now, moving together, feeling our passions rising as the climax approaches. His strokes become harder, shorter as his cock jerks inside me. My bud thrills to the pressure of his body as he rubs on it just as the head of his erection hits home, creating divine pleasure for me. I sense through my own waves of enjoyment that he's approaching a peak as well. Just as my orgasm engulfs me, making me dig my nails deep into the flesh of his arm, I feel him swell even more within me and then shoot out his climax inside me. He sinks down on me, groaning with the force of his orgasm as my vagina convulses around him, tightening with the waves of my powerful crescendo.

We don't speak for a long time as our breathing returns to normal. He lies between my legs, his weight heavy upon me, his cock still sheathed inside me. I stroke a hand across the broad back that's now dewy with the sweat of our exertions.

'That was glorious,' I say softly.

'You are a delight,' he replies, his voice tender now. 'I meant to be much more restrained, but I couldn't stop myself.' He nuzzles into my neck. 'I think that is probably more than enough education for now.'

I make a small noise of agreement. My eyelids flicker and close. I'm worn out by the bouts we've just enjoyed and now that the fire has died right down to little more than a red-gold glow, the room is almost completely dark. I'm warm from the love-making. Miles slowly withdraws and I'm too tired to bother with the need to tidy myself up. I curl up into his broad warm chest and fall asleep.

I don't know how long I sleep for but when I wake it feels like the middle of the night. I'm desperate for a pee. Miles is still asleep and it's almost completely dark in the little hut. It's so quiet that I feel almost suspicious. What's wrong? What's missing? Then I realise: I've been used to the sound of the wind buffeting the little hut but that noise is gone. We're in absolute quiet. I've never gone so long without access to my telephone or email or the Internet but it turns out that the world goes on without all the endless chatter and distraction. My life seems so full and busy but maybe real existence is this quiet isolation and my noisy, social flitting is the illusion.

I can make out some shapes in the darkness and I find the bucket in the corner. God, if it weren't for this, I would be able to put up with this place a lot more easily. I pee as quietly as I can, and then go back to our bed. It's chillier now, and all the sleeping bags are underneath us. Miles's body emanates a good heat: he must be a warm-blooded creature, while I'm more prone to cold, always suffering with chilly toes and fingers. I snuggle up against him and fall back to sleep.

I wake to feel his mouth at my earlobe, tugging gently. He kisses the skin just below and then buries his face in the place where my neck and shoulder meet. He has wrapped me in his strong arms and I feel tiny in his muscled embrace. Hot against my hip is his hard erection.

'Winter, are you awake?' he murmurs.

'Mmm,' I say, coming to a little in the darkness, my skin awakening to the touch of him.

'You're so beautiful, so enchanting. I can't resist you . . .'

'Do I have another lesson?'

'Think of it as revision,' he murmurs. 'Nothing new to learn, just consolidating . . .' His cock is hard against me. I turn so that I'm facing him, and lift one leg up so that it rests on his thigh. He sighs with pleasure as he understands that I'm open to him now. He manoeuvres the head of his cock so that he's at my entrance again. Just the feel of that great smooth head pushing at me sends judders of delight twisting through my stomach. I don't think I could ever get tired of this delicious sensation: the pushing of his giant battering ram against the lips of muscle that guard my entrance, the stretching as I engulf it and he thrusts the thick shaft in as far as it will go, so that I'm impaled on him.

He's in me suddenly, pushing through and into my vagina, filling it up with his cock. He pushes it home hard and I gasp. He pushes again, fast and fierce, driving the breath out of me with an 'Oh!' He's clasping me fiercely, one hand cupping my buttocks, the other wrapped around my waist so he can move me up and down on his erection. There's none of the slow savouring of our last encounter. He's driving me hard – I understand now what riding means – he's riding me – or I'm riding him as I take him into my very depths and thrust my hips to spur us both on.

'Oh my God,' I groan, throwing back my head. He's consumed with passion now, sinking into me to the root, driving back and doing it again. His mouth finds mine and we begin to devour each other, our tongues twisting together, our saliva mingling as we ride the heat of our desire. He's going hard and fast, it won't be long before he comes, I can tell. This is not part of my education so much as him slaking his need.

'You're delicious, you're so sexy,' he says in my ear. 'I can't resist you . . . God, you're making me come . . .'

The realisation that his orgasm is building floods me with hot excitement but before I can reach my own peak, he groans loudly and says, 'Yes, oh . . . I'm coming now,' and his thrusts become shorter and sharper and then he bursts a jetting climax inside me.

'Oh . . . oh . . .' I moan, inflamed by his passion.

Swiftly he thrusts again, his cock still huge and swollen inside me, and reaches down with one hand. The balls of his fingers find my throbbing clitoris and he begins to massage it hard, stroking and tickling and rousing it to an unbearable state of excitement. My thighs tighten, my fists clench and I cry out sharply as he strums my bud to beyond what it can bear and a delightfully sharp, electric orgasm shoots through me, stiffening my limbs in convulsive spasms. I'm left panting and replete. Miles pulls his cock slowly out of me.

'Thank you,' he says, kissing me lightly. 'I love it when you come.'

'I love it when I come too,' I say, and he laughs.

'A willing student. I can't ask for anything more.'

We doze off again in one another's arms.

When I wake, Miles isn't beside me. The hut is full of a grey light. It's day now and the storm is evidently over. I shiver, cold without his body to keep me warm. I've covered myself with some of the sleeping bag but not enough to be properly cosy.

Where is he? I wonder. Probably he's gone out to relieve himself. No humiliating bucket for him. Men are so lucky that way. I wish he was with me. I'm engulfed with desire for his body, the warmth of his nearness.

Have I really had three orgasms since last night?

When I was with Jacob, I'd insist that I couldn't possibly orgasm more than once a night, and when he'd tried to persuade me otherwise, I'd only ended up sore and grouchy. But now I understand that was because I'd never known what real desire – or real fucking – actually was. Now I think I'm probably capable of four orgasms or more, if only it's Miles who's fucking me . . .

141

The memory of our delightful night-time bout excites me.

Oh that cock – that utterly bloody magnificent cock. I sigh and flush at the thought of it and my sex prickles with longing. I laugh at myself. *Ready for another go?*

You bet I am. Where is he?

I want to sit with him, drink coffee with him, touch him, kiss him, taste him, fuck him. I remember the sight of his dark head buried between my legs. I could never tire of the delicious feelings he roused in me with his magical tongue.

I can hardly stand the way the recollection makes me feel. I shiver and stand up, taking one of the sleeping bags with me, wrapping it round me.

I can hear a strange noise: a thumping, thudding kind of noise, like a flag fluttering hard in a strong wind. I frown, wondering what it can be, and go to the window to look out but I can still see nothing but whiteness. It fades a little and then gets louder again. I'm still scrutinising the sky when the door of the hut opens and Miles comes in in a gust of freezing air. He's dressed again and is smiling broadly at me.

'Morning, lovely. How are you? Did you sleep all right?'

I nod, still frowning. 'Yes, but . . . that noise, can you hear it?'

'I certainly can. Don't you know what it is?' His eyes are bright.

'No – what?'

'It's a helicopter. If I'm not much mistaken, we've been found. If they've got heat-seeking equipment, the fire that's been burning in the hearth will be lighting this place up like a Christmas tree on their monitors. If they don't know where we are yet, they will very soon.' He walks up to me and throws his arms around me. 'Don't you see? We're going to be rescued! It's going to be okay.'

'Oh,' I say weakly. 'That's . . . that's fantastic.'

But my heart is sinking. All I've wanted since the accident is for us to be found. So why do I now feel so utterly depressed?

CHAPTER NINE

'Freya, honey! Oh my God, I'm so happy to see you!'

My father is advancing towards me, his face split by a beaming smile, his small brown eyes almost lost in the creases of his eyelids and the folds of his cheeks.

I'm wearing a white hospital gown and lying in a bed between pristine white sheets, a blood pressure sleeve around my upper arm that automatically squeezes me every few minutes and updates the information on the monitor at my side. I've no idea what the numbers mean but the nurse who regularly glides in to examine them doesn't seem particularly concerned, so I guess I'm all right. I was brought straight here after we were rescued this morning, and I've been thoroughly examined, tested and monitored ever since.

'Hi, Dad.' I smile wanly as he comes up, drops a kiss on my cheek and grasps my hand. He sits down on the chair by my bedside, leaning in towards me.

'How are you, sweetheart? Are you okay?' He scans me anxiously. I think I can see the signs of strains on his face: his eyes are bloodshot and dark bags puff out underneath them, his forehead is lined and his complexion has a grey-ish tinge.

I smile up at him, comforted by the fact that he's clearly been worried about me. 'I'm fine, Dad, really. I'm very lucky.'

'I'm so relieved to have you safely back where you belong. What the hell happened to you?' He squeezes my hand a little tighter, gazing into my eyes. 'Tell me the whole story.'

I stare back at him, almost helplessly. The two days since the crash were the longest of my life. So much happened, and every moment is vivid in my memory. But when my father asks me about it, all I can see is Miles: his piercing gaze, the rippling muscles, the glory of his huge cock and the sight of his dark head between my thighs . . . My stomach somersaults in agonised pleasure at the recollection, forcing me to close my eyes and gasp involuntarily.

'Was it that bad?' Dad asks tenderly. 'I can't imagine what you've gone through.'

Well, that's a relief . . .

'So,' he continues, 'start at the beginning. You were supposed to be getting a flight to LA, right?'

I see myself in the back seat of the Mercedes as I was that day. It's as though I'm looking at a different person as I remember how I ignored Miles or treated him with utter disdain. I can picture the back of his dark head and broad shoulders, his huge hands on the steering wheel, as I rapped out my orders.

God, I was awful. I can hardly repress a shudder as I think of it. *What did he think of me? He must have held me in complete contempt.*

I open my mouth to start the story, suddenly realising that I'm desperate to tell it, but just then the door opens and the nurse bustles in, so I close it again. I've learned to keep quiet when strangers are about, unless I want to see details of my life appearing in gossip columns. However, this nurse is exactly the kind of efficient, discreet person I'd expect to find in a Swiss private hospital. She comes over and examines the monitor by my bedside, just as the sleeve around my arm judders into life again and starts squeezing me. As it releases its hold, she looks at my blood pressure reading and nods.

'How is she, nurse?' asks my father.

'She's going to be fine,' the nurse replies in faintly accented English. 'There's nothing to worry about, all signs are normal.' She turns to me and smiles. 'Considering you've just spent two days in freezing temperatures, you couldn't be better. You were obviously well looked after.'

I smile back at her, longing to tell her all about Miles and how amazing he is: how he rescued me, found me shelter and made sure I was safe. But I don't want to say anything in front of my father. It seems really important to keep all that to myself for now.

The nurse turns back to him. 'There is the bruising, of course, but it doesn't seem to have caused any serious damage.'

Dad frowns. 'Bruising?'

'Across your daughter's chest. The cause appears to be the seatbelt of the car. The doctor has examined her thoroughly and is confident that she will heal quickly.'

'Oh, honey.' Dad turns back to me, his eyes moistening. 'You were hurt! I can't bear to think about it . . .'

'I'm fine,' I say reassuringly. 'And things could have been a lot worse than that. I was lucky to get out of there with just a bruise.'

As the nurse makes her exit, my father's face darkens and he says, 'Believe me, I've thought very hard about how things might have turned out. I can't believe that I came so close to losing you. There are questions to ask about how this happened, you can be damn sure about that.'

His belligerent expression frightens me: it tells me that Dad intends to make someone pay for this episode. Any hint of danger to me, or my sisters, brings out the worst in my father.

Oh God, there's only one person he's going to blame for it – and it isn't going to be me . . .

I push myself up on an elbow in my desire to start explaining that the accident was entirely my fault, when the door to my room opens again and I see a sight that completely takes my mind off the urgent need to defend Miles.

There she is: slender with knockout curves emphasised by one of her trademark bandage dresses. She stands precariously balanced on huge heels, her toffee-coloured hair spilling over her shoulders in glossy waves, false eyelashes framing her wide green eyes. She pouts and says, 'Hi, Freya. How are you?' before wiggling into my room and sitting down in the chair next to my father's, right next to my bed.

I'm speechless with fury. What the hell is she doing here – in *my* hospital room?

Dad turns to look at her with that stupid cow-like expression he has whenever Estella is anywhere near him. 'Baby, that's so sweet of you. Freya's going to be fine, aren't you?'

I nod, not looking at her. I know my expression must have become sullen because my father says, 'Estella wanted to come and see how you were herself. She's been worried sick, haven't you, baby?'

Estella pouts again and nods, fluttering her ridiculous lashes. It makes me want to grind my teeth in fury. How can my father not see through this pathetic act? It's like the vamp ABC, a childish idea of what a sexpot is – all cartoon curves and breathy voice and vacant expression. Estella was not like this when she was assistant to my sisters and me; then, she was a smart cookie who had an obvious sharpness about her. That was before she sensed that my father was lonely and vulnerable and might be susceptible to her if she drew a bit more attention to herself. Suddenly, she changed: her skin became a dark golden brown with as much of it on display as possible, from pumped-up décolletage to long gleaming legs. She gained caramel highlights and hair extensions, whiter teeth and long varnished nails. She layered on make-up, and her usual low-key wardrobe was ditched in favour of figure-hugging dresses and sky-high heels. Sure enough, Dad couldn't help but notice the change as she made a special point of leaning towards him, touching his arm and giggling girlishly whenever he was about. I was furious he couldn't see through her obvious game, but there was nothing I could do. I wanted to warn him against her, and tell him that she was only after him for his money but by the time it was evident that Estella's tricks were working, my father was already enchanted and would not have listened to a word against her. Besides, he seemed to think that she was really in love with him. How could I tell him that she was faking it? Surely he could work that out for himself? I mean, I love my dad but he's a short, stocky man in his late fifties with thinning hair and a thickening middle. He's not exactly love's young dream, and if he weren't rich, a woman like Estella would not look at him twice.

But here she is, insinuated into my father's affections. And if he's bringing her to my bedside in the hospital, then

I have to contemplate the likelihood that Estella might be a permanent fixture.

Possibly even my future stepmother?

I want to shudder at the thought.

'I'm so glad to see that you're okay,' Estella says in her breathy voice. 'We've been so worried about you!' Her big green eyes stare at me, wide and seemingly innocent.

'Thanks,' I say through clenched teeth. I can't bear seeing her here.

This is hardly appropriate, for crying out loud! I'm in hospital, recovering from a frightening ordeal. The last person I want here is Estella.

I look pointedly away from her and say to Dad, 'Where are Flora and Summer?'

'They're at home,' he replies. 'Flora was in Paris but she flew back today. Summer never left, first because of the weather and then because you were missing. She's been by the phone the entire time, desperate for news about you. She wanted to come here, of course, but I told her it would be better to wait until you had a chance to recover. The doctor says he expects you'll be out soon.'

I nod. I didn't expect to be in the hospital for long. I'm perfectly fine, for one thing. But they were determined to check me out thoroughly, no doubt to justify the enormous bill. 'Dad . . .' I say hesitantly. I wish Estella weren't here. Despite her village-idiot act, she's no fool. But I can't hold out any longer, I have to ask. 'Where's Miles? Is he okay?'

That hard look comes into my father's eyes again. 'He's fine. He's back at the house.'

'What is it?' I say quickly. 'Is something wrong? Was Miles checked out by a doctor?'

'Oh yes. He's got a clean bill of health. He's perfectly able to answer the questions Pierre and I will be putting to him.'

'Dad, you mustn't blame Miles for this. It wasn't his fault. It was mine.' I gaze at him beseechingly. 'I made him drive me to the airport even though he told me that the weather conditions were unsafe. I even told him to go faster. He was obeying my orders.'

'Maybe,' my father says, his tone harsh. 'But he's the expert. He should have used his judgement and refused. That's what I pay him for. He put your life in danger, honey. That's hard to forgive.'

I sit up even straighter. 'No, he didn't! He saved me. I mean it – I wouldn't take no for an answer, you know what I'm like. And once the car began to skid . . . well, you should have seen him. He was magnificent. He couldn't stop it going over the edge but he saved our lives by limiting the fall as much as he could, and then he rescued me from the car before it toppled further down the mountain. Because of him we found shelter and made it through the hours until we were found. Without him, I'd be dead!'

My father shakes his head. 'Without him, you'd have been safely at home! Not setting off on some fool's errand to get to the airport. No – believe me, Miles Murray will be answering some hard questions right now. Pierre is going to question him thoroughly about what happened.'

I'm filled with anxiety. My father's head of security is one tough nut. Just the sight of him makes me fearful, and I'm the last person who should be frightened of him considering that he's paid a great deal to make sure that no one harms me. I hate the idea of Pierre, with his rugged face, meaty body stuffed into a tight jacket, and that salt-and-pepper shaved head of his, sitting in front of Miles.

But Miles can handle him. He can handle anyone.

The thought is comforting but nevertheless, I'm still anxious. What if my father decides that Miles's services are no longer required? Not only would it be incredibly unfair after what Miles has just done for me, but my heart goes cold at the idea. I'm desperate to see him again even though it's only a few hours since we were separated.

I'm about to protest and tell my father that he must not, on any account, sack Miles or punish him in any way, when I notice Estella's eyes fixed on me, interest sparking in their sea-green depths. Immediately I bite my tongue. She's sharp and no doubt has noted my eagerness to defend Miles. Her cogs will be whirring and I don't want to give her any hint of what's happened between Miles and me. I sense that she'll always be on the lookout to turn any situation to her advantage. So I say airily, 'Oh, well . . . I'm sure Miles will give a good account of himself. Maybe you're right – he should have talked me out of the journey to the airport.'

Estella listens carefully. I hope it's enough to put her off the scent. Just then the door to my room opens and in comes one of the consultants who examined me so carefully this morning.

'Doctor Schulmann,' my father says, standing up and looking a little anxious. 'Is everything all right?'

The doctor, white-haired and wearing gold-rimmed spectacles, smiles and says, 'Of course, Mr Hammond. I just came to present you the hospital's compliments and to tell you that Miss Hammond is free to leave whenever she wishes.'

'Are you sure, Doctor? Shouldn't she stay in for the night to be observed? I've just heard about this bruise she's sustained—'

'Hello!' I say loudly. 'I am here! You can talk to me, you know.'

The doctor turns to me with that friendly smile and chuckles. 'Ah, Miss Hammond, you are quite right. Now if you wish, you can of course stay the night—'

'I don't wish,' I interrupt. 'I want to go home.'

'But, as I was saying, you are in very good health and there is no reason at all not to allow you home.' The doctor continues to smile with his best bedside manner.

My father looks doubtful. 'I'm not sure ... I'd feel happier if you were being observed for a little while longer, sweetheart. This bruise they mentioned ...'

'Dad, I'm fine. Please! I want to go home. I want to sleep in my own bed.' To my surprise, I'm telling the truth. I never thought I might consider that mountain eyrie to be my home, but now I'm longing to return. Perhaps it's not entirely unrelated to the fact that Miles is there.

'Well, honey, if it's what you want ...'

'It is.'

The doctor gives a little bow. 'I shall inform the staff you are ready to leave,' he says, and goes out.

'All right, then. Jane-Elizabeth is downstairs. I'll tell her to organise a car.' Dad stands up. Estella totters to her feet as well.

'Aren't you going to wait for me?' I ask. I imagined I'd go home with my father.

He turns to Estella with a smile and chucks her cheek as if she were a little girl. 'I can't, honey. I promised my angel I'd take her shopping this morning. She's been my rock over the last few days and she's going to get a little reward.' He turns to me and bends down to kiss my cheek again. 'I'll see you at home later. We'll all have a nice family dinner together, okay? You, me, the girls and Estella.' He beams, obviously unable to imagine anything nicer.

I don't look at Estella but I can sense her triumphant expression even if I can't see it. She's delighted with the way things are shaping up and she knows there's not a thing I can do about it.

'Bye,' my father says, slipping his arm around Estella's slender waist. He looks at me a little dewy eyed. 'I'm so happy to have you back, Freya. I can't believe I nearly lost you.'

'I'm still here,' I say, mustering up a smile even though I feel miserable inside, then I watch as he and Estella go out together.

As soon as I'm alone again, I fall back on my pillows and gaze out towards the window with its view over white rooftops towards snowy mountains beyond. I yearn for Miles. It feels like so long since we were parted. For the whole time we were lost, I wanted only to be rescued but as soon as I heard the thwacking blades of the approaching helicopter I realised what it would mean: Miles and I were going to be separated. We were together for the last time for the flight back in, but we weren't able to speak over the sound system, not when everyone else in the aircraft could listen in. As we landed, I looked over at him and our gazes locked. The look in his blue eyes made me shake inside with excitement and desire, but there was something in his face that filled me with apprehension. It was as though, somehow, he was saying goodbye, and the thought filled me with a panicked horror.

153

We had no time to speak to one another when we touched down, as I was immediately whisked into an ambulance and driven at top speed through the city streets to the hospital. I don't know what happened to Miles. I haven't seen him since.

Dad said he was at home. I'll see him there. It will all be okay, I'm sure of it.

But though I try to convince myself, I can't help the dark fear crawling up through my stomach and creeping over my skin.

A few minutes later, the door opens and Jane-Elizabeth is standing there. I'm so happy to see her that my eyes fill with tears and, as she comes towards me with her arms open, I realise that she is crying too.

'Freya, you naughty girl!' she says through her tears, enveloping me in a huge hug. 'How could you put us through that? I thought we'd lost you! It was terrible. Oh, I'm so happy to see you!'

She holds me tight and kisses my hair, and I feel the first real comfort since Miles and I were separated. Jane-Elizabeth has been a part of my life for so long, and she's the closest thing to a mother that I've got now. Just the sight of her is reassuring. She always dresses the same, in narrow black trousers that show off her legs and baggy black tunic tops that hide her slightly bigger middle, and beautiful scarves to provide a note of colour: bright Hermès silk in the summer, and soft printed cashmere in the winter. Her hair is naturally dark but threaded with grey and she has a terrific grey quiff at the front that looks like it's been dyed in but is completely natural. She has soft brown eyes in a face that's remarkably young-looking. Jane-Elizabeth says it's down to the fact that she hasn't had children, but that looking after us has given her the grey streak. She pulls back now to look carefully at me, scrutinising me for any signs of harm. 'Are you really all right?' she asks. Her tears have dried now, but her eyes are still damp and she sniffs a little.

I nod.

Her brow creases in a worried frown. 'What happened to you out there, Freya? We thought you must be dead.'

'It was . . . frightening,' I reply. I have a flashback to the moment that the car left the road and began to plummet towards the earth. I remember the blind panic, the strange slow-motion of it, the desperate desire not to die and, as it comes back to me, I begin to shake. Jane-Elizabeth notices and clutches my fingers tightly, murmuring soft words of comfort. Tears spring back to my eyes and I'm seized by an urge to let it all out and cry, but I swallow it down. 'I thought it was all over for me. I really did. But, thank God, Miles was there and he saved me.'

Now I recall the feeling of his arms around me, the warmth and comfort of his body as he carried me through the buffeting wind and driving snow. I remember his words of encouragement, the delight in his eyes when he found us the hut, the way he laughed and his down-to-earth practical approach to our ordeal. I see his face hard with fury, his eyes angry and accusing, and his expression of hurt bewilderment at the things I said to him. Then, my inside clench with painful pleasure as I remember his mouth, his tongue thrusting into mine, the feel of his hands on my body, the hardness of him pressing against me. Oh God, it's almost too much. I remember that physical yearning I felt for him before he'd ever touched me: it's a hundred times more powerful now I've tasted the delights of what he can give me. Jane-Elizabeth hugs me again. 'It sounds like Miles was a bit of a hero.'

A delicious warmth fills me at the sound of his name. It feels as though I can't hear it enough. 'He was. But I'm worried that Dad wants to blame him for the whole thing.'

'Your father was very frightened, Freya. He genuinely thought you'd been killed. It was awful to witness.' She pulls away to gaze into my eyes, her expression serious. 'That man adores you, Freya, you've got to believe that. I've never seen him more close to the edge than I did over the last few days. He wants to punish someone for those awful feelings – but he'll calm down. He'll soon realise that Miles is the one who brought his daughter back safe and well.'

'I hope so. I couldn't bear it if Dad punished him for something that was my fault.'

Jane-Elizabeth raises her eyebrows. She looks surprised. I start to flush. I suppose she hasn't often heard me admit that something might be my fault, particularly where members of staff are concerned.

'I mean . . . I . . . well . . .' I'm not quite sure what to say to recover myself, and I can feel my blush growing stronger. 'I should have seen for myself what the weather conditions were like,' I finish lamely.

'Mmm.' Jane-Elizabeth is still looking at me oddly. Then she gives my hand a squeeze and says, 'Why don't you get dressed, and we'll go home. I've brought some fresh clothes for you – they're in the bag in the corner – and the car is waiting downstairs. And I mean it, Freya, about your father. He was distraught over you.'

I get out of bed and go to pick up the bag of clothes. 'Yeah. I noticed by the way he couldn't wait to go off shopping with Estella rather than take me home.'

Jane-Elizabeth sighs and says, 'I'm afraid that Estella is a cross we all just have to bear.' I see the sadness in her face and remember that Estella has trampled all over her life too. She adds gently, 'It doesn't change what your father really feels for you. You must remember that.'

I say nothing, but take the bag into the bathroom to change.

Twenty minutes later, after leaving the hospital through a flurry of flashbulbs, television cameras and shouted questions from reporters, Jane-Elizabeth and I are being driven through the city streets in another of my father's black Mercedes. I think of the one buried in snow at the bottom of the mountain and wonder idly if it will ever be recovered. The storm has well and truly passed, and a wintry sun is doing its best to illuminate the grey-white sky. It will be a drive of an hour or so back to the house but the roads are clear of snow. It's hard to imagine it was such a short time ago that the storm was brewing up and my life was about to change for ever.

I lean my head back against the headrest. It's so good to feel clean again. I had a long, steaming hot shower, scrubbing off the dirt of two days but also washing the traces of Miles from my body with something almost like regret. The whole experience in the hut is becoming increasingly more dream-like. Although it's all so vivid, there's a kind of unreality to it. Were we really shut away like that, just the two of us? Did we really do all those delicious things to one another?

157

Now that I'm stepping back into my old life, being chauffeured in a pristine car back towards my luxurious mountain home, I'm feeling increasingly disconnected from what happened. But my body hungers for Miles in a way that reassures me that it was all darkly, passionately real.

Miles, where are you? Are you thinking about me? Do you yearn for me like I'm yearning for you?

I picture him suddenly, talking to me in those headily exciting moments before he began to give me my first lesson. I hear his deep voice growling in my ear and even though it's just a memory, my body throbs in response. He's saying, 'When we get out, normal relations will be re-established, and everything that's happened here will be forgotten.'

My desire is forgotten in a jolt of panic. *Forgotten? Really?*

That's what I agreed to. It's what he said.

A voice cries out in my head: *No! No way. He can't forget everything just like that . . . can he?*

I know for certain that I can't. But the idea that Miles might fills me with dread.

'Freya?' It's Jane-Elizabeth, sitting beside me, unaware of what's churning inside me.

'Yes?' My voice sounds breathless and anxious but Jane-Elizabeth doesn't seem to notice as she opens her handbag and pulls out something small, slim and black.

'Here. This is for you. A new telephone. Your old one was lost, wasn't it?'

I nod, and take it from her. 'Thanks. I appreciate it.' I gaze down at its smooth, gleaming surface. I can tell it's ready to spring into life, and reconnect me with everything and everyone from before. I don't turn it on. I know that hundreds of emails and notifications will have arrived for me since I went missing. I'm not sure I'm ready for all that just yet.

'Is it all right?' Jane-Elizabeth asks, watching me as I stare at the phone. 'It's all connected and ready to go.'

'Oh – oh, yes, it's great.' I slip it into my pocket and go back to staring out of the window. All I want is to be home again, and to find Miles. I have to see him as soon as I possibly can.

If I don't, I feel like I'll go mad.

CHAPTER TEN

'Freya, you're back!'

'Welcome home, we're so happy to see you!'

The minute Jane-Elizabeth and I emerge from the lift into the main hallway, I'm engulfed by two pairs of arms, and two smiling faces are pressed against mine as my sisters run over and hug me hard. We haven't been this united for a long time. I suppose that coming back from the dead does have its upsides: everyone feels all warm and fuzzy about you.

Flora pulls away from me, a beaming smile on her face. 'I can't believe what you've been through! It's amazing that you're okay. Dad said your car crashed right off the mountain!'

'We want to hear *all* about it,' chimes in Summer.

'It was kind of incredible,' I reply, laughing at their puppyish enthusiasm.

'Girls, let Freya get her breath back before you mob her!' reproves Jane-Elizabeth. 'Why don't you all go through to the snug and I'll have some tea sent in for you?'

'That sounds great,' I say happily. 'You know what? I'd love some hot chocolate.'

'Done,' says Jane-Elizabeth. 'I'll ask for some food as well.'

She goes off to talk to the cook as we head to the snug, the cosiest room in this chilly glass palace. As we go through the house, I think that the staff are smiling at me in a way I've never been aware of before – as though they're genuinely pleased to see me.

Miles's remarks about what the people who work here really think of me come floating into my mind and I feel a hot burn of shame. I don't like the way that makes me feel so I banish it quickly from my mind. I'll think about it later, but in the meantime I resolve to be nicer if I can. At least my rescue seems to have put everyone in a good mood with me, which is a start.

Where is he? I wonder. A tremor shimmers over my skin as I imagine him somewhere close. Dad said he was here at the house but I don't think there'll be any sign of him here in this part of it. The bodyguards are rarely seen on this floor, though I've never really thought about that before. They've always just disappeared when they're not required, reappearing when necessary. It's never occurred to me to wonder where they go. Now I imagine Miles several storeys beneath me on one of those floors I've never visited.

If only I'd known what was here all along. If only I'd realised . . . How can I see him? What's he doing right now?

I have a delightful image of Miles in the shower, soaping his muscled arms and torso, hot water streaming over his dark head and running down his pecs and the hard solidness of his thighs. *Mmm. That's delicious.* His eyes are closed as he turns his face to the shower of hot water. He's clean and wet and incredibly enticing. In my imagination he turns his back to me so I can see the firmness of his buttocks with the dip on each side by the glute muscles. *Turn around for me, Miles, show me that magnificent cock of yours . . .* I imagine myself stepping naked into the shower with him, pressing myself against his back, the water dousing me in a hot stream. He turns, surprised, and I sink down to my knees to kiss his cock into stiffness, letting water fill my mouth and then treating him to his own personal bath inside my hot wet mouth. He's magnificent, his length growing strong and hard, swelling under my ministrations as I lick and suck him . . .

'Freya, are you all right?' Summer is looking at me quizzically. 'You've gone all glassy eyed.'

'What?' I jerk back to reality, almost startled to find I'm not in a hot shower administering tender oral attention to Miles's erection. 'Oh . . . sorry . . . just a flashback.'

I'm forced to drag my thoughts away from Miles by my sisters who bombard me with questions, not letting me get an answer out before they ask something else.

'Girls, one at a time!' I say, holding my hands up and laughing. 'Please! Let's get settled and I'll tell you everything.'

In the snug, we sit down on the sofas in front of the fire. Three of them are placed around the fireplace and we each take one. Summer is facing me on the opposite sofa, her legs pulled up in front of her, her arms wrapped around her knees. 'So come on!' she urges. 'Start from the beginning.'

Flora lounges over hers, her russet brown hair spreading out on the cushions. She has a taste for striking attitudes, it's all part of her dramatic nature. 'We need to know everything,' she announces.

'The inside story,' adds Summer. 'Did you know you've been all over the news?'

'I wondered when I saw the welcome-home committee outside the hospital. How did they all find out?'

Flora shrugs. 'Who knows how any of them ever find out anything? Dad tried to keep it quiet but once the search was on, the word spread very quickly. You can imagine how much the press loved the story. It was good enough when it looked as though you'd plummeted to your death off the mountain. It's even better now that you've been miraculously rescued. Look.' She picks up the television remote and clicks the TV on. Footage is playing and there I am, coming out of the hospital, Jane-Elizabeth at my side looking fierce as she holds up a hand to keep the reporters out of my face. Our driver is on my other side, one hand on my elbow as he steers us through the melee. I look pale but my dark glasses cover up most of my face. I'm just glad I washed my hair and put some make-up on – but I make a mental note to make an appointment with the hairdresser. My brown hair needs a proper blow-dry and some fresh lowlights to restore its sparkle, and my fringe definitely requires a trim.

The voiceover is explaining that Freya Hammond was missing for two days after a car crash during an alpine storm. 'Miss Hammond is said to be in surprisingly good health after her ordeal. Despite claims of a near-fatal crash and two days in sub-zero temperatures, there are no outward signs of injury. In fact, some sources are suggesting that this could be an elaborate stunt to win back her former boyfriend, Jacob Amsell.'

I laugh out loud as the screen fills up with pictures of me and Jacob during our days together, frolicking on yachts, sunbathing on beaches and turning up to film premieres as the voiceover gives a précis of our relationship. It never occurred to me that anyone might think I'd somehow arranged to fake a crash – after all, it would be incredibly difficult to do such a thing even if such a crazy idea had occurred to me. I'd certainly have needed Miles's cooperation and it's hard to imagine getting him to agree to let one of my father's cars topple over the edge of a mountain just because I said so, and then disappear with me for two days. The press have an even wilder imagination that I gave them credit for – but I can see that it's a good story. As for the pictures of me with Jacob – just a short time ago, I'd have been cut to the core to see them and now I don't care at all. He's in the past. He was an asshole and now he's history. A learning experience. One of the guys whose role in life is to teach us what we don't want in a man.

Now . . . there's Miles.

I lean over and click the remote. The sound stops abruptly and the picture vanishes.

'It's a good story,' Flora says softly, looking over at me. 'But there's nothing in it. Right?' She lifts her eyebrows enquiringly.

I open my mouth to rebut the suggestion that I might have faked a car crash and put my family through hell just to win back that ridiculous lowlife, then stop. My sisters don't know the truth about why Jacob and I broke up. Miles doesn't know the full story either, even though I confided part of it to him. No one knows, except Jacob, my father, our lawyers and me. Oh, and some hookers, if they ever recognised Jacob and heard what had happened between us.

Maybe this story might be a good way to deflect attention from the truth.

At the moment, everyone is just happy to see me back in one piece, but my father intends to find out what happened, and so do my sisters. Once it's known that Miles and I spent two days and nights holed up together in a snowed-in mountain hut, surely it won't be long before people begin to ask what happened between us during those long, dark, cold hours . . .

'You didn't!' Summer says disbelievingly. 'You didn't cook this up, did you?

She looks indignant and I can't blame her. It would be terrible thing to do, and tempting though it might be to throw up a smokescreen, I can't do it.

'No,' I say. 'Of course I didn't. It's a stupid idea. The press will get over all this in a day or two and all the ridic-ulous gossip will die down.'

'They have a point, though, don't they?' Flora says, looking at me intently. 'I mean, you look absolutely fine. You don't have a mark on you.'

I say nothing but unbutton my shirt and open it to display the livid bruise, now an interesting melange of purple, green and yellow, that crosses my chest, disappear-ing under my bra and coming out the other side.

Summer gasps. 'What's that?'

'The mark from my seatbelt. If I hadn't been wearing that, then believe me, we wouldn't be having this conver-sation. And the car took most of the impact – you should have seen it. You wouldn't have believed we could get out of there. But we did.'

Flora bites her lip as she regards the mark on my chest. The twins really look nothing like each other. Summer has that blonde blue-eyed prettiness, but Flora has a pale russet look that's not exactly beauty but is very arresting. She has almond-shaped eyes and spikes her lashes out with lots of mascara to create a feline look. Now her eyes, brown like mine but speckled with hazel, look worried. 'I didn't really believe those stories about you faking the crash,' she says, almost apologetically. 'And now I can see that bruise . . .' She gazes at me as I button up my shirt again. 'I realise what a lucky escape you had.'

'It wasn't just luck. It was Miles too.' I try to keep my tone and expression neutral. I don't want anyone speculating about us, not when I have no idea myself what is happening between us, but I can't help talking about him.

'Miles?' says Summer, frowning. Then her face clears. 'Of course – you set out with the bodyguard you can't stand.'

'I know. And I'm counting my blessings I did.' I tell them about the crash and how it was the most frightening thing that's ever happened to me. They listened in wide-eyed silence as I describe the sensation of the car leaving the road and the impact that followed. I describe Miles getting me out of the car just moments before it slid off the plateau to vanish in the snowy valley below, taking our phones with it. I'm almost reliving it as I tell them about the terrible weather, the icy, penetrating cold, and the sense of fear and despair as Miles disappeared into the storm to look for shelter.

Summer's eyes are wide as she listens intently. She says, 'That must have been weird. You hated him – and he saved your life!'

I nod. 'Yeah.' I try to sound casual and laugh lightly. 'I suppose he's not so bad after all. I owe him a lot.'

Flora has been gripped by my narrative and she leans forward to say urgently, 'But what happened? Did he find the shelter?'

'Of course!' I laugh again. 'Do you think I'd be in such good shape if he hadn't? We had the most amazing piece of luck.' I tell them about the shepherd's hut and they are gripped by my description of its privations.

'Tinned food,' says Flora, pulling a face.

'No running water!' breathes Summer, her eyes wide.

'No nothing,' I reply. 'No *bathroom* at all . . .' I look at them both meaningfully and they gasp as they take in the implications.

'So how did you . . .?' Flora can't articulate it but we all know what she means.

'A bucket.'

They both gasp again and Flora shudders. 'How awful,' she says. 'In front of the bodyguard?'

'He went outside.'

'Thank goodness for that,' Flora says and Summer nods in agreement.

'Luckily we weren't there for too long. I didn't think I could stand going without a shower for much longer.'

Summer says, 'You were so lucky though. Thank goodness for that hut.'

'And the fact that Miles is trained in arctic weather and mountain survival.' I can't resist saying his name. I know that the real story of the crash is not the filthy sleeping bags and the nasty food or even surviving the storm against the odds, but I don't want to give them any clue of what is, so I start to describe the rescue and they are quickly diverted. When I finish, I realise that Flora is crying.

'What is it?' I ask. 'I'm fine, you don't need to cry!'

'I know, it's just . . .' She gulps and sniffs. 'You could have died if hadn't been for those bits of luck that saved you – the car landing on the plateau, and then finding the hut. I can't help thinking that someone was looking out for you.'

I get up, sit down next to her and wrap my arms around her. She clings on to me and sobs.

'I think that maybe . . . Mama was protecting you,' she whispers.

I feel my own eyes fill with tears and a tightness form in my throat. I can't speak. The same thought had occurred to me but I'd hardly acknowledged it until Flora said it out loud.

Summer gets up and joins us, clutching my hand and Flora's. 'Maybe Mama is your guardian angel,' she says.

I say, 'If she's looking out for me, she'll be looking out for all of us.'

Flora sobs again. 'I'm sorry,' she says. 'It's a happy thought, not a sad one, and yet . . .'

'I understand,' I say quietly, hugging her tighter. 'We all do.'

We sit quietly for a while, bonded by the memory of our mother.

I barely have a moment to myself for the rest of the day. Not surprisingly, I'm inundated with calls and messages as soon as I switch on my phone. I find myself telling the same story over and over until I begin to suspect that it's taken on a whole new life that is completely removed from what actually happened. Everybody is clamouring to see me, to invite me here and there, but I have no appetite for it. I put them all off, telling them I have to rest and get back to my old self, which seems to satisfy them.

When my father gets back from shopping with Estella, he calls me to his study so that I can recount the whole thing again from beginning to end. I go there excited, hoping that Miles might be there, but he's not. Instead, I'm treated to the grizzled, menacing presence of Pierre, who listens in silence as I tell my story. I know that they're trying to discover exactly what Miles's role in the whole thing was, so I make sure that I play up the way he saved my life, the fact that his training and knowledge brought us safely through the whole ordeal, along with a helping of good old-fashioned luck. I paint the relationship between us as that of a damsel in distress and the heroic, utterly chivalric knight who saves the day and protects the maiden and her purity with complete, unquestioning devotion. By the end, my father seems happier. It's impossible to tell what Pierre thinks; his face is so creased and lined and battered that it's difficult for emotions to make any impact on it, but that doesn't really matter. He'll follow my father's orders. As long as Dad is happy, that's all that counts.

Dad sits back thoughtfully behind his huge desk and frowns. 'Well, as it seems as if Murray did play a crucial role in getting you through this.'

'I'd be dead without him,' I say frankly.

'Yes but . . .' He presses his fingertips together. 'That doesn't change the fact that it was his driving that took you off the side of the mountain. That's the problem for me. The whole thing was his fault, even if he managed to save you from the consequences.'

I lean towards my father and say urgently, 'No, Dad. You've got to believe me. It was my fault. Don't blame Miles. I should never have demanded to be taken to the airport, or insisted he speed up, in those conditions. He was obeying my orders.'

169

Dad glances over at Pierre and they seem to exchange meaningful looks but I can't work out what they're saying by them.

'Where *is* Miles?' I demand, unable to wait any longer. The whole day he's been on my mind, lingering in the shadows of it, like a dark and delicious secret. 'I want to see him.'

'Why is that?' my father asks.

'Why?' I shoot him a look of frustrated bewilderment. 'Because he saved my life! I haven't had a chance to thank him properly yet, that's why. Once we were rescued, we never had another moment to speak. And—' I've tried to be calm and persuasive but I can feel anger building up in me now. *Why won't my father treat me like an adult?* 'I want to make sure that you haven't sacked him or decided to punish him for this! I've told you that it wasn't his fault. Do you believe me or not?'

Dad looks at Pierre again and then back at me. 'Of course I do, sweetheart,' he says slowly, as though I'm a child needing to be pacified. 'I know you want to protect Miles Murray, and that you feel strongly about it. But you've been through an ordeal and it's our job to make sure that this is what it seems, that's all.'

I frown, trying to decipher what he's saying to me. 'You mean – you think that there might be more to this than just an unfortunate accident? You're crazy! I was there, and I can tell you exactly what it was like. That car was completely out of control. It was only Miles's skill that managed to stop us being killed in it. I was frightened – really and truly frightened! There was no fakery about it, I can guarantee it.'

'We know what you believe, honey,' my father says, and the patronising tone in his voice just infuriates me more.

'This is ridiculous!' I declare. 'You're paranoid!'

'I don't think so,' my father replies. 'Remember what happened in the past.'

I go quiet, not knowing what to say to this. Things that happened long ago still have the power to leap out and control the present. They're still shaping my future too. I close my eyes for a moment as powerful emotions grip me: a mixture of fear, confusion and horror. Things I've tried to block out of my memory rise up and clutch at me, delighted to be resurrected and to prove their power to control me no matter how hard I try to escape. My hands ball into fists and my nails cut into my palm. I'm glad. I want the pain to bring me back to the here and now. I open my eyes and take a deep breath. 'That doesn't have anything to do with what just happened to me. I know it – with my whole being.'

Pierre speaks at last. 'We have to investigate.' His harsh, rasping voice, heavy with its French accent, always sounds as if it's rusty through lack of use. 'We have to be sure.'

I turn to him. 'But you hired Miles. You investigated his background. You know that he's one hundred per cent trustworthy.'

Pierre stares back at me, impassive as a rock. His face, craggy and scarred, repels me.

'Well?' I demand. 'Isn't that right?'

'We have to be sure,' he repeats, with a finality that tells me he won't be saying any more.

I swing back to look at my father. 'Dad, tell him all this is a waste of time. Where is Miles? I want to see him.'

'Miles will be staying here until we've concluded the investigation,' says my father, his voice grave. 'But I'm sorry – you won't be able to see him.'

'Why not?' I stare at him, horrified. I'd been sure that I would see Miles today. It's all I've been hanging on to.

'We have our reasons.' My father speaks in a tone I know well. It means I won't be getting anything more from him. 'And once I'm satisfied that you're all right, I think you should leave here. You'll be better off somewhere else – a change of scene – until we get this sorted out.'

I gape at him, appalled at the idea that I might be separated from Miles for . . . how long? For ever?

No! I have to see him!

'Dad,' I say urgently. 'Please . . . just five minutes with Miles . . .'

He shakes his head. 'No, honey. I'm sorry. I can't allow it. It's not going to happen.'

I go back to my room in a daze, trying to think everything through. My father evidently has very strong suspicions that something is going on and that Miles might be involved.

I remember the television reports and their suggestion that my crash was faked. *What's wrong with everyone? Why do they have such vivid imaginations?*

I don't know what my father thinks might have gone on, or how he believes Miles hoped to profit by the whole thing, but that's not my main focus right now. I'm horrified by the realisation that I've been forbidden from seeing Miles. I didn't dare beg too much in case it made my father even more suspicious. After all, beyond common politeness, why should I be so concerned with seeing Miles again? According to my account, he's just a member of staff who was doing his job. A hero, maybe – but he's paid for his expertise. My father would expect no less from him.

Oh God, what am I going to do? How am I going to see him?

I throw myself on my bed and groan. My longing for him is so intense I can hardly stand it. He's here, somewhere, in this very building. I wonder if he's thinking about me, wondering how I am. Maybe he's seen that nonsense on the television – I imagine how that will make him laugh and say something cutting in the Scottish accent that always gets stronger when he's being sardonic, with a lift of that eyebrow to underline his scorn.

I close my eyes and begin to dream of him, remembering every inch of his skin, his taste and his feel. The events of the day have exhausted me and I quickly slip into sleep, and the most vivid dream I've ever known. I'm lying asleep on my bed, just as I am in reality. A presence comes into the room and even though I'm not awake, I'm alert to it, aware of it approaching me, coming closer to the edge of my bed. It's a vast, massy presence but I can't turn to see it. Instead I feel as though I'm paralysed. I wonder who or what this presence is. Friend or foe? I long for it to be Miles come to find me, but if it were him, surely he would speak to me, and this presence is silent apart from the sound of regular breathing. It's closer now, sitting down on the bed. I feel the weight of it close to me on the mattress. The breathing is louder. I want to speak and move but I can't. I'm frozen, my limbs as heavy as lead, and a sense of horror grows inside me as I realise that whatever is with me is not a benevolent presence but something that means to harm me somehow. My heart races with fear, I try to scream but I'm unable to open my mouth or even move a muscle. Panic begins to overwhelm me as I feel that great shape leaning over me, closer and closer . . .

My eyes flick open and I'm awake, panting, my heart pounding. I'm alone in my dark bedroom. The presence is gone. I dreamed it. I must have. It's the only explanation.

I clutch at my chest, trying to regulate my panicked breathing. *Oh my God, that was horrible, horrible . . .*

Despite my efforts to reassure myself that it was just a dream, I'm still shaky with the after-effects of my fear. I get up. It's late, after one o'clock in the morning. They must have decided to let me sleep and not disturb me for dinner. I open my bedroom door and look out into the corridor, lit with the gentle glow of lamps at intervals along the hallway. It's so quiet out there. Everyone has gone to bed.

I step out into the corridor and without really thinking what I'm about to do, I walk quickly and quietly towards the elevator. A little red light flashes near the ceiling and I notice the security camera, small and black, tucked away by the coving. I walk close to the wall so that it will catch as little of my image as possible, although it's futile to try and hide completely. As soon as I stand in front of the elevator doors, I'll be visible, and inside there's another camera. Whoever is observing the CCTV screens will be certain to see me.

But why should I be afraid of that? This is my home! I should be free to move around as I like.

I summon the elevator, and when it arrives, I step inside. I stare at the buttons for a moment and then press the one marked '2'. A floor I've never visited before.

What the hell am I doing? This is crazy.

But I can't stop myself. The doors slide shut and the elevator glides downwards, coming to a halt with a tiny chime. The doors open again and I'm looking out into another corridor, but where the ones in the main house are lit by the golden glow of lamps, this is lit with the cold grey light of recessed bulbs: functional but unwelcoming. I step out, looking around me. No one is in sight. I start to walk down the corridor, wondering what I'm doing. I don't even know what's on this floor, but I'm guessing that the first floor will be more utilitarian, and this floor will have the staff bedrooms on it.

I glance up and see more red lights twinkling on the side of CCTV cameras, their dark glass lenses observing the corridor. I can't go anywhere in this place without being seen. I think suddenly of the hut, its utter remoteness and isolation. It was completely private. No one could track me there or watch my movements.

Voices spill from an open doorway but as I get closer, I realise it's a television. I stop by the doorway and glance inside. The interior is semi-lit, partly by the bright glare of the television in the corner and partly by the grey light from the bank of screens that show the images from the cameras throughout the house. A security guard sits in front of the screens but he's not looking at them at all. His attention is completely focused on the television and the late-night show he's watching.

That's good. He might not have seen me leave my floor and arrive here. I guess it's a boring job looking at corridors that are empty most of the time.

I take the opportunity of a burst of noise from the television to dash past the doorway. It's like being some kind of spy. I have to remind myself that I'm in my own home. I have a right to be here. Or do I? This feels disconnected to the life I know upstairs, with its light and luxury. I have a feeling the staff would not be happy to see me on their territory, and I hope that they're all asleep.

I pass a kitchen, a large dining room with half a dozen or so small tables each set for four people, and then a sitting room, where another television is playing and a man I don't recognise is asleep in front of it in an armchair.

I had no idea my house was so full of strangers.

I'm obviously in the staff quarters but how am I going to find Miles? I turn a corner and come to a wide hallway, with a table against one wall and above that, some rows of pigeonholes, a few stuffed with envelopes. I go over and examine them. Each pigeonhole has a name and number below it. This must be where the staff receive their post and internal communications. I scan them quickly, my heart beating faster. At first, I can't see Miles's name and have to calm myself and look again more slowly and carefully. Then, I find it: M. Murray. There's no number next to his name. *The numbers must be room numbers. Why isn't there one for Miles?* The pigeonhole is empty.

I look quickly at the other names. There are at least two dozen. Is that really how many people it takes to run my family's life? And that's just here at the mountain house. There are more throughout the world at my father's many properties. All this staff, just to look after four people. I shake my head at the oddness of it, and push it out of my mind as I do a quick process of elimination on the numbers I can see against the other names. The numbers seem to run from one to twenty-five, and three numbers are not listed: 17, 21 and 24. So if Miles doesn't have an allocated room, perhaps he's in one of these others.

This is completely crazy. But I'm going to see what I can find.

Two corridors lead off from the hall, one labelled 1–15 and the other labelled 16–25. I head down the second one, guessing the labels must be directing towards the room numbers, and sure enough I soon pass a grey door numbered 16, then another, number 17. This place is like a dour hotel, I think, stopping in front of 17, the first of what I guess are the unoccupied rooms.

My palm feels clammy as I reach out and take hold of the doorknob. Very carefully, I twist it but I only manage half a turn before it stops. The door must be locked. I daren't force the handle or rattle the door in case there is someone inside. I let it go, and release a breath I didn't know I was holding. Then I turn and walk on further down the corridor, passing 18, 19 and 20, coming to a halt in front of 21. I'm even more nervous this time. What if it's open, but the person inside is not Miles? How on earth will I explain myself? I can't even begin to think of the questions that will be asked if I'm discovered here.

I steel myself, take hold of the handle and twist it. The same thing happens. A quarter turn and then a dead halt. It's locked. I try again but with the same result. That leaves only one room left that isn't occupied by someone else, at least as far as I can guess. I walk on towards the last four doors. I'm already giving up on this foolhardy mission but I've come so far, I may as well go on. The security guard is probably still watching his television show or no doubt he'd have come to investigate by now.

I'm standing in front of room number 24. The door looks identical to the others, with its chrome number, peephole and doorknob. Could this be the one with Miles behind it? There's only one way to find out. I'm about to reach out and take hold of the handle when I'm grabbed swiftly from behind, my head is jerked back and a hand is clamped hard over my mouth. There's no time to make a sound and before I can work out what is happening, I'm being pulled along the corridor the way I came, and then through an open door and into a dark room. The door is kicked shut and I'm enveloped in complete blackness, my eyes wide with panic but seeing nothing.

'What the hell are you doing here?' says a voice in my ear. 'Don't scream, do you understand?' Then the hand over my mouth relaxes its grip and I'm let go.

I'm panting hard with shock, adrenalin racing through me and making my hands shake and fingertips prickle as I turn to look at my assailant, but I've already recognised the deep voice and the Scottish accent. 'Miles?' I gasp.

A switch is flicked and a cool white light shines down upon us. There he is, standing right in front of me in a narrow hallway, his eyes hard with suspicion.

'You heard me,' he says roughly. 'What the hell are you doing here?'

CHAPTER ELEVEN

'I came looking for you!' I say, joy bubbling up in me at the sight of him. He looks so gorgeous in a pair of loose cotton pyjama pants and a white T-shirt that shows every bulge of muscle beneath. I throw my arms round his neck. 'I'm so glad I found you! I thought we were going to be kept apart and I couldn't stand it. I had to see you.'

Miles is standing still and unresponsive. Then he reaches up and takes my arms from around his neck.

I gaze up into his face, worried. His expression is stony, his blue eyes almost black in the white light from the overhead bulb. Despite its hard set, his mouth is still unbearably sexy.

'What is it? Aren't you pleased to see me?'

There's a pause that seems far too long, making me jittery with nervousness, before he says, 'I don't know if I'm pleased to see any of the Hammonds right now, if I'm honest.' He turns and walks away from me, down the short hall and into the main room. It's like something in a basic hotel, with a small double bed and some functional furniture. Miles sits down in a bucket armchair, looking far too big for it, and throws his arms over its back. I follow him.

'Why?' I ask, dismayed. 'What's wrong?'

'Wrong?' He glares at me. 'How about being interrogated for hours about the circumstances of our crash?

How about being treated like some kind of criminal? I haven't heard so much as a "thank you for saving my precious daughter's life".' Miles looks angry now, and all I can think of is how amazingly sexy it makes him. His blue eyes start to flash and his hands ball into fists. 'Your father hasn't said as much but he's making out that I'm some kind of blackmailer or kidnapper – I can't quite work out what crazy ideas are floating through his head. He seems to think I'm guilty of *something*, anyway. And now they're holding me as though I'm under some kind of house arrest.'

'Arrest?' I echo. 'But you can leave if you want to, can't you? I mean – you came out into the corridor to find me. They haven't locked the door.'

'It wouldn't matter if they had. If I wanted to go, a locked door isn't going to keep me in.' He laughs mirthlessly. 'But that arsehole Pierre has made it very clear that I'm not to go anywhere. I was just in the middle of deciding whether I'll oblige him or not.' He looks over at me. 'I'm sitting here thinking about heading off when I see the handle of my door turning. Nice and quiet and sneaky. So I wonder if there might be some dirty tricks going on and slip out to have a look. And there you are, down the hall. You're lucky I recognised you or it might have been rather nasty.'

I stare at him, horrified by his implication. 'You mean – you might have *killed* me?'

He glares back and then suddenly a huge smile breaks up his angry expression and he laughs, properly this time. I'm filled with relief as he says, 'Ah, ignore me. I've been sitting here, working myself into a fit of paranoia as bad as your father's. I'm not angry with you. I'm fucked off, it's true, but it's not that bad. I just resent being treated like a suspect for some unknown crime when I thought I'd done pretty well at bringing the boss's daughter home with nothing more than a bruise.'

Miles stares over at me and our gazes lock. The atmosphere changes and I feel the charge of sexual tension fill the room. We're both remembering that the boss's daughter came back with a whole new education.

'So,' he says softly, still staring at me. 'You decided to come and find me, did you?'

I nod, my mouth going dry. I've been enjoying my fantasies of Miles but the reality is both infinitely more complex and much more exciting. He hasn't fallen on me, telling me I'm the woman of his dreams and he has to have me now. In fact, when he thought I was a danger to him, he was more likely to strangle me than kiss me. But I can't help preferring this flesh-and-blood man to my imaginings, whether he refuses to act like my romantic hero or not. My gaze travels over him, taking in the way he looks so heart-poundingly sexy in his cotton pyjama pants and T-shirt.

He says, 'I guess you're not exactly used to this part of the building, are you?'

I shake my head, not able to speak. His gaze is raking over me, taking me in. I wish now that I'd inspected myself in the mirror before I set out to find him, but the whole thing was so impulsive, I didn't think of it. I'm wearing the clothes that Jane-Elizabeth brought me earlier: ballet flats, black skinny jeans and a loose silk top printed with a pattern of birds.

Miles says softly, 'I'm honoured. You came to the staff quarters. It must be a first to see a Hammond on this floor.'

I manage to find my voice at last. 'I had to see you.'

'Did you now?' He smiles, a lop-sided half smile of amusement. 'We only saw each other this morning. You're not going to tell me you can't live a day without me, are you?'

I can hardly believe that it was only this morning that we woke up together in that hut. Could he have forgotten what he did to me in the night? I can almost still feel the swollen sensation that lingered for hours after he pounded me with his huge prick. The thought makes me pull in a sharp breath. 'I don't know how we left things,' I say at last. 'I wanted to know what you think.'

'What I think?' He stands up, and I'm almost over-whelmed by his physical presence. He's tall and broad, making me feel small and fragile by comparison. He takes a few steps closer to me and I start to tremble. How on earth does he have this effect on me? I'm eaten up with longing for him. I have the most tremendous urge to leap on him, kiss him, hold him – but I know instinctively that this would be the wrong approach. I say nothing but look up at him. He reaches out a finger and strokes it along my jaw, leaving a trail of tingling nerve ends where he touches me. 'I think,' he continues, 'that we had an agreement. What happened in the hut stays in the hut. Right?'

'That was what you said,' I say, my voice loose and shaky with the effect he's having on me. I can't seem to breathe properly and my whole body is alive with excitement.

'So . . .' His blue eyes search my face. 'Is there anything more to say?'

You know there is! There must be! We can't just leave it like that!

The words shriek inside my head but still I say nothing. I can't, not while I'm working so hard at controlling my breath and the racing of my pulse. I long for him to touch me again so badly, it's all I can do not to grab his hand and press it to my face.

I close my eyes, concentrate hard and take in a deep breath. When I've released it I say quietly, 'I don't think my education is complete.'

His eyes flicker with something I can't identify. 'Oh, really? But the terms of my tuition were very clear. Do you mean you want to change them?'

I drop my gaze. 'Yes. Yes, I do. I want to finish what we've started.'

He says nothing and when I look up, his eyes are burning into me. 'It's not that easy,' he says. 'Things are different outside the place.'

'They don't have to be,' I say quickly.

'But they are. You're Freya Hammond here. I'm your bodyguard. That's not a situation I find conducive to . . . instruction.'

'Please,' I say weakly. 'I . . . I must . . . I want . . .'

His expression changes at once and he says roughly, 'I don't obey orders like that, you ought to know that by now.'

'I'm sorry!' I look up at him beseechingly. 'I didn't mean to express it like that! I'm not ordering you, I promise. I would never do that now.'

He turns and walks away from me, going over to the bedside and switching on a lamp. The light from it is warmer than from overhead; it touches his skin with a golden glow. 'Good,' he replies. 'Because it will get you precisely nowhere.'

'Please, Miles. I . . .' I lick my lips, looking for the right way to express myself. 'If you would be kind enough to consider it, I'd like to continue what we started. I would like to carry on learning what you can teach me.'

He comes back towards me, his expression softening. 'You know what? You surprise me. I thought when we got back here, it would be like it was before. You'd go back to being haughty Miss Hammond and you'd look right through me. When your dad started questioning me, I even wondered if it was at your instigation, so you could get me fired and not have to remember the humiliating episode where you made the mistake of fucking the staff.'

I gasp. 'No,' I say quickly. 'It's not like that. I've done everything I can to persuade him that the crash was my fault.'

That eyebrow goes up. *Oh God, it slays me.* A rush of pure desire courses through me so fast it almost knocks me off my feet.

'Really?' he says in a low voice. He looks sceptical.

'Yes. I promise. I don't know what my father is thinking but I told him I owe you my life. I've made it clear that you've been nothing but honourable.'

Miles walks towards me again, sending my senses soaring. 'I don't know about that,' he says in that sexy deep voice, the Scottish accent rolling off his tongue. 'Maybe "honourable" isn't quite the right word . . .'

I turn my face up to his, desperate for him to kiss me.

'You really want this, don't you?' He's scrutinising my face as if trying to read my mind.

I nod.

He seems to let his guard down just a fraction more. 'You are a very hot girl, Freya Hammond, in more ways than one. A man has to be careful before taking you on. You have a protective cordon around you like a concrete fence.'

'They know nothing,' I say vehemently. 'They can't stop me getting hurt, no matter how much they try. Besides, they have no right! I don't need them. I want to make my own choices, live my own life. I'm damned if I'll let them control me.'

He seems amused by my outburst. His face is close to mine now. I can see the gorgeous angles of his cheekbones, the long straight line of his nose, the dark stubble bristling on his chin. And those beautiful lips are so near, it's driving me mad with need. Then, suddenly, he takes my head in his hands and pulls me to him, landing his mouth on mine with an unexpected ferocity. My nerves sing out with the delirium of his touch, and everything responds to the pressure of his mouth, the taste of his tongue as I open to it and he pushes deep into me. My eyes close as I surrender to the wonder of his kiss and the feel of his hand on my skull, his fingers twisting in my hair while the other hand clasps my waist. I put my own hands up to his jaw, caressing the roughness of his stubbled skin as I pull his mouth as deep into mine as I can.

We kiss for a long time and when at last his lips slowly leave mine, I can read his desire in the way his eyes have turned a darker blue. I'm panting for more, wanting only to return to the exquisiteness of his mouth, but he shakes his head and smiles.

'Oh no, Winter. No more. Not here. This is not the right place for us.' He turns, goes to the desk by the wall, picks up a scrap of paper and a pen. 'Do you have a new phone yet? Give me the number.'

I pant out my phone number, dazed by the sensations coursing through my body and still coming to terms with the fact that he's just told me that there won't be any more.

But he called me Winter . . . Excitement stabs me in the core. *I know what that means.*

'Can you get away from here?' he asks as he scribbles down the number.

'Yes . . . yes.'

'Good. Because I don't intend to stay much longer myself. I'm sorting out a new phone. When I have it, I'll be in touch. Okay?'

I nod, torn between desperate disappointment that we won't be taking advantage of the bed and a delicious anticipation of what will happen next.

He comes over and takes my hands. 'I'm happy to continue your education,' he says, 'on my terms. Do you understand?'

'Yes,' I whisper.

'This place drains me. We'll continue somewhere else.'

'I understand.'

'Good. Now let's get you back to where you belong.'

My private helicopter flight lands in the early afternoon and a car waits for me on the edge of the landing site. It's a sunny day, with the jagged, snowy peaks of the mountains clearly defined against the clear blue sky. The pretty village of Klosters nestles among the pine-covered slopes, a collection of traditional chalet-style and more modern hotels and houses, all covered in a thick layer of pure white snow. We drive through the village. Through the tinted windows of the car, I see the winter tourists milling about, heading for the ski slopes or wandering out to the shops and restaurants. This place attracts a wealthy crowd and I wonder if I'll see anyone I recognise. A group of girls in chic ski clothes, fur hats and sunglasses make me tense but as we pass them, I realise I don't know any of their faces.

I don't want anyone to know I'm here.

I told my father and sisters that I was going to stay with my friend Lola for a few nights at her place in St Moritz but my flight actually brought me here. No one, not even Jane-Elizabeth, knows where I really am. It was hard to persuade my father to let me go without a body-guard but I needed to travel alone so I lied and told him that Lola was supplying both the helicopter flight and the security. He knows that she comes from a family almost as paranoid about security as ours, so that allayed his fears a little. I can only hope now that he doesn't decide to check up on me. The truth is that I booked a company that I use all the time in the skiing season, when I flit from one resort to another for parties. The owners know me and no one seemed to think it odd that I didn't have anyone with me.

'I know I suggested a change of scene,' Dad said when I told him I was leaving. 'But I was thinking of somewhere hot and very private, where we know you'll be completely secure. An island. A private resort.'

'Just a few days,' I wheedled. 'Lola and I are going to have a very quiet time, with massages and spa treatments. I need to relax after what happened.'

He considered it, and seemed happy with the idea that we'd be lying on massage tables being treated with face masks and oxygen therapies. 'Okay, honey. You're right, you need a good rest and Lola will look after you. But stay in touch, all right? And just a few days.'

'Okay,' I said, too happy to have won my freedom to show my irritation at the way my father was being more controlling than ever.

Of course he had no idea that I wasn't going to be with Lola at all.

The driver has the address that I'm going to. I hope he knows the way because I have no idea where it is. He takes us on the road out of the main part of the village. The chalets we pass are picture perfect, like something from a story book with their carved shutters and balconies. Thick pine forests slope away from the road and as we climb higher, I get a strange frisson of sick fear remembering the last time I was in a car on a mountainside, even though today is nothing like that stormy, snowy morning. A short way out of the village, the driver takes a turning and then another and we are suddenly on level ground, following a curving driveway round until we see before us a beautiful chalet. It's very traditional, the bottom storey in light stone, the top storeys in dark wood with bright red shutters at the windows and a wooden balcony facing out towards the village that lies prettily below. The sloping roof is laden with at least a foot of pristine snow, and the place is ringed with pine trees at the sides and back.

The driver gets out and opens the car door for me. I climb out, blinking in the afternoon sun. This is a beautiful place, close to the village and yet completely isolated too. The driver takes out my suitcase.

'Shall I carry it inside, madam?' he asks.

'No. Don't worry. I'll take it myself.' I press a tip into his hand. He murmurs his thanks and gets back into the car. A moment later, he's driving away and I'm left here alone in front of the chalet.

This is the place. Step one complete.

I pick up my bag and walk up to the front door. I'm jumpy with nerves and the tingling of a pleasant excitement as I ring the bell, but there's no answer. After a few moments I try the door handle. It turns under my hand and the door opens. I step into a hallway.

I gaze around the room with its tiled floor, white walls and simple wooden benches. It's completely empty. A staircase leads away in front of me to the next floor. I wonder if this is Miles's home. 'Hello?'

There's no reply. Mystified, I head for the staircase and soon I emerge on the first floor to find myself in a large room with spectacular views over the mountains. The wooden floors are covered in rugs, and cosy armchairs and sofas piled with cushions are grouped around a fireplace where flames flicker over logs. Lamps glow on the side tables. Through an archway I can see a dining room and beyond that a kitchen. Another staircase leads upstairs. It's beautiful but not the kind of place I'd imagined Miles to own.

'Hello?' I call again, but there is still no reply. I put down my case and walk through the room to the dining area where a carved wooden table is surrounded by chairs upholstered in red-and-white cushions. On the table is a note. I pick it up.

Winter
  Make yourself at home. Prepare for your tutorial. It will start at four o'clock precisely.

I feel a lazy somersault of exhilaration turn in my stomach and wonder what Miles has in mind to teach me today. Four o'clock. I have less than an hour. I return to my bag, pick it up and go upstairs where I find the four bedrooms, each one with a beamed ceiling and furnished with comfortable-looking beds, antique chests and soft armchairs. The main one has a huge bed covered in a beautifully embroidered counterpane. Vast lamps sit on tables either side of it and it faces a fireplace with a stone surround. Before the hearth is a huge white fur rug. I shiver, unable to help imagining all the delicious things that Miles might do to me in this room.

I've been riding high on my excitement ever since yesterday morning when I received his text. It had been agonising saying goodbye to him in the silent corridors of the staff quarters.

'Don't worry about the security cameras,' he'd murmured to me when we reached the elevator. He dropped a kiss on my cheek. 'I'll deal with them.'

'What are you going to do? How will you get away from here?'

'Don't worry about that. I'll sort it. Just wait for my message.'

With a final swift kiss, he'd ushered me into the elevator and I'd watched, racked with longing, as the doors closed on him. I hadn't expected to sleep that night but I'd reckoned without the accumulated exhaustion of recent events and as soon as I climbed into bed, I fell into a deep sleep that lasted well into the next day. I spent that day and the next resting up, returning calls and messages and waiting fretfully for Miles to get in touch. I had no idea where he was. He might still be on the second floor for all I knew. He had my number, but I didn't have his.

At breakfast on the third day, I gazed at my phone which was still stubbornly without messages from Miles.

Flora had already eaten and there was no sign of Summer. I was wondering if I should take my handset to Jane-Elizabeth and ask her to check that my phone was working okay when Estella wafted in wearing a white silk robe, her hair tousled from bed.

I cast a quick look at her. *Oh, nice. Just to remind us all she's been sleeping with our father.*

'Morning, Freya,' she said, going to the sideboard to pour herself some coffee from the pot on the hot plate. 'How are you?'

'Fine, thanks,' I said as briefly as I could without being too rude.

'Recovered from your . . . *ordeal*?' She gave a special emphasis to the last word that made me look up sharply.

'Yes, thanks,' I said, trying to sound casual. 'It wasn't so bad, you know. I was lucky.'

'You certainly were,' drawled Estella, coming to the table with her coffee cup in one hand. She sat down at an empty place and looked around impatiently. 'Where's the maid? I want my grapefruit salad.'

I tried to hide my irritation. It wasn't so long ago that Estella was meek and eager to please, always rushing off to do our bidding. Now she was very much the lady of the house. *Let it go. You can't do anything about it.* I ignored her last comment and drank my own coffee. Now that Estella was here, I wanted to be off as soon as possible.

She fixed me with a knowing look and said in her languid drawl, much less breathy than the voice she uses with my father: 'So . . . tell me, just what was it like, being rescued from death by a hunky bodyguard like Miles Murray?'

191

A warm flush started to creep up my neck and I did all I could to halt it, breathing regularly and trying to keep calm. 'He was extremely professional. As you'd expect.'

'I don't doubt it.' She smirked. 'And it can't have been all bad, being trapped with him for two days. I mean . . . I'm sure he was very good company. And you must have found *some* way to occupy your time.'

I stared back at her and said nothing, but inside I felt sick. Of course Estella would think that way. It's how her mind works. As long as she contented herself with making comments to me, and not confiding her suspicions to my father.

'We managed,' I said. 'I was very scared a lot of the time.'

Her expression became sympathetic but it didn't look all that sincere to me. 'Yes. So traumatic. Lucky you had someone like Miles to help you through it.'

At that moment, the door opened and the maid came in.

'My grapefruit salad! At last,' said Estella but the maid came over to me, a parcel in her hands rather than a bowl of grapefruit.

'This arrived for you, miss, by special courier.' The maid put the parcel down beside me, a well-wrapped box hand-addressed in capital letters.

I looked at it curiously, wondering what it could be.

'Aren't you going to open it?' asked Estella, her interest evidently piqued. 'And bring my grapefruit!' she called to the maid, who was on her way out.

'Maybe,' I said. I put one finger under the flap of gummed-down brown paper and began to lift it. At that moment my phone made the swishing sound that meant a text had arrived. I picked it up. The number was unknown. I pressed to open the message.

A parcel will arrive for you this morning. Don't open it in public.

I almost gasped but managed to restrain myself. Slowly, hoping that I looked normal, I picked up my coffee cup again and drained it before saying, 'Actually, I think I'll open it upstairs.'

Estella shrugged but she looked disappointed.

Good. You can wonder.

I stood up, thankful that the text had arrived just in time, and headed up to my room with the parcel under one arm. It had to be from Miles. Sure enough, when I unwrapped it in the privacy of my bedroom, there was a box inside, wrapped in black crepe paper and tied with a black silk ribbon. Tucked under the ribbon was a note: *To be worn for your lesson.*

Now, in the luxurious chalet bedroom, I take the box from my bag and place it on the bed. I texted Miles back when I'd opened it but there was no response for several hours and after that, just a short message giving me the address of this place and a time to be here.

So here I am. What now? Shall I just get ready for him?

I notice that a small table is placed by the hearth where a fire is laid ready to be lit, and on the table a paper scroll wrapped with a red ribbon has been tucked into a glass vase. I go over and take it out, pull the ribbon open and unroll the paper. On it is written in clear black handwriting:

Your lessons will consist of learning the four classical elements of our world:
Fire, water, earth and air.

Be ready for your tuition.

I read it twice, trying to understand. I know what each of these things is, so what can Miles teach me about them? And I was expecting something a little more . . . physical.

Trust him. I'm sure I'm going to enjoy the lesson.

I look at my watch. Still a little while to go before Miles arrives. I decide to have a shower and prepare for him. After I emerge wrapped in a towel and damp-haired from the shower, I go to the box on the bed and open it.

There is the costume that Miles wants me to wear for the lesson today.

My uniform.

I laugh. It's nothing like a uniform or anything that plays to ideas of schoolgirl skirts and long socks. It's more like something a goddess would wear. I lie it out carefully on the bed and look at it. A thrill of excitement turns in my belly and sends out tingling messages all over my skin. Only half an hour until my lesson begins. I'd better get ready.

Twenty minutes later, I've dried my hair into a wavy bob and made up my face, curling out my lashes with mascara, adding sparkle to my lids with a golden shimmer that makes my brown eyes look positively velvety, and painting my lips in a dark vampish red that somehow seems suitable for the goddess gown Miles has sent me. Now I'm ready to put on my costume.

I walk over naked to the bed, noticing a large cheval glass mirror facing it. I glimpse my own form as I approach the bed: my long body with its flowing curves, the full breasts and round bottom. My bruise is almost gone but I look at the traces with fondness: it's the proof of what happened to me, and what took place between Miles and me. I hope he'll run his fingers down it, perhaps trail his lips along its fading path and make the skin there burn and tingle under his touch. I've prepared for today, getting myself soft and smooth with lotions and scrubs and oils, and I hope that I look my best. Now it's time to get dressed.

The first thing to put on are the knickers, a flimsy piece of pale gold shimmering mesh on silk ribbons that tie at each side of my hips. A rush of arousal goes through me as I slide them on and tie up the little ribbon at each side; it's hard to not imagine Miles's fingers undoing them. Now for the gown. There's no bra to wear underneath. Instead, the pale gold silk tulle fastens in a halterneck and then falls in soft pleats over each breast, giving more than a hint of the rounded flesh and dark nipples below. It meets again in the middle of my stomach and joins the most interesting part of this dress, the pale gold leather belt with gold buckles at each side. The contrast of leather and metal with the delicate softness of the fragile material is striking. The tulle fastens to the belt at my waist and then drops in a long narrow waterfall of fabric to my feet, a sparkling drapery that just covers my knickers. At the back, a matching flow of material falls over my bottom to the floor. I put on the dress, working out as I go along how everything goes together. As I fasten the belt's little gold buckles on each hip, I notice each has a golden ring hanging from it. My eyes fly to the box where my accessories await: a pair of high-heeled shoes and two gold leather buckled cuffs to wear on my wrist. They had looked purely decorative but now I see that they have tiny metal fasteners that can link them to each other. Or something else.

I gasp. I can't help it. *Is Miles . . . kinky?*

I've heard of people who like dressing up, spanking games, and all that bondage stuff, but it's never appealed to me. I've only been able to imagine them as faintly embarrassing and a little humiliating, not a turn-on at all. But now, as I look at the pretty wrist cuffs with their shine of hard metal against the muted glow of the tinted leather, my heart starts to race.

What will he do with me?

The idea of Miles restraining me as he teaches me new lessons in pleasure is darkly exciting.

I promised to do as he says and take everything he wants to give me.

I've never surrendered myself like that before, and never wanted to. I've always fought hard for my own independence, resenting my father's control and running shy of any man who looks as though he want to do the same. But that's how I ended up with Jacob, weak-willed and pathetic. Maybe my need to feel strong and in control of my destiny has been leading me in the wrong direction. The idea is an intriguing one.

My fingers are trembling very slightly as I put on the golden cuffs, buckling them snugly around each wrist. Then I slide on the dark nude peep-toe stilettos that came in the box. They are exactly my size.

I gaze at myself in the long mirror. The gown is beautiful, the fall of the fabric emphasising my curves, revealing my hips and the gleam of my legs. The leather and metal give a hint of a princess from a science-fiction fantasy, while the silk and heels add a dollop of Hollywood glamour. I feel intensely feminine and very sexy. I hope that Miles will like the result of his choice.

Miles. My eyes fly to a clock on the chimney piece over the fireplace. It's one minute to four o'clock.

I go back to the staircase and walk carefully downstairs, holding the delicate tulle of the dress out of the way of my heels as I go. In the sitting room, the fire is still burning, flames lapping at the logs. It is darker outside and the lamps glow even more golden, sending out pools of yellow light. I stand by the fireplace, looking around the beautiful room and wondering what will happen now.

Another clock chimes four times.

I hear the front door open.

He's here.

CHAPTER TWELVE

The door downstairs closes and a heavy tread approaches on the stairs. My breathing is coming faster but I try to control it. I stand by the fire, trying to adopt the stance of a model to show myself off to best advantage.

Miles walks into the room and stops as he sees me, his gaze intense beneath black brows. He looks gorgeous, more handsome than I remembered. There's nothing of the bodyguard about him today; he is wearing a sharply cut charcoal grey coat, dark trousers and polished shoes, and looks as though he's come from a smart gentleman's club or a business meeting. His blue eyes shine in the lamplight, a bright blue against the sombre colours of his clothes. His expression is impassive as he looks me up and down. Then he nods slowly and smiles.

'Hello, Winter. I'm glad to see you obeyed my instructions. It's good to see you. Very good indeed.'

'It's good to see you too,' I reply softly. 'Tutor.'

He advances, unbuttoning his coat. His steely gaze softens as he takes in the sight of my body, hidden and yet revealed by the golden gown. 'I hope you've come ready to learn.'

I nod. 'Oh yes.'

'Excellent.' Miles takes off his coat, revealing a soft blue shirt beneath a grey cashmere jumper, and throws it over the back of a chair. He turns to look at me. He's close to me and my skin is prickling with anticipation of his touch, my sex already tingling and alive to his presence. He stares deep into my eyes. 'You've shown your commitment to my instruction. I'm impressed. You know, Winter, I wasn't sure you'd take to this as wholeheartedly as you have. I thought you might be a dilettante, not prepared to see it through. You've surprised me.'

'I hope I'll go on doing that,' I reply, dropping my gaze. I want him to see that I'm prepared to hand him control in return for the exquisite pleasure he can bring me and the erotic lessons he can teach me. When I look at him again, he's observing me with a strange expression: tenderness mixed with a kind of surprise. As soon as he sees me watching him, his expression changes again, this time to that cool detachment I've seen previously.

Miles walks through the sitting room and dining room and into the kitchen. I turn to watch as he opens a huge fridge and removes a bottle of champagne. A moment later he's returning with it, two glasses in his other hand. He puts them down on a side table, picks up a small remote and directs it towards some hidden equipment. At once, piano music fills the room, delicate and delightful.

'Chopin,' he says, and smiles at me, the eyebrow lifting slightly. 'In case you didn't know.'

'I didn't.'

'All part of your lesson.' He opens the bottle of champagne in two deft movements and pours us each a glass. He hands one to me, then lifts his glass to mine and says, 'To you, Winter. You are an able and beautiful student.'

I lift my glass in return and smile. 'Thank you.' *My God, I want him so badly*. But I know that this slow lead-in, with me in this incredible outfit, is all part of the fun.

199

We sip our champagne. The icy bubbling liquid fills my mouth with small serried explosions. It's delicious. I look around the room and say, 'Is this place yours?'

'No.' He smiles at me. 'It belongs to a friend. I like it, but it's not really my style.'

'What is your style?' I ask, and take another sip of the champagne.

Miles raises his eyebrow again. 'I think we'll leave that lesson for another time. Did you see my pointer on what we'd learn today?'

I nod. 'Fire, water, earth and air. The four elements.'

'That's right – the elements that the ancient Greeks believed were the basis of everything in the world. Aristotle added a fifth – the quintessence, or fifth element – which he called *aether,* the heavenly substance that forms space and everything else they couldn't explain. The stars, for example.' Miles lifts his glass to me. 'I like to think of anything that adds to the joy of life as part of that heavenly substance.'

I take another drink. The crisp, biscuity liquid fires its volleys of bubbles over my tongue. 'Then we should add champagne to it. I suppose you could say that it's a little like drinking stars.'

He smiles. 'Yes. I like that. We think the same way, Winter.' His gaze travels appreciatively over me again. 'You look like a heavenly body yourself, Winter, in that dress. Like the goddess you were named after.'

'You chose well,' I reply softly.

His gaze becomes intense suddenly and fires off an answering tumble of excited butterflies in my stomach. 'I think we should begin.' He puts his glass on the side table and says lazily, 'So . . . where shall we start? Earth, air, water or . . . fire . . .?' His eyelids drop a little, making his gaze more hooded. A rush of desire flows through me. I can feel my nipples hardening, my nerves awakening to a greater pitch of alertness.

Miles takes a step towards me and says, 'I think fire first . . . Yes. Fire is the best way to start.' He takes me by the hand and leads me towards the fireplace where the flames are still flickering around an almost consumed log. Leaning down, he picks up another and throws it into the molten orange heart of the fire, making sparks crackle and explode as fresh flames leap up around it. Miles moves to stand behind me, his body very near to mine. I can feel him achingly close, the soft cashmere of his jumper almost touching my bare shoulder blades. His mouth is close by my ear.

'Watch the fire, Winter. Amazing, isn't it? It's fascinated mankind since we first discovered it, although the Greeks would have us believe that Prometheus stole fire from the gods, an act that earned him the peculiar torment of having his liver eaten by an eagle, only for it grow back so it could be eaten again the following day.'

The buzz of his voice in my ear is a torment too. I long to turn my face to his so that he can kiss me, or so that I can at least feel the touch of his lips on my cheek, but I daren't move.

'Heraclitus thought of the soul as a mixture of fire and water, the hot, dry fire being the noble part, the one that contains our passion, energy and drive. Appropriate to start here, then, where our passions are kindled.'

His mouth is tantalisingly close to my ear. I'm breathing faster, my breasts rising and falling rapidly under their light covering of golden tulle. I can feel the heat from the fire on my bare skin, and an answering warmth inside as my body prepares for pleasure.

'Today, we can describe fire in a series of chemical equations, explaining everything about it: the light, colours, heat and growth of the flames. We know that it's precious but also deadly. It provides heat and comfort but also it's also searing, burning, destroying. Perhaps that's why it symbolises passion so perfectly . . .' His lips close around my earlobe and I gasp as I feel the light touch of his teeth on it. He sucks gently, his tongue caressing it. I sigh with the exquisite sensations he's provoking in me just with the small sucks and licks on my ear.

I feel a movement at my waist and realise that he is deftly clipping my wrist cuffs to the golden hoops on my belt and that my arms are now tethered. My insides clench with surprise and a rapid whirl of excitement.

'Can you feel the heat?' he asks. His hands are on my flesh now, running along my arms. His fingertips trail over the skin on my hip. 'Yes. You're warm.'

My lips are dry and I lick them, my pulse racing at the touch of his fingers. I want those fingers all over my body, I want them to press inside me.

'Fire is about volatility. Transformation.' His voice is low, hypnotic. 'Not all transformations are good: from untouched to burnt. From whole to destroyed. But others take us to places we never dreamed existed.'

Take me to those places, Miles.

I want to speak, but I can't. The heat from the fire plays over my skin while Miles's proximity is making my back burn and tingle. I'm aware of my wrists tethered to my belt. *Holy hell, what's he going to do now?*

'Take off your shoes.'

I obey, stepping out of the stilettos and feeling the soft white rug beneath my feet. I'm about five inches shorter now, and Miles seems bigger and more powerful than ever. Suddenly his hands are on my shoulders and he's pushing me gently downwards. I sink to my knees, my gaze fixed on the golden flames leaping in the fireplace. Now he's beside me, taking me further back so that I'm lying on the soft white rug in front of the fireplace, my legs bent beneath me as if I'm offering myself in supplication to the fire. I can see him now, half-kneeling behind me, looking at my body with its golden drapery, my nipples already erect and pert against the silky fabric that covers my breasts. I stare up at him, longing for his touch, feeling at once intensely vulnerable and strangely in control. I want this. My body urgently needs him, and I'm offering it in all its vivid femininity.

Miles leans down and kisses me on the mouth, his tongue sliding between my lips. His face is inverted to mine, so his chin touches the side of my nose as he explores my mouth. The sensation of his tongue being upside down in my mouth is curious, the probing, exploring kisses provoking a strange excitement. He kisses me, reaches down and places his hand over my mound. I twitch with the sudden, unexpected touch so close to my core. He slides his hand down over the swelling sex with its delicate covering of golden mesh and presses it between my thighs. Then, gently but firmly, he moves my legs apart, first one thigh and then the other. Now I'm open to the heat of the fire and I can feel it playing over my sex, warming me where I'm already hot and needy.

He pulls away from my mouth, and looks down at my prone body, the wrists bound to my sides. 'You look very beautiful,' he murmurs. 'Now . . . let's learn a little more about fire.'

I feel a thrill that has a shimmer of something like fear inside it.

He goes on: 'Fire is considered a masculine element, and in the pagan world, its tool is the candle.' He reaches over to a candlestick on a low table by the fire and plucks the white stem of a candle from it. 'Not surprising, really, when you consider how the candle carries and contains a flame.' Miles put the candle lightly against my lips, drawing it over them so that I can feel the smooth waxy cylinder. I'm seized by the impulse to lick and kiss it, but I restrain myself. He runs the candle over my mouth, down my chin and neck to the base of my throat, then further to my right breast. Slowly he puts out one hand and draws the loose pleats of tulle away from that breast. I hear him draw in a breath as he exposes the full curve and I guess that he's looking at the erect nipple that's been straining at the cloth. He takes the candle and runs its circular edge around the sensitive area that surrounds my nipple, tickling me lightly with it. Now he pulls aside the fabric that covers the other breast and I'm entirely exposed to him. I can feel the heat from the fire flickering over my skin, and the nipples become even tighter and more erect. I long to touch Miles, or even touch myself, but my wrists are bound, there's nothing I can do.

Miles gets up and goes to the fire, leaning over it so that his large form blocks it out. When he turns back, he is holding the candle upright so that the orange flame on its tip burns strongly, taking hold of the wick. He kneels down in front of me, between my open thighs, and I gaze at him. I'm utterly prone before him, my sex still covered with the mesh knickers and silk drapery but my breasts exposed, cupped by the fabric that's tethered to the belt just below my wrists.

This is so exciting. But what is he going to do with that candle?

He's staring at me intently, his eyes dark with lust. Then he says softly, 'Like so many things, fire can bring pain . . . and pleasure.' He brings the flickering candle up towards my chest. 'You just have to know how to control it.'

The golden light jumps and sways before me. Beneath, a shimmering pool of molten wax is gathering. Miles moves the candle smoothly so that it is directly above my left breast. Then, slowly, he tips it so that a drop of the liquid wax trembles on the candle's rim and then falls, landing exactly on my nipple.

A sharp, burning sensation floods out over the sensitive bud and I gasp loudly.

'Shhh,' he says soothingly. 'Don't respond at once. Control yourself. Let yourself feel it.'

I bite my lip to stop any more sounds escaping, and close my eyes instead. The sensation of pain subsides, leaving a delightful throbbing in my nipple, and an answering clench below, where my sex is swelling and growing juicy. I can feel the mesh of my knickers getting damp as desire floods me. I open my eyes again. Miles moves the candle to my other breast and does the same as before, tipping it slowly so that I can watch the clear blob swell on its rim and then fall, encasing my nipple with a hot coating of wax. As I gasp and moan again at the stab of pain and the echo of pleasure, he pours a stream of wax down my cleavage towards my waist. Then he blows out the candle and puts it on the hearth.

'Fire causes a change of state,' he murmurs, 'from solid to liquid, and when the heat is removed, the liquid becomes solid again.'

Miles brings his face close to my left breast. I can see that the nipple is covered in a white cap of wax. He carefully puts his forefinger and thumb on either side of it and tugs gently so that the cap comes off, making my nipple tingle with delight as it's freed. Immediately he takes it in his mouth, sucking and pulling hard on the pert bud so that I can't help moaning again. It's beautiful. I had no idea my nipples were capable of giving me so much pleasure. The yanking pull of his mouth on my breast is exciting, making me move my hips in time with the deep sucks on my nipple. When it's exquisitely tormented, he moves to the other, repeating the process of freeing it from its waxen prison and then sucking it into reddened torment.

When I look down, I can see Miles kneeling between my legs, his form dark against the flickering firelight, his head bent over my breast as he sucks it. I wish I could touch him and caress him but I can't move my wrists from the side of my dress. I can only writhe with the effect of the wild sensations he's causing in my body, and gasp with the intensity of what I feel. In my core, I can feel a mad longing building.

I have to have him. This need has to be slaked.

I want him to release my hands so that I can tear off his clothes, dig my nails into the skin on his back, find his hard length and pull it into my depths, where I'm so hungry for it. At the very least, I wish he would press himself against the swelling mound where my clit is already stiff against the gold mesh of my knickers, and give me a little of the relief I crave.

I mustn't force it. I have to wait.

At last he releases my nipple with a tiny popping sound and turns his attention away from my breasts. Now he follows the waxen trail down between them, and his hand plays lightly around my belt and then at the silken ribbon of my knickers. I bite my lip again as he runs his finger under the ribbon, tantalisingly close to my mound but still so far away. Then he takes hold of the end of one of the bows I tied earlier and tugs so that it slips free.

I can't help myself whimpering with anticipation as he folds the triangle of golden mesh gently away.

'Oh, Winter,' he murmurs. 'You're ready for me, I can tell. You're learning very well about the transformative power of fire.'

'Please,' I say, my voice light and breathless, 'I need more.'

'All in good time. This is your lesson, not mine. Relax and surrender to it.' His voice is low and hypnotic. I close my eyes and relax my head, letting the tension out of my body. 'That's better. Only when you stop fighting it can you begin to experience it.'

I know I'm not fighting anything, except my own desire and need to move things along at the frenzied pace my body is demanding. But I understand: Miles is dictating the order of events here, not me. The more I surrender control over what is happening, the greater the heights I'll climb to.

'There's plenty to learn, Winter. No need to hurry it.' His tone is gentle, caressing. Now his hand begins to play over me, touching me lightly, stroking me. I feel completely exposed to him, my sex now open to the fire and to his gaze. I open my eyes and see that he's looking at me, his

207

dark blue eyes fixed on mine. He smiles and says quietly, 'I love to see the pleasure on your face when I touch you.'

The pressure in his fingertips grows as his hand roams over me. Now he's touching the wet slit of my sex, trailing a burning zigzag over it. It feels as though his fingers are on fire as he moves them over me, toying with my need as the longing within me builds up to a frenzy. I'm lifting my hips to bring myself closer to his probing fingers, unable to prevent myself twisting them against his hand. I don't think I can wait any longer. Then I feel him push his fingers between the hot lips of my sex to the entrance. He presses one finger hard inside me and it feels so good, it's all I can do not to cry out. He slides it deep inside, letting it move effortlessly into the dark groove within me. Oh God, that's all I want and more ... He pushes another finger in and then another, stretching me as he presses inside, fucking me hard with his fingers. I want him, as deep and hard as he can give, and I thrust up to meet him. The fact that I can't move my arms from my waist becomes unbearably exciting as I realise that my body is entirely at his mercy, and that I won't be able to resist the pleasure that he's intent on giving me. Now the ball of his thumb is on my clit so that as he fucks me with his fingers, the cushion of his thumb strums and rubs my bud, creating a point of hot pleasure under it. I'm gasping now, panting hard as my need for him increases. The heat from the fire seems to grow more intense as my sex gets hotter and needier. Miles's hand plunges in and out of me, his thumb tweaking me with ever more exquisite pressure until I can take it no more. I tense and my hips buck. I can't help throwing back my head as I shout out, 'Oh God, I'm coming, Miles!'

Then the pleasure explodes over my body and I can only surrender to its delectable convulsions until the boiling torrent subsides and I'm left, breathless and replete. When I open my eyes again, sighing happily, Miles is staring at me.

'An excellent start,' he murmurs, his eyes dark with desire. 'Do you think you've learned a little about fire, Winter?'

I nod. 'Oh yes. I've learned a lot. It . . . it turns solids to liquids with devastating effect.'

He smiles. 'Very good. You're going to be an A-grade student, I can tell. We'd better not leave it too long before your next lesson.' He drops a kiss on my belly and then on each of my breasts and finally on my mouth. 'But first . . . a little break.'

I'm feeling deliciously satisfied as we sit down by the fire with our glasses of champagne, still fizzy if not quite so ice cold as before. Outside, the day has darkened to a navy-blue night and the twinkling lights of Klosters are spread below us under their snow-capped roofs. In the distance, the mountains stretch away to great dark shapes clad in the shadows of pine forests.

Miles disappears upstairs for a few minutes, leaving me time to enjoy the view. When he's back, I say, 'Who did you say this chalet belongs to?'

'I didn't. It's a friend of mine, called Dominic Stone.'

The name means nothing to me, but I nod politely.

Miles sits down and says, 'May I say that you're looking even more gorgeous post-lesson?'

I laugh, a little embarrassed as I remember that only a few minutes ago I was thrashing on the rug with Miles's

209

fingers buried deep inside me. The atmosphere is luxurious now, after my fierce orgasm, but still charged with tension. I might have slaked the first furious fires of my desire but I'm still hungry for the sight of Miles's muscled body and the touch of his warm skin. 'I have a feeling I don't have any lipstick left,' I say flirtatiously. My dress has been restored so that my breasts are covered again and I've retied the silk bow of my knickers. But my hair is most likely tousled and the high-heeled shoes are still where I abandoned them in front of the fire.

Miles is gazing at me with an unreadable expression in his blue eyes. Whatever it is, it makes my insides turn in lazy circles of lust. 'Are you ready to move on?'

'What's next?' I ask playfully, and take another sip of champagne. It's loosening me up deliciously but I don't want to get drunk and impair my ability to enjoy this sensory experience to the full. I remember suddenly how drunk Jacob and I used to get before we had sex, on huge bottles of Kristal and litres of iced Grey Goose. Then we frolicked around madly pretending we were having the best sex in the world when really we hardly knew what was going on half the time.

It didn't have one quarter of the excitement I experience with Miles. One kiss from him is sexier and more arousing than a whole night with Jacob.

More and more I'm amazed by the very idea that I might ever have loved Jacob. He seems like a lifetime ago and the person who loved him is not the girl sitting in this beautiful chalet in front of a fire, dressed in an extremely sexy gown with the handsomest, most desirable man in the world sitting opposite. I stare over at Miles, who's looking back at me with an amused expression in his eyes, his mouth twisted in one of those half smiles I like so much, and one dark eyebrow lifted just a touch.

He's lovely. He's everything I want.

The thought surprises me. So far, I've been entranced by Miles's body and his overwhelming physical presence. At least, that's what I thought. But now, as we look at each other with a kind of sexy conspiratorial amusement, I realise that ever since we've met he's pushed my buttons in other ways. First, his arrogance disturbed and annoyed me. Then his calm capability and straightforward approach to saving my life made me feel safe and secure. His failure to pamper and indulge me riled me but really I wanted his attention: I wanted him to see me as a woman, not as the boss's precious, untouchable daughter. Most of all, I wanted him to want me – not just as a sexual object but for something else.

My mouth goes dry with the realisation.

Oh my God. I want him to love me.

It explodes in my brain like a light flashing on in a dark room. I feel stunned by the revelation and the next question follows like night following day.

So do I love him?

The idea sends me into a whirl of mad hope and wild confusion.

Won't that make things very complicated?

But what am I doing here if I don't feel something for him? Would I really come all this way, risk as much as I have, just for sex?

For my lessons, I remind myself, and a voice replies in a knowing way, *Yeah – if you want to call it that.*

I realise that Miles is speaking and I drag my attention back to him, still feeling dazed by what I've just been thinking.

'We're going to follow up fire with air,' he's saying.

'Oh?' I frown. 'Air?' I look towards the outside, where the temperature is clearly extremely low, if the crisp clear sky and the layers of snow are anything to go by. Does Miles want to make love out there? I'm up for most things but my skin goosebumps just thinking about it.

He sees where I'm looking and laughs. 'Don't worry, we're not going outside. Not yet. I'm not thinking of cold air. Quite the opposite.' He stands up, drains his glass and puts it down, then fixes me with a challenging look. 'Follow me, Winter. It's time for your next lesson.'

I get up, rearranging my drapery so that it fall seductively down my legs, and follow him as he turns and climbs the wooden staircase to the next floor.

We're going to the bedroom?

That doesn't seem very airy to me, unless he's planning on opening the window.

But Miles takes me to a door I hadn't noticed, and opens it to show me a small vestibule with a bench, hooks and shelves of white towels. On the far side is another pine door, this one with a small window in it.

Oh, now I understand.

I smile at him.

'I see you know what kind of air I'm talking about, Winter. You'll understand how suitable this is when I tell you that Aristotle categorised air as both hot and wet, as opposed to fire, which is hot and dry. It's associated with blood and in pagan thought, its tool is the sword, probably because it is considered sharp and able to penetrate.'

I look around, almost as though expecting to see a gleaming weapon on the bench.

'I don't want you to take it too literally,' he says softly, and that eyebrow rises again as he smiles. 'Now, take everything off, put on a towel, go in and wait for me. Oh – and inside you'll find a blindfold. When you're settled, put it on and lie down.'

I nod. 'Yes, M— Tutor. I'll do as you say.'

'Good. I'll be back.'

With that, he goes outside to the hall and closes the door. When he's gone, I unfasten my gown and step out of it. My cuffs are already gone, taken off by Miles when he untethered me earlier. The silken knickers fall away when I undo the ribbons and I'm quickly naked. After I wrap a towel from the pile around me, I open the second door and step on to the hot floor inside the small, wood-lined room. There are two levels of pine benches that run the length of the far wall, and in the corner a pile of hot, steaming rocks, a pail of water next to it with a wooden ladle beside it. The air inside is hot and dry with the tang of eucalyptus to it. I breathe, feeling the sharpness inside my nostrils as the heat hits them.

The Ancient Greeks were right – it is sharp.

I go over to the bench and sure enough, a soft white blindfold is lying there. I sit down on the bench and pick it up. My skin is already prickling in the heat, beads of sweat rising on my nose and legs as my body registers the temperature. I take the blindfold and put it round my eyes, tying into a knot at the back of my head. The dark is freaky and a stab of panic hits my belly.

Do I want to do this?

I've never worn a blindfold before and never understood why anyone would want to. Why put yourself at such a disadvantage? I've always wanted to be the seeker not the hider. I'm not sure I'm ready to take on this role.

Wait. Trust Miles. Don't you think he's going to take you on a journey you'll enjoy?

I know that's right. The sensation of being tethered in front of the fire was what rushed me to that incendiary orgasm. I leave the blindfold on and breathe deeply to calm down.

I'm ready now. All I can do is wait.

CHAPTER THIRTEEN

I sit for a while in the heat of the sauna, then on impulse I lie down on the long bench, still wrapped in my towel, the blindfold keeping the world in darkness.

It feels like an age before I hear the door open but the sound of the hinges and a gust of cooler air make me aware that Miles has come in.

At least, I hope it's Miles. I can't see a thing with this blindfold on.

I make an effort to calm myself. There isn't anyone else it could be. Of course it's Miles.

I sense the presence in the room. He goes over to the boiling rocks, lifts a ladleful of water and spills it over them. At once there is a fierce hissing and wet steam fills the room. It rolls into my nostrils and lungs, piercing the delicate internal membranes with its eucalyptus sharpness. The hot moisture envelops my skin and my perspiration rises to meet it. I'm hot. Very hot. It's cleansing but hard to bear as steam coats me inside and out. I try to breathe regularly and keep myself serene in the darkness beneath my blindfold but every nerve ending is alert to where Miles might be. It seems a long time before I sense him close by. There's a slight creak and a minuscule movement in the bench below me and I guess that he's down by my feet. I have a sudden memory of my nightmare a few nights ago, and the strange threatening presence on my bed. My heart starts to race with fear.

Stop it! It's nothing like that. Be calm and see what happens.

I pull the image of Miles to the front of my mind: tall, handsome, that straight nose, those cheekbones, the dark eyebrows and the sparkling blue eyes underneath with their sardonic expression, and the perfect lips made to be pressed on mine. I want to see his shoulders, stroke my finger down his chest and run it into the trail of dark hair that leads down to his fantastic cock. The thought makes my own heat turn dewy inside my sex.

As I'm thinking this, I feel the towel around me move. I give a small gasp as it's pulled gently away, exposing my entire body. The hot air engulfs me. The steam has almost subsided now, leaving the hot, cutting air behind that pulls the perspiration from my body so that I feel simultaneously wet and dry. My hair is sticking in tendrils to my face and I guess that my body is beaded with the cleansing pure sweat of the sauna. Now I can feel him close to me, the added heat of his body almost too much to bear. He's leaning over me, breathing softly on my face, a steady stream of cool air playing over my cheeks and tickling my eyelids. Now he's taking it down my neck and over my chest, stopping to blow the stream on my nipples, cooling them deliciously in the broiling atmosphere. The jet plays over the damp skin of my belly and down to my mound.

I moan lightly.

Oh Miles, don't play with me too much. I want you so badly.

As if he can read my thoughts, the stream of air stops. Now he's very close to me his flesh brushes lightly against mine and I realise that he's naked too. Delight courses through me. That body, the one I've dreamed of and longed for, for so many hours now, is close to me, without the frustrating barrier of clothes. I reach up to touch him, to find that smooth, muscled flesh in all its tantalising hardness, but his hands at once clasp themselves around my wrists and push my arms back over my head onto the smooth wood of the bench. As they do so, Miles's body presses down on mine, and his lips find my mouth. With a sigh of pleasure, I open my lips to him and his tongue pushes hard inside, finding mine with a questing strength. We kiss hard and wet, as though the steaming atmosphere has made us reckless with moisture. His whole weight lands on me, the hard square chest pressed on my own softness, his firm belly on mine, his thick hard thighs heavy on my legs. But best of all, I can feel that thick girth digging into my stomach.

His cock.

God, it's delicious, that long, hot, velvety length pressed hard against me. I moan again, the sound disappearing into his mouth. He's still holding my hands above my head as he moves firmly against me, driving his erection into the softness of my belly. So close to my longing sex, and yet so far . . .

The heat is so intense and so tropical, it sends me wilder than I thought it possible for hot air to manage. I move against his delicious weight, revelling in the sensation of his huge maleness against me. Oh, that body. It's broad at the chest and narrow at the hips, firm and smooth. I want to feel its power driving into me, I want to know that the strength in his thighs and back is dedicated to driving that glorious length deep inside me.

We carry on kissing, our tongues embracing wildly, and now I can feel him take his weight on his knees, lifting his cock away from my belly, and then he's pressing my legs apart with his thigh so that one leg is pressed against the wall, and other dangles over the side of the narrow bench. It ought to be uncomfortable but it's not, it feels wildly erotic to be taken like this in the hot intensity of the sauna, pressed against hot wood on one side, and the fierce warmth of Miles's body on the other. Then, suddenly, his erection is at my entrance.

Oh God, yes, I remember now . . .

The moment the tip of his shaft plays at the way into my sex, I remember that exhilarating feeling of his girth stretching me to accommodate him, and just as I remember it, it begins in reality. The probing smooth head is between my lips and then pushing forward into the hot wetness. As he enters me, he releases my wrists at last, taking his weight onto his arms, and I'm able to put my hands onto the bulging muscles of his upper arms, pushing myself downwards to force him deeper inside. His thighs press against mine and their hardness is deliciously exciting: I love the contrast between his solid masculine body and my own soft curves. I want to open to him as far as I can but the narrow bench restricts me. Even this gives me new, unexpected sensations of pleasure: I feel that his body is more joined to mine somehow, as though I'm squeezing tighter around his incredible girth as he pushes in hard, making me gasp with every thrust home. With my blindfold on, my other senses are heightened and I'm aware of every way that his body touches mine: the thrill of the grind of his pubic bone on my clit, the press of his balls against my buttocks as he goes as far as he can. I want him in the very heart of me, as deep as he can go. I want us to be joined into one thing, each experiencing these exquisite sensations in magnificent unison.

'Oh Miles,' I gasp, as that incredible cock plunges inside me again, fulfilling a hunger within me I never knew I had until now. I feel almost drunk on the pleasure he's giving me in this hot, wet room, our bodies growing slippery against one another.

'Don't speak unless I ask you to,' he says. 'Who is the tutor here?'

'You are. Oh, *you* are.'

'What are you learning about air, Winter?'

'Fucking in the hot air is amazing.'

'Fucking you anywhere is amazing, Winter.'

'Oh God,' I moan, as he hits home again. Is it legal for someone to have such a glorious cock? It's too much, it's driving me wild. I had no idea I could take something of this size and length, but I can, and love it too. I want him to go harder, faster, to go on giving me these waves of delight that are making me moan and buck my hips to meet him. Despite my blindness I feel as though I can see him, his blue eyes turned dark with lust, his mouth tight, not with anger but with the extreme sensations he's experiencing in my hot, tight depths.

Suddenly I feel his head at my chest and his mouth closes over one of my nipples, sucking it in a rhythm with his thrusts, so that as he hits home he tugs firmly on it, making pleasure sizzle from my breast to my clit in a gorgeous sharp ripple.

Oh God, this is almost too much.

I'm trembling on the brink of beginning my climb to an orgasm, but I want to stay on this wonderful ride for longer. I'm not ready for it to be over yet, I can't get enough of Miles's body. I run my hand over his bulging forearm and under it to the hard curve of his chest; then over the broad, muscle-hard surface of his back and down to the dip on the side of his buttocks where I can feel his muscles flexing as he fucks me.

I had no idea that touching someone else's skin could be so exciting.

This is the kind of elemental experience I've been longing for: the simple, fierce union of our bodies.

Elemental. Appropriate somehow.

He seems to be swelling inside me, and I gasp. I didn't think he could get any bigger but he's thicker now, moving faster, as though he's not far from a climax himself. I wonder if we're going to come together: I know I could, in an instant. It's taking an effort to stop myself flying off wildly into ecstasy as it is. Then suddenly, he pulls out of me, leaving me bereft. I want his cock back. I reach out my hand for it, desperate to feel its length slick with my juice. Miles grasps my wrist and pushes my arm back over my head.

'Not yet, Winter,' he growls. His body moves away from mine. I lie there, unseeing, panting with everything I've just experienced, knowing I'm totally exposed to him, my sex wet and swollen. It makes me throb with pleasure to think of him looking at me, enjoying the sight of my naked body open to him. I feel his huge hands at my waist. He's turning me over. I help him, moving on to my hands and knees as gracefully as I can, my palms flat on the smooth wood of the bench. I know my back is slick with sweat: I can feel trickles of it running over my lower back and my buttocks. He's kneeling behind me, and I can tell that he has one leg on the bench, the other foot on the floor. He's running his hands over my skin, round the curves of my hips and buttocks, letting them slide in the moisture on my flesh. His finger begins to follow the trails of the droplets as they run with a delicate tickle over the surface and into the cleft between my buttocks. He takes his finger further and further down the cleft, exciting me as I feel him approaching my eager sex. He smoothes downwards with his fingertip, and then I feel it at my entrance, pushing gently inside, first one finger and then two. Then he takes them out again, running them over my lips and rubbing the juices up and over my electrically charged clit. I moan as his fingertips rub and play at my bud, taking my own lubrication to massage and tantalise it. His hand disappears entirely and to my astonishment I find it at my face, his fingers on my mouth. He inserts them, wet and tangy with the flavours of my sex between my lips, pressing them in. I close my mouth around them and suck hungrily, tasting my own arousal and becoming more excited in the process. I can't help pushing my bottom backwards as I suck and I find the tip of his jutting cock with a kind of exhilaration. I want to manoeuvre it home somehow but I know that Miles is the one in control and if he doesn't want to enter me yet, then I will just have to wait in the kind of delicious torment he loves to inflict on me.

I suck on his fingers hard, letting my tongue roll and play on them just I would love to do to his cock and I can hear his breathing thicken and come faster. He pulls his fingers out. Then the velvety head of his cock is at my entrance and I press back again, helping it find the place where I can welcome it in. He lets it ram gently against my lips and then against the little valley between my vagina and bottom, and it touches my bottom for one strange but unexpectedly exciting moment, before returning to the entrance of my sex.

I want to moan and beg him to take me at once, but I daren't say a word in case he decides to punish me by removing his cock altogether and I couldn't bear that, so I bite my lip hard to keep quiet.

One large hand is on my waist. I try to move my thighs apart as far as I can on the narrow bench and then, at last, he thrusts hard, making me take him in one push. I cry out as his length forces itself into my depths, further than it did when I was lying down. The sensation is rapturous and yet almost unbearable as he uses all his strength to plunge hard in and out, making me gasp with the painful pleasure as he rams inside. He seems to be reaching almost to my ribcage, forcing the air out of me in a loud moan.

It's beautiful and terrible at the same time. Oh God, don't stop, please!

I hear him grunting as he rushes his cock into me, one hand still on my waist and the other on my shoulder, forcing me back onto his length. Then that hand is reaching round me, finding my clit, rubbing it hard and yet with masterful, arousing strokes that are going to take me all the way to the edge of pleasure. He strums me as that magnificent cock fucks me as hard as I could desire, and I feel the bliss building up in the velvet darkness.

Oh yes, my wonderful, my gorgeous Miles . . . That's so beautiful. I can't bear it but I need it so badly. Oh, touch me there, rub me harder, right on the tip of it, make me come . . .

I can't speak aloud, my panting is too fierce even if I wanted to, but I'm begging him to keep up that exquisite movement, working in my sex and on my clit at the same time until I begin to wail with the strength of what I'm feeling. He thickens inside me again and I know that this time we won't be able to stop. His thrusts become shorter – faster and more fierce, if that were possible – and he flicks hard on my clit and I can feel the torrent rushing up to take me with it. I collapse forward as my orgasm explodes inside me and his grasps him at the same time. We whirl wildly into pleasure, his orgasm pouring out inside me as I convulse with mine, crying out with its force as his weight lands on me and we lie panting as the sensations subside.

It's some time before either of us can move.

'It's late.'

Miles is looking at me with a tenderness I've never seen before. I'm sitting across the table from him, wrapped in a fluffy white robe and eating a plateful of delicious food.

'Is it?' I say, smiling broadly at him. 'I hadn't noticed.'

He laughs, pushing his own empty plate away from him. 'Well, it is.'

'And we've only covered two of the elements,' I say mischievously. 'Where did you get this dinner from, by the way?'

'Dominic's chef left it here. All I had to do was put it in the oven. I'll pass on your compliments.'

'Do. Or maybe all food tastes better after amazing sex.'

'I expect it does.' Miles glances around the dining room, where the wood burning stove emits a cosy heat and the windows look out over the valley below. 'A little different from our last billet, eh, Winter?'

I laugh and nod. 'You better believe it. Decent bathrooms.' I've already showered off the effects of our sauna session, which is why I'm folded up so cosily in this white robe.

'I thought you'd appreciate that.' He takes a sip of his red wine and then says idly, 'So how long can you stay?'

'As long as I want,' I reply.

He fixes me with one of those looks. 'Really?'

'Well . . .' I don't want to talk about circumstances outside this charmed chalet where I'm experiencing such bliss, but I suppose we have to face reality. 'I can't really be away for too long. My father will be wondering where I am. He thinks I'm with Lola at the moment but if he discovers I'm not, there'll be hell to pay.'

Miles looks puzzled. 'Look, I know you girls are under a constant kidnap threat. All kids of famously rich men are. But even so, your dad takes things to extremes. Right from the start, we were told that you girls had to be protected to a greater degree than I've ever experienced. There's a virtual full-time surveillance operation mounted on you. Why is your dad so paranoid?'

I turn back to my plate, my carefree mood evaporating. 'I . . . It's hard to explain. It's because . . . of something that happened.'

Miles frowns. 'What? What happened? You can tell me, you know that.'

I rest my elbow on the table and prop up my head with my hand. I feel jittery inside. I've never talked about this with anyone outside my immediate family – if you don't count the shrinks they sent me to. 'It's because . . .' I take a deep breath and start looking with intense interest at the grain in the wood of the table. 'Years ago, I was kidnapped. My mother and I were taken hostage.'

'What?'

I look up to see Miles looking genuinely astonished. 'They didn't tell you, then?'

'No, they bloody didn't! Why didn't anyone say anything about this? How come I've never heard anything about it?'

I feel a strange dragging sensation of fear and loss, the one that always comes when I think about the events of my childhood. It's why I try not to remember them. 'It was all hushed up. It wasn't difficult because no one even knew we were taken. It was in Italy, where my mother and I were staying at some grand villa. My sisters weren't there, I can't remember why. It was just Mama and me. One night, when I was sleeping, I was woken up and there was this huge man there, sitting on my bed and watching me. When he realised I'd woken up, he clamped his hand over my mouth, picked me up and rushed me out to a van where my mother was already a prisoner. They tied us up and put tape over our mouths and drove us in our pyjamas to the mountains. They kept us there in a cave.'

Miles is open mouthed. When he can speak, he almost splutters. 'But this is bloody awful! You were *kidnapped*? What the hell happened?'

I trace the patterns in the wood with my forefinger. My heart is racing at the memory and the nightmare images that play in my mind: my mother in her blue dressing gown, bound, her frightened eyes staring at me above the gag across her mouth; the dark interior of the van; the silhouette of olive trees against a greenish sky as we're hustled to the cave and dumped deep inside with frightened young men armed with knives as our guards. I try to tell him about it but I can't summon up the words to convey the terror. When I talk, I begin to stutter and choke.

'Hey, hey, hey.' He's beside me in an instant, his arms around me, hugging and comforting me with the warmth of his body, the touch of his cheek on mine. 'Hush, hush,' he soothes. 'There's no need to say anything you don't want to. It sounds like a nightmare, sweetheart. A terrible ordeal. No wonder you were messed up by it.' He pulls away and fixes me with his concerned blue eyes. 'But you were okay, right? You and your mother got out okay?'

I nod. 'Yeah. We were rescued after a while.'

'How long?'

'Two weeks.'

'*Two weeks?*' He looks horrified. 'Christ, if I'd known this had happened to you, I would have handled our crash differently. No wonder you were so terrified.'

'They found us eventually,' I say in a flat voice. 'The guards didn't struggle, they gave us up so easily that I think they were relieved it was all over. I'd already guessed that most of them weren't happy with the whole thing. It was one leader who made them all go through with it. But the men who looked after us, they were kind mostly. And they could tell that my mother was sick and getting sicker.'

'Oh no . . .' Miles's voice is tender as realisation dawns in his eyes.

I nod. 'She was on medication to control a condition that I didn't even know she had. Without it, she began to deteriorate. By the end of the fortnight she had sunk into a coma. When they found us, it was too late for her.'

'Freya, I'm so sorry.' Miles pulls me close into his arms and my head rests against the solid security of his chest. I want to cry but my eyes are dry. I've not cried about it for years, not since I swore I wouldn't it let it hurt me. I took the memories of my mother's last weeks and shut them away. 'That's a terrible story.' He sways with me for a few minutes, comforting me with his body. Then he says softly, 'But how come it was kept a secret? Why wasn't it discovered?'

When I speak, my voice is a little muffled by his chest. 'Because it was an inside job.'

'What did you say?' He pulls back to look at me.

'One of our bodyguards planned the whole thing and carried it out. The kidnappers demanded absolute secrecy and we gave it because my father suspected from the start it was one of the guards. Instead of involving the police, he tried to use local contacts to infiltrate them with bribed informers.'

'Did it work?'

'I don't know. But he found us. Eventually.'

Miles stares into my eyes and then says in a low voice, 'That guy was evil. The guards you have at home, all around you . . . we're not like that. You have to believe me.'

'I believe you're not,' I say softly. 'I can't imagine you ever doing such a thing.'

He looks fierce. 'Of course I bloody wouldn't! I ensure people's safety and nothing else! For Christ's sake!' He hits the table suddenly and violently, making me jump. He's breathing hard as he looks at me apologetically. 'Sorry, sweetheart. I don't mean to frighten you. It's just . . .' He looks away, his expression inscrutable. 'Bastards like that make me fucking furious, that's all. You're safe with me, you know that.'

I nod. 'I do know that.'

'Good.' He strokes my hair gently and smiles, evidently calmer. 'Good. I'm glad to hear it. Now . . . you must be tired.'

'*You* must be tired.' I smile back, relieved we're on happier ground.

'You know what? I think two lessons are enough for today. We should save something for tomorrow.'

'Hmm, let me see, what have we got? Oh yes – water and earth.' I smile again, glad to put the horrible memories I've conjured up back in their rightful place, shut away in the depths of my mind. 'You've already surprised me with fire and air. I can't wait to see what you do tomorrow.'

Miles wraps his hand round mine and squeezes gently. 'Got to keep you guessing, right? Boring, predictable lessons are never effective, or so I believe. Come on. Let's turn in.'

'Can we have some revision before tomorrow?' I ask meekly, getting up to follow him.

'Your thirst for knowledge is insatiable,' he says with a laugh, taking my hand to lead me to the upstairs bedroom. 'It does you credit.'

'It's because I have the best teacher,' I return. 'You stimulate my . . . mind.'

Later, after a soft and tender bout of lovemaking, I'm lying in bed, looking up through the skylight in the beams at the gleaming stars so far above us. Miles has his arms around me and I'm gently running my finger up and down the smooth flesh of his arm.

I remember how, according to Miles, Aristotle said that space and the stars were made of aether. The stuff of heavenly substance.

I lean towards him. He's more than half asleep, his eyes closed and his breathing deep and regular. 'I've thought of something else.'

Miles grunts. 'Uh? What?'

'Something else to add to the things made of aether. You know, heavenly things.'

'Uh.'

I can tell he's almost asleep but I can't help whispering on. 'Well, you know, I think that the experience of an orgasm – that's heavenly. Should we add that?'

'Mmm. Let's.'

'Good. Champagne, stars and orgasms. But there's something else, even better than orgasms.'

After a deep sigh, he says, 'Is there?'

'Yes.'

I wait for a long time. When I'm sure he's asleep from the pace of his breathing, I say gently, 'I think it's love.'

The word hangs there in the warm darkness, filling me with strange excitement. I can hardly believe I've dared to say it. I only did it because I was sure he wouldn't hear me but I wanted the pleasure of hinting to him how my feelings for him are ripening. I breathe a long, happy sigh, contented in my body and heart. Somehow the experience of telling him about my mother and what we endured has lightened my soul a little. Five minutes seems to have achieved what hours of therapy could not. My body luxuriates in the feel of his, and my sex aches a little with the use I've put it to today.

More tomorrow, I hope.

I close my eyes.

'Goodnight, Winter.'

Miles's voice makes my eyes flick open with surprise. I turn towards him. 'Are you awake?'

There's no answer, just another deep, slumbering breath.

Oh God, did he hear me? Did he hear me talk about love?

I can't know. Not now.

There's more to learn tomorrow.

CHAPTER FOURTEEN

I'm lying in darkness, surrounded by cool, fetid blackness. Nearby I can feel the damp chill of a rock wall. I blink, trying to make out what or who is around me. I can feel their presence although I can't see anything. I'm paralysed by the darkness, and by the fear growing inside me. The presence is close. I can hear its breathing.

I manage to move. I can stretch out a hand and touch something. It's a rough fabric, like towelling, and underneath it is a firmness. I must be touching someone – a body – but it's almost too cool for that. Where is the body heat? Why is there no warmth? My fingertips run lightly over the roughness.

'Mama?' I whisper.

There is no answer, just the faintest hint of a sigh on the night air. And then, from nowhere, a hand grabs my wrist, seizing it with a hard, iron grip. My eyes fly open in shock against the darkness and I gasp, and then scream in utter terror—

'Freya, Freya! Wake up, sweetheart, you're all right. It's just a bad dream. I'm here, sweetheart, I'm here.'

Strong arms are wrapped tightly around me, and at first I struggle, trying to fight off the horrifying grip in my dreams. I'm blinded by fear, gasping and crying.

'Freya! You're all right! I'm here . . .'

At last his voice penetrates my consciousness and my terror subsides. I slump into his arms, panting and sobbing as I realise, with a drenching relief, that I'm safe. Of course, I know where I am. I'm in the beautiful master bedroom of a chalet just above Klosters. I'm in Miles's arms after spending the night with him. I ought to be in a state of bliss but here I am, still gasping after my nightmare, my eyes streaming.

'Oh God, I'm sorry,' I say between intakes of breath. 'I'm sorry!'

'Don't be sorry,' he soothes me, 'it's fine, it's okay now. Did you have a nightmare?'

I nod.

'It's because of what we talked about last night, isn't it?' Miles says softly. His blue eyes gaze into mine, tender but questioning.

'I guess it must be.' I take a deep breath and let out a long sigh, trying to get my breathing back on track and restore myself to calmness. 'Sometimes I get these flash-backs. They're so powerful. They must be dreams but they feel so real. At first I dream that I'm sleeping and then, in my dream, I wake up. But it feels exactly like what waking up is like, and so when the bad stuff comes I truly believe in it.'

'That sounds awful, you poor wee thing.' Miles's voice is so gentle, his Scottish accent so sweetly comforting in the way it rolls softly, enveloping me like a soft duvet.

'And I can't describe the presence – I can never see it. It's near me and it's so real, I can hear its breathing and feel its mass – sometimes its weight if I'm on a bed. It's watching me and I can't move, and at first I don't know if it's good or evil, it just seems curious about me. Then . . . then . . . I realise it wants to harm me.' A sob in my throat catches me by surprise and I hunch forward. Miles's arms tighten around me and he hushes me quietly, as I shake off the nauseous feeling that comes with the memory of that awful thing.

'I don't have to be Doctor Freud to interpret that dream,' Miles says in a low voice, rocking me a little. 'Not now you've told me about what happened in your past.'

I nod miserably. 'I know. So often I'm back there – in that cave. With my mother.'

'You're safe with me,' he says firmly. 'I'll always keep you safe.'

'Well . . .' I sniff and manage a laugh. 'You *are* a bodyguard, aren't you? It's your job.'

He looks at me solemnly, his blue eyes as serious as I've ever seen them. 'But we both know that you've got a good reason to be suspicious of bodyguards. No wonder you always had such an attitude towards me and the others.'

'I suppose I have found it hard to trust after what happened. The fact that we were betrayed by someone who was supposed to keep us safe was very scarring.'

'Well, I know that now.' He shakes his head. 'Personally I think we should have been told about this event. It would help us all understand your father's paranoia and over-the-top demands. The security checks he insists on would put a military installation to shame. And it might make relations with you, our charges, a little bit easier if we knew about the history involved.'

'You mean you all hate us!' I say, with a weak smile.

He grins back, that gorgeous half smile that twists his lips and makes my heart do little flips. 'We don't hate you. But let's just say you don't always make it easy to be enamoured of you.'

233

'I suppose not.' I feel calmer now, almost back to my old self. I lie back on the pillows. This room is so serene. It's luxurious but very natural too, with the plain wood walls, the embroidered fabrics and the hand-carved furniture – an expensive take on a traditional Swiss chalet. Above me, sunshine floods through the skylight, illuminating the room with gentle golden glow.

'We don't talk about it to outsiders,' I say, staring upwards. 'My father's channelled all his anger and fear into trying to keep us safe and making sure nothing like that ever happens again. But I think he felt guilty too because he couldn't save us in time. All his money and power, and it turned out he could do nothing against a gang of kidnappers in the Italian mountains.' I turn my head so that I can look over at Miles. 'He's never forgiven himself for my mother's death. He's afraid that if we talk about it to the outside world, it will give the impression that we're weak and vulnerable. And someone might try again. So we have to pretend that our security has never been breached and we're absolutely impregnable. That way no one will bother us.' I shrug. 'That's the idea anyway.'

Miles nods. 'I can see that.' He rubs one hand slowly across the top of his head, ruffling up the short dark hair there. His bare arm bulges with muscle and I have a strong desire to touch him, to bury my face against his smooth skin and inhale the scent of him. 'I really do.'

'And if we told employees, it would be bound to leak out. For some reason, we're objects of fascination. I mean, we're only people like everyone else but the papers are obsessed with us. I don't welcome it, it just happens. They get so much gossip about us, some of it invented, and some of it true. I have no idea where it comes from.' I blink at him slowly. 'It makes all of us paranoid. Maybe our friends are selling stories about us behind our backs, or perhaps someone's listening in to phone calls or bugging rooms. That's partly why we hardly ever talk about what's really going on in our lives, even to each other, in case someone's eavesdropping and it leaks out. Imagine if you saw your private life all over the papers, to be pored over and laughed at. I'm not an actress or a politician or a model, or someone who's asked for attention.' I shrug. 'I'm just a girl!'

Miles smiles at me. 'Not just a girl, Freya. Never that.' His gaze runs over me, taking in the curves of my bare shoulders, the rise of my breasts above the sheet, my dark hair spilled out over the snow-white pillow. 'I never saw how beautiful you are until now. When you were Miss Hammond, I never even thought you were very attractive.'

I laugh. 'Oh, thanks!'

He goes on, ignoring me. 'But now . . .' That raking look again, the one that sends my stomach into ecstatic raptures. When he speaks again, his voice is husky with desire. 'Now I think you're the most beautiful thing I've ever seen.'

A delicious shiver sweeps over me at his words. I beam at him, hoping I don't look too stupidly happy at his compliment. I remember last night, when I couldn't resist the temptation to open my heart just a little and whisper the word 'love' to him. A kind of hot but almost pleasurable flush creeps over my cheeks. There's a very good chance that he did hear but I've no idea how I'll find out one way or the other.

'Is it time for our lesson?' I ask, hopefully. My gaze shifts to the door to the bathroom. If the lesson today is on the theme of water, then perhaps he'll be asking me to accompany him into the shower . . .

Miles laughs, his eyes glinting mischievously as he shakes his head. 'Uh uh. Let's not rush things. You know, a lot of people believe that you learn better if you've had a healthy dose of exercise.'

My eyes gleam. 'Well, luckily for us, our lessons are all about exercise, aren't they? Two birds with one stone.' I raise my eyebrows at him. 'So what are you waiting for?'

'I'm thinking about an entirely different sort of exercise, you incorrigible girl.' He picks up a snowy white pillow and tosses it on to me. 'I think we need to get outdoors and work up an appetite for later – in more ways than one.' His blue eyes are twinkling with humour now. I love that look: warm and merry. I feel as though I'm being allowed to see a Miles that very few other people have ever seen. I'm one of the lucky few.

I wonder who the others are . . . The thought flies lightly across my mind and I felt a nasty tang of something like jealousy at the thought of other women Miles might have laughed with and loved. I put it out of my mind before it can poison our blissful morning together.

'We are going to get up,' says Miles as I squeeze the pillow to my chest, 'and I'm going to make you coffee and eggs just the way you like them. Then we're going to get dressed and go on the mountain.'

'The mountain?' Amid the happiness, I feel a small pang of anxiety. 'You mean skiing? What if I see someone I know?'

Miles purses his lips and frowns. 'Let's keep off the busy slopes as much as possible. In fact, we'll go off-piste if you can manage it. You'll be in ski clothes – Dominic's girl-friend has some here that you can borrow – and goggles, and as long as we don't hang out at any of the cafes or restaurants, you should be fine.' He leans over and kisses me. I adore the taste of him on my lips and long for more, but he pulls away. 'I think we should risk it. No one assumes you're here, and that means they won't expect to see you. In my experience, very famous people can walk about quite naturally if no one assumes they're there.'

'Okay, then. Let's do it. I love skiing. And didn't you say something about eggs? I'm starving . . .'

A few hours later, I'm revelling in the sensation of taking the slope at speed, guiding my skis to move exactly as I want, hitting the snow with a steady hiss and glide as I fly down the mountain. Ahead of me is Miles's dark form. I thought I was pretty good at skiing – I've been doing it since I was three, after all – but I've got nothing on Miles. He's better than any instructor I've ever seen as he takes the slope at the kind of speed only an expert can manage. His tech-nique is perfect, even awe-inspiring. It looks deceptively easy as he moves in lazy-looking zigzags, his body almost skimming the ground at every turn, his poles barely touch-ing the snow. Only the wake of white powder from the blade of his skis shows how sharply he's cutting through it.

If he ever gets tired of being a bodyguard, I think, he could easily get work as a stuntman in the movies – in his black ski gear and sunglasses, he looks like nothing so much as James Bond as he skis effortlessly down the mountain.

When I come to a halt beside him, I'm breathless but exhilarated. I love this kind of exercise, out in the open air, enjoying the ice-blue sky, the liquid sunshine and the crisp white snow. It's also very sexy, perhaps because of our form-fitting ski gear. Miles found me a great outfit: an all-in-one ski pant suit in red with a matching ski jacket. With it, I'm wearing a red hat and a pair of sunglasses. I feel sleek and athletic, and with Miles all in black, we make a striking pair against the white slopes.

'You're amazing!' I say, breathless as he smiles at me. 'I had no idea you could ski so well.'

'Training,' he says drily. 'A lot of it. We were made to master the toughest slopes in the world.' He looks up the mountain, sunlight glinting off his metallic aviator shades. 'This is kind of child's play after that.'

I laugh. 'Of course it is.' I stick my poles in the snow and take off my sunglasses. 'What are we going to do now? I'm starving.'

'Starving?' Miles frowns. 'We only just had breakfast.'

'Four hours ago!' I exclaim. 'And skiing always makes me ravenous.'

'I was worried that maybe you didn't eat enough this morning.'

'Don't be silly, it was delicious and I ate plenty.' I grin at him. 'I'm only glad you've turned out to be so good at the stove. I'm utterly useless.'

'Why am I not surprised?' He laughs, driving his ski poles into the snow. Then he grabs my hands and pulls me so that my skis glide gently between his open ones and my body bumps softly against his. He wraps his arms around me, puts his mouth close to my ear and murmurs, 'But you're far from useless, Winter. I happen to know you're very talented indeed.'

My stomach tightens and my heart starts to race. There's an answering tingle between my legs. His nearness and the timbre of his voice close to my ear are almost unbearable; my skin prickles with the sensation.

'Really?' I whisper. 'Am I learning well?'

'Very well. You're going to pass the course with flying colours.' His mouth is almost touching mine now, making me dizzy with longing.

'I think I'm ready to start my education again,' I say, my voice weak with the power of my desire for him.

His mouth lands on mine, my lips open and our tongues meet. We start to kiss deeply, oblivious to everyone else around us – not that where we are is busy place. Because we were off-piste, it's a very quiet part of the mountain and as far as I can see, there's no one about. I relax into the deliciousness of his kiss, savouring his taste as he possesses my mouth with his.

When he pulls away at last, he has a lazy look of promise in those blue eyes. 'Shall we go back to the chalet, Winter? I think it might be time to resume your lessons.'

'Yes, please,' I say. 'Let's go right now.'

Back at the chalet, the chef Dominic called in for us has been in the kitchen during our absence and a delicious-looking lunch has been left out for us: a cold chicken and ham pie, tempting salads of roasted vegetables and balsamic vinegar, wild rice with charred beetroot and nuggets of feta cheese, and peppery rocket with sweet tomatoes. Freshly baked bread sits in a basket with a dish of Alpine butter, and there's a board of Swiss cheeses, along with a plate of tiny chocolate-covered choux buns to have afterwards. There's far too much for just the two of us but the skiing has had its usual effect on my appetite and I eat heartily.

'Oh my goodness,' I say, leaning back in my chair. 'I'm stuffed. I've been terribly greedy.'

Miles pushes his plate away and smiles at me. 'Too full for lessons?'

I groan. 'You know what? I might be!' I'm taken unawares by a huge yawn. 'In fact, yesterday's activities have made me quite sleepy.'

'Then I think you should have a rest. I don't want you falling asleep on me later. Come on.' He gets up and puts out a hand. 'Lessons can wait. I want you on good form for the next one, it's going to take all your concentration.'

I get to my feet. I wanted Miles so badly only a short time ago. Now I can hardly keep my eyes open. 'Mountain air,' I say apologetically.

'You've had a very exhausting time lately,' he says as we head for the stairs, his arm around me. 'I don't just mean our lessons. You're probably still recovering from the trauma of our accident.'

'What about you?' I ask, yawning again. 'You went through the same trauma.'

'Not exactly,' he says gently. 'I'm trained for crises, and I don't have the kind of childhood baggage you have. Anyway, I'm going to stay awake so I can look after you.'

I rest my head on his shoulder, loving the way he makes me feel. I do feel safe. Properly. Not guarded or monitored or filmed – but really safe, deep inside. I don't remember ever feeling so calm. 'Thank you,' I whisper.

'For what?'

'Oh – everything.'

We reach the bedroom and I'm so tired, I'm almost completely floppy. I sit on the bed and let Miles slowly peel off my clothes until I'm in a T-shirt and my knickers.

'This is almost more than human flesh can stand,' he says, his eyes glittering as he looks at me. He lifts the covers so I can slide underneath. 'You're extremely tempting. I hope you realise what a measure of self-control I'm exerting.'

I giggle as he pulls the covers over me. The sheets are smooth and cool against my bare legs. 'You can ravish me if you like,' I say invitingly. I'm already damp just looking at him. Then I'm ambushed by another enormous yawn.

He laughs. 'I don't think I can face the possibility you might fall asleep while I do it. I'll wait until you're refreshed, I think.' He drops a kiss on my cheek and smiles. 'Sleep tight.'

I sigh happily as he turns to head for the door. Just then, his mobile rings. I hear him answer it as he goes to leave but before I can make out anything further, I'm fast asleep.

CHAPTER FIFTEEN

When I wake it's dark outside. It's late afternoon and the sun is dropping behind the mountains. I come to my senses gradually, shaking off the strange feeling that sometimes comes with sleeping in the daytime.

I pull on a robe and pad downstairs to find Miles. He's outside on the balcony with a glass of wine, reading and seemly oblivious to the startling sky above him: it's a streaked glory of pink, lavender, blue and gold, the mountains dark against it. In the shadows at their feet, just below us, the little town is beginning to glitter as the lights twinkle in the growing gloom.

I open the door and put my head out into the cold evening air with a shiver. 'Brrr. It's freezing out here.'

Miles turns around quickly at the sound of my voice, his handsome face breaking into a smile as he sees me. 'Well – is that surprising?' He gestures to the snowy mountains surrounding us.

'I suppose not.' I laugh. 'But I've just been tucked up warmly in bed. The contrast is pretty noticeable.'

He puts his book down and gets up. Coming towards me, he holds out his arms and in a moment he's engulfed me in a hug. I nuzzle into his jacket, but its surface is chilly. 'Come inside,' I coax. 'Don't sit out here in the cold any more.'

'How can I resist?' he says, raising his eyebrow at me.

In the sitting room, he's already lit the fire and it's crackling away merrily as it burns around a large log. Once the doors are closed and we're out of the icy air, I relax again. I sit down on the sofa opposite the fire and beckon him to me, then pull him down so we can cuddle up together.

'Take off that jacket!' I command.

He starts to slide it off but says, 'Watch out now ... Don't forget yourself and start issuing orders.'

'Of course not!' I say quickly. 'It's not an order – more of an invitation.'

'Now, those I like,' he says, and pulls me into his broad warm chest. 'Even if you have made me leave my book and my drink outside.'

'Aren't I more interesting?' I ask, putting my lips to his cheek. The skin is a tantalising mixture of smooth and rough, with the softness of his cheek tempered by the prickle of stubble.

'Of course you are,' he murmurs. His arm tightens around me. 'Listen, it's lovely being cosy on my own with you up here but I wondered how you feel about going out for dinner. I'm okay with eggs, but not very good with anything else, so it would either be a disappointing supper, or we'll have to call on the services of the chef again.'

I open my mouth to say that of course we'll go out – then I close it. What if I'm seen and word gets back to my father? I can hardly wear a ski hat and sunglasses through dinner in a restaurant, and I'm well enough known to be recognised, especially here in Klosters. 'I'm not sure,' I say, frowning.

'I know what you're thinking – it's safer to stay here. But my friend Dominic is in town—'

'Dominic who owns this chalet?' I say, mildly panicked. Does this mean our delightful sojourn *à deux* is over? Will we be sharing this place with Miles's friend? The thought is not a pleasant one. I don't want any intruders but it's hard to see how we could refuse someone entry into their own chalet.

Miles sees my expression and says quickly, 'Yes, but he's not staying here. He and Beth are just passing through and he suggested dinner. He knows that we've got the chalet, and doesn't expect to come up here. It's fine.'

'But still . . .' I frown again. 'A restaurant?'

'Dominic knows a very sweet little place in the mountains – we'll have a room to ourselves. We won't see anyone else.'

'I don't want to see anyone but you,' I say.

'I know.' He covers my hand with his large one and squeezes it gently. 'But you'll like them, I promise. And you'll get a much better dinner than you will with me, I can assure you of that!'

I smile at him. It suddenly occurs to me that if Miles is going to introduce me to his friend, then surely that means I'm someone important in his life, someone he wants people to meet. Or am I reading too much into it? 'Okay. It sounds fun.'

'Good. Then we'll go.'

I'm putting a last slick of gloss on my lips when I hear the jingle of sleigh bells outside. Curious, I put my lip gloss in my purse, pick up my shoes and hurry downstairs. Miles is waiting at the bottom, wearing a black coat with a fur collar, thick leather gloves and a black wool hat.

'There you are,' he says. 'Come on, we're going.'

'Who's at the door?' I ask, putting on a pair of fleece-lined boots and a thick sheepskin coat with a deliciously soft, woolly collar that encases my neck in warmth. I slip my shoes into a bag and pull a soft cashmere beret over my hair. 'Sounds like Father Christmas has just arrived.'

'Not exactly.' Miles grins. 'But I don't want to drive so we're going the traditional way.' He opens the chalet door and I catch a glimpse of the dark shapes of horses shaking manes, hear the thud of hooves, soft whinnies and the muted jingle of bells on the harnesses. A driver, well wrapped up and wearing a brimmed hat, sits at the front of the sleigh, a long slender whip in his hand, lit by two glowing lanterns hanging from the curved prow, one on each side.

I laugh as I step outside the chalet. I usually get around in four-wheel drive SUVs, leaving the sleigh rides for the tourists, but there's something very charming about the old-fashioned vehicle. Miles locks up the chalet, then opens the little door in the side of the sleigh and helps me in. The seats are well upholstered and fur-lined rugs are provided; he settles down beside me on the padded seat and tucks the rugs around us.

'*Wir sind fertig,*' he tells the driver. '*Schloss Marika, bitte.*'

'You speak German,' I say admiringly.

'A little.' He smiles back. The driver flicks the reins and the pair of huge brown horses toss their heads, and begin to trot. The sleigh jerks a little as the horses find their rhythm but as soon as they have their pace, we glide over the snow and into the darkness. I sigh happily. This is very romantic, I have to admit that. The view is stunning. The moon is up and is touching the snowy mountains and the pine forests with its icy beams. The sky is a silvery grey, bright with the moonlight, but we are gliding through the cold shadows of the forest, our way lit by the now golden light of the lamps. Every now and then, the driver urges the horses on with a click and a crooning sound, and the world is quiet except for the thudding of the hooves and the hiss of the sleigh's runners on the snow. We're heading away from the town that's sparkling below us, a fairyland of white-capped roofs.

'It's so beautiful,' I say to Miles and he nods.

'Aye. It makes me remember home just a little.'

'Really?'

'Pine trees always make me think of Scotland.'

I press into him and he puts an arm around me. 'I'd like to go there.'

He laughs and I feel it rumble against my chest through the thickness of our coats. 'You wouldn't find my village quite as glamorous as this place. I mean, I love it but fondness helps the eye along quite a bit. The land around is beautiful, though, there's no doubt of that.'

We sit close together, soaking in the atmosphere, listening to the jangle of the bells and the snorting of the horses, as the sleigh climbs the winding road. Just as I'm wondering where on earth we could be going, the driver turns off between two old stone pillars topped with stone griffins, and a pair of open wrought-iron gates.

'Ah. We're almost here,' Miles says. 'I don't know about you but I'm ready for dinner and much as I'm enjoying this ride, I could also do with getting inside somewhere warm.'

I don't feel the cold at all, except for the slight numbness in my cheeks. I gaze ahead into the darkness at the end of the curving drive, half wanting us not to arrive somewhere

I'll have to share Miles with other people. But before too long we round the bend and I see before me the turrets and stone walls of a schloss.

'Here we are. Schloss Marika,' says Miles.

The castle windows glow golden against the night and the large arched wooden front doors stand open to a brightly lit hall. Within a few minutes, the driver has brought the sleigh to a halt in front of the steps that lead up to the door. Miles has leapt down and helped me out of the sleigh and we're walking up the steps and into the huge hall, with its iron chandelier glowing with candles. I take off my coat, hat and boots in the ladies' cloakroom and return pink-cheeked in the dress I chose for this evening: a simple black silk shift with red satin heels embroidered in glittering jewel-coloured thread, and an evening purse also exquisitely embroidered.

'You look beautiful,' Miles whispers to me, as he takes me by the arm and we follow a waiter down a winding stone staircase to a private vaulted room at the bottom.

'Thank you.' I feel a rush of pride that he might want to be seen with me on his arm.

As we walk in, I see a couple are already waiting there for us. The man is tall and dark, with noticeably beautiful brown eyes and olive skin. As he sees us, he stands up, a broad smile on his face, his arms out to Miles, and a merry greeting on his lips. Behind him, sitting at a beautifully laid table is a pretty girl: she's fair with shoulder length hair falling in soft waves, and wide grey eyes. I guess at once she's English: she has those pink-and-white looks. But as she turns to us with a smile, I have the impression that she's tougher than those big wide eyes and the full, rather rosebud-ish mouth might suggest, although I don't know why I should think that. She's smiling very brightly with a glow about her that might just be the candlelight burnishing her fair hair. She gets to her feet too and I see that she's shorter and curvier than I am, wearing a knee-length dress in black-and-white chevron stripes that shows off a small waist and round hips.

'Miles, you old reprobate! How are you?' Dominic is good-looking and well-built, but for me, he doesn't have Miles's magnetism or the tough muscled body of the ex-soldier. He looks over at me. 'And you must be Miles's friend . . .'

I nod, smiling back.

Miles says, 'This is Freya.' He doesn't explain our relationship and there is no follow up question to find out more. Perhaps Dominic's been told not to ask questions – or perhaps he already knows everything. 'Freya – Dominic.'

'Great to meet you, Freya. Welcome. This is Beth.' He gestures to the girl still standing at the table.

She smiles broadly and I feel instantly welcome. 'Hi, Freya.'

We take our seats as we swap polite information about our journeys and the weather. Beth asks me solicitously if I've warmed up and compliments me on my dress. When we're settled, the waiter stands ready to take our orders for drinks.

Dominic says expansively, 'Is it all right with you if we order a bottle of champagne?'

'Of course,' says Miles. I nod my agreement. I'm feeling rather shy in the presence of these confident, rather charismatic people. I have no idea if they know who I am but I'm enjoying the feeling of anonymity. I get the impression I'll be judged on myself, rather than on my father's money or perceptions gained from the media.

When Dominic's ordered a bottle of Krug, Miles says, 'Is there something to celebrate?'

I notice suddenly that Beth is not just glowing from the candlelight but from the illumination that comes with sheer happiness. She and Dominic look at one another and I know at once that they share something special.

Dominic doesn't take his brown eyes off her as he says, 'The truth is – I've asked Beth to marry me. And she's said yes.'

Beth laughs joyfully, puts out her hand and takes Dominic's. Then she says, her gaze still fixed on him, 'Yes. I can't believe it but we're engaged.' She shakes her head. 'I didn't realise it would feel so different.'

'Congratulations!' says Miles heartily. He's beaming at them both, and seems genuinely delighted. 'What wonderful news. I'm really happy for you. Dominic, you're a very lucky man. Beth – I hope you know what you've taken on!'

'Of course I do,' she says, laughing.

'Congratulations,' I echo, moved despite the fact that I hardly know them. It feels a little odd to be here sharing their big moment when I'm a virtual stranger. Their happiness is almost palpable. I smile at Beth. 'Do you have a ring?'

She nods, her eyes shining with pleasure, and holds out her left hand. A beautiful emerald-cut diamond glitters on her finger with a setting of tiny diamonds on either side of it, all on a band of platinum.

'It's stunning,' I say sincerely, admiring the ring's elegance. I notice that it sits on her finger above another ring: a hoop of diamonds, small but very sparkling. 'Oh! You've got two rings!'

Beth's gaze moves back to Dominic and her eyes soften as she says, 'Yes, that's right. The smaller one is my promise ring. Dominic gave it to me a while ago to signify a promise to one another.'

I'm a little confused. 'I thought that an engagement ring was a promise ring – a promise that you'll get married.'

'Yes, of course. But we had an earlier promise too – it signifies something to us.' She flushes very lightly and I get the impression that this is more than a straightforward engagement.

But why, when they look so happy? Why should they have needed a different promise altogether? I'll ask Miles to tell me what he knows, I decide, intrigued.

They're still looking at each other, lost in the happiness they so clearly feel. I feel a pang deep inside me. *I want that.* I can't help the thought as I see the pure love between these two, and I glance at Miles. He's staring at his friends, that half smile of his twisting his mouth but there's a stillness about him and a look in the depths of his eyes that I haven't seen before.

'When will you get married?' I ask, feeling that I need to say something.

Beth looks back at me. 'We haven't even discussed that! Dominic managed to take me by surprise. I had no idea he had a proposal on his mind right now – he's working so hard, flying all over the world. We'll have to talk about it.'

Dominic leans even closer towards her, holding her hand more tightly. 'Was it really a surprise?' he asks, smiling at her.

'Completely!' She laughs merrily. 'Didn't you notice how flabbergasted I was?'

'Maybe just a little.'

'So where did it happen?' asks Miles.

'Right here! About an hour ago,' Dominic says. He looks at me. 'Have you seen outside the schloss?'

I shake my head. 'Just the front, but I could hardly see that in the dark.'

'Come and see this.' He gets up and leads the way out of the private vault and up the winding staircase. Halfway up it, set in the thick stone walls is a small window that looks out over the back of the castle. 'Look,' says Dominic, making space for me to peer out.

Beneath us, the view is illuminated by the cool white moonlight. Pine forests iced with snow stretch away up the mountain, towards its craggy, white-capped peak. Below us is the stone terrace of the schloss and a tower connected to the terrace by a flight of stone steps. The crenelated top of the tower is lit by storm lanterns holding fat candles, one between each crenulation, casting a pretty golden light over the snow.

Beth has come up behind us and stands next to me to look out of the window, her expression tender. 'We were standing there together, on the top of the tower with that incredible view, and the castle behind – and then he pulled me into his arms and kissed me and said that . . . well . . .' She blushes again, looking prettier than ever. 'Well . . . he said some lovely things . . .'

'And luckily she said yes,' Dominic cuts in with a laugh.

'He had the ring ready for me.' She glances down at it as though she still can't quite believe it's on her finger. 'It's just . . . perfect.'

'That's so romantic,' I breathe, looking down at the exquisite scene. A proposal on the tower of an Alpine schloss sounds amazing – a lifetime memory.

'But I have no idea when we'll find time for a wedding, or where it will be,' Beth says, as Dominic puts his arms round her.

'You should get married here in Switzerland of course,' I say. 'A beautiful Alpine winter wedding.'

'It sounds lovely,' Beth says, as we all begin to descend the stairs back to the private room. 'But I've got family in England, Dominic's sister is in New York, and the whole thing would be a nightmare to organise.'

'It sounds like it's going to be tricky wherever you hold it.' We go back into the vaulted room where the champagne is now waiting for us. 'Maybe you should make everyone come to you.' I take my place at the table, putting a white linen napkin on my lap.

'That's a point,' Beth says. 'Somewhere equally inconvenient for everybody!'

We both laugh.

'Are you two going to be talking weddings all night?' Miles asks drily, as the wine waiter returns to open the bottle for us.

'I think it's virtually required, isn't it?' Dominic says. Good humour and happiness are shining from his face. All this bliss is catching, and I feel as though I'm walking on air myself. The waiter pulls the cork with a satisfying 'pop' and the foaming liquid gushes into the waiting flutes. Dominic holds up his glass. 'Now, this might seem a little formal but this is a very special occasion, so I'd like to propose a toast to my beautiful, amazing fiancée, Beth. She's agreed to be my wife.' He says the word 'wife' as though it's a precious jewel he can hardly believe he owns. 'I'm the luckiest – and happiest – man in the world. To Beth.'

'To Beth,' chorus Miles and I, and we all sip our champagne while Beth looks bashful.

Miles clears his throat and says, 'I think it's only right that we both drink to your health and toast the future union of two very special people – so here's to Dominic and Beth, and the future.' He lifts his glass high.

'The future,' says Dominic, staring into Beth's eyes.

'To you,' Beth returns, her face glowing with pleasure.

'To the future,' I echo, and I realise that I'm not quite sure whose future I mean.

On the way home, Miles doesn't put on his gloves, but holds my hand under the fur rug. His thumb rubs gently across the top of my hand in smooth but pressing strokes that serve to heighten my anticipation for what will surely be coming next, when we get home. As we left Dominic and Beth at the schloss, climbing into the sleigh for the return journey, I turned to wave at them and saw that they had already forgotten us: he was turning her face up to his and gently dropping his mouth to hers in a tender kiss, the light from the open doorway gilding their figures.

I felt strange as I turned back to face the oncoming darkness lit only by the dim glow of the lamps. In a way, I envied them their obvious happiness in one another. But in another way, I was full of a kind of dark thrill at the thought of Miles and me being alone together again.

Dominic and Beth showed a polite interest in me and my relationship to Miles but the excitement of their engagement had, understandably, taken centre stage. I was relieved really – it meant there were fewer awkward questions to answer. They seemed to take it for granted that I was Miles's girlfriend, not the daughter of his boss. When I thanked him for the use of the chalet, Dominic had said casually that he was happy for Miles and me to use it – Miles needed a proper holiday after refusing to take one for years.

'Why has he refused to take a holiday?' I asked, as Miles talked to Beth.

'Oh . . .' Dominic made a face and looked at the table-cloth. 'You know. He ought to clear his head really, and try to relax. But he won't do it. He's too stubborn. He says he's worried that if he clears his head, he won't know what will pop into it.' Dominic gave me a look as though he oughtn't to say more. 'But you know what I'm talking about. All that stuff in Afghanistan—'

'What?' Miles had stopped talking to Beth and was suddenly alert to my conversation with Dominic. 'What's that about Afghanistan?'

'Oh – I was just saying to Freya that you still haven't taken a proper holiday since . . . well, since—'

'I'm taking one now, aren't I?' Miles said pleasantly but I sensed a kind of warning in the tone he used to Dominic. 'You should be pleased. And that chalet's a peach. It's just the ticket.' He looks at his watch. 'Talking of which, we should really be getting on our way . . .'

It wasn't long after that we said our goodbyes on the stone steps before the schloss and Miles and I climbed back into the sleigh for the return journey.

'They seem very nice,' I said to Miles, feeling his thumb moving insistently over my hand. 'I liked them both very much.'

'They're good people,' Miles replies. He's staring ahead with no outward sign that he's caressing my hand under the fur rug.

'There seemed to be a story behind their relationship.'

'Isn't there one behind every relationship?'

'Yes, but . . .' I feel a little deflated by Miles's taciturnity. 'You know what I mean.'

He turns to me, almost apologetic suddenly. 'Yes – and you're right, it hasn't been straightforward for them. Do you know Anton Dubrovski?'

'Of course!' I think of the very handsome Russian billionaire I've seen once or twice at parties. 'I went to something he held in Moscow – a big party to raise funds to support an orphanage he sponsors. He's a friend of my father.' I frown. 'Although I haven't seen him for a while.'

Miles says, 'It's a complicated story but Dominic worked for Dubrovski for a while and managed to get mixed up in a very strange money-making scheme, which he got out of as soon as he could. He and Dubrovski went their separate ways but there was some nastiness over the whole thing. It ended with Dubrovski retiring from the public scene for a while to lick his wounds and let a potential scandal die down.'

'What does that have to do with Dominic and Beth?' I ask. I'm not that interested in Dubrovski's fate. Russian billionaires have a habit of disappearing – either they mysteriously commit suicide or get on the wrong side of their government and then find themselves in prison for corruption or tax evasion.

'I think the whole thing put a strain on Beth and Dominic's relationship for a while. But they're through that now. I've never seen them happier. I think this is the real thing for them both.'

'Do you think they wondered . . . about us?' I ask.

He turns to look at me, his eyes intense. 'I don't know. Let them wonder. Maybe we shouldn't have come out. Perhaps it would have been better to keep ourselves shut away from everything.'

'Well, I . . .' I can't get any further for Miles suddenly takes me in his arms and kisses me hard. When he pulls away he says:

'We're nearly home, Winter. Are you ready for our next lesson?'

I feel my stomach go liquid with longing. 'Ready and waiting,' I whisper back.

CHAPTER SIXTEEN

When we get back, Miles tells me to go upstairs and get changed.

A tingle of anticipation goes over me as I climb the stairs, wondering what he means. Should I put on the Goddess dress I wore on our first night here? But in the bedroom on our bed is another black box with a note on it. I pick up the note and read it.

> *Winter*
> *Put these on and pin your hair back. Come downstairs to the sitting room.*
> *Bring the tape and the other box with you.*

I open the box and discover inside a set of pale pink underwear – a bra and knickers – made out of PVC. Beneath them is a packet of hair pins, a large roll of black sticky tape and a smaller black box that's sealed with a ribbon in pink PVC. I don't open it, but feeling breathless, I quickly take off my clothes and pull on the underwear. The sensation of putting PVC close to my skin is strange but arousing: it sucks on to me, locking on with a plastic grip, showing every curve and creating a surface of smooth, shiny perfection. My breasts look even riper and rounder when encased in pink rubber.

There is nothing for my feet, so I pin back my hair, pushing the pins in close to my scalp so that my short bob is even shorter, pick up the tape and the other box, and hurry back downstairs, wondering what Miles has in mind for me. I'm feeling pleasantly fuzzy inside after the champagne and the fine red wine we drank at dinner, but I'm in no way numbed. Every nerve is tingling as I try to imagine what lies ahead for me.

Water. What could he be going to teach me about that? I had assumed that water meant we'd be in the bathroom, perhaps in the shower, but that isn't the case if we're going to be in the sitting room. I'm intrigued, which adds to the sense of excitement as I walk into the main room. Miles is sitting there, soft music playing from the speakers. He's got a glass of whisky in his hand and is watching the fire glow and dance. He's obviously spurred it back into life. He looks up as I come in.

'Ah, Winter,' he says, his eyes travelling down my body from the shiny cups of my PVC bra to the triangle that encases my mound, and down my bare legs. 'You look exquisite – better than I could have imagined, and believe me, I enjoyed imagining how you would look in that outfit.'

I turn around for him, saying, 'I've never worn PVC before.'

'Really?' He smiles, raising an eyebrow. 'It can be very appealing, believe me. And it has a pleasant snap.'

A delicious sensation seizes me and my whole sex quivers and swells into life as my pulse begins to race.

'Come here, Winter.' His blue gaze is boring into me, as though he knows exactly how my skin is alive to him, my heart pounding and my breathing coming faster. It's as though he even knows that, down below, I'm growing slick and ready. The PVC rubs tight and delicious on me as

I walk, making my clit thrill to it. I walk towards him and when I reach him, he nods to the floor. 'Sit down there, where I can see you.'

I sit at his feet, curling my legs up under me and looking up at him. He smiles at me and says, 'The traditional place for the student to sit, yes? At the feet of the master.'

I love being so close to him but I can't yet touch him, even though I would love to undress him so that I can press myself against that hard body and inhale his intoxicating scent.

Miles holds his glass of whisky up to the light so that it turns a honeyed amber colour and swirls it around. 'See this, Winter?'

I nod.

'Whisky. The finest Scotch there is. In some cultures spirits like these are called "water of life" – the kind of liquid that burns the throat and tongue, and that works a strange transformation on the brain, making the drinker more expansive, more merry before beginning to have the opposite effect altogether.' He stares at the whisky as it eddies in his glass. 'Too much and you'll go mad. A little more than that, and you'll die.' He looks at me with a wry look. 'A poison, you see. We drink our poison very carefully – but we still drink it.'

He passes the glass down to me and I take it. I take in the strong, dense aroma. I've never drunk much whisky. I've had Jack Daniels and Coke, but not Scotch, and certainly not neat.

'Try it, Winter. It's Talisker, the whisky made on the Isle of Skye, and this one is twenty-five years old, older than you are. It's a single malt, which means it has just malt barley grain and water. Very pure. And the water

259

used comes from springs that run over peat. That gives its particular flavour.'

I lift the glass to my lips, feeling the burn of the fiery liquid even before I've drunk any. Then I sip. A smooth strange flavour fills my mouth, burning along my tongue. It's smoky and intense but honeyed and smooth too. I let it rest in my mouth for a moment, and then swallow. I cough a little with its strength but at once warmth fills my veins and the burn subsides to a pleasant tingle. I lift the glass again.

'That's enough,' Miles says, reaching down to take it from me. 'You'll get drunk very fast if you're not used to it. It's strong.' He puts the glass down on a side table. 'And I don't want you to miss anything tonight. But you see how water can be so potent. Now.' He stands up. 'We're going to continue your lesson outside.'

'Outside?' My gaze goes to the darkness beyond the doors to the balcony. I can see the glitter of the lights from the town below, and the moonlight on the snowy rooftops and the peaks of the mountains, but nevertheless, it's dark and very cold. I'm wearing very little.

Miles is watching my expression with amusement. 'That's right.' He nods to a robe on the sofa. 'Put that on and go outside. You'll see what to do.'

I want reassurance that I'm not going to freeze to death if I do as he says, but I know that will spoil the mood, and besides I'm supposed to do as I'm told, so I get up and put on the robe. Then I go to the door and look out. There's a thick layer of snow along the balcony railing, though the balcony itself has been swept clear of snow. It's still glittering with frost, however. I shiver just looking at it, my skin goose-bumping. I glance back at Miles, who's watching me carefully. He nods, so I pull open the door and step out into the icy air. My feet touch the deck and I want to jump back but I take a deep breath and force myself. At once my attention is drawn by a light to my left and I turn to see what it is. There is an almost eerie sight – a swirling mass of fog that's lit from beneath so that it seems almost like a ghost swaying in front of me. I gasp and then realise that I'm looking at the Jacuzzi pool which is at the far end of the balcony raised on a wooden platform, and the cover has been lifted so that the steam from the hot water rises into a sultry cloud above the pool. It's illuminated by a dozen small lanterns that glow with candles on the side of the hot tub.

I understand now.

I walk towards the pool, bracing myself against the bitter cold, and drop my robe as I climb the steps. The freezing air grips my body as I step in, feeling the delicious contrast of the warm water surging around my ankles and then my calves as, slowly, I go down the Jacuzzi steps and lower myself into the hot tub until I'm submerged in its luxurious heat. It's a wonderful sensation to be outside, and to be so enveloped in warmth.

The door to the chalet opens, and Miles steps out. He's wearing a robe himself now, and the idea that he's naked underneath makes a thrill clench my stomach. He walks towards me and I realise he's holding the box and the tape in one hand and his whisky glass in the other.

What's he going to do to me? What's in the box?

He puts the two objects and his glass next to a lantern at the side of the pool where they can be easily reached, and lets the robe slide from his body. He reveals his muscled torso with its sprinkling of dark hair, and the smooth mounds of his biceps. His abs are toned and defined above the line of the dark swimming shorts he's wearing – *not naked, not yet . . .* – and his thighs bulge out firmly below them.

Oh my goodness, he's so amazingly well built . . .

My mouth is a little dry at the sight of him. No man has ever been able to reduce me to a state of quivering lust like this, just by displaying his body. I've lain on enough yachts in the millionaire playgrounds to see some buff men showing off their gym-honed physiques, but not one has inspired this level of desire in me. Something about Miles encapsulates masculinity for me – or perhaps it's because I know what he can do with that powerful form, and what heights he can drive me to with it.

He steps into the hot tub and sits down beside me. I feel inexplicably shy and stare down. A light glows in the base of the pool, sending strange shadows swirling in the water.

'Winter,' he says softly, his voice low and caressing.

I look up at him.

'This is your element, you know. Not only is water associated with the season of winter, but it's also considered a feminine medium, connected with those who have intuition, who are emotional, sensitive and artistic. The water signs in the Zodiac show that. You'll know that water is vital – a colourless, odourless compound made up of hydrogen and oxygen that forms the basis of all life. It covers seventy-one per cent of the earth's surface.' He suddenly grins at me. 'And I would say that at the moment, it covers approximately ninety per cent of you.'

I blush a little. I'm feeling very shy, though I can't think why. The Talisker is still in my veins, warming and relaxing me. I'm aware of the tightness of my PVC underwear, which seems to be gripping me even more in the warm water. My nipples, erect after the cold air and now the stimulation of the water, are erect, rubbing on the bra.

'We are made mostly of water,' Miles continues, his Scottish accent stronger as it always is when he drops his voice down low. 'Imagine that, Winter. You and I are mostly water. So when I kiss you, it's amazing we don't merge into each other entirely.'

He puts his hand under my chin and turns my face to his, staring into my eyes. Then he slowly lowers his mouth, touching his beautiful lips very gently on mine. His tongue darts out and he licks the surface of my lips, pressing lightly inside, just far enough to tantalise me. For a few delicious minutes he toys with me, flicking his tongue around my lips and teeth as though he hasn't decided whether to commit to a kiss or not. Then he pulls away and says, 'Let's share some water of life.'

Reaching for his glass, he takes a sip of the golden-brown whisky and holds it in his mouth. When he returns his mouth to mine, I open my lips and this time his tongue comes in strong and hard, bringing with it a gush of fiery liquid so that his tongue itself seems to be setting mine on fire. We kiss, pushing the whisky from mouth to mouth, pressing it around our tongues and letting it slide down our throats until it's disappeared. We're kissing hard now, and his hands are roaming over me beneath the water, feeling the smooth curve of my hips and the expanse of my stomach, caressing my arms and reaching down my legs. I can't have enough of his touch and I long to touch him in return. I reach and smooth my hand along the hard strength of his arm as his mouth continues its fierce possession of mine. At once he pulls away.

'Oh no, Winter. Not yet. I've got plenty to teach you first.'

'But I want you so much, I *need* to touch you,' I say longingly. The hunger I have to feel his flesh is almost overwhelming.

He smiles at me. 'Soon. But not yet. Put your arms up on the side of the pool.'

I do as he says, reaching out so that both arms stretch out along the edge of the Jacuzzi. Miles lifts himself out of the water long enough so that he can reach the roll of tape that he left on the side, and sweeps up a towel from a pile on the steps. I glimpse the hardness in his swimming shorts as he gets back into the water and a thrill of excitement throbs in my sex, encased in the tight PVC knickers. Then he dries my forearms and the side of the pool around them, and a moment later, he has pulled a long strip of black tape and is taping my wrists to the wooden surround of the Jacuzzi. He rips off several lengths so that my wrist is well tethered and then repeats the process with the other arm, going around me in the water to reach it. I feel strangely excited by the way my arms are now completely out of my control. With them along the poolside, my lower body feels curiously weightless, as though I'm going to float up to the surface of the water, but I keep myself on the seat in the pool.

'Just right,' Miles says, with a smile. He comes to where he can face me and looks at the way my new position means that my breasts are raised and thrust forward, the PVC wet and dripping and the skin above beaded with water. 'You're so beautiful,' he murmurs admiringly. 'Gorgeous. Look at these.' He reaches out and caresses my breasts, running his hands over the smooth shiny surface of my bra. My nipples are so hard beneath the tight latex that they are almost painful. 'I want to teach you what pleasure you can have in water, my darling. It's our natural element, after all. We're made in water, from water. No wonder it's the most delicious element to make love in.'

With a deft movement, he parts my legs and glides in between them so that he's pressed against me. My body is alive with excitement as I feel his wet flesh on mine and the hardness of his erection pressing on my mound.

I want you – right now. Oh, Miles!

I want to speak but I can barely catch my breath, my heart is racing so fast. The pressure of his hard cock on me is unbearably tantalising but I know that he doesn't intend to let me have what I want quite yet, and I don't mind – I just want something to happen so that I can begin to quell the fiery desire that's building up inside me.

He kisses me again, our mouths embracing hard, our tongues wild now as we possess each other. Our faces are damp and the wetness around us seems to drive our kisses on to become open-mouthed, our tongues roaming everywhere as we taste and lick each other. His hands are on my breasts again, his hard body against me, then carried away by the movement of the water, then ramming back on me again. I feel his hands at my back and realise he's undoing the bra, pulling it away from my pert nipples. It's a delicious relief to feel the tight PVC peel away from my skin, leaving it with a sting that's almost like taking off a sticking plaster. My skin thrills to the rush of warm water, and my nipples sing in the soft bath after their encasement in the bra. *God, that's beautiful.*

His head dips down and he takes a nipple into his mouth. It's already aroused from the bra and now the water, and the pull of his teeth around it makes me groan. I watch his head as he sucks hard on me, nibbling on my delicate rosy bud, then taking as much of my breast in his mouth as he can. His fingers toy with my other nipple, rubbing it between them, pulling it lightly, then caressing the soft underside of my breast. My whole sex is alive with need, the tingling between my legs growing from a gentle tickle to a pulsating torment of longing. The intermittent touch of his cock against me is torturing me in the most delicious way possible, as the work of his mouth on my nipple sends electric currents of lust to my groin. The immobility of my arms adds to the erotic effect – I feel as though my body is offered to him for his pleasure and mine, as though I'm utterly open to him, ready to be his when he thinks that the time is right. I'm wet all over, but if we weren't in the pool, I know that my juices would be making me slick with readiness for him.

He stops playing with my breasts, letting my nipple slide from his mouth with a tiny pop, and then puts his mouth to my ear.

'Are you ready, Winter? Are you prepared to find out what pleasure water can give you?'

'Yes,' I pant, even though I've already experienced something of it. 'I'm ready.'

'Good. Stay very still now.'

He leaves me for a moment and I feel bereft without his body next to mine, but he's back in a moment with the small black box which he puts close by on the edge of the pool. Then his hands are all over me again, smoothing my skin and delighting in my curves. They're at my knickers. He's slid his fingers in under the band. Oh my goodness . . . the water has made the PVC cling so tightly to me that I'm not sure for a moment how he will get them off. But he has soon worked them free of my skin and is peeling them away from me, very slowly, taking his time to expose every centimetre of flesh. As he exposes my mound, I feel a fresh rush of arousal. The warm water floods there, bathing me and playing gently across my swollen parts. My clitoris stands proud as the pink PVC pulls away from it, and then he slides the knickers down my legs and lets them float away in the pool. I'm utterly naked to him now, the water more delicious against my skin than I could ever have imagined. I feel as though the swirling movement and its gentle heat, could lift me to orgasm quickly with little trouble. I'm gasping with the intensity of it.

Miles reaches for the black box, opens it and takes out a device that's made of black silicon and is shaped like a flattened C. I wonder what it can be as he puts it down, takes a bottle from the box and pours something from it on to his palm. Then he puts down the bottle, takes up the C-shaped thing and rubs it in the liquid. I catch a glimpse of it in his hand – it's smooth and shiny now, well anointed with the liquid. *What is he going to do with it?*

He's close to me now, his mouth at my ear again.

'Are you ready, Winter?'

I nod, panting.

He puts his mouth on mine and starts to kiss me with the same wild intensity as before. Our tongues writhe together, hungry for one another, and as we kiss I feel his hand on my mound and then his fingers at my slit, playing there. His thumb rubs over my clit, sending delicious sensations shooting through me and I moan lightly into his mouth. He strums me there a little longer, making my bud unbearable sensitive, then his fingers are back at my slit and he's pushing them in, fucking me with them. *Oh yes. Harder. Do it harder, Miles, make me feel you . . .*

Then, his fingers vanish, and to my surprise I feel something else at my entrance – thicker, smoother. I realise it's the oiled device Miles prepared and that he's going to push one end of it inside me. It's at my lips for a moment, pressing forward with little tantalising movements, and then it's sliding easily inside me. One side of the C is now deep in me and Miles moves the other so that it falls into place, pressing down firmly over my mound and on to my clit. *Oh . . . oh, it feels nice!* I find the simultaneous inward and outward pressure delightful. He pushes it in and out of me, making it rub over me, sending exquisite sensations through me. Then he presses it so that it is as far as it will go inside me and it's also firmly placed over my clitoris.

'Enjoy the ride,' Miles murmurs as he kisses me and then, to my surprise, the thing begins to vibrate.

Holy shit! That's . . . oh wow . . . that's . . .

I start to moan. The device is finding some sweet spot deep inside me that fills me with sensations of delectable pleasure as it whirrs hard against me. I put back my head, resting it on the side of the pool, and close my eyes so that I can surrender myself to the joy I'm getting. The side pressing on my clitoris is vibrating deliciously, making me throb to it in an almost unbearable, ceaseless pulsing of intensity.

Miles is close to me again, his fingers reaching for the little device. Now suddenly, the pulsing changes: it comes in waves that build in intensity and then drop off before beginning again slow and soft, then getting harder. I sigh with pleasure as my whole body is filled with the resonance of its stimulating throbs.

Oh my goodness, I've never felt anything like this ...
The internal massaging is taking me to heights of bliss
while I'm trembling with the force of the erotic effects of
the pressure on my clit.

I'm going to come soon ... I won't be able to help it.

I open my eyes and see that Miles is close to me, looking down at me as I move my hips to the delicious rhythm
of the little whirring friend he's put inside me. I long to
touch him but my arms are still spread along the poolside,
firmly tethered by the black tape. Then I see that his shorts
have gone and he's holding his impressive shaft as it rears
up under the water. The sight of it, long and magnificent,
swollen to a huge girth, makes me moan and lick my lips.
God, I want it ...

Before I can say anything, Miles kisses me. It's so beautiful, I would cry out if he weren't already in possession of
my mouth. I thrill to his tongue and the taste of him as he
devours me, moving between my parted thighs.

Yes, Miles, please, do it now ... I need you so much.

Can he really enter me while the little device is busy
there already? I feel his tip at my entrance and then he's
pushing his shaft inside, alongside the slim wand of that
pulsating machine.

Oh ... oh ... it's almost too much!

I'm stretching to engulf him, feeling that incredible sensation of being filled by his huge cock, now given even more
girth by the small obstacle in his way. I moan through our
passionate kisses as he keeps thrusting forward until I feel as
though he's filling up my entire body. I want him so much –
as much as he can give me. I want him in me right to the root.

I can hear him panting and groaning as he gets in me to
the hilt, and the knowledge that his excitement is growing

makes me shudder with even more of my own. He loves being in me, I can tell that, and I open my legs even wider to him, so that he can get as much of me as he wants. The warm water around us is beautiful, as soothing and delicious as a warm bed, and it feels utterly natural and right to be making love in its gentle embrace. The friction of our bodies is different in the water, though – but the whirring little machine is giving me all the friction I could wish for on my swollen bud. Miles seizes me around the waist so that he can push me up and down on his huge length and he begins to fuck me hard and beautifully. My legs wrap around his strong thighs so that I can urge him on, his cock hard against the vibrating toy inside me. He moans with delight, and I know that he's getting pleasure from the little device whirring against his shaft too. He kisses me rampantly as he fucks me, then dips his head to suck my nipples, anointing each one with his tongue and grazing them with his teeth, before returning to claim my mouth.

Oh, it's divine . . . it's amazing . . .

We buck hard against each other, riding the waves of our passion. I don't want to come yet. I open my eyes. Miles's face is pressed to mine, his eyes closed as he savours the sensation of my tightness and the vibrations pulsing between us. I look past his broad naked shoulders to the view beyond: the startlingly beautiful night with its dark navy sky, the looming mountains, the snow touched with the hard glitter of moonlight. It's surreal to be outside, naked, so warm and in such heaven, with the freezing air all around us.

'Oh Miles,' I gasp. 'Don't stop . . . oh my God, your cock, it's so wonderful . . .'

'I love fucking you,' he says roughly, his voice thick with lust. 'You're gorgeous. I can't get enough of you . . . oh *Christ* . . .'

We're both gasping and moaning with ecstasy as he thrusts hard and deep, his cock stabbing into me with all the vigour he can summon, the water washing around both of us, splashing over my breasts and neck.

I'm so close now, with the tiny vibrator buzzing on my clitoris and Miles's cock inside me. I don't know how long we've been going, I'm in a daze of furious excitement as I approach an explosive climax. This little thing working its magic on me from the outside and the inside is driving me wild, even without the action of Miles ramming home, his excitement enhanced by the throbs within.

'Oh God, Miles, I'm going to come . . .' I stare up at him with wide eyes, glassy with the pleasure I'm experiencing. 'I'm going to come . . . oh *God!*'

It's beginning. It's almost more than I can stand. I can feel Miles's cock swelling to an even thicker girth as his excitement is moved up a notch by my approaching orgasm. The feeling of him thickening and throbing inside me sends me whirling over the edge. The little machine doesn't stop – it propels me into an orgasm of such incredible intensity that I scream, my head thrown back, my body bucking in the water under Miles's deep thrusts. Great waves of bliss crash over me, the velvet darkness of extreme pleasure littered with exploding stars engulfs me and I shudder again and again with the force of it.

My scream fades away with the orgasm, just as Miles's mouth finds me again. He kisses me deeply as his fingers find my little silicon friend. The whirring stops and he pulls it out from inside me, dropping it on the poolside, without taking his cock out of me. His mouth is close to my ear, his breathing fast, as he says, 'You're driving me mad, Winter, I'm close now,' and then he starts to fuck me hard again, his cock moving easily in the natural lubrication produced by my fiery orgasm. He rams in and out as I push my body up to him, offering him everything, his belly pressing on mine, his chest crushing my soft breasts as his strong arms enfold me. I can feel his great shaft throbbing and stiffening even more as he begins to approach his climax.

'Oh God,' he groans. 'Oh you're beautiful, you're making me come . . .'

'Come now,' I urge him, 'pour it into me.'

It's all he needs and he explodes inside me with half a dozen hard, slow thrusts, then sinks down on me, his eyes closed, breathless with the force of his climax. Then he opens his eyes with a smile and kisses me slowly and luxuriously, our tongues twirling around each other. The water swishes around us.

'That was amazing, Winter,' he says, stroking me and gazing into my eyes.

'Next time I want to touch you,' I say longingly.

He reaches up and pulls away the tape so that my arms are free. I've not noticed even a little discomfort until now, but I'm suddenly stiff and strained in my upper arm muscles. I flex them, submerging them in the water to help them relax.

Miles kisses me again and says, 'I think that could well be part of our next lesson.'

'I liked learning about water,' I say with a laugh. I can feel his erection subsiding within me.

'I liked teaching you,' Miles returns. 'But before we both turn into prunes, we'd better get out.'

I laugh and reach for a towel.

Later, showered and dry, we lie in each other's arms, pleasantly exhausted. I'm languorous with the kind of delicious torpor that comes after sex of that intensity. But part of me is bleak with misery. The day after tomorrow, it's time to return. I can't stay locked away for ever, not answering messages. The flight back is booked. I've not yet asked Miles about what he's planning to do but I assume that he'll also be taking up his bodyguard duties at some point in the near future.

What's going to happen to us? I wonder, as sleep begins to creep softly into my mind.

Then, just as I fall asleep, I remember that there is one element left.

Miles still has to teach me about earth.

CHAPTER SEVENTEEN

The next day we wake up very late – our long night and all the activity we've engaged in has made us very tired, so we sleep and sleep, sometimes wrapped around each other and sometimes apart, one waking and then the other, until we finally wake up together.

I love the lazy luxurious morning we share, talking and laughing, being playful. Miles asks me to make us some coffee and I pretend to be asleep, so he picks me up and carries me carefully to the bathroom, puts me in the shower and turns on the spray. When I squeal as the jet of cold water hits me, he laughs and I can't help joining in. Later, when I'm in my robe and drying my wet hair, he says, 'You are the perfect screwball heroine, you know that?'

'Am I?' I smile back at him. 'What do you mean?'

'You're the heiress – that's a condition for lots of those crazy society comedies of the Thirties. Weird, really, when you think about that state that most Americans were living in during the Depression – they seemed to love seeing those girls dripping in diamonds and furs, falling in and out of love.'

'I don't drip with diamonds!' I say indignantly. 'And I never wear fur, I'm against it.'

He gives me a sideways look. 'Maybe not diamonds and furs. But that handbag you carry . . .'

'Prada,' I say, puzzled.

'How much?'

'How much?' I think. 'I don't really know.'

'I'd guess a lot. Maybe two thousand dollars.'

I shrug. 'Maybe. I just put it on the card.'

'Uh huh.' He nods. 'Your clothes and shoes – all designer, I suppose.'

'Yes.' I'm puzzled. 'Of course – where else would I shop? What's your point?'

'Not everybody can.' He looks away and seems very interested in the piece of toast he's buttering.

'I know that!'

'Do you?'

'Yes!' The answer comes so easily and I'm so sure of it, but suddenly a doubt niggles at my mind. Do I really know how lucky I am? Do I truly understand what it's like not to have anything I want? I have a sudden flash of the boy Miles growing up in his Scottish village outside Edinburgh. I don't know anything about his background but I can guess that it was nothing like mine. I'm used to being surrounded by people who've grown up the way I have, with money and homes all around the world, and constant travel. But to Miles, it must look crazy that we all have so much without even thinking about it.

'So you see – rich and spoiled, but smart and funny as well. Like I said, you're the ideal screwball heroine. Beautiful, too,' he says casually.

'Really?' I say, feeling ridiculously flattered. *Smart and funny as well!* I decide to ignore the 'spoiled' remark and hope it's more about my bank account than about my character. *And he thinks I'm beautiful. Not just during sex but all the time.*

275

'Yes.' He nods with a little shrug that makes me feel even more delighted. 'Of course. I think so anyway.'

'And you?' I gaze at him flirtatiously. 'If I'm the spoiled heroine, who are you?'

'Oh.' He grins at me. 'The butler. Or the unsuitable suitor. That sort of thing.'

'You're not unsuitable!'

'Your father might think differently,' he says with a lifted eyebrow.

'I don't care what he thinks,' I say stoutly.

'That's just the way it should be for the screwball film.'

'So . . .' I lean against the table on my elbows. I don't want to talk about my background or my father anymore. 'Does the screwball film include a Jacuzzi?'

He laughs, throwing back his head. 'Not usually!'

'And . . .' I take a bite of my toast and eat it slowly and thoughtfully. 'Don't you still owe me a lesson?'

Miles raises his eyebrows. 'Have you managed to take in what I've already taught you?'

'Hmm, let me see. Fire was extremely powerful – very vigorous. Air was a hot and humid experience. And water . . .' I sigh. 'I loved water.'

'Water? Or a little silicon friend of ours?'

'That was a great enhancer of the element,' I agree, nodding. 'I did enjoy it.'

'Darling, I noticed.' He smiles at me, his blue eyes merry.

My soul thrills to being called 'darling'. *Does he really mean it?* 'So,' I say casually. 'Isn't there another lesson? Fire, air, water . . . what about earth?'

'Ah.' He nods slowly. 'Earth.'

'So . . .?'

'So . . . are you ready for your last lesson, Winter?'

'As I'll ever be,' I declare. 'Teach me what I need to know.'

We're in the bedroom, and I'm lying on the white fur rug, wearing a leather bra made of thin straps that criss-cross my chest, moulding gently round my breasts but leaving them more or less exposed. My nipples, pink and already stiff, poke through the slim thongs of leather. Around my waist is a slender leather corset tied tightly but not uncomfortable. Small straps attached to it reach downwards to the tops of my thighs, where silk stockings are fastened to the ends, and I'm wearing spike-heeled black stilettos. The area between the corset and my stocking tops is bare, exposed entirely to view. I feel luxuriant and sexy as I lie on the white rug, the soft fur caressing my exposed buttocks. The only light comes from pillar candles burning on the hearth and the skylight in the ceiling where the soft afternoon sunshine is already beginning to fade into twilight.

My teacher stands by the fireplace, dressed in a black silk robe, a leather mask concealing his eyes. He looks sterner and stricter than I've seen him before. In his hand is a long, slender whip, the end of it a mass of soft-looking black leather fronds.

I lie quite still and wait to hear what my teacher has in mind.

'So, Winter,' he says. He's running the slender whip across his palm. 'You've been an excellent student so far. But you have one lesson left to learn. The lesson of earth.'

I look up at him. The glitter of his blue eyes behind the leather eye-mask is deliciously exciting and a pleasant shiver runs over my skin. I love the sensation of being at his mercy, knowing that whatever lesson he has planned for me will give me exquisite pleasure.

My teacher continues. 'Earth is the last element we will be exploring and it is linked in classical teaching with the sensual aspects of life, so it's particularly suitable for our lesson. It's the heaviest of all the elements, and carries associations with the underworld – and its erotic potential. Sex is our consolation for death, isn't it, Winter? We all know that our mortal body will eventually pass away, but while we inhabit it we may enjoy its pleasures. In classical myth, the goddesses of the earth are those of fertility and agriculture, helping the earth surrender its bounty of food. Mother Earth is the goddess from whom all life and all good things flow.' My teacher seems to be warming to his theme, drawing the whip through his hand a little faster. 'Today, Winter, you're wearing leather and silk – provided for us by the beasts of the earth. I hope you will appreciate their beauty. You will also learn to value some of the fruits of the earth, and the use to which we can put the precious metals, mined from its depths.'

Oh my goodness . . . What has he planned for me? I can see that there is a large bowl on the table near the fireplace and my belly fizzes a little at the anticipation of what is in it, and what uses my teacher will find for the contents later.

'But first.' He plants his feet a little further apart. 'There is another and powerful tradition that runs alongside the classical ones and that also has a firm connection to the earth. It is the Wiccan, or pagan, tradition. In the pagan mind, the symbol of the earth is the staff, the rod.'

Does he mean the whip? I shiver lightly again. *I've been a good student, I've done all he's asked. Is he going to punish me?*

I don't feel frightened. I'm know I'm safe in the hands of my teacher. I watch as he moves across the room to a large armchair and sits down. He regards me gravely for a while, and I feel his gaze moving over my body, from the pert nipples poking through the thin strips of leather, to the tight corset and my exposed body below, down my stockinged legs to the spike heels. My sex tingles and I can feel my juices rising to the surface, making me ready for whatever lies ahead.

From his seat my master says, 'You want to touch this time, don't you, Winter?'

'Yes,' I whisper.

'Good. Come over to me on your hands and knees.'

Obediently, I roll over, on to my front and raise myself up into a crawling position. I move towards him slowly, feeling my hips sway with every forward movement. I sense that he's watching the curve of my bare bottom as I approach, but my head is low and I can't see him. When I reach his feet, I stop.

'Very good,' he says in a low voice. 'Now, you will be granted your wish, Winter. You can touch me – but within limits. You may only touch the rod, do you understand? The rod and the balls. And you may use your mouth. Consider it the fertility rite of the earth goddess.'

I nod, excitement swirling in my belly. I can't wait to touch and kiss him. I've been longing to play with his magnificent cock for so long, but my teacher has not allowed it until now. I understand that I'll be worshipping his staff, and I can't wait to start paying homage to it.

'You may begin, Winter.' His voice is deep, caressing.

I lift myself to my knees and pull aside the black silk of his robe. Behind his mask, his blue eyes are watching

279

me carefully as I draw in a delighted breath at the sight that greets me. His huge cock is standing stiff and ready for me, its velvet tip, smooth and shiny, rearing upwards. He's a beautiful sight: so firm and thick, his balls large and ripe beneath. I lick my lips. I can't wait to get started.

I grasp the stiff shaft in one hand, relishing its heat and the smooth skin, and begin to move my hand up and down it. As I rub gently and rhythmically, I dip my head to the satiny soft tip, and run my tongue over it. I play around it, running round the rim, over the top and tickling in the tiny slit there. As I rub and tickle with my tongue, I feel the great thing twitch and respond, throbbing under my hand. When I've anointed it with my tongue for long enough, I finally let the whole of the top slip into my mouth, engulfing him with my lips. I hear a gentle sigh escape my teacher's mouth as the top of his shaft disappears into the warm wetness of my mouth. As I suck on him, I caress and tickle his balls with one hand and tighten my grip at the base of his cock with the other. The great length responds by growing even stiffer and throbbing magnificently under my touch.

'You are doing very well,' says my teacher, his voice thickened by the sensations he's experiencing. 'I'm pleased with you.'

A judder of excitement goes through me. My juices are flowing hard now, I can feel the moisture between my legs, making me slippery and ready for this beautiful machine of his. But it's in my mouth for now, filling me up, as I put my hand back on the shaft, rubbing harder and more rhythmically. I want to take him into my mouth to the root but I'll never able to – he's far too big for me. Instead, I concentrate on licking and toying with the great head of it, my tongue roaming over it, flicking around it, tickling that little slit and playing at the rim, while my hands are busy on the stiff length and his tight balls.

I lose all sense of time as I close my eyes and worship the cock that has already brought me so much pleasure. I adore touching him, tasting him, giving him a little of the joy he's given me. I can hear my teacher's breathing coming faster and I take as much of him as I can deep into my mouth, thrilling to his groan of ecstasy as I engulf him in my mouth. I can't keep him there for long, he's too big, so I let the shaft slide slowly from between my lips and go back to concentrating on the top while my hands work on his length.

I don't know how long I'm sucking and rubbing and kissing and tickling, but when I feel his huge cock swell even more under my hand, and feel his balls tighten with the force of his approaching climax, I feel almost disappointed that my work will soon be done. I've enjoyed it so much, I don't want him to come – and yet, it's also the ultimate tribute, that he'll surrender himself to the climax I've brought about with my mouth and hands. The sense of his approaching orgasm is deeply exciting, and my clitoris twitches and swells with the effect.

My teacher has begun to move now, pushing out his hips so that his cock goes deeper into my mouth as I suck, sliding him in and out, my head dipping rhythmically in time to my hands rubbing hard on his shaft. He groans. His hands touch my head, as though he wants to push me further down his shaft, but he doesn't exert any pressure.

This is beautiful. Come for me, Miles . . . I want every drop you can give me . . .

I know it's coming now. He's thrusting up into my mouth, I'm gripping him harder, working him faster, my tongue tickling hard. He's like a rod of iron now.

Yes, my darling, give it to me, please . . .

Then he groans deeply and throws back his head, his mouth open, as the great cock stiffens and shoots out the swift jets of his climax. The hot, salty liquid floods my mouth as it spurts out, his shaft throbbing with each explosion.

I take it down, swallowing it all, licking the head of his cock for more, relishing it.

When at last his erection has stopped throbbing, I let it slide slowly out of my mouth and let go of him. I look up at him, panting, my lips and chin wet with saliva.

He stares down at me with a half smile. When he speaks, his voice is replete. 'Very good . . . That was most enjoyable, Winter.'

I smile up, my eyes bright. I'm so happy that I've pleased my teacher. But I know that the lesson isn't over yet.

'The earth doesn't just provide seed,' he says. He stands up, pulling his robe closed, and steps around me to go to the table. 'It is rich with metals as well, the deposits that we mine from it and turn to our own use. Gold, silver, bronze.' He looks back over his shoulder at me. 'Did you know that most of the earth's gold deposits are at the core? Too deep for us to reach. Most of the gold we've mined so far is thought to have been brought here by meteorites crashing into the earth's surface.' He gestures to the bed. 'Go and lie down. You're going to experience a little of what the earth's metal can do for you.'

I do as he says, going to the bed and lying on my back on the bare sheets. He comes over carrying a bowl and looks down at me with approval.

'Yes,' he says. 'Yes.' He puts the bowl on the bedside table and takes a small square object from it. It's made of a dull metal, and from each corner of the square juts a tiny spike pointing inwards. 'This is bronze, Winter. The metal of the ancient civilisations, an alloy of tin and copper.'

I wonder what the small object is for, but my teacher will not let me wait for long. He bends down and deftly puts the square over the nipple of my right breast, so that the bud emerges from between the four inward-jutting spikes. The spikes press into it with a kind of sharp, buzzing tickle. I gasp. It's painful but not unbearable and the initial sting quickly becomes a kind of ache that makes my sex throb in response. With a deft movement, my teacher presses another square on to the nipple of my left breast, and I pant as the hot sting hits the delicate bud.

'Can you feel the bite of the bronze?' he asks in a low voice.

I nod. 'Yes, Tutor.'

'If you misbehave, Winter, then I'll have to make it bite a little harder. Like this.' He turns one square, and the rasp of the spikes across my nipple makes me moan out loud. 'But I think you might enjoy it too much for it to be an effective punishment. And besides, you're such a compliant student.' He swiftly turns the other square, making the other nipple sing as well. I writhe a little under the sensation. I've never understood the concept of pleasurable pain, until now.

'The Bronze Age is considered a factual period in history,' says my teacher, 'but the Gold and Silver Ages are mythical. Nevertheless, these precious metals must be represented. They too can bring great pleasure.' He lifts another small object from the bowl, this one made of sparkling silver. It's a kind of long hoop, with indentations near the top, and small tassels of silver chains hanging from the ends. I have no idea what it might be. 'This little object, for example.'

He holds it to my chest, the metal cool on my skin, the little chains snaking over my flesh with a delicate tickle. He runs it downwards over the leather corset around my waist, and down again to where my sex is ripe and ready, swollen with heat and desire. I'm breathing fast, my heart racing. Is he going to press the little thing inside me? It doesn't seem the right shape for that. Then, to my surprise, he presses the hoop over my clitoris, the indentations closing around it so that it's almost encircled by the slender metal. The sides of the hoop run down me towards my entrance, the little chains lying around my wet lips. My clitoris throbs to the tight embrace of the metal clip.

'Delightful,' says my teacher. 'Open your legs for me, Winter.'

I part my thighs even further, so that he can see me utterly exposed to him, my sex now dressed in its sparling clitoral clip and tassels of silver chain. My silk stockings rub pleasurably on my skin as I move my legs apart. The bronze nipple squares bite hard on my little buds and I moan softly, gripping the sheet with both hands, drawing it up into my clenched fists.

'Gold,' says my teacher. 'Something golden for you.'

He dips into the bowl again and this time brings out something that makes my eyes widen: a huge golden dildo with a handle shaped with a grip. I know at once that is so the dildo can be plunged in and out with force.

I moan again.

My teacher sits on the bed beside me, and grips the handle so that the dildo seems to be emerging from his knuckles. It glitters, vast and thick. I'm panting at the sight of it, my clitoris twitching inside the clip that heightens it's very throb.

'I think you should kiss this beautiful thing,' he says and brings it to my lips. I open my mouth and let the cool metal slide inside. I suck it longingly, remembering my teacher's huge cock. When it's well anointed with my saliva, he pulls it from my mouth and trails it down my body, its hard length exciting me unbearably. He toys with it over my mound, pressing it down on my clit with delicious pressure, rubbing it around my wet lips until it's oily with my juices as well as my saliva.

I want it, I'm desperate to be filled up . . . Fuck me with it, please . . .

I can't speak but he must know from my face and the longing expression in my eyes that all I want is for him to send that golden shaft deep inside me.

Its cool head is at my entrance now, dallying among the silver chains from my clit clip, their roughness stimulating me beautifully. Then, at a slow, tormenting pace, he pushes the huge dildo deep inside me.

I cry out with the pleasure of it as he begins to fuck me with it. I writhe and twist under the onslaught of sensations: the bite of the bronze around my nipples, the embrace of the silver clip on my clit and now the incredible sensation of the golden dildo my teacher is thrusting in and out of me. My fingers grip the sheets even tighter, my head twisting with delight as I moan, opening my legs wider to him so that he will press that delicious thing in and out faster and harder. I can't stand this for long, I'm too aroused by the process of this lesson, the way he's watching me from behind that mask as I respond to what he's doing to me.

Oh God . . . this is too much for me, I'm going to come . . . Fuck me harder . . .

The clip seems to tighten around my clit as it swells again, making divine sensations wash over me. It's no good, I'm going to come, I can't help it . . .

He seems to see how close I am and the dildo drives even deeper inside me, thick and hard. My limbs stiffen as the bliss builds in my pelvis and with a shout I'm possessed by great shudders of delight as the orgasm grabs me and shakes me in its ecstatic grip. The waves come again and again until, at last, I'm left panting and helpless.

My teacher pulls out the shiny dildo, wet with my honeyed juice. Then he opens his robe and reveals his own hard shaft, standing upright and ready.

I sigh with pleasure and let my knees fall open on the bed. *Oh yes, please . . . I want this . . .*

In a smooth movement, he's between my legs, his chest hard on my breasts, making those little bronze squares nip me even harder. The clit clip is still there and now his groin is pressing hard on mine, his cock at my slippery entrance. Then his magnificent erection slides up inside me. I groan as it hits the top of my vagina, squashing the little tassels against my soft flesh. Then he begins to fuck me, his mouth taking possession of mine. I hold him to me, my hands roaming over his broad back under the silk robe, clasping his firm buttocks, urging him deeper inside.

We fuck hard and fast, kissing and moaning, our bodies giving each other the greatest of pleasure as his cock dives into my velvet depths. On and on we go, thrusting in time with each other until, at last, we dissolve into the beauty of our mutual orgasm, both surrendering to the joyous bliss we've given one another, collapsing under the force of our ecstasy until we lie together, panting and spent.

When we're showered and refreshed, we make supper from leftovers in the fridge, and eat them while chatting idly and laughing. We don't talk about the extraordinary lesson he's just given me. The teacher and Winter are part of a particular existence. Now we're Miles and Freya.

Later we watch a movie cuddled up together on the sofa. It's one of his favourites, *Sullivan's Travels* directed by Preston Sturges.

I'm enjoying the movie, luxuriating in being near him, feeling the pounding of his heart through his cashmere jumper, when I'm struck by a strange thought.

This isn't a lesson. This is ... romantic.

An odd sensation courses through me, as though I've just missed my footing or had a rug slip beneath me. The agreement was that we would have our lessons, there was never any promise of anything else. And yet – so many of the physical things we've shared over the past few days have been spontaneously affectionate. Yes, they were all laced with the sexual desire we feel for one another. We can't get close to each other without the air crackling with the electric hunger we have for one another's body. But when we kissed on the slopes yesterday, or in the sleigh on the way home, anyone would have taken us for a couple in the grip of a love affair, not simply sharing their sexual needs.

And look at me now – I'm in a borrowed robe, and we're snuggled up in front of the fire. I shake my head. *This is weird.*

287

'What is it?' he asks, noticing my movement, distracted from the film. 'Are you okay?'

I feel shy suddenly. I'm staring down at the belt I've tied around my waist and the way the pattern on the fabric disappears in the knot. 'Yes, I'm fine,' I say quietly.

He clicks the movie on to pause, and squeezes me again. 'Come on, sweetheart. What is it? You can tell me.'

'I . . .' I take a deep breath and glance up at him, catching those intense blue eyes before looking quickly away. The power of them is sometimes too much for me. 'I just wondered about what's going to happen when all of this is over.'

There. I said it.

He's looking at me, his eyes expressionless. 'No one knows what happens when all of this is over. Maybe nothing.'

My heart sinks and I can feel my face fall in disappointment.

He continues, 'It all depends if you believe in God or not. Or maybe in reincarnation. Or the spirits of the trees and the stones. But to be honest, I don't have a clue.'

I see a glint of mischief in his eyes and pound him crossly, laughing despite myself. 'Not when *life* is over! I mean this! Our time in this beautiful place.' I look around at the pretty interior of the chalet, with its nod to the Swiss peasant culture in the red and white cushions and the heart-shaped cut-outs in the chairs. First we were in a kind of hovel together, shut away from the world and everyone's prying eyes. Now we're here, in a more beautiful and comfortable version of the same thing. *With proper bathrooms this time, thank goodness. And without the fear of imminent death.* Nevertheless I am afraid; I'm worried that this is the last time Miles and I will be together like this and that this lovely dream is nearly over. I'm supposed to be heading back. Soon I'll get an email from Jane-Elizabeth, under instructions from my father, wanting to know my whereabouts and what my movements are. I gaze at Miles, hoping my vulnerability isn't showing in my eyes. 'What's going to happen to *us*?'

Just as I feared, Miles's eyes darken. When that happens, they seem to go a shade that's almost navy, the dark rim around his iris fading into the muted colour. He looks away from me.

My throat is dry suddenly. I should never have asked him this question, not yet. I should have kept my worries to myself and let him bring it up in his own time. Now he's going to feel pressured. Our beautiful arrangement based on pure longing for one another will be ruined, because of my thoughtless questions.

'The truth is, Freya,' he says at last, 'the truth is that I don't know.'

My fingers are fiddling nervously with the knot on my belt. 'You don't know?' I ask hesitantly.

He shakes his head, his lips in a straight line. His arm slips away from around my shoulders. 'I can't pretend to you – well, I guess I could but I don't want to. What we've been doing is glorious, amazing, mind-blowing.' There's a tiny pause as we both remember some of the more exquisite moments we've shared in the last few days. 'But . . .'

The but. Oh no. Not the but.

He hesitates. My stomach is doing all kinds of wild gymnastic routines while I wait the age it takes for him to speak again. When he does, his voice is low and he is still studying something of intense interest on the floor.

289

'I don't know what you want, but you're very young, Freya. I'm older than you, and a lot more world-weary. I've seen a lot of bad things in my time. Believe me, you don't know how bad.' He pauses and I wait, desperate for him to continue. I want to say something but I bite my tongue, sensing that I have to let him speak in his own time. 'There are reasons why it suits me to be employed by your father. His intense need for privacy and security work for me right now.'

'Why?' I ask timidly, unable to hold it in. 'Are you running away from something?'

He glances at me swiftly and laughs one of those hollow, mirthless laughs. 'You could put it like that. Yes.'

'Is it . . .' I don't know why the thought strikes me, but it does. '. . . A woman?'

An awful expression crosses his face. It's so brief I almost think I imagined it but I know I didn't: it's utter pain.

'Yes,' he whispers. 'In a way. Yes.'

My heart plummets. I replay that fleeting expression in my mind again. It was a look of unbearable trauma. Whoever she is, it's clear he still loves her, or, at least, isn't over her.

Bleak disappointment races through me. *That's why he wanted this situation to have limits. That's why we had to agree that what happened in the hut would stay there. He belongs to someone else.*

The minute I think it, I can't believe I haven't considered it before. Then I remember our time together in the hut, when he told me that he didn't have a girlfriend. *But that doesn't mean he's not still in love with an ex.*

A cold thought hits me like a punch.

And despite everything that's happened between us, it hasn't been enough to shake her from his heart. All this time he'd rather have been with her.

What hold must this woman have over him?

Miles is staring at me, and I suppose he must be watching a variety of emotions flit across my face. He says, 'It's not what you're thinking.'

I look up at him with hope in my eyes. 'She's not on the scene any more?'

'Nope.' He shakes his head slowly. 'She's dead.'

I gape at him, horrified. 'Oh my God, Miles, I'm so sorry. That's terrible.'

He looks away. 'It's fine, really. Do you mind if we just watch the movie now?'

Later that night I'm dozing in Miles's arms, still wondering what his dead girlfriend means to him. I don't know how I can live up to a woman who might well have attained saintly proportions by now. Despite loving the movie and enjoying the way I was sharing one of Miles's passions with him, I couldn't help the bleak feeling that kept creeping into my heart. After all of this, it seemed that it had meant nothing to Miles. Maybe a sticking plaster for a wounded heart, but little more than that. We would go home now and things would return to normal.

Normal?

I picture my everyday existence with its flurry of activity that really adds up to nothing much: the whirl of socialising, the preening and pampering, the rounds of shopping to keep up with the very latest of everything. And for what? What does it all really achieve? It doesn't make me happy, I know that. Beneath the cheerfulness I summon up to show my friends, I feel constantly sad and angry – something I can hardly admit even to myself.

Miles has made me happy. He really has, and not just because of the divine sex he's introduced to me. Even though I always knew that this was no-strings attached, he's made me feel cherished and loved in a way I haven't for ages. For as long as I can remember, in fact. And he's made me feel protected too. The idea of losing that feeling is like walking naked into a snowstorm. I don't want to return to the chilly loneliness of my daily life.

I look at him as he sleeps beside me. He's turned towards me so that I can see the finely moulded shape of his lips and his long straight nose, his eyes closed. One arm is bent under his head and the other is flung out towards me, the fingers reaching out over the sheets as though he wants to touch me even in his sleep. I reach out my hand and brush the tips of his fingers with mine. His hand twitches and he sighs.

Oh Miles. What am I going to do without you?

I tell myself that he'll still be close to me, that perhaps we can continue our lessons in other places – at home, in planned locations – but I fear that Miles won't want that. He's suggested nothing of the sort.

A tear leaks out from under my lashes, followed by another.

I don't want to lose you. I'd give anything to be back in the storm in that hovel, if it meant I could be with you.

CHAPTER EIGHTEEN

The next day we pack up to leave the chalet.

The chef arrives to make us breakfast, as Miles thinks we require a little more than eggs on our last day. He's a tall, red-faced man with enormous ears, who says little but produces a hearty meal to sustain us on the journey home.

It's only when our bags are at the door and we're upstairs waiting for our cars to collect us that I say casually to Miles: 'So – what happens after this?'

I'm sitting on the sofa while he's standing by the window looking out over the magnificent view, clouded over today with a hint of bad weather to come. He looks ready to be on his way in a Belstaff black leather aviator jacket and sunglasses. My skin tingles at the sight of him, remembering the delicious early morning sex we shared when we woke up. It was not the long, erotic experience of my lessons, but the kind I love almost as much: straightforward but intense as he kissed me deeply, parted my legs and pushed in the hot hardness of his morning erection. I wrapped my legs around his thighs, and we ran a fast course of deep, satisfying fucking that ended in crackling, electric orgasms that exploded swiftly over us.

I wanted to speak to him then, as we pulled apart in that hot post-sex sweat and dampness, but he was out and striding to the shower almost at once. The time wasn't right to broach the issue.

He turns to me now, his expression inscrutable and his eyes hidden behind the mirrored shades. 'After this?' He smiles suddenly, making happiness course through me. I'd do anything for that smile. 'Well, Winter, I think you've learned just about all I can teach you for now.'

'I don't think so,' I say softly. 'I think there's more to learn. And I need to consolidate my knowledge. You don't ask a girl to take her driving test after just one lesson.'

He laughs. 'True.' Pulling off his shades, he walks towards me and sits down beside me on the sofa. 'But how long can this go on for? We can't both keep escaping from our lives like this – even though it's been a beautiful experience.'

'Has it?' It comes out almost in a whisper and I realise how badly I want him to have loved this as much as I have.

He takes my hand. 'Of course it has.' His other hand reaches out to stroke my hair and he looks at me with tenderness. 'You've trusted me completely. That's meant so much. You can't know how much.'

'I feel so safe with you.' I gaze up at him, hoping to convey the things I dare not say to him.

The expression in his eyes changes again, and I see a glimpse of that awful sadness, darkening his eyes like a cloud blocking out the sunshine.

'What is it?' I beg, feeling as though I've blundered somehow. 'What have I said?'

He looks away. 'Nothing. Nothing. Really.' He gazes back and I can see he's made an effort to put whatever it is out of his mind. 'Freya, I've been a coward. I've been putting off talking about this with you because I've enjoyed our lost weekend so much.'

Oh no! My heart begins to pound and a sick feeling makes my hands clammy.

'But . . .' He stands up. 'I don't plan to work for your father any more.'

'What?' I jump to my feet. 'Why not?'

'Because he's lost his trust in me. I can see that. He and Pierre suspect me somehow, even though there's no proof and no reason to. Now that you've explained what happened in the past, and the fact you were once betrayed by a guard, I can see where your father's coming from. But the years have made him paranoid, and Pierre isn't helping matters. He seems just as crazily suspicious – his job depends on it, I think. Pierre gets paid extremely well for reflecting back your father's fears and, of course, making sure none of them are ever realised.' Miles sighs and walks over to the fireplace where the hearth is now cold, scattered with the black ashes that are all that remains of the burning fire of last night. He picks up a poker and stirs them, but they remain cold and dead.

'This is ridiculous,' I say urgently. 'Of course you must come back. They'll soon realise they've been mistaken. I'll tell my father and he'll understand. I was there when we crashed, I know how it happened and it's mad to think you could have somehow staged it. What do they think you hoped to gain out of it?'

He turns and looks at me with a long, penetrating stare and then says, 'You. You, of course, Freya.'

'Me?' I blink at him, stunned.

'Yes. You were out of his control for a couple of days while we were lost. Have you ever heard of Stockholm Syndrome?'

I shake my head, still taking in what he said.

'It's when someone is kidnapped, and they end up form-
ing a relationship with their kidnappers, espousing their
cause and turning to their side. Sometimes they can even
end up falling in love.'

I feel a violent blush explode over my cheeks and I say,
'That's ridiculous.'

Miles doesn't seem to notice my scarlet face but says,
'They might think that a version of that has happened to
you. They may even doubt there was a crash at all. They
might think I pushed the car over the cliff and took you to
the hut to brainwash you there, so that you'd back up my
version of the story.'

'But why? Why would you brainwash me?'

He smiles and says, 'I love the way you can't think of a
reason. Why would a man want to brainwash a woman
like you?'

My heart sinks as I realise that, of course, it all comes
back to the same thing: money. *My father's fortune. The
whole reason I lost my mother, why I live in fear of my life,
why people blackmail me and ruin my relationships* . . .

'That's right,' Miles says softly, seeing the expression on
my face. 'Money. That's what they think I want.'

'But . . .' I sigh hopelessly, looking around the room as
though there is an answer hidden there. 'I know that's not
true! I can tell them!'

'The more you try to tell them, the less they'll believe
you and the worse it will look for me. Why would you go
to such lengths to protect a bodyguard, considering the
way you usually treat the staff? They'll look on that as
proof of my guilt and decide that I've got to you somehow
and I'm using you for my own ends.' He walks towards
me, his eyes tender again in that way that makes my

stomach melt and my knees go weak. His nearness is enough to drive me mad with longing. 'And you see . . .' He puts out his arms and I fall into them with something like relief. 'They're not entirely wrong, are they?'

'What do you mean?' I say into his jacket, inhaling the masculine smell of the leather.

'Well – look at us. Here we are.' He smiles down at me. 'What would they think if they could see this?'

'But I made you do it!' I say hotly. 'It was all my idea – you would never have done anything if I hadn't suggested it – and even then, you didn't want to go against your ethics.'

He laughs. 'If you told them that, they'd simply think I was even cleverer than they thought – managing to make you think that *you* engineered what *I* wanted. Sweetheart, you're young and they'll think that makes you impression-able, someone who doesn't know her own mind. You told me about that boyfriend . . .'

'Jacob,' I supply.

'Yeah – you said that you found out he slept around and cheated on you. Does your father know about that?'

I nod slowly.

'Unfair as it may seem, that will help him come to the conclusion that your judgement may be a little immature.'

I feel caught in a whirl of frustration. I'm trapped – I can't help my father change his mind about Miles because one way or another, I'll always confirm his suspicions. 'They *are* wrong, though! What do you mean by saying that they aren't?'

He blinks and gives me that beautiful half smile of his. 'Because of this. Because of what we've been doing together.'

'It's not wrong!' I say in a choked voice. I can feel those damned tears stinging thickly behind my lids. 'We're two adults! Why can't we make our own choices? Do what we want?'

He strokes my hair again. I love it when he does that, feeling the heavy comforting weight of his hand touching me so softly. I always feel calmer inside.

'I wish it were that easy,' he says huskily. 'And perhaps it might be if you weren't Miss Freya Hammond. But you are.'

'I don't want to be!' I say, turning my face back into his chest so that my voice is muffled by his jacket. 'I'll give it all up if I have to.'

'We both know you can't walk out of your life.' His arms wrap round me. 'No one can. It always comes to get you in the end.'

'Please, Miles, please . . . Please don't leave your job right now. I can't bear it! After everything that's happened – the accident, the way I've talked about the past – I can't take it if you go right now!' I start to shake. I'd hardly realised how strongly I feel about it but now I know for sure that I can't stand it if he goes. 'It isn't about the lessons, or having sex with you – I mean, of course, those things are glorious and I don't want to stop – but it's more than that! I . . . need you.' I lift my face from his jacket and gaze up at him, my eyes damp with unshed tears. 'Don't go yet, I beg you. Stay a bit longer, until I'm feeling more stable. Please!'

He gazes down at me and I can read conflicting emotions in his eyes. Somewhere a little voice is whispering to me: *if he loved you, he'd stay without question. And look at him! He clearly doesn't want to.*

Then he frowns and groans. 'Oh God, Freya Hammond, you put me in a quandary, you really do. Every instinct in me is telling me to shake the dust of your family's house off my feet. And I've learned to trust my instincts. And what's more . . .' His face contorts in an agonised expression as though painful thoughts are crossing his mind. I wait to hear what it might be that makes him feel that way, but he just sighs a short sharp sigh of exasperation and says, 'You're a lady who's difficult to resist, do you know that?'

A wave of hope rushes over me. 'Am I?'

He nods. 'But listen: if I come back to your father's place, there has to be a condition.'

'Of course,' I say breathlessly. Anything to make him stay. 'What is it?'

Miles raises one eyebrow at me. 'No sex.'

I gasp. 'What?'

'Not at your father's house. I can't have us creeping about, having sex in secret and hoping no one notices. For one thing, they will, and for another, it's not my style. On Hammond premises, we keep our distance, all right?'

'Oh my goodness!' I groan. 'That will *not* be easy . . .'

'Maybe not – but those are my terms. Understand?'

I nod. Just having him near will be worth the tantalising prospect of having to hide my desire for him. And besides, my heart sings with the implication that we will be having sex somewhere that isn't my father's house. *So he must want this to continue!* 'Okay. I accept the condition. Yes. No sex under my father's roof.' I laugh lightly. 'It sounds so weird.'

There's the roar of an engine as a car comes down the drive and halts in front of the chalet.

'I expect that's your ride,' Miles says drily. 'To take you to catch your private flight.'

'I wish I was coming with you,' I say wistfully.

'On a public plane? You'll be more comfortable your way.' He drops his mouth on mine and kisses me, softly at first and then with gathering passion. He pulls away and gazes at me, his blue eyes intense. 'Thank you for everything, Winter. These two days have been heaven. You were my goddess. I mean that.'

'Thank you,' I whisper, longing to know more about how he feels. 'I've loved it.'

I want to say 'you' – I've loved you . . . no, I love you . . . but I can't. I'm too afraid.

The raucous noise of a horn sounding from the car below breaks the atmosphere.

'I'll see you back at the house,' he murmurs. 'Now – you'd better go.'

For the return flight, I keep my eyes closed and listen to the music that plays through my headphones. I'm listening to melancholy love songs that sum up my mood. I don't even know if I should be happy or sad. Am I at the start of a relationship, or at the end of it? Does Miles feel anything for me other than lust, or does the spirit of his dead girlfriend, whoever she is, stand between us, keeping us permanently apart? I have no idea, and the very fact of that is exhausting. If only I knew what I should feel! I end up veering between sadness at our parting and joy at the memories of what we've shared, and a vague formless fear of those unknowns that threaten to keep us separated forever.

One of my father's regular bodyguards is waiting with a car for me at the heliport, and before long I'm on the familiar route home. It already feels as though my reunion with Miles was a lifetime ago.

As I exit the lift and walk into the hall, Jane-Elizabeth comes out of the main sitting room to meet me.

'They said you were here!' she beams as I walk through the hall. She holds out her arms for a hug. 'How are you, sweetie? Recovered a bit? Did you have fun with Lola?'

I nod. I don't want to lie to Jane-Elizabeth, but I can hardly tell her the truth – she'd be honour bound to pass it on to my father and besides, I don't think she would understand. Miles's explanation of how everyone would think he had somehow brainwashed me is still ringing in my ears. I don't want to risk his position any more than I have to.

'And are you feeling better?' persists Jane-Elizabeth, standing back to get a good look at me. 'You do look much better, I must say. Fresher. There's a light in your eyes. You two girls must have thoroughly enjoyed that spa. What was it called? Perhaps I should go there myself!'

I freeze, then turn away, flicking through a pile of unopened mail on the hall table to gain some time. 'Er . . . it was called the . . . the . . .' My mind is a blank. 'I really can't remember. I'll ask Lola to send me the details.'

'Yes, do,' Jane-Elizabeth says cheerfully. She doesn't seem to suspect a thing, which makes me feel dreadful. I've never lied to her before but what can I do?

'Are the twins here?' I ask, to change the subject.

Jane-Elizabeth shakes her head. 'Flora's gone back to Paris. Her acting course starts soon.'

'Oh yes.' I'd forgotten that Flora has decided that she's going to make a go of an acting career. She has the talent if her appearances in college plays were anything to go by,

Sadie Matthews

but I know that our father is against the idea. 'And Summer?'

'She's gone on a skiing vacation with one of her friends. She'll be back at the end of the week.'

So I'm alone in the house, apart from my father and Jane-Elizabeth. *And Estella. I mustn't forget her.* My heart sinks. I feel as though there is nothing to look forward to. What am I going to do with my life? Before there was Miles, I was about to jet off to LA for fun with Jimmy, but what was I going to do after that? What real plans did I have?

None. Nothing. I'm wasting my time. At least Flora has an ambition and is doing something about it. What am I going to do?

A picture suddenly floats into my mind, and I recall the way that Dominic and Beth looked at each other that night at the schloss. Their love gave their life a meaning and I suddenly wish more than anything that I could know what it was like to have someone love me as thoroughly as Dominic loves Beth.

Miles.

His name echoes through my mind like a sigh. I suddenly wish I could see Beth again, so that I could talk to her, confide in her, ask her advice. She's the only person I know, apart from Dominic, who knows Miles, properly, as a friend.

Just then Jane-Elizabeth says, 'Oh, I thought you might be interested to know that your bodyguard is coming back here. Miles Murray. He was on a few days' unpaid leave, but Pierre told me he's returning tonight. I think there was a question mark over whether he would stay or not, but apparently he wants to.'

My whole being thrills to the sound of Miles's name and the knowledge that tonight we'll be sleeping under the same roof again. Not in quite the same way as we did at the chalet but even so, I'll be comforted knowing that he's near me.

'Oh,' I say casually. 'That's interesting. I'm glad he didn't leave.'

'Yes, after what he did. We're all in his debt, aren't we? Now, dinner's at eight, as usual,' Jane-Elizabeth says as I head for the stairs. 'Your father will be so pleased to see you.'

My father is pleased to see me, as Jane-Elizabeth predicted, but even so most of his attention is reserved for Estella, who claims to have a bad headache and whose every moan and groan extracts my father's solicitous attention, as he gets her water, moves the flowers further away from her, calls for her soup to be taken away and replaced with plain crackers, and whatever else she demands. In between he asks me questions and I answer, trying to feel grateful to Estella for at least taking some of my father's attention away from me and the lies I have to tell him about my trip away. I paint a picture of Lola and me relaxing on our own, shut away in our spa most of the time, indulging ourselves with treatments.

'Well, I'm glad you're back,' Dad says. 'Is that better, darling?' He's talking to Estella now. 'More water? Sparkling this time? Of course.' He turns back to me. 'Flora's gone to Paris, I expect you know.' He shakes his head. 'Ridiculous. I don't approve.'

'We have to do something with our lives, Dad,' I say, 'and Flora's got a passion for acting. It's the perfect thing for her. Especially as she doesn't have to worry about how she'll survive from job to job like most actors.'

'I don't like her drawing attention to herself,' Dad says frowning.

'I want Badoit!' says Estella imperiously, pushing away the glass Dad has given her. 'Not this awful muck. Badoit only.'

'Yes, my darling, I forgot.' He calls for Badoit and the maid goes rushing off to get it.

'I envy her sense of purpose. I need to do something with my life,' I say, and then wish I hadn't as Estella turns to me with a kind of smirk.

'Yes, you must,' she says in a honeyed voice. 'Let me see . . . what could it be? Charity work, perhaps . . .? Very suitable for a girl like Freya.'

I feel a rush of fury. I don't want Estella involved in my life at all, and I can't help feeling that she doesn't wish me well.

Dad says, 'Yes, that would be very suitable. Perhaps you could set up your own charity, Freya. Help some good causes.'

I don't say anything but fidget a little. We already have a family foundation dedicated to charitable causes and I suppose I could get more involved with that. It would give me a worthwhile role in the world. 'I'll think about it,' I say, reluctant to seem enthusiastic about Estella's suggestion, even if it is a good one.

'Perhaps you could help fallen women,' says Estelle sweetly. 'All the Mandys in the world who've had to turn to prostitution to make ends meet. Give them a chance in life.'

I look at her with a stony expression, wondering why she should say such an odd thing.

'Or,' she adds with a strange little smile, 'you could save the rhino.'

'Whatever you choose, I'm sure it will be an excellent cause,' says my father. 'Now – Estella, my love, shall I ask the kitchen to make you some plain steamed fish? I know you like that.'

Later that night, I'm lying in my huge bed, more aware than ever of the great yawning space around me. Was it really only this morning that I woke with Miles's arms around me? It seems like a lifetime. I close my eyes and try to conjure up the sensation of his embrace and the pleasure of his warm body against mine, but it's no good. I can't make it feel real.

I sigh with longing. *Oh Miles. When am I going to see you again?*

Just then, my phone beeps with a new text. I pick it up. There is a text from Miles.

Winter. I'm back. I'm downstairs in my old room and I'm thinking of you x

My stomach clenches in delight. He's here! And he's thinking about me!

I'm thinking about you too, Miles.

Suddenly I feel comforted and for a moment, I remember with such clarity how it was to have his arms wrapped round me that I'm cheered by a burst of happiness.

Tomorrow I might see him.

I imagine how it will be: the two of us pretending that nothing has happened, that we're simply employer and staff. Perhaps Miles will be detailed to drive me around.

Perhaps we'll drive out somewhere deserted and have mad sex on the back seat of the Mercedes. The thought excites me, and I dream of it happily as I fall asleep.

But nothing about my dreams will come true.

The next day, all hell breaks loose.

CHAPTER NINETEEN

I'm enjoying a leisurely breakfast alone in the dining room, wondering what Miles is doing and whether I'll see him today or not, when Jane-Elizabeth comes into the room. She looks just the same as usual, with her black jeans, velvet slipper shoes and oversized black tunic top, but her face is pale and strained, her brown eyes anxious.

'Oh, there you are, Freya,' she says breathlessly as she sees me. 'I've just been to your room.'

'Well, I'm here,' I say, sipping my coffee. 'What's wrong?'

'Oh dear.'

The look in her eyes suddenly makes me nervous and I put my cup down on it's saucer with a loud clink, some of the coffee spilling over the edge. 'What is it? Tell me.'

'Freya . . .' To my astonishment, she looks hurt as well as worried. 'How could you?'

'How could I what?' I'm getting really anxious now.

She doesn't answer but says, 'Your father wants to see you. Right now. He's in his study.'

'Jane-Elizabeth!' I stand up, feeling slightly sick. 'Tell me what it is.'

But she just shakes her head sadly and says, 'Right now, Freya. Go at once.'

I stride along the corridor, my heart pounding and my stomach churning with a horrible nauseous feeling. All I want now is to get this over with and find out whatever it is that's making Jane-Elizabeth look so grim. Am I being blackmailed again? Has the whole nasty episode with Jacob raised its nasty head once more?

My hands are trembling slightly as I reach the study door and rap on its smooth surface.

'Come in!' calls my father from inside.

I turn the knob and push the door open. I can see my father behind his desk, which sits opposite the doorway across the room. He's looking at me with a stern expression and cold eyes. Then I see that there are two other men in the room with him. One is Pierre, looking as dark and menacing as ever in his black suit, the shoulders stretched across his meaty back. He turns to look at me with a cool expression. Then I gasp. The other man is Miles.

I am flooded by mixed emotions: joy at seeing him, and the delightful somersault in my stomach that I always experience when I see him after a break. But also a kind of horror. Why have I been summoned like this, only to find Miles here? After what he said to me, it can't be good news. It just can't. I look away immediately, knowing I mustn't betray myself.

'Ah, Freya,' says Dad, and I realise he's been watching my reactions very carefully. 'You're here. That's good. You've got some explaining to do, my girl.'

'What do you mean?' I say as boldly as I can, advancing into the room and trying to hide the tremor in my fingers. I need to brazen out whatever this is until I can find out more. *Innocent until proven guilty, right?*

My father picks up a newspaper that's on his desk and tosses it towards me. 'I mean – *this.*'

The paper lands on the floor at my feet and I look down at it. There's a huge picture on the front – a couple on a snow-covered slope, dressed in ski gear. They're kissing passionately and the dark headline is stamped across it: *LE KISS!!* Under that in smaller letters it says *THE HEIRESS AND THE BODYGUARD – THEIR SECRET PASSION* and I see that there are lots of pictures of the couple laughing, staring at each other, embracing, and more of that kiss. It's us, of course: Miles and me, together, on the slopes at Klosters, in shots taken only two days ago.

I stare at the front page, stunned, my mouth open. I simply do not know what to say. I had planned to answer my father with a denial, to lie my head off if I had to, in order to make sure that Miles and I remained a secret. But I can hardly lie when the proof is all over the front page.

'That's not all,' says my father in a grim voice. 'It's been picked up somehow. That rag has the exclusive – the best shots. But it's everywhere.'

My gaze moves involuntarily to Miles but he's staring stonily at my father, his body completely still. I look back at Dad, and I know that my expression is far from defiant now. I can tell that the blood has drained from my face and my eyes are wide and scared. If I could have picked the very worst way for my father to find out about Miles, this would have been it. I blink, as though I can get rid of the images on the front of the paper that way, but when I look again, they're still there.

LE KISS!! LE KISS!! LE—

'Freya!' Dad's voice is cold. 'Explain, please. Murray refuses to say a word.'

'I . . . I . . .'

Pierre is staring at me, and I think I can see a kind of sneer in the set of his lips.

'Spit it out!' shouts my father. He leaps to his feet and bellows, 'What the hell have you been playing at?' He picks up another newspaper from the pile on his desk and throws that one at me too. 'A lovely trip with Lola? You *lied* to me, Freya! You've been with *him*.' He shoots a look of pure hatred at Miles, who stares back, his gaze still hard as granite.

'I . . . Yes, I was with him!'

'How could you lie to me?' shouts my father. 'How?'

'Because . . .' I feel fury building now. My fear is beginning to turn into rage as I wonder why I felt the need to lie to my father and the answer comes rushing into my mind. The words suddenly flow from me in an angry flood. 'Can't you see why, Dad? Because of this! Because of the way you're treating me like a criminal for living my life! I've done nothing wrong. You force me to lie to you because of the way you treat me! I don't live in a home, I live in a fortress! It's been like this for so long, I can't remember what it's like to live without the feeling of being watched. You wonder why we flit across the world, always on the move, never able to settle. I'll tell you why! It's because we don't have a home – not a real one, where we can be ourselves. And it's to escape your control, because all you want to do is make us live our lives on your terms. Why shouldn't I be with a man I like? Why shouldn't I have some fun and love and laughter in my life? I'm young! I want to live, not just to exist in this god-awful house shut away on the top of a mountain!'

I run out of breath and come to a stop, my breath coming fast and my eyes blazing.

My father looks furious. My tirade has obviously done no good at all – he hasn't listened to me, he hasn't understood. 'You ungrateful child!' he yells. 'With everything you have, you're still unhappy! I grew up with nothing, and you have everything!'

'No!' I yell back. 'You had your freedom! Don't you see? That's the one thing you won't let me have!'

'Freedom?' Dad snaps. His eyes are narrow now, bright with his anger. 'You've got your freedom! All I want to do is protect you, and keep you safe!'

'Then why are you so furious that I've been with Miles? He's a bodyguard! He'll keep me safer than anyone!'

'Because . . .!' my father splutters. 'Because . . .!' He shoots another vitriolic look at Miles, who is watching proceedings with an impassive expression. 'Because he can't be trusted!'

'That's ridiculous,' I retort. 'Of course he can! You and Pierre hired him, you must have trusted him.'

'That was before your accident,' says my father, stressing the word 'accident' as though he means something entirely the opposite.

Pierre suddenly speaks up, his harsh voice crackling through the air. 'We've investigated Murray since that event,' he says in his strong French accent, 'and other things have come to light. Things that cause to us to wonder if our initial trust in him was misplaced.'

'What things?' I demand.

Pierre looks over at Miles and says nothing. Miles slowly turns and looks at Pierre with an expression of utter contempt. 'What things?' I demand, louder.

'Think before you repeat your baseless allegations,' Miles says in an icy voice.

I stare at them both, puzzled, and then my father says, 'You don't understand, Freya. I'm angry with you because

311

you lied, because you've let yourself become a target of the paparazzi. Of course you want to live your life – I'm offended that you should think I would want to stop you, or your sisters, from doing so.'

'But you *do* stop us!' I say, my voice pleading now. 'Can't you see that?'

'I keep you safe,' Dad says obstinately. 'As any loving father would do.'

'You stifle us.'

We stare at each other, incomprehension and hurt flickering between us. Then my father looks at Miles again and says, 'That man has betrayed the trust I placed in him. He has seduced you while in my employment. That is unforgiveable. It's a gross dereliction of duty, and I intend to make sure that he never works for any reputable family again. He's dismissed at once.'

'Why?' I shout, furious again. 'What's he done?'

My father's face becomes angry again too. 'What's he done? Freya, he's taken advantage of you for his own ends!'

'You don't know that!' I cry. 'You have no idea what happened!'

'We can guess only too well!' retorts my father. 'An older man, and a young *rich* girl? Oh please! It's obvious that he's manipulated you and made you fall for him.'

'And what about an older rich man and a young *poor* girl?' I shoot back. 'You don't expect us to question Estella's feelings for you. Why should you question Miles's for me?'

My father's expression turns icy. 'What?' he hisses. 'What did you say?'

'You heard me!'

'How dare you compare my sweet Estella to this man!'

I'm speechless. I don't know where to start. I can't find the words, I'm so angry. My father takes advantage of my inability to speak.

'You're a thankless, ungrateful daughter!' he yells, his face turning puce with anger. 'You lied to me about your whereabouts, and you've let yourself be made a fool of by this man. You're not just a fool to me – you're a fool in front of the whole world!' He snatches up another newspaper and lifts it up.

In one smooth movement, Miles is on his feet. His fists are clenched but otherwise he seems completely in control as he says in a low, menacing voice, 'Mr Hammond, if you throw that paper at Freya, I swear I will knock you down.'

Pierre leaps to his feet. 'Murray, sit the fuck down! You'll regret this.'

Miles turns to him, his face set hard. 'You're quite wrong if you think I'll ever regret anything you can do to me.'

'You're fired!' screams my father, almost spitting in his rage. 'You get out of my property and never set foot in it again! If you come within one hundred yards of my daughter, I'll have you sued! Imprisoned! And if you think you're going to get a job in this country now, you're completely mistaken!'

'I kind of had the impression already that I was fired,' Miles says, a tiny smile playing near his lips. 'Okay. Fine. I've done nothing but care for Freya and protect her. You're wrong about me, and I think that deep down you know it.'

'I know nothing of the sort,' Dad bellows. 'Now get out!'

'Okay.' Miles puts out his hands in calming gesture. 'I'm going. Don't take this out on Freya, that's all I ask.'

'You're in no position to ask for anything, Murray. And don't you ever come near my daughter again.'

'I think that's down to Freya, actually,' Miles says in a pleasant voice. He turns and begins to stride to the door. He stops opposite me and our eyes meet. His gaze makes me want to melt and he says in a caressing voice, 'Don't let him upset you, angel. Live life on your own terms, not his.'

'Don't go, *please* . . .' I whisper, my voice drenched with longing.

'I have to. You see that, don't you? But keep the faith. You'll be okay.' He smiles at me, that gorgeous half smile I love so much. I want to rush to him, kiss him, hug him and feel his strong arms around me. But I can't move. 'Bye, angel.'

He walks to the door, opens it and strides out. I feel as though my heart is being torn from me.

My father says in an icy voice, 'Freya, you will never see him again, do you understand?'

I can't speak. I'm watching the empty doorway where Miles has just exited.

'You will never see him again,' my father repeats. 'He's a traitor and a liar. Can't you see that, Freya?'

But I can't say anything. My throat is constricted and my eyes swimming. The vision of a life without Miles in it is too much to bear.

'If you do,' my father says in a tone I've never heard before, 'you can leave this house and never come back. Do you understand, Freya? That man or your family. That's your choice.'

I feel as though my heart will break.

Miles, I need you! Please . . . please . . . don't leave me.

CHAPTER TWENTY

I really don't know if I can take this.

My emotions have been in a heightened state – one way or another – for so long that I'm exhausted. I'm so strung out by everything that's happened that, even though I'm wound up to the point of tears, I can't cry.

Miles walked out of my father's study this morning, and out of my life. I couldn't help wondering if he was glad that my father had dismissed him like that: he'd only come back because I'd begged him to, and I always knew, somehow, that he wouldn't stay long. I've learned that Miles is a proud man, a man of principle and integrity. There was no way he would stay working for my father and Pierre when the two of them suspected him of duplicitous behaviour.

But what makes me lie on my bed, frozen and grieving, is fear. I'm afraid that Miles doesn't feel anything for me. I replay every minute of our time together in the chalet, recalling what he said to me. He didn't give much away, but I recall the look of pain on his face when I asked him if he was running away from a woman – the woman who, it turned out, was dead.

It's hard not to leap to the conclusion that he still loves this dead woman, whoever she is.

But does that mean he feels nothing for me?

I bury my face in my pillow, and remember the moments of tenderness: the sweet snuggling in front of the fire, the

breakfast he cooked me, the way he held my hand under
the fur rug during our sleigh ride. He didn't have to do
those things. He wanted to do them – we both did. We ate
and drank and laughed together; we made love and then
slept wrapped up together, waking to the delight of sleepy
smiles, lazy kisses and warm flesh.

Like a couple. A normal couple.

I remember how, when we talked about our future,
Miles reminded me that I'm Freya Hammond, and told me
I simply couldn't walk out of my life. Maybe that's it.
Perhaps he won't let himself fall for me because he believes
it's impossible that he and I could ever be happy together,
ever have a future.

'Miles, you're wrong,' I whisper into my pillow. 'We do
have a future – because I can't imagine my life without you
in it. I can't go back to how things were, because my life
simply wasn't worth living. And I'll do anything it takes to
show you I mean it.'

The little voice in my head asks me: *what about the
dead girlfriend? How can you compete with her, if he still
loves her?*

All I know is that she's not here, and I am. Surely I have
a chance – as long as I can show Miles how much I love
him.

But where is Miles? His phone is switched off and he's
not replied to any messages. As far as I know, he's simply
disappeared.

The exhaustion of everything that's happened catches up
with me and I fall asleep on my bed for a few hours. When
I wake up, groggy, it's the early afternoon and my phone
is flashing madly with an onslaught of messages. I sweep it

up and scroll through them all, hoping desperately that one will be from Miles.

None of them are. They're from friends demanding to know all the gossip about my love affair, or media outlets also demanding the same (as though I'd spill my secrets to them!), or just the usual crazy stuff from people who somehow manage to find out my email address and think that makes us soul mates.

There's one from Flora:

OMG, you dark horse!!! So all along you and that hunky bodyguard were getting together! You kept that quiet. Sorry to see you're the latest splash, honey. Come to Paris if you need to escape it all . . . xxx

And from Summer, who's a little more succinct:

I THOUGHT YOU HATED HIM!!!! Xxx

I groan as I read the messages. Of course, I'd forgotten that the whole world now knows about my liaison with Miles. *Le Kiss!* It seems there's no escape. I'm under scrutiny wherever I go. But who on earth recognised me, and was quick-thinking enough to take those long-lens shots when Miles and I kissed? The paparazzi have an extraordinary talent for sniffing out pictures that will make them money, that's for sure.

And all my privacy disappears.

Only a day ago, my whereabouts were a secret and only two people knew I was with Miles in Klosters – Beth and Dominic. And now, anybody who can pick up a paper and read it knows. The papers will no doubt be in a frenzy of speculation over what that says about the accident and my romantic future. Well, let them obsess. I can't care, or I'll go mad. I just have to shut it all out and concentrate on what the hell I'm going to do next.

I ring downstairs for lunch to be brought to my room – I can't face Jane-Elizabeth and her disappointment over my lies right now – and while I eat it, I answer the messages my friends have sent, usually with just a few words along the lines of how crazy the world has gone if I'm front-page news. I keep trying Miles but his phone remains off and none of the texts or messages I send are answered. All I want to know is where he is. I know so little about him, I can't even begin to guess where he might have gone after leaving this place.

I'm staring at my phone, willing it to flash with a message from Miles and feeling utterly powerless. Then a thought strikes me.

I leap up and head for the door. Clutching my phone, I march to the lift and summon it. When it arrives, I take it down to the second floor and when the doors open with their tiny chime, I stride out, not caring if the cameras spot me or not. Last time I came to this floor furtively, secretly, but this time I'm reckless. Damn them all, why should I creep about in my own home, for God's sake? I walk past the guards' room with its bank of screens relaying all the activity through the property and then past the kitchen where there are preparations going on for the evening's meal, judging by the aroma of cooking, then past the dining room and into the staff sitting room, where the television is playing. The atmosphere is livelier than when I was last here, but it's still fairly quiet. A man in one armchair is reading a newspaper, while another is sprawled over the sofa, watching the game show on the television.

I walk in and say loudly, 'Hi!'

Both the men turn to look at me enquiringly, and then leap to their feet when they see who I am. I recognise one as Thierry, a bodyguard and driver, but I don't know the other.

'Hello, miss,' mutters Thierry. The other just stares at his feet.

'Sorry to interrupt you,' I say cheerfully. 'I've got a quick question, that's all. Do either of you know where I can find Miles Murray? Do you know where he's gone?'

The gaze of the second man slides to the newspaper he was reading and which now lies abandoned on the floor where he dropped it. There's the picture of Miles and me kissing on the snow slope. He looks back at me, wide-eyed, and shakes his head.

'What about you, Thierry? Don't you bodyguards tell each other things?'

Thierry also shakes his head. 'Sorry, miss. I saw him this morning, but he didn't say anything about his intentions.'

'You saw him?'

'Yes. He came down here with a look on his face like nothing I've ever seen. He went to his room and left a few minutes after that with his bag. I don't know where he went.' Thierry shrugs helplessly. 'Sorry.'

His room. Of course. I'll look there.

'Okay, thank you. Apologies for disturbing you, go back to your TV show.' I smile at them, then stride off out of the room and down the corridor. Thierry doesn't do as I suggest but comes out after me, calling, 'Miss, where are you going?'

'Nowhere,' I say, picking up my pace. I know exactly where Miles's room is, thanks to my last foray here.

'You can't go down there!' protests Thierry as I forge ahead, through the hall with the staff mail boxes and down the corridor towards room twenty-one. 'Miss, stop!'

I turn around to face Thierry, who's hurrying after me, his expression anxious. 'Thierry – whose side are you on?' I say pleasantly. 'Mine and Miles's – or my father's?'

Thierry halts in the corridor and stares at me, his brown eyes confused. His mouth opens but he doesn't say anything. I can tell that he's thinking about the fact that while he might want to help Miles and me, it's my father who pays his wages and it's more than his job's worth to be found permitting this kind of audacious act. 'Sorry,' Thierry says, 'I'll have to tell the house manager what you're doing.'

'Fine.' I whirl round and am at the door of room twenty-one before he can do anything to stop me. The door stands ajar so I push through and slam it shut behind me. I know it won't be long before Thierry fetches the house manager, who'll have spare keys for the room, so I've only got a few minutes. I begin to search frantically, not even knowing what I'm looking for, except that there must be some clue to Miles's whereabouts here. The room is almost completely bare, with only a few signs that someone recently occupied it. The sheets on the bed are rumpled – I long to inhale Miles's scent but there's no time for that – and the pillows dented. On the bedside table is a half-drunk glass of water. In the tiny bathroom, a towel has been thrown over the side of the shower and a bar of soap left in a dish on the side of the basin.

Other than that, there seems to be nothing. I hurry to the wardrobe and open it, then pull out all the drawers, but everything is bare. I've been less than five minutes but I can hear footsteps pounding along the corridor outside and a hand shaking the handle from the outside.

'Hey there, open this door!' comes the cross voice of a woman.

I abandon the drawers and stand in the middle of the room, looking about. Surely there must be something that will help me find out where Miles has gone!

'I've got a key and I'm going to use it,' says the voice outside, and immediately I hear the key being inserted in the lock.

Then I see a paperback propped on the shelf near the television. It's a spy thriller. Perhaps it belongs to Miles, or perhaps just left here by some other occupant. It's the only thing I can see, anyway, so I pick it up and flick through the pages. Two thirds of the way through is a slip of paper that must be marking a place. There are some letters and numbers on it, so I fold it quickly and slip it into my pocket, just as the handle turns and the door opens to reveal the house manager, her face flushed and angry, with Thierry standing just behind her.

'What are you doing here, miss?' the house manager says, trying to balance out her obvious annoyance with politeness. 'You shouldn't be in here.'

'Just looking around,' I say airily. 'I found this – it's been left here.' I toss the paperback on the table. 'You should try it. I hear it's very good. Well, I'll leave you to it. Sorry to disturb you.'

I walk out past the house manager, shooting Thierry a look as I go past him. I know I can't expect him to risk his job for me but even so – he wasn't willing to help his colleague either. They watch me go, frowning, as though wondering what on earth I'm playing at, but I don't care. I don't know if the slip of paper I've found will help me, but I do know it's all I've got right now.

In the privacy of my room, I take out the little piece of paper and unfold it. It's been scrawled on in pencil, as though the writer was taking up the first thing he found to write with while he was on the phone. It reads: *D – new* and then a string of numbers which I guess is a mobile phone number with the British code in front of it.

I only know one friend of Miles and that's Dominic. Could he be *D*?

I wish I could investigate Dominic a little more, but I don't know where to start. I don't even know his surname, or the address of the chalet where we stayed. I wonder if he might still be at the Schloss Marika, but I'm sure that's a dead end. He and Beth were only going to be there briefly.

I stare at the piece of paper and the numbers written on it.

What the hell. What's the worst that can happen?

Impulsively I snatch up my mobile phone and tap in the number. It takes a few seconds to connect and I realise that my heart is pounding. Then it rings and after an agonising wait, it is suddenly answered.

'Hello?' says a male voice.

'Hello – who is this?' I ask.

'Who is *this*?' comes the reply.

It's a fair question but I don't want to reveal anything about myself in case this is a strange number. I strain to recognise the voice but I can't. 'Is this . . . Dominic?'

'Who wants to know?' shoots back the voice.

I suppose I can hardly expect anything else but I don't know how long I'll be able to keep this cat-and-mouse game going. 'Listen, I don't know who you are, but I've found your number and I think you may be the friend of a friend of mine. My friend is called Miles. Do you know someone called that?'

There's a long pause and then the voice says in a different tone, 'Freya? Is that you?'

I take a deep breath of relief and laugh. 'Oh yes! Yes, it is – is that Dominic?'

'Yes!' He sounds astonished. 'How did you get this number? Hardly anyone has it, it's new.'

'Miles wrote it down somewhere and I found it.'

'Is everything all right? Why are you calling? Are you okay?'

'Yes, I'm fine but . . .' I flush a little even though Dominic can't see me. 'Have you seen the papers?'

'Ah. Now you mention it, Beth did draw the story to my attention. I'm sorry for you both. What a rotten stroke of luck to have a photographer catch you in Klosters. Unbelievable.'

'Do you know that Miles has left here? He went first thing this morning after he and my father had a showdown.'

There's silence at the other end of the phone.

'Dominic, do you know where Miles is?'

He still says nothing and I say, flustered, 'You do know, don't you? Please, Dominic – he's not returning my calls or texts and I'm desperate to speak to him.'

At last Dominic says, 'I'm sorry, Freya. I do know where Miles is but I can't tell you. I've promised I wouldn't. He needs some time away from the madness to recover.'

'Please!' I'm agonised by the fact that I'm so close to finding out what I want to know, but now Dominic is refusing to play ball.

His voice is firm. 'I'm sorry – but no.'

'At least give him a message from me!' I cry, worried that he'll ring off and I'll have lost my chance.

After a moment, he says, 'All right. I don't see how that can hurt.'

'Thank you,' I say breathlessly, and then wonder what on earth I want to say that Dominic can relay for me.

'Yes?' he prompts.

'Tell him – tell him that we can weather the storm together – if he wants. Tell him to call me. I . . . I *need* to talk to him.'

'Okay.' Dominic sounds sympathetic but I know he's unshakeable. 'And Freya?'

'Yes?'

'I'm sorry. I really am.'

I know that I have to come out of my room and face real life again soon. I can't stay here for ever, moping over my phone and wondering if Miles will call. But what am I going to do?

My father is furious with me. My sisters are far away. I was supposed to visit Jimmy in LA. Perhaps I should do that – escape this awful winter and go somewhere hot and sunny. But being so far away doesn't appeal to me right now, and the idea of fun in LA seems flat without Miles to share it with. I decide to make a plan to visit Flora in Paris. I love that city and perhaps I'll be able to shake the press off my tail for a while. They'll certainly be waiting around to see whatever I'll do next and lying low until something else comes along to distract them seems like the best option.

It's late when I finally emerge from my room to see if the family are gathering for dinner. Jane-Elizabeth is in the drawing room, sipping on a gin and tonic and reading a magazine. She jumps up when she sees me.

'Are you all right, darling?' she says, all concern, and I remember why I love Jane-Elizabeth. She doesn't hold grudges and she always puts our well-being before everything else.

I nod. 'I'm sorry I was a bit devious about going away for the weekend. I just didn't want to involve you in lying to my father.'

She smiles. 'That's all right. I can see why you did it. You looked so much better when you got back, you obviously had a marvellous time with him. And why not?'

I smile a wobbly smile back. Jane-Elizabeth's understanding is breaking down my defences. 'It was lovely. *He's* lovely. He's not what they think he is, I promise!'

'I'm sure he's not. You're having a hard time,' she says sympathetically. 'Your father's told me some of it and naturally he has no idea why you're so upset. He can't understand it. Now, I'm going to get you a gin.'

She bustles about at the drinks tray while I say, 'Dad thinks Miles has brainwashed me. But he also just doesn't see that I need to be able to live the way I want.'

Jane-Elizabeth nods as she puts ice into a tumbler. 'You know why he's so protective, and why he doesn't trust anyone. He's terrified of losing you.'

'But he can't keep me under glass for the whole of my life! I have to take risks, and get hurt, and make mistakes and all the rest of it.'

Jane-Elizabeth pours out the gin, tops it up with sparkling tonic, drops in a slice of lemon, and brings it over to me. 'I know that, Freya, my dear, but your father feels he gave you some freedom over that affair with Jacob, and look what happened.'

'That wasn't my fault – it's Dad's blasted money that makes me vulnerable to all this! That's why I'm chased all over the place, and photographed without my permission and blackmailed!'

'And that's exactly why he doesn't trust Miles,' Jane-Elizabeth says softly. 'But you know very well that the money brings blessings as well. Your father told me you're thinking of working for the Foundation.'

I nod. I'd forgotten all about it with the furore of recent events but it's still a good idea.

'I think that would be an excellent thing to get your teeth into. And if you still feel the same way about Miles in a few months, perhaps your father will relent.'

'I can't wait a few months!' I say, agonised at the idea. 'I need him now!'

Jane-Elizabeth fixes me with a solemn look. 'If you're really serious about this, you'll need to be prepared to wait, Freya. Your father will not come round in a matter of days. I've never seen him so angry – it's a symptom of his fear, not an indication of his lack of love for you, but he's furious. He considers Miles disrespectful.'

'That's not true!' I burst out. 'Dad has been completely disrespectful of *him*! You should hear the way he spoke to Miles, and what he said. Miles has been nothing but honourable!'

Jane-Elizabeth holds up her hands. 'All right. I'm sure that's true. But the fact is, he's the last man on earth your father would want for you right now. And that's not going to change overnight.'

The atmosphere at dinner is icy. My father is stony-faced and barely speaks to me, while Jane-Elizabeth looks uncomfortable and miserable as she picks at the food put in front of us. Only Estella seems at all chirpy. In fact, I'd say that she's positively revelling in the situation. I wonder what my father is going to say to me – surely he'll speak to me before this meal is over and ask me what I've decided to do. I don't want to start more rows and conflict, or make him angrier, but I can't lie to him either. I've had enough of all that.

We're listening to Estella babble on, talking about how there were hordes of press photographers at the gate of the house when she left it this morning, as though we all need reminding of the fact, when my phone vibrates in my pocket. There's a strict no-phones-at-the-table rule, which is why it's on silent, but I can't ignore it. What if it's Miles?

'Excuse me,' I say, standing up and hurrying out of the dining room, taking out my phone as I go. I don't recognise the number but answer anyway, as soon as I'm far enough away from the dining room not to be heard. 'Hello?'

'Hi, Freya,' says a voice I can't place. 'I hope you don't mind me calling. It's Beth.'

Beth? For a moment I'm confused and then realisation washes over me. 'Beth! Hi, how are you?' My pulse quickens and I can feel a tremor in my fingertips.

'Listen, Dominic told me you called him wanting to know where Miles is.'

'Yes, that's right.' I'm breathless. 'He wouldn't say.'

'I know. He feels bound by that bond of brothers thing. He knows that Miles is desperate to go to ground for a while, until all this blows over. But . . .'

'Yes?'

'I can guess what you're going through, being parted from him. I could see you're crazy for him. And I can also understand it – I don't know Miles well but he seems like a fantastic guy. Very attractive too.'

'Yes,' I say, pierced with longing as the memory of him fills my mind. 'Do you know where he is?'

'I don't know where he is this very second,' she replies, and my heart sinks. 'But I do know that he's coming here for a few days from tomorrow.'

'Really?' I'm filled with joy again. At last, I'll find out where Miles is.

'He's going to stay with us while he makes various arrangements.'

'Where are you right now? At the chalet?'

'No,' Beth says. 'In Paris.'

'Paris?' I blink as I take this in. Paris is perfect. I was considering going there in any case. I say quickly, 'I'll be there tomorrow.'

Beth laughs. 'I guessed you'd say something like that. Okay – call me when you get here and we'll sort things out.'

'I will,' I say, my heart suddenly light and full of happiness. 'I'll see you soon.'

'Sure – and it's between you and me for now, okay? I guess I'm just an old romantic after all . . .'

CHAPTER TWENTY-ONE

My news causes a thaw at the dinner table. My father is glad to hear that I'm going to Paris to stay with Flora. But he has a condition. I'll have to take Thierry with me as my security.

'Dad, I don't need a bodyguard,' I say, exasperated.

'Don't be silly, of course you do. More than ever, now you're front-page news. I won't feel happy unless I know you're being looked after.'

Being spied on, more like, I think to myself but there's no point in fighting my father on this. Things are bad enough between us, and I'm happy to see that his mood towards me lightens as I tell him my plans.

'I need to put some space between me and everything's that happened,' I explain. 'If I'm going to move on with my life.'

'Yes,' my father says.

'And as the Foundation's headquarters are in Paris, I might drop in and see if there's a role I can play,' I say, as the idea occurs to me.

'Even better,' says my father.

'And you'll stay with Flora?' puts in Estella, who's been listening carefully, her good mood a little deflated by the way my father is relenting towards me.

'Yes, for now,' I say airily. 'It depends on how long I end up staying there.'

Estella nods.

'Shall I make the arrangements?' asks Jane-Elizabeth. 'When would you like to go?'

'First thing in the morning,' I reply.

'Of course. I'll get on to it,' she says, without batting an eyelid. Impulsive travel is part of what my family does.

'Thanks, Jane-Elizabeth.' I smile gratefully as I stand up. 'Now if you'll excuse me, I'm going to pack and turn in. I want to be up bright and early for my flight.'

Thierry doesn't say anything in particular but I can tell that he's keeping an especial eye on me from the way he keeps glancing over his shoulder at me as I sit in the back seat.

Another guard drives us to the airport, and then Thierry carries my bags from the car to the small private plane that will take me to Paris Charles de Gaulle. On board, Thierry sits at the back while I relax into a large cream leather seat and refuse the champagne I'm offered.

I'm keyed up and excited, delighted at the thought that I might be seeing Miles again very soon. How will he react when he sees me? I imagine us rushing into one another's arms, and him sweeping me up with a laugh of happiness and a kiss as he vows we'll never be parted again. My imagination soon begins to take me to more fevered places than that, and try as I might, I can't stop myself thinking beautiful thoughts of making love to him with all the need that has built up over the last few days.

One of the cabin crew comes over to me and says politely, 'Can I offer you a paper, madam?'

'Thank you,' I say as she puts it down on the table in front of me. 'Could I also have some water, please?'

'Certainly,' she replies with a smile. 'And we'll be taking off in approximately ten minutes.'

I hardly hear her. I'm looking at the front page of the newspaper. To my horror, there's a large photograph of me and next to me – not Miles, as I might have expected, but a picture of Jacob, my ex. The headline screams at me: *Freya boyfriend HIV shock!!!*

I'm gasping and confused as I try to take in what the newsprint is saying, but it swims in front of my eyes.

HIV? What . . .? How?

I force myself to calm down and read the article that's under the pictures. And there it is, in cold, hard print: the whole story of Jacob's dalliance with prostitutes, the fact that he was filmed and how I was then blackmailed to buy the film and hush the sordid business up. The HIV reference comes from the fact that I had to be tested for all the known STDs once we found out what Jacob had been up to. To my huge relief, the story is not claiming that Jacob has HIV which he's passed to me – although the attention-grabbing headline is obviously meant to imply that – but only that it was a possibility. Still, the article takes great pleasure in describing Jacob's predilections and detailing what he got up to with the girls he hired.

I realise my hands are shaking as the stewardess sets down a bottle of water and a glass beside me, pretending not to notice that my face is staring up at her from the newspaper. As she leaves me, I slump back in my seat. The plane is beginning its taxi to the runway for departure but I'm barely aware of it. I'm aghast. How has this happened? Who on earth has let the cat out of this particular bag? Surely not Jacob, who has nothing to gain from all this . . . In fact his father, a very strict and morally upright man, will be appalled by the scandal, I'm certain of that. I feel sorry, suddenly, for Jacob – not an emotion I ever expected to feel. It's bad enough for me, but at least I'm the injured party. For Jacob, it's deeply humiliating.

I pick up my phone to text him and then put it down again. I expect I'm the last person he wants to hear from right now.

Just then the little plane takes up its position and a moment later, we're roaring along the runway and up into the air, towards Paris.

By the time we arrive just over an hour later, the messages are pouring into my phone. My life is turning into a very amusing soap opera for the entertainment of my friends – at least, that's how it feels. There's a general expression of astonishment as those not in the know suddenly understand why Jacob and I broke up, and an outpouring of sympathy from those who knew why we didn't want the circumstances to get out. Lola wants to know if she can find out tomorrow's splash first, so she doesn't spill her coffee at breakfast, like she did this morning. At least that makes me laugh, even if a little ruefully.

All of this is only going to fan the flames of the media attention, and make it harder to get about without attracting the press. I remember that Paris is where Jacob's parents have their main home, and suddenly wonder if coming here was such a good idea.

But I only heard from Beth yesterday evening. I had no idea then that Paris might be tricky.

It's too late now, I think, as we land smoothly at Charles de Gaulle and Thierry ushers me from the plane to a waiting car. There are paps with long-range lenses trained on the plane and they start snapping the minute I step out.

How the hell do they know? If I weren't too old and wise for such stories, I might start to believe in witchcraft, with the way they anticipate my every move.

I'm in the car quickly and as fast as we can get out of the airport, we're on our way to the city centre.

'This is madness!' I say to Thierry, who's sitting in the front besides the driver.

'I know,' he says grimly. 'Crazy.'

We've got a couple of pap outriders for a while, chasing us on their little buzzy mopeds, but we lose them quickly. I know it won't do any good. They'll be phoning contacts in Paris, telling them we're on our way and which road we're on. They'll pick us up close to the city centre and then stay on our tails until they find out where I'm staying. I call Flora.

'Hi!' she says, sounding a little dozy. 'Are you here already?'

'Flora, it's almost nine o'clock. Are you still in bed? We've just left the airport. The thing is, I'm on the front pages again today.'

'What for? More gossip about the bodyguard?'

'Not this time. It's about Jacob. I'll explain when I see you but I've got photographers on my tail and I don't want to lead them straight to you. I'll be there as soon as I can but I might have to take a roundabout route.'

'No hurry,' says Flora. 'I need to get up anyway.'

'You students! Shouldn't you be at your course?'

'No lessons today,' Flora says with a laugh. 'Call me when you arrive.'

'I will.'

I click off the call. 'Thierry, we can't take these guys to my sister's house. We're going to have to come up with a plan. You need to let me out early, before the paps pick us up again.'

'I don't think so,' Thierry says uncertainly. 'That's not in the schedule.'

'Thierry, it's much more unsafe to lead the press straight to my sister's flat. Listen, I'll get out and go to Flora's by public transport. I can easily slip onto the train or metro somewhere. You take the car to the Ritz – I'll call there and make a booking. Go to the back as though we're going in privately. They might see I'm not in the car, but by then, they'll be good and confused. Okay?'

'My orders are to accompany you at all times—'

'Your orders have changed,' I say crisply. We're on the outskirts of the city now. There isn't much time. I see that we're approaching a red light and the car is slowing to a halt. This is my chance. Just then the light turns green and the driver makes to speed up again. Before he can, I open the door and jump out. 'Stay at the Ritz till I contact you,' I cry as I hit the road and slam the door shut behind me. The car has to move off and I'm forced to dive between the traffic, before I'm caught in a rush of moving cars. With a dash and an apology to the barrage of horns, I make it to the pavement in time to see my car taking Thierry away into town.

I'm free!

I'll go to Flora's but not yet. Thierry knows her address, I'll be easy to find there. I need to use my freedom while I have it.

Two hours later, I'm strolling into a pretty café in the Marais district of Paris. It's a chic place that looks more like a sophisticated sitting room than a coffee shop, with book-lined walls and velvet sofas.

I found a station without too much difficulty using my phone, and as the train took me into the city, I called Beth to arrange a meeting. From the station, I took the métro but got out early so that I could enjoy my walk through Paris, a city I've always loved. The weather is cold but bright, and I'm perfectly equipped for a city walk, with my flat biker boots, jeans and belted quilted jacket with a fur-edged hood. Over my shoulder is my bag – my luggage is still in the car with Thierry – and I feel as though I could go anywhere and be anyone. Except, that is, for whenever I pass a newsstand and see my face and Jacob's staring out at me. Then I'm glad for my cashmere beret and the big pair of dark glasses I'm wearing.

I spot Beth as soon as I go into the warmth of the café. She's engrossed in something on her tablet, her fair head bent over it. I feel a rush of affection as I see her, as though I'm meeting an old friend, which is odd because we've only met once before.

'Hi!' I say, taking a chair at her table.

She looks up and beams at me. 'Freya, you made it. Lovely to see you.'

We drop kisses on each other's cheeks in greeting and Beth orders me a coffee.

'You seem very occupied,' I say, nodding to the tablet.

She flushes happily. 'Wedding plans,' she explains. 'It's easy to spend hours looking at all the different options. But I have a good idea of what we want, so it's just a question of locating it.'

'You're not wasting any time,' I say, smiling.

335

'No – we don't want to. We want to get married as soon as we can, now we've decided. I'd love to have a Christmas wedding.'

'Very romantic – but Christmas isn't that far away. Can you really plan everything so fast?' I think about the enormous parties my father has held, or the ones I've attended all over the world, ones that are months in the planning. 'What about your dress? It can't be made in time, can it?'

She laughs merrily. 'Your face is funny! You look really worried! I'm not expecting to wear haute couture, handmade in an atelier in the rue Cambon. I'll be happy with something beautiful that I find in some quirky little shop somewhere. And I could organize it all for next week if I had to – we don't want a huge wedding, just our closest friends and family.' Beth looks thoughtful. 'That's why getting married here in Paris may be best.'

'Can you just decide that?'

'Well, we have to be resident in this country for a while but as Dominic keeps a flat here, that's fine. There's a bit of official documentation we have to sort out – medical certificates, birth certificates and a legal affidavit, but nothing we can't arrange fairly fast.'

I look at her, impressed. She seems completely unfazed by the idea of marrying in a city she doesn't know well at very short notice. 'Let me know if I can help,' I say.

'Maybe we can go wedding dress shopping together,' she replies with a smile, as the waiter brings my coffee.

'That sounds fun,' I say, meaning it. 'I'd love to.'

Beth sips at her own coffee before she says, 'But you haven't come here for that, have you?'

It's my turn to flush now. The question has been burning in my mind. 'Is Miles in Paris yet?'

'He's arriving at the flat today,' she says. I can see sympathy in her eyes: she must know what it's like to feel the way I do – mad about someone but somehow not able to be with him.

'Where's he been?'

'I have no idea. I know that he's been footloose for a few years while he's been a bodyguard. Since he returned from Afghanistan and left the army, he hasn't settled, according to Dominic. I think he has a place somewhere in Scotland but he never goes there.'

I lean towards her, eager to learn all I can about Miles. We've experienced such amazing intimacy together and yet I know so little about him. 'What happened in Afghanistan? Dominic hinted about something that took place there.'

'I really don't know, I'm afraid,' Beth says apologetically. 'Miles is an old friend of Dominic, but he hasn't talked about him much and we've barely seen him together. But now you mention it, I think I have heard Dominic say something about it all . . .'

'What?' I stare at her, willing her to remember. She thinks hard but still looks blank.

'I'm sorry – I really don't know. I can ask Dominic if you like, but I have a feeling that he won't tell me.' She gives me a sideways look. 'You and Miles – this is all very new, isn't it?'

I nod. 'It's crazy, the way it happened.'

Beth leans towards me, now, her eyes bright. 'Tell me the whole thing. I love a good romance.'

It's almost an hour later when I finish. We've had another coffee each in the meantime while I opened my heart to

Beth and related the story of our crash, the sojourn on the mountainside and everything that's happened since.

Beth has listened, asking the occasional question, with rapt attention and now she shakes her head. 'Wow. That's amazing. You two have been through so much already – talk about a fiery start!'

'I'm worried it's all over,' I say gloomily. 'I don't have a clue how Miles feels about me, or if he can overlook the fact that I'm a Hammond, and the daughter of a man he now despises.'

'I'm sure he doesn't despise your father,' Beth reassures me. 'He knows your dad just wants what's best for you. It sounds to me like your father has a lot of other influences on him too – this Pierre man doesn't sound very helpful.'

I nod. 'He feeds Dad's paranoia – it keeps him in a job, after all.'

'I hadn't realised you were one of the Hammond sisters,' Beth remarks, stirring the foam on her coffee. 'It certainly makes things a little less straightforward for you. The press watches your every move, doesn't it?'

'Yes!' I exclaim. 'It's a nightmare. And somehow my private life ends up there for everyone to read. The latest is a story about my ex and me – it's on the front pages! Intimate details of my life served up for everyone like I'm some kind of real-life soap opera.'

'It must be horrible,' Beth says sincerely. 'I'm really sorry.'

'No wonder Miles doesn't want to be a part of it,' I say, my shoulders slumping.

'Don't worry about that – Miles is a stubborn character. He wouldn't let things like that stand between him and what he wants.'

I look up at her, my expression pleading. 'So why has he just walked out of my life like this?'

'You shouldn't rush him,' Beth says gently. 'I know you want everything to happen right now, but this is all very sudden. You both need time to adjust to this. He just left his job yesterday – he must have a lot on his mind.'

I feel selfish and stupid. 'Of course. You're right. I'm only thinking about it from my point of view.' I shut my eyes and sigh. 'I feel like I'm going to mess this up. I really do.'

Beth puts her hand over mine and shakes it comfortingly. 'You won't. But you need to calm down and not rush things too much.'

'Beth . . .' I hesitate, not sure how to ask what I feel I need to know. 'Miles has said to me that there was a woman in his past . . . a woman who died. Do you know anything about that?'

She looks back at me, her grey eyes wide. 'I don't. How awful. Dominic hasn't said. I'll ask him and if I find anything out, I'll let you know.'

I look at my watch. 'I ought to go. My sister's waiting for me, and my bodyguard will be getting frantic.' I sigh. 'I'd better put in an appearance so that I can be safely accounted for and monitored.'

'It's so strange that you're not free to do as you want.' Beth shakes her head. 'I can't imagine it.'

I smile at her. 'That's why it's great to be here with you, free and unnoticed. Just doing a normal thing like having coffee and chatting.'

Beth looks aghast. 'Oh my goodness, that's awful! You can't do something as simple as this without being watched?'

'Not usually. If my father could relax our security and let us sink more into anonymity, things might be easier. But he feels the risks are too great. And besides . . .' I shrug. 'The press aren't going to lose interest in us anytime soon. I know I just have to live with that.'

Beth's expression becomes determined. 'That's just terrible. If I can help you, I will. We'll sort something out, I promise.'

Beth's words cheer me up, and when we say goodbye and she promises to let me know what she can as soon as possible, I feel a little more light-hearted. She's right, I mustn't pressure Miles before he's ready. We've both got a lot of stuff to process, after all. But I can't help longing to see him as soon as I can.

I text Flora to tell her I'll be with her within the hour, and then wander through the streets of Paris, watching people going about their lives, making my way towards Flora's flat in the Marais. When I check my phone, there's a message from Lola.

Freya, I've just had Jacob call me wanting to know where you are. He's in a terrible state about this story in the papers. I told him I don't know. Has he tried to call you? He might be trying to reach you. Speak soon Lx

There's a message from Jane-Elizabeth too:

I hope you had a good journey to Paris. We're all horrified to see the newspapers today. Your father is investigating the leak right now, and limiting the damage. By the way, Jacob called, wanting to know

340

your whereabouts. I told him you're in Paris, I hope that's all right. He might want to contact you. Let me know if I can help. Love J-E

I read the messages twice, wondering why Jacob hasn't called me himself. He knows that I wanted to keep this out of the papers as much as he did, but it's out there now, and who knows how? It's hard to trust anyone – someone in the lawyers' offices might have leaked it, or one of the girls involved might have decided to make some money out of her connection to me. Even though Jacob betrayed me and caused me such pain, I feel sorry for him now. He's been publicly humiliated and I don't think he deserves that, even if he is a selfish playboy. Besides, it will hurt his parents deeply, and they don't deserve that either.

I'm wondering whether to call him myself when my phone rings. I don't recognise the number and when I answer, it turns out to be a very panicky Thierry on the other end, wanting to know where I am.

'I'm fine!' I soothe. 'I'm on my way to Flora's right now. Everything's okay. I'll let you know when I'm there. Just sit back and enjoy the hotel. I'm sorry the Ritz is closed for refurbishment – I'd forgotten about that – but I'm sure you'll be very comfortable at the Hôtel de Vendôme for now.'

'I can't enjoy myself,' he says, exasperated. 'My job is to look after you.'

'Relax, Thierry, really. It'll all be back on track soon, you'll see. I'll call when I get to Flora's.'

'I'll go there now and wait for you.'

'No – there's no need. Flora's got her own security. It's really not necessary. Bye, Thierry!'

When I end the call, I think for a second and on impulse I summon up Jacob's number and ring it. He doesn't answer and I don't leave a message on his voice mail. If he wants me, he can call me himself. I'm not sure what I want to say to him anyway – just to sympathise, I suppose, and tell him that my father is trying to discover who leaked the story. Even though I feel for him, I still remember how much he hurt me with his behaviour. If he hadn't done it, we wouldn't both be in this situation.

I put my phone away and press on towards Flora's flat.

CHAPTER TWENTY-TWO

When I turn into the road where Flora's flat is, I come to a dead stop. Flora lives not far from the Place des Vosges, in a small winding little street lined with beautiful old buildings in mellow stone that reach up several storeys, each with narrow, elegant windows adorned with tiny wrought-iron balconies. Outside Flora's building, photographers are hanging around, smoking and chatting, their huge black cameras round their necks. The sight makes me feel physically sick, my hands prickling with sweat. I dart into a doorway and call Flora.

'You've got a press pack outside!'

'I know,' she says apologetically. 'They turned up this morning, I've no idea why.'

'Because I'm on the front page again, that's why!'

'Oh, yes. I forgot about that. I haven't seen the papers yet.'

'How do they all know where you live?'

'I've no idea.' Flora's tone is weary. 'I've given up wondering about it. Just come inside. My door code is 1509.'

I realise that I'm shaking. 'I can't. I can't face them.'

'Just walk past them and don't look up! You know the drill.'

'Flora, I mean it – I really can't!'

There's a pause and I can sense her exasperation. 'Then what are you going to do?'

'I don't know. I'll think of something.'

'You shouldn't have given your security the slip like that. You need your bodyguard to get you past them without being hassled.'

'I just need to be free, Flora! You must be able to understand that. I have to be able to live like a normal person.'

'Of course I understand. But you and I both know it's not going to happen.'

'I'll call you later,' I say, leaving the shelter of the doorway and marching in the opposite direction, away from Flora's flat. 'When I've figured out what I'm going to do.'

I don't know where I'm going, I only know that I've got to get away from the press. I can't take them right now. If they get my picture, I'll be on the front pages again tomorrow, the subject of frenzied speculation about what I'm doing in Paris, and what state my love life is in.

I just need some time and space to sort myself out! I can't live with this kind of scrutiny.

I'm filled again with a wild longing for Miles. I want the security of his presence, I yearn to feel that deep inner sense of safety that I have when I'm with him.

Where are you, Miles? What are you thinking? Are you wondering about me? I'm sure that if he knew how I felt right now, Miles would be with me in an instant, wrapping his strong arms around me and reassuring me that I don't have to worry.

But he also knows I can cope. He knows I'm strong when I have to be.

The thought floats into my mind and comforts me. I pull out my phone again and ring Beth.

'Hi, Freya.'

'Beth . . .'

'Are you all right?' She picks up on the anxiety in my voice at once. 'Where are you? Haven't you reached your sister?'

'The press are all over her street. I can't bear them to find out where I am – I won't have a hope of any privacy if they do.'

There's a tiny pause and then Beth says decisively, 'Come here.'

My heart flips over. 'Is Miles there?'

'Not yet. Dominic's not here either. Come right away, I insist.'

'All right,' I say, grateful of the refuge, and she gives me the address of an apartment in the smart area of St Germain-des-Prés. 'I'll be there as soon as I can.'

I make my way towards Bastille and on the Boulevard Beaumarchais I manage to find a taxi. It's only a short drive along the Left Bank to the beautiful, polished district where Beth and Dominic's apartment is situated. We stop in front of a huge flat-fronted building in beautiful pale stone, with a vast double door of glossy black wood. A smaller access door is cut into it, with a buzzer set in a brass surround on the wall nearby. I ring the buzzer and a moment later the small door swings open, revealing a concierge, an old man in a grey uniform.

'*Oui, Madamoiselle?*' he asks, fixing me with a piercing gaze.

'*Je voudrais visiter l'apartement C, s'il vous plaît.*'

'*Vous êtes . . .?*'

'*Mademoiselle Hammond.*'

My name doesn't seem to register with him, but he returns to his small office just inside the door and checks a list. I'm on it, evidently, because he comes out again and beckons me in. Inside the door is a lush courtyard, the building around it rising up five storeys. The concierge indicates a wide hallway to one side, where an old, very broad and uneven wooden staircase leads upwards. '*Le deuxième étage*,' he says, and I start to climb the ancient stairs. They're highly polished, their unevenness part of their charm. I love the way Paris has these beautiful places hidden away, little oases of calm and beauty so close to the busy city streets.

When I reach the second floor, I tap the brass knocker on the elegant white front door. A moment later, the door is opened and Beth stands there, beaming at me.

'You made it! And you're alone . . . no press?'

I shake my head. 'Mission accomplished. No one has a clue where I am.'

'Excellent. Come in. Would you like some tea? I was just about to have some myself.'

'English tea?'

'Of course.'

'Yes please. I love English tea.'

I follow her through the stylish apartment. It's light and spacious, with classical proportions and signs everywhere of its venerable age: marble fireplaces, ornate plasterwork and antique shutters at the windows. But it's been decorated in a cool, modern style that makes it feel calm and fresh. The kitchen is small, clad entirely in black marble and supplied with high-spec chrome appliances. I lounge against the marble counter as Beth makes the tea.

'I take it you weren't expecting the press to know you were going to your sister's flat,' she says as she gets out the cups.

I shake my head. 'No. I've no idea how they found out.'

Beth frowns. 'Have you told anyone that you're here?'

'No one. Friends and family know I'm in Paris, but not exactly where.'

'Then you should definitely keep it that way. There're obviously some leaks going on.'

I rack my brains, trying to think about which of my friends might be passing information about me to the press. I suppose it's not unlikely that one of my many acquaintances might be amusing themselves and earning a little money by informing on me. But only my closest friends know the latest news, and I trust all of them because they suffer from media attention almost as much I do. Why would any of them suddenly decide to start betraying me? 'I can't think who it might be. No one who knows my intimate business would want to spill the beans.'

Beth puts tea bags into the cups and says, 'So this morning you find that information about your ex and you is all over the papers. Who knew about that?'

'Only me and my father, some of our lawyers, our head of security . . . and, of course, Jacob and whoever he told.'

'I see.' Beth makes a face. 'Tricky. It could be anyone. If the papers are prepared to pay well for information, there could be any amount of people who can get access to it.'

'And even if they don't have informants, they can find out anyway,' I point out. 'I was found by a photographer in Klosters even though no one knew I was there. Not even my family or closest friends.'

'That *is* strange,' Beth says, frowning.

'Miles one day, Jacob the next. It all feeds the appetite for information about me.' I take the cup of tea that Beth offers me and follow her down the hall to the sitting room. 'And you can imagine what kind of trouble it causes – I've fallen out badly with my father over Miles, and my ex might be a greedy playboy, but he doesn't deserve this, and neither do I.'

'So you guys appearing in the papers is what's made all this go so crazy – with Miles walking out on his job and all the rest of it.'

We sit down opposite each other on white sofas. I nod and sigh. 'It's unbelievable.'

'I hope you can both sort it out, that's all,' Beth says fervently. 'I'm afraid I've got no more news for you. Dominic was out when I got back this morning and I don't know when he'll be home. He could be meeting Miles right now, for all I know.'

I feel a prickle spread over my skin as I consider the possibility of Miles walking in through the door at this very moment. A deep hunger for him possesses me, something so fundamental that I feel as though I couldn't go on existing much longer without him.

I say softly, 'I just hope it hasn't gone so far that Miles wants to bail on me.'

'He's not like that,' she says adamantly. 'I'm sure of it. You wait and see.' A thoughtful look comes over her face. 'I've just had an idea. No one but me knows you're here right now. Why don't you draft three or four different messages, each saying that you're going to a different location? Send them to the people closest to you and see what happens. If the press pack goes to one of those locations, you'll know that they're the leak.'

I gasp. 'That's a good idea. But who shall I send them to?'

'Send them to your most trusted first, so they can be

eliminated. Then go through your address book until you find the source!' Beth smiles triumphantly.

'Okay,' I say, enthused. 'Let's do it.'

We draw up a message that reads:

Hi, Flora's flat here in Paris is surrounded by press, so I'm going to sneak off to the ... I'm sure they won't find me there. Speak soon. Love Freya.

We insert the names of six different hotels and send the messages off: to Jane-Elizabeth at home who always deals with my travel arrangements and passes on to my father whatever he needs to know, to Summer, to Flora (with the message altered to read 'your flat') and to my three closest girlfriends, Lola, Eugenie and Stephanie.

When the messages are sent, I sit back and say, 'How long do you think it will take?'

Beth shrugs. 'I've no idea. Hopefully the press pack will stay right where they are, or just disperse and not turn up at the other locations. That way you'll know you've got a watertight inner circle of trust.'

We drink more tea and I get some replies to my messages, most just acknowledging the one I sent. Beth and I talk about Miles and about Dominic and the forthcoming wedding. She tells me some of the story of her own romance, with its rocky beginnings, and how her and Dominic's lives are now more settled, although full of constant travelling because of Dominic's work.

'I've learned to adapt my own career to moving around. And if I need to, I can settle in London or New York for a while on my own. But we both hate being apart for too long. We need each other,' she says simply.

I nod. I feel I understand, even though my own feelings for Miles are relatively new. When your world is centred around another person, what's the point in being away from them?

The telephone rings suddenly and we both jump. Beth goes over to answer it and it's clear at once that she's talking to Dominic.

'Yes, okay . . . I see. That's fine. I'll see you later, darling. Goodbye.' When she's put the phone down, she turns to me and says, 'He's with Miles now.'

My stomach spins over in a whirl of delight. Miles! 'Will they be here soon?'

Beth shakes her head. 'I don't think so. Dominic says they're stopping to eat before they come back here. I got the impression there are things they want to discuss in private.'

Now my excitement is turning to fear. 'What things?'

'Miles has got to think about his future, I suppose,' Beth replies.

I don't say anything, but I feel a veil of misery falling over me. I hate the idea that he might be considering a future without me. I don't want him to discuss it with Dominic, I want us to plan a future together.

Beth can see my expression and she says in a comforting voice, 'Don't worry – you're already assuming the worst. That doesn't mean it will happen. Just wait and see.'

At that moment my mobile rings and I pick it up. Flora's number is on the display. 'Hi, what's up?'

'Well . . .' Flora sounds bemused. 'I know you've decided to stay somewhere else, but if you want to change your mind, you can. All the photographers have just left.'

'Really? The press have gone?' I raise my eyebrows at Beth. 'Where do you think they've moved to?'

'I've no idea, unless they're at the George V. That's where you are now, isn't it?'

'Er . . . yeah. Listen, I might come to you after all. But I'll be a little while, all right?'

Flora sighs. 'All this toing and froing is very confusing. Lucky for you I planned to be in today. Just come over whenever you like.'

I put the phone down and gaze at Beth, who's staring back wide-eyed. 'Did you hear that? The press have left Flora's flat.'

'So where have they gone?' Beth says breathlessly. 'We need to find out. Then we'll know who's behind the leaks.'

I feel excited but also bleak. I've sent my fictional whereabouts to my very closest contacts, including my own sisters. It looks as though one of them is a traitor. Beth and I pull up a map of Paris on her tablet and we note exactly where to find the hotels I've used as possible destinations.

Beth says, 'We need to get to each one as quickly as possible to see where the press pack has gathered.'

'Shall we split up? Look, I'll go to the Hôtel George V, Le Meurice and Hôtel Le Bristol – they're all fairly close to one another. You go to the others, and the first one to spot the press calls the other. I don't think it will take long.'

Beth nods. 'It's the quickest way. You can borrow a slouchy hat so that you're even less recognisable. Come on, let's go right now.'

Ten minutes later, I'm striding down the Avenue George V towards the first hotel. Beth's hat is covering me very effectively and my sunglasses lend another layer of concealment. I don't think I can be recognised. Besides, it's cold and the afternoon is darkening, which means I can walk along in the shadows. When I reach the impressive exterior of the huge Hôtel George V, with its grey frontage and rows of windows, I'm filled with relief. There's no one outside – no shabby photographers with their ubiquitous mopeds, anyway. Flora is in the clear. I knew she would be. Just at that moment I get a text from Beth.

No one here. Summer is not the source. Heading to the next.

I take a turn to the right, heading towards Hôtel le Bristol on the rue de Faubourg Sainte-Honoré, a magnificent hotel in a classic Parisian building of plain grey stone with the high leaded roof broken by garret windows. It only takes about ten minutes from the Avenue George V before I see it in the distance. The light is fading now as I approach and I have to take off my dark glasses to see where I'm going. There seems to be something going on near the entrance, and I blink hard into the twilight to see what's happening. A text comes through just then from Beth.

Your friend Stephanie hasn't told the press – still no sign of them. Two down, one to go.

I click off the message, my heart sinking. I can see that a doorman is outside the hotel remonstrating with some photographers, a couple of whom I recognise from earlier in the day. He's asking them to leave but they evidently have no intention of doing so. I stand as near as I dare on the pavement and watch, the familiar sick feeling curling in my stomach. I can't stand the sight of these men, with their cameras and their utter ruthless devotion to getting that shot. But this time, it isn't them causing my nausea.

I reach for my phone. Beth picks up on the second ring. 'Freya?'

'They're here. I've found them,' I say through dry lips.

'Oh no. Oh my God. Where are you?'

'I'm at the Bristol.'

There's a pause as Beth takes this in. 'But that means . . .'

'Yes. It's Jane-Elizabeth. She's the leak. No wonder they've been on my tail so fast. She knows everything, everything about me.' My hands are shaking and now I feel truly sick, as though I want to throw my guts up right there on the street.

'Oh my God. I'm so sorry.'

'Don't worry about it,' I say hopelessly. I feel as though my world is turning on its head. Jane-Elizabeth is the closest thing I have to a mother. How can she betray me like this? I'm too shocked and appalled to cry.

'I'll meet you back at the apartment,' Beth says. 'If you want to come back to our place, that is? Or do you want to go back to your sister's?'

I open my mouth to reply, but before I can, I'm grabbed from behind, as a blunt-nosed object is pressed into my back, and a voice hisses in my ear, 'There you are, you bitch. I knew you'd come here.'

'What?' I cry, startled. 'Who are you?'

'Shut up,' orders the voice. 'Don't open your mouth again.'

353

I hear the faint sound of Beth's voice coming from my phone but I'm being hustled to a waiting car and I can't lift the phone to my ear. The next moment I'm thrown on to the back seat, the door is slammed shut and we're driving off.

CHAPTER TWENTY-THREE

Fear is coursing through me. I have no idea where I'm being taken and I'm too scared to look at the man sitting to my left. He's clearly anxious from the sound of his breathing and the way his limbs are fidgeting. Then, slowly, as my own agitation subsides, I realise that I know this person. His presence is familiar to me. I slide my gaze over and catch a glimpse of his profile against the window.

'Jacob?' I say wonderingly.

He turns towards me at once, his eyes glittering dangerously. 'Shut up.'

'Where are you taking me? What is this?' My fear subsides a little as I realise that the man who has forced me into this car is my ex-boyfriend and surely he can't mean to hurt me. But in answer Jacob shoves viciously with whatever it is he's been pointing into my side. 'Ouch! That hurt!'

'You heard me! I said shut up!' he shrieks. 'Don't try and talk to me – you *will* regret it, I promise.'

I'm startled by the sudden pain he's inflicted on me, and by the fact that I've never seen Jacob like this before. He looks different – wild-eyed, pale, sweating. He's not the smooth-faced playboy, swaggering about in his designer clothes and showing off his credit cards and fast cars. Not at all.

I glance down at my phone. The screen is blank, my call to Beth ended somehow in the tussle to get me into the car.

I don't think I can contact anyone without attracting attention. The screen will light up in the darkness and be instantly noticed. In fact, I should hide it in case it rings and Jacob remembers that I have it. I slide my phone underneath my thigh, hoping that's enough to muffle the sound if it should ring. Surely Beth must be wondering what's happened to me?

I want to ask Jacob where we're going and what he wants me but the wild note in his voice means I take seriously his order not to speak to him. Instead, I try to work out where we're going but the darkness outside means I soon lose my sense of direction and have to keep alert for landmarks that will help me. Jacob leans forward and mutters to the driver and we keep on going through the falling night. I wonder if I can jump out when we stop at lights but I have a feeling that the doors are centrally locked and I don't want to try and fail.

I feel the phone vibrate before its ring fills the air but there's nothing I can do to stop the sound. As soon it rings, Jacob stiffens. He holds out his hand, his expression like nothing I've ever seen before. 'Don't answer it! Give that to me,' he barks.

I pull my phone out. It's Beth's name on the display. 'Jacob, it's my friend, she'll be worried about me. Let me answer and tell her I'm safe—'

'I don't give a shit!' shouts Jacob and he goes to snatch the phone from me. As quickly as I can, I press to connect the call and cry out, 'Beth, I'm with Jacob, he's got me!'

But I don't know how much she can hear, if anything, before Jacob hits me hard across the face with one hand and takes the phone with the other.

I gasp with pain and shock as the sting of his flat palm burns over my cheek. I turn to stare at him. His face is a mixture of anger and fear, as though he can hardly believe what he's just done.

'Jacob!' I say in a stunned voice. 'You hit me! What are you doing? What the hell are you thinking?'

He looks like a frightened boy for a moment, and then his face becomes maddened and resolute. 'Don't you talk to me like that,' he hisses. 'You're to blame for all this shit! You've ruined my life and you're going to damn well pay for it!'

'What are you talking about?' I demand, angry now myself. 'How have I ruined your life? I didn't force you to sleep with those prostitutes!'

He looks furious and I wonder for a moment if he intends to hit me again. Then he pulls back, and says, 'Don't say another fucking word, Freya. I mean it.'

I decide to keep quiet for now. Jacob is clearly in a volatile state and I don't want to make things worse. I knew he would be upset by the press reports, but his reaction seems out of all proportion – and how can he think of blaming me for it? I have the distinct feeling that I need to find out more about what's brought him to this, but that I'll need to tread carefully while Jacob is this agitated.

I gaze out of the window, continuing to wonder where we're heading. I wanted to get close to Miles and instead I'm being taken further away from him. Is this how it's going to be for us, with the world doing its best to keep up apart? He doesn't even know yet that I'm in Paris. What will Beth do about the fact that I've disappeared? She doesn't have a way to contact my family. But then, I remember with a fresh hit of despair, I can't trust

Jane-Elizabeth after all. A piece of the jigsaw falls into place – how would Jacob have known how to find me if he hadn't been told about my whereabouts by the one person who knew I might be at the Hôtel le Bristol? Who, of course, is Jane-Elizabeth.

The whack that Jacob gave me across my face counts as no pain at all compared to this awful blow.

The car comes to a halt in front of a row of garages in a back street. I wonder where on earth we can be and the unsavoury atmosphere of the location makes me even more apprehensive. The next moment Jacob is round at my side of the car, opening the door and hauling me out.

'What are you doing?' I shriek, really scared now. 'Let me go!'

He grabs my arms and I realise that the driver has got out and has opened one of the garage doors. Jacob pushes me over towards the dark space beyond.

'Jacob!' I cry, bewildered. He isn't the man I remembered at all – the old Jacob would never treat me like this. *What on earth is he capable of now?* 'Stop it! No!'

He won't listen and he's far too strong for me. Against my will, I'm half pushed and half pulled to the sour-smelling darkness, then he shoves me hard so that I fall down on to the cold concrete floor. He steps back, slams down the door and just as I shout 'No!' one more time, it closes with a crash and I'm alone in complete blackness.

I sit on the chilly concrete for several minutes, trying to take in what's just happened. I'm completely bewildered by how everything has transformed for me in such a short time. Just over an hour ago, I was drinking tea with Beth in a luxurious flat in St-Germain. Now I'm alone in the dark in a freezing garage in God only knows where, with no phone and no way out. I'm half terrified and half confused. I can't believe that Jacob would really hurt me, and yet he's already struck me a hard blow across the face. Why is he so angry? How can he possibly blame me for the revelation of his sordid past? He must realise that I had nothing to do with it.

I'm shivering, despite my warm coat and hat. The darkness is beginning to oppress me and awful feelings of fear are swirling up inside me. I'm alone. I know this terrible sensation from all those years ago, but somehow the fear is magnified by the blackness I'm surrounded by and the utter isolation. I'm shaking all over, on the edge of hysteria and total panic.

Stay calm, stay calm! I pull in a deep gasping breath and release it on a shaky exhale. I do it again and again. I hear a voice in my mind.

Winter, you're brave and strong. Don't be afraid. Don't let them break you.

'Miles?' I whisper. 'Miles?'

There's no answer from the silent blackness but I feel some measure of comfort somehow, as though Miles is thinking about me and sending me strength. I know I can endure this if I have to because I'm certain Miles believes I can.

I don't know how long I'm alone in the darkness. At one point, I try to get up and find my way to the wall so I can feel my way around and maybe locate a light switch but the enterprise is too difficult and dangerous. There are obstacles in my way and I have no idea what I might be grasping hold of. I sink back to the floor and wait, passing the time by thinking about Miles and recalling every moment we've spent together since that day when we plunged down the mountain together.

Keep the faith, Miles said to me as he left me yesterday morning, and I'm going to do that. We might not be together at this very moment but I can still take strength from him.

I will keep the faith. I won't let anyone break me again.

It feels like about three hours later when the sound of an engine outside brings me back to the present moment. I'm instantly alert. I've thought hard about what Jacob's motives could be for imprisoning me like this, but I've drawn a blank. I need to make sure he stays calm now – I have a feeling he's teetering on the edge of doing something stupid in retaliation for whatever it is he thinks I've done to him.

There's a crash and the garage door opens, revealing the dark shape of a man. I blink hard, trying to make out if it's Jacob.

'Get up,' says a harsh voice in heavily accented English. It's not Jacob's.

'Who are you?' I call. 'Where's Jacob?'

'No questions,' he retorts. 'I take you to Jacob.'

I realise he probably doesn't have enough English to answer me anyway, and his mention of Jacob reassures me a little. Besides, I'm desperate to get out of here. I've been as strong as I can, but the cold, lonely darkness is almost more than I can stand.

The voice says more sternly, 'Come out here. Get in the car.'

'Okay, I'm coming.' I'm stiff with the cold of sitting on

the concrete floor and I stagger as I get up. The man grabs my arm and yanks me hard, so that I almost fall before I catch my balance. Then he pulls me out of the garage and into the street, where the dim light from the street lamps on the road is incredibly comforting after the pitch black inside the garage. A car is waiting, its engine purring and the back door open. The man thrusts me on to the back seat of the car and I catch a glimpse of him: he's a meaty type with a buzz cut and the kind of stupid mean face that gazes out of pictures accompanying stories about mindless killers. He slams the door shut, climbs into the front seat and we're driving off, heading somewhere else entirely.

I don't think there's any point in asking this thug questions: he doesn't seem like the confiding type. I wonder if I should try to escape, but I'm so tired and stiff now, I wouldn't be likely to make much of a fist of it. Besides, they're apparently taking me to Jacob, and he'll be able to explain what's going on. It's been a very long day, and the cold and shock I've suffered have exhausted me. The purring engine of the car is soothing and I have a deep desire to sleep but I know I must fight it. Rather than waste my energy trying to run, I should keep my wits about me. It's what Miles would tell me to do, I know that.

Stay alert, Winter. Where are they taking you and why?

We're back in the busier streets of the city now. There are bright lights and people everywhere. Where are we going?

I try to think it through as we go. Would Jacob really want to hurt me? He's vain and cocksure, but he's essentially weak. Despite the slap he gave me, I can't believe he would harm me. It doesn't fit with anything I've known about him.

I can hear Miles's voice again, almost as if he were at my ear, talking softly.

Maybe he's changed. Perhaps he's fallen in with a bad crowd. Maybe there are tough guys who've got close to him for the sake of his money. Don't take anything for granted, Winter. Do you understand?

Jacob must blame me for the story getting out. But what good will it do to hurt me after the event? It's out there now. We both have to face that. The only way to deal with it is to live it down in silence and with as much dignity as we can muster, until it's yesterday's news and no one cares.

I think of Jane-Elizabeth, and imagine her sending emails and making furtive calls to contacts in the press, passing on my secrets and no doubt getting a handsome payback at the same time. She is probably the source of this whole scandal as well. Should I tell Jacob that, to convince him I'm not to blame?

The thought of Jane-Elizabeth's betrayal feels me with deep, almost unbearable sadness.

Why, Jane-Elizabeth? Do you really hate me that much? Does Dad not pay you enough to secure your loyalty?

I realise that the car is pulling to a halt again, this time outside a place I recognise, except that we are not stopping at the front as I expect, but around the back. I'm hustled out of the car and through a side entrance, then into a service elevator where my new friend presses the penthouse button. I know where we're going now, and I stand straight and silent, not willing to speak to the thug at my side. It's not as though he has anything to tell me anyway. The elevator begins its glide towards the top of the building.

Where are you, Winter?

I'm at Jacob's apartment. I know this place.
Stay alert, okay? I want you to look after yourself.
I will.

The conversation that's going on with Miles in my head is keeping me calm. The service elevator opens and the hard guy with me pushes me out and along a corridor. We walk along at a quick pace, and I can tell he's nervous that we might be seen. Hence the service elevator, I suppose.

I suddenly think about Thierry. He must be having one hell of a terrible day. From the moment I leapt out of the car and headed off alone, he must have been sweating with anxiety. And now his worst nightmares have come true. The boss's daughter has been abducted on his watch. He might not even know. He might still pacing the suite at the Hôtel de Vendôme, wondering where the hell I am and when he has to make the phone call to Pierre that he's dreading, the one where he confesses that he's fucked up badly. I feel bad that I've put him in this position but I really had no choice. I'll sort things out for him if I can.

I wonder what Beth is thinking now, and how much she heard of my shouted message. What good will it do anyway? Perhaps she's called the police. I hope fervently that she hasn't. It will be world news within the hour if she has, and that will do no one any good.

We're at the penthouse door now, and the guy knocks on it lightly, his head flicking from side to side as he glances up and down the corridor. A few moments later, the door opens: another heavy, this time in a black suit, but with the same mean expression on his face, though this one doesn't seem quite as stupid as the other, perhaps because of a cunning look in his piggy eyes.

Oh God, you were right, Miles. Jacob is in with some

tough guys. What's he thinking of? He's not like this, he's really not. He's just a kid.

And now he's a kid out of his depth, Winter. He's going to be scared and that will make him dangerous. Stay very calm, do you understand?

'This way,' grunts the man in the suit, and leads me up the stairs. I don't need him. I know this apartment well. I've been to lots of parties here, with more spoiled kids than you could count, when the music's thumped and the drinks have flowed, and the drugs have spilled out over the glass coffee tables. Drugs aren't my scene but I've seen plenty of people indulging, getting high as they stare out over the magnificent view of Paris through the floor-to-ceiling windows. I've also been here alone with Jacob, watching movies with him on his cinema-screen-sized television, while the maid brought us cold beers or tubs of popcorn or whatever else we wanted. I can't believe how many vapid hours I've wasted here.

And now I'm back. And there's Jacob, sitting in his big black armchair, the one he liked to call his Bond villain chair, with one leg crossed over the other. Despite his tan, his face is pale, his skin sweaty and his pupils dilated. His light brown hair looks dingy and he's fidgeting badly. He doesn't look right at all.

The two heavies have escorted me so that I'm standing right in front of Jacob, beside one of his low glass coffee tables on the white Mongolian goatskin rug. Outside, Paris shimmers in blue and gold and touches of neon, a sparkling blanket laid out below us. I can see myself and Jacob and the two meaty men reflected in the black windows.

This feels so unreal. Maybe it's why I'm calm.

Jacob is staring at me, an aura of agitation around him. 'Hi, Freya,' he says at last.

'Hi.' I smile at him. I'm going to be calm and friendly. I don't want to give him an excuse to get angry with me. I realise now that I'm not dealing only with Jacob but with his two friends here too, the kind who look like they hurt people for a living.

Jacob coughs. He looks away as though he can't quite meet my gaze. 'Do you want something? Water? Coffee?'

'Water would be nice, thanks.'

Jacob looks at one of the heavies, who goes off without a word. He looks back at me and coughs again, while I study him intently, looking for signs of his state of mind. 'I . . . I guess you're wondering what you're doing here,' he says slowly.

'Yes.' I smile again. 'It's nicer here than in the garage though.'

He glances up at me and away. I can tell he doesn't want to think about that.

Why was I there?

Thinking time, Winter. He doesn't quite know what he wants to do with you. He's not in his right mind. Watch out.

Jacob gets up suddenly and wanders over to the window. I get the impression he's psyching himself up somehow, and when he turns back his face is twisted with anger. 'You deserved that!' he shouts. 'A few hours in that garage to think about what you've done to me!'

'What have I done?' I ask gently. 'You know I've never hurt you, Jacob. You were my boyfriend. I loved you.'

'Don't give me that!' he yells back. I wince, feeling that I've somehow made a mistake and helped to fuel his rage when I was trying to do the opposite. 'Don't give me that love stuff! You've hated me ever since I fucked those girls: Mandy and the others. You've never forgiven me, have you? You just had to have your revenge and tell the papers.'

'That's not true, Jacob,' I say firmly. 'Yes, I was hurt. But I was as desperate as you to keep the whole thing out of the press. You know that.' I don't want to tell him that I suspect it was Jane-Elizabeth who put the story out there. I have a feeling that to Jacob it might be virtually the same as me leaking it myself. 'How do you know it wasn't one of the girls?'

'No,' he says dismissively. 'I paid them off very generously and they knew what would happen if they ever told. They had no reason.'

'Then it was your lawyers? Someone at their office, maybe?'

Jacob shakes his head scornfully. 'I don't know who the hell your father uses but my dad's lawyers don't break client confidentiality. Ever.'

'Okay, okay.' I try to soothe him but I can see he's shaking and sweaty. The guard returns with a glass of water for me. I take it and drink it gratefully while I watch Jacob. He turns back to look out of the window, and he lifts his arm to run a hand through his hair, ruffling it so that it stands up straight. As he does, his shirt sleeve rises and reveals the tattoo of a rhinoceros he has high on his left bicep. I'd forgotten he had it until now, but as I notice it, I can't help remembering the last time I saw it. It was on that tape, the one that showed Jacob being serviced by his call girls. I'd been most gripped by the sight of the tattoo on his thigh, the tiny padlock with the 'F' inside that he'd had put there for me, to show his devotion. That was how I'd known for sure that the man I was watching on the sex tape was my boyfriend. But I also saw that rather crappy little rhino when it came into close-up as the camera focused for a moment on Jacob's arm.

At that moment, I hear a voice in my head but I can't recognise it or make out what it's saying. The voice floats on the outskirts of my consciousness, playing over and over like a snippet of tape that I can't quite decipher.

Jacob turns to face me. 'No, Freya. I've looked at it from all angles and it has to be you who told the papers.'

'But why would I do that?' I ask, putting the glass down on the table. I notice suddenly that my mobile phone is sitting on it, by a carved wooden bowl.

'I don't fucking know!' he roars, burying his head in his hands. I scoop up my phone and slip it into my pocket while he's not looking. The guards haven't noticed. 'Why don't you fucking well tell me?'

'I didn't do it, Jacob, I swear to you.' I stare at him, confused. 'But what does it matter? I know it's bad and humiliating but it will be forgotten. Why is it worth *this*?' I gesture at the heavies who are standing silently, watching.

Jacob walks back towards me and slumps down in his armchair, rubbing his hand compulsively across his head. He looks up at me and I can see something awful in his eyes. Utter fear. He leans towards me and says in a strained whisper, 'Freya, my dad did not know about those tapes. I cleared up the fallout without him ever knowing. My mother didn't know either. But they do now. And . . . well, you know what they're like. They're very straight, very religious. I've sworn to them that I don't misbehave, that I don't take drugs. Christ, they don't even know I've got tattoos. Now they've seen the papers. My dad got a copy of the tape from the lawyers and he watched it. He knows how much I paid the girls to buy them off afterwards. He's . . .' Jacob's face contorts, and when he looks at me, I think he's about to break down and cry. 'He's told me that's it, Freya. He's going to take away my money, my apartment, my cars . . . everything. He's told me that I have to make it on my own now, prove to him that I've changed my ways and that I can make a go of life without him.'

I nod. It's clear now. The newspaper scoop hasn't just humiliated Jacob, it's destroyed the pleasant, protected existence he's enjoyed till now. His money, gone. Everything he's taken for granted and considered his due, taken away. All that cocksure arrogance and swagger vanished, just like that. He's the same as any guy on the street, maybe worse because he's never so much as had to lift a finger to earn a penny that he's spent over the years.

And me? Am I like that too? Would I be destroyed like this without my daddy's money?

The question pierces me to the heart. I don't know. I hope not. I hope I could make it on my own. Then I realise that I've already taken that risk by pursuing Miles against my father's orders. I'm filled suddenly with a kind of elation. *I've made my choice and I chose my heart. I'll never let myself be destroyed the way Jacob has.*

I gaze at Jacob. 'You can do it!' I say firmly. 'This might be the start of something amazing. Show your dad you have the potential to do the same thing he has and make a success of yourself.'

Jacob's gone white. He's still whispering as though he doesn't want the heavies to hear what he's saying. 'You don't understand. I can't just have the tap turned off like that. I have obligations. There's stuff I have to take care of.' He nods almost imperceptibly in the direction of the two men.

Oh God. Oh Jacob. What have you done?

'I have to get money from somewhere,' Jacob says in a low, urgent voice, leaning towards me. 'A lot. And soon.'

'What are you mixed up in?' I say in a whisper, my voice sounding frightened.

He ignores my question. 'You're my only hope. Can you see that? I need money. You've got more than you need. Your dad's even richer than mine. You owe me, Freya.'

'I *owe* you?' I'm astonished.

'That leak didn't come from me. It came from you. You're the reason I'm in this fucking mess so you'd better get me out of it. And if you don't –' he leans towards me, his eyes flashing now. I can sense the depth of his desperation, '– you will be sorry. I mean it, Freya. Don't mess with us. These guys will have acid in your face before you know where the hell you are.'

I gasp. It's a terrible threat. For a second, I wonder what's happened to the sweet, slightly silly Jacob I fell in love with. Then I know: he's been lost in a dark world of drugs and crime and greed and money. There's some story of stupidity and hubris that I don't know but that I can guess at. And it's led Jacob to this – threatening me with mutilation if I don't give him the money that he's convinced himself is his due.

'I want to help you, Jacob,' I say in a shaking voice. 'But I don't have access to a lot of money in one go. You know what it's like. I get an allowance.'

'I need what you can give me right now. And then you'd

better ask your dad for the rest. You'll think of a way to persuade him.' Jacob talks in a dull, flat way as though this is something he needs to happen and he can't be bothered with the particulars. 'It will be easiest if you tell him that we're back together. You've forgiven me and you're going to come and live here with me.'

'What?' I stare at him, utterly astonished. 'You can't be serious, Jacob. Get back together? Live together? Are you crazy?'

'It's the best way,' he says with a shrug. 'You can see that, can't you? Maybe we should even get married.' A small spark shows in his eyes, the first I've seen tonight. 'Hey, that's not such a bad idea. My dad would love that. It might be the way to put everything right, too. I bet he'd forgive me if I told him we were getting married.'

I gape at him, unable to believe my ears or that he can really be serious. Then suddenly I hear a voice behind me.

'I hate to interrupt this touching proposal but I'm afraid Freya is otherwise engaged.'

I spin round in time to see the two heavies also swing round to confront whoever is in the room. My heart is racing and a thrill of joy explodes over me.

Even before I see him, I know who it is.

CHAPTER TWENTY-FOUR

Even though I've been surrounded by guards since I was tiny, I've never seen one actually holding a gun. Maybe I saw a bulge under an arm, the smooth black leather of a holster, or a glimpse of cold metal, but that was all. When we were kidnapped in Italy, I never saw a weapon. I think they knew a small girl and a sick woman were helpless enough without being menaced with guns or knives. The people who rescued us must have been armed, but the darkness and confusion meant I didn't see it.

Miles is standing there with a handgun pointed directly at Jacob's forehead.

The colour has drained from Jacob's face and his eyes are wide and staring. His hands grip the arms of his chair but he's sitting as though frozen.

Even though Miles has his weapon aimed at Jacob, I can tell that all of his attention is focused on the two heavies who are both on high alert, ready to reach for whatever they've got concealed about them.

'Put your hands up and then stay absolutely still.'

The men slowly obey him, though I can tell they're both assessing the situation and when they might be able to make a reach for a weapon.

'Move a muscle,' says Miles coldly, 'and your little golden goose here gets it. Then we'll see how useful he is to you.'

The heavies don't move, their small mean eyes fixed on Miles and their expressions stony. They don't bother to say anything. I guess words don't achieve much in their world.

Miles keeps his eyes fixed on them. 'Freya,' he says, 'go and open the window to the terrace.'

I obey at once, feeling strangely calm despite my pounding heart. My fingertips are shaking but I manage to undo the clasp of the glass door and slide it back. A blast of icy air hits me.

'Good,' says Miles. 'Now, come here. Get behind me.'

I move at once, striding across the room. I smile at him but his face stays impassive. There's just a flicker in his icy blue eyes and a tiny lift of his eyebrow.

'Right, guys – out – and keep your hands where I can see them.' Miles waves the barrel of the gun to indicate that they should all move out on to the terrace. I don't think the guards are going to obey him but then there's a high zipping sound and a bullet lodges in the white fur of the Mongolian goatskin rug. They move swiftly, Jacob leaping out of his chair as though it's just delivered him an electric shock. In a moment all three of them are on the terrace, and Miles has slid the window shut and locked it.

He turns to me. 'I don't think they're armed, but we won't risk it. Get out of the apartment as fast as you can. Take the main lift. I'll be right behind you.' He keeps his gun trained on the people outside as they stare in, the two heavies with furious expressions and Jacob's terrified. They look eerie through the glass that's darkened by the lights inside. 'Go.'

I do as he says, dashing down the stairs and out of the front door, running as fast as I can for the lift. I press the button to summon the elevator and wait, flooded suddenly with adrenalin. I'm panting hard and shaking from head to toe. Then I see Miles emerge from the flat just as the elevator pings and the doors slide open. I step in and hold the doors as he strides down the hall towards me and into the lift.

We stand and stare at one another as the doors shut, then his arms are round me and I'm lost in the warmth of his chest. I tip my head back and his mouth lands on mine. He kisses me hard and I return it with all my strength, my nerves tingling with the onslaught of delayed reaction to the situation and the delicious sensation of the kiss I've been yearning for. A great well of joy fills up inside me. We're together at last, and it feels like I've come home.

When we pull apart, I say, 'I knew you'd find me. I felt like you were with me all the time.'

He stares down at me, his expression solemn and loving at the same time. 'I had to come. From the moment Beth told me you were in danger, there was nothing else I could do.'

'What happened up there?' I ask him, wide-eyed. 'Did you kill them?'

He smiles. 'I try to make it a general rule not to kill people. They're stuck out there for a while but I don't think it will be too long. One of them will have a phone. That's why we've got to get out of here as soon as possible.'

I sigh with happiness at being so close to him. I feel as though nothing can go wrong with the world when I'm with Miles. His lips touch mine again just as the elevator comes to a stop and the doors open. He takes my hand in his.

'Come on.'

'Where are we going?'

'Somewhere private.'

A prickle of delight runs over me. 'Really?'

We walk swiftly out of Jacob's building and on to the brightly lit boulevard. In a side street beside the building, a taxi is waiting, its engine running. Miles strides over and opens the passenger door so I can climb in. As Miles gets in beside me, he says, *'Le Meurice, s'il vous plaît.'*

'That's funny. I nearly went there today,' I say, relishing the deliciousness of Miles being near. His presence is making my head whirl and my skin tingle.

'Yes, I've heard. I made Beth tell me exactly what the two of you had got up to today so I could work out what had happened.' He puts his arm round me as the taxi heads off, and we press close to one another. 'Jacob found you at the Bristol, didn't he? Beth heard something then, and then again when you managed to shout to her that you were with him.'

'Clever Beth,' I say gratefully. 'And you used that to find me?'

'It wasn't that hard. Jacob is no master criminal. Taking you to his own apartment made it easier, and I've got contacts, don't forget. I put the word out and I got some answers very quickly. Jacob's been making a name for himself, but not in the way he would like.'

'Poor Jacob,' I say softly, rubbing my cheek across Miles's shirt.

He laughs and I can hear the sound rumbling through his chest. It's beautiful and his warmth and the fresh, clean masculine smell of his skin are utterly delicious. I feel as though I can't get enough of him. 'Poor Jacob,' he says.

'He's been a complete prick to you, but you still feel sorry for him? Freya, you're gorgeous.' He kisses me again, softly and tenderly.

My heart swells with love and happiness. 'Because I can tell that he's totally useless at whatever it is he's trying to do. The idea that I might give him cash, or live with him, or *marry* him even!' I stare up at Miles, wide-eyed. 'It's ludicrous. Surely he can see that?'

Miles looks suddenly grave. 'He's out of his depth. And he's not in a fit state to distinguish between fact and fantasy. I just hope that whatever thugs he's got mixed up with can see how pathetic he is and feel sorry for him. Poor kid. Another example of what too much money can do.'

'I hope they don't hurt him!' I say, suddenly appalled that all this might actually result in real harm. It seemed like a game, or a play-acted scene when we were up in that apartment. Miles is making me realise that it was horribly real. This is how people get killed.

He hugs me. 'I hope so too, sweetheart. But you're my priority now.'

The journey to the Meurice goes quickly. We're engrossed in one another, kissing and touching, revelling in our reunion and the beauty of being together.

The driver has to cough loudly when he pulls up in front of the hotel, and the doorman opens the door of our taxi to help me out as Miles pays and we enter the building. I've put my sunglasses on and keep my head down but no one seems at all interested in us. I guess all the photographers are still waiting at the Bristol, hoping that I'll turn up there. If they knew that the heiress and the bodyguard are checking in right now at a hotel only a short distance away, they'd be cursing and leaping on those mopeds to get here as soon as possible.

Let them freeze outside the Bristol.

My elation is suddenly shattered by the memory of how the press knew where I was. It was Jane-Elizabeth who started this whole thing and who leaked the details of Jacob's peccadilloes to the press – it's the only possible explanation. She's the only one who had any access to the information. Jacob was right about one thing – it was my side who sold him down the river. What I can't understand is why Jane-Elizabeth has turned against me like this: why has she decided to ruin my relationship with my father, put me in danger even, by revealing my whereabouts to the media, and to Jacob?

It doesn't make sense.

I haven't got the first idea what I'm going to do about it, or how I'm going to confront her. I also don't want to think about it now, not when I've got this sweet reunion to enjoy in one of the most luxurious hotels in Paris.

'Come on, sweetheart,' Miles says, taking me by the arm. We follow a bellboy who leads us to an elevator which we take up to the second floor. A few moments later, he's opening the door to a beautiful suite, classically elegant and decorated in muted silks and velvets, with a view over the Tuileries gardens. A bottle of champagne sits chilling in an ice bucket and on the floor, to my astonishment, is my luggage, which I haven't seen since the morning. There's another black bag there too.

Miles tips the bellboy, then turns to see the expression on my face. He laughs as he closes the door. 'Surprise!' he says.

'You're right it's a surprise,' I say, going over to make sure that it is my bag I'm looking at. 'How did this happen?'

'It was all arranged.' Miles shrugs a little.

'So you were pretty sure that you were going to find me?' I say, laughing.

'Winter, I wasn't coming back without you,' he says, wrapping me in his arms again. 'I found out that Thierry was your security. I tracked him down at the Hôtel de Vendôme – where you apparently sent him and where he was practically chewing the carpets. He was somewhat relieved when I told him everything was all under control.'

A thought strikes me. 'I have to let Flora know where I am! She must be worried sick.'

'Beth's in touch with her. She knows you're okay and you're with me. But no one knows exactly where we are.'

'That's a relief,' I say with a sigh. 'I've begun to understand that the happiest times of my life are when it's just you and me, without the world knowing about it.' Tears suddenly fill my eyes and my lip wobbles.

'Hey, hey – are you all right? What's wrong?' Miles looks down at me anxiously.

'I . . . I found out who's been betraying me. How the press have known where to find me.'

'I know. Beth told me. I'm sorry, sweetheart.'

I sniff and try to hold in a sob. 'I haven't been able to think about it with everything else that's going on. But I can't believe that Jane-Elizabeth would do this to me!'

'Are you sure it's her?' Miles asks. 'It seems out of character to me as well. From what I've seen of Jane-Elizabeth, she's completely devoted. Unquestionably loyal.'

'I know.' I sob again, feeling the punch of betrayal all over again. 'I don't know who I can trust in the world if I can't trust her.'

Miles hugs me tighter, rocking me a little as though to calm me with the gentle movement. 'We'll work it all out. It'll be okay.'

I sniff, comforted a little. Whatever else has happened, I'm with Miles and that's the most important thing. 'Miles . . .?' I look at him, my eyes still damp.

'Yes?' He looks down tenderly.

'Is there any chance we can get some dinner? I haven't eaten all day and I'm absolutely ravenous.'

He smiles down. 'That was my very next suggestion. We're going to eat right here.'

I take a bath in the Italian marble bathroom while the hotel staff set the dining table in our sitting room and Miles orders dinner.

When I emerge from the bedroom, dressed in a simple navy-blue silk dress, there are candles flickering on the table by the French windows that give on to the Tuileries gardens, and two glasses of fizzing champagne waiting. Miles is standing looking out over the view, changed into dark trousers and a crisp shirt. He looks gorgeous against the window, broad and strong, his muscles just apparent beneath the cotton of his shirt. When he turns, I almost gasp at the sight of his handsome face and those moulded lips. He smiles at me and my whole body responds with a shimmer of delight and excitement.

'You look beautiful,' he says.

'Thank you.' I shake my head. 'When I left for Paris this morning, this is what I dreamed might happen tonight. But I had no idea what we'd have to go through to get here.'

Miles picks up the glasses of champagne and walks over, handing one to me. 'I didn't even know you were coming to Paris this morning. But I did know that I had to sort my head out. I needed to work out how I felt about you and what kind of future we might have.'

'What did you decide?' I ask softly, almost nervously, as we touch the rims of our glasses together. I hope that what happened today means that Miles has decided that he wants to be with me, but I can't take anything for granted. My heart starts to race with the fear that he might be about to let me down somehow and tell me, sweetly and gently, that it isn't to be.

Miles hesitates, looking down at the table, and then lifts his gaze to meet mine. His blue eyes are intense, a deep navy blue.

'Everything was decided the moment Beth told me you were in trouble. I felt . . . like the bottom of my world had been ripped out. The idea I might lose you was so terrible that – well – it crystallised what I thought might be the case.'

'What's the case?' I ask, gazing at him, my insides fizzing with anticipation.

'Freya, I knew I love you.'

'You knew that?'

'I . . . *know* that.'

'You love me.' I sigh happily. I feel as though some missing piece of my life has just slotted into place and made everything complete.

He presses his face to my hair and murmurs, 'I love you.'

I close my eyes and feel his fingertips stroke along the skin of my arm. Every hair stands up with excitement and

I release a long breath. His closeness is driving me wild. I want him right now, I don't think I can wait any longer.

There's a knock at the door.

'Ah,' says Miles, pulling away from me with a mischievous look in his eyes. 'I think that must be dinner.'

We eat a delicious feast, served to us on huge platters under silver cloches that are pulled off to reveal magnificent dishes. I'm starving and every mouthful is ambrosial, the pleasure heightened by the fact that I'm sitting opposite Miles. Every now and then I remember those soft murmured words and my insides roll over with pleasure and I sigh happily.

Meanwhile we talk, about Jacob and about how our relationship unfolded and then ended. Miles tells me about his plans for the future, now that he's not working for my father any more. He owns an estate in the wilds of Scotland – 'not like the kind of estates your friends own,' he says with a laugh – and he's dreamed of spending a few years there, running a very specialist survival school, passing on what he learned in the SAS.'

'A little time out of the rat race,' he says with a smile. 'No constant round of travel. I need to get away from mansions and penthouses and fancy hotels. A man can have a little too much of all that. It can leave him jaded, you know?'

I nod, thinking that wherever Miles is will be heaven, as far as I'm concerned.

'And what are you going to do, Freya?' he asks.

A stab of fear pierces me. 'What do you mean?' I'd just assumed we were going to be together now. 'Are you going to leave me?'

He smiles at me. 'This isn't going to be simple, sweetheart. That's why I left you at your father's – so that you could think clearly for a while about what you really want. You know what it will mean if we decide to be together. Your father won't like it. You could find yourself cut off, like Jacob.'

'I don't mind about that,' I say vehemently. 'I've thought about my old life – and I was totally miserable. Everything feels right with you and I can't give that up to go back to that other existence. It might be luxurious but it's empty and meaningless and unhappy. I mean it, Miles, don't make me go back!' I gaze at him earnestly, desperate for him to understand how much I mean this. 'Take me with you, wherever you're going.'

He stares at me, thoughtful. Then he takes a sip of his wine and says, 'If you're serious, and you've thought about what it might mean . . . then it might be an idea for you to disappear for a while. This fuss with Jacob isn't good. It needs to blow over and you can't be involved in it. I don't like what happened today one bit.'

'You mean . . . come away with you?' I catch my breath in excitement. Then my pleasure is doused. 'But they'll find me. I'll have to tell my father I'm safe, Jane-Elizabeth will know and then . . . then the world will know about five minutes after that. How can I get round it?'

'Leave it with me, I'll think of something. There's always an answer.'

I feel comforted again, and my happiness returns. I lean towards him, pushing away the remnants of my pudding. 'I would expect nothing less from a teacher. You're supposed to have all the answers, aren't you?'

He smiles at me, his eyes filling with desire mixed with tenderness, and its potency makes my pulse race with excitement. 'I may not have all the answers, Freya, but I have the one to the question you're asking right now.'

'Do you?' I say softly. 'Prove it.'

He stands up and walks round to me, lifting me to my feet in a smooth, strong moment, and pulling me to his chest. 'You'd better come with me,' he said. 'This lesson is a practical.'

CHAPTER TWENTY-FIVE

Hotel suites are made for love. The bed is huge, the linen luxurious, and we are utterly private. We kiss hungrily as we go from the table in the sitting room to the bedroom, taking off our clothes and strewing them behind us. We move together, not wanting to take our mouths from each other, as we unzip, unbutton and pull off our clothes with eager fingers. Miles's crisp shirt is left draped over the damask sofa, my navy dress is soon a silken puddle on the pale wool carpet. Each time a new bit of his skin is revealed, I want to worship it: the curve of his shoulder, the hard bulge of his bicep, the dark nipples in the sprinkling of black hair, the rippled torso. He's as hungry for me as I am for him, moaning with pleasure at the sight of my breasts rising from their black satin bra and running his hands round my waist. His tongue probes my mouth as I welcome it, relishing his taste, the passion in the way he wants to explore every part of me. My hands roam over his broad back as we reach our bedroom. We abandon our shoes in the doorway. I'm in my underwear now; Miles is still wearing his trousers but I don't want that to be the case for long. My hands are busy at his waistband and zipper. My fingertips brush against the hardness inside his boxer shorts and I'm filled with a rush of hot excitement.

Oh God, I've wanted this so much.

I'm shaking with need as I undo his trousers and push them downwards. He steps out of the trousers, leaving them on the floor. I can see the evidence of his desire now, the rearing erection that's pushing out the soft cotton of his shorts, and it makes my stomach flip over with longing. My sex pulses in response to the sight of Miles's massiveness, the iron-hard rod that I hope he'll soon be plunging into me.

He pulls me to him, pressing the hot length against my belly. It seems to reach all the way from the top of my mound to past my belly button and I gasp with longing for it. His strong arms envelop me, his mouth roughly taking possession of mine.

He lifts me up and I wrap my legs around him, then, still kissing me, he carries me with ease to the bed and lies me down there, our mouths parting reluctantly. I gaze up at him, panting, ready for him right now and yet not wanting to hurry this exquisite moment when we're burning with the anticipation of what's to come.

Miles reaches for two of the pillows and puts them under my bottom, raising me up to him so that my sex, still encased in black satin, is tilted towards him. Then he sinks down, his hands caressing my thighs, pushing them open slowly so that he can cover the soft skin with kisses. His tongue comes out to lick me. He kisses my knees, licking just underneath before nibbling with delicate tickling bites at the flesh of my inner thighs.

I'm gasping with the pleasure of it, arching my back as the light butterfly bites and kisses flutter up the inside of my legs, as his hands run down my calves, massage my feet and caress my toes. This feels so beautiful. One of my hand plays in his dark hair as his head moves about, tasting my skin, and other is at my breast, feeling my own curves, pinching the hard nipple under its satin covering, or running over my neck, my fingers at my mouth, feeling my tongue come out to play over them. I want Miles everywhere at once, his lips and fingers busy at every pleasure point. But he's tantalising me deliciously as he rubs his face across my thighs, sucking the skin, grazing his teeth over it. He's so close to where my hot juices are welling up, coating me with readiness for him. I'm twitching with the desire my little bud feels to have some of the attention Miles is lavishing on my legs. He pinches my toes and scratches lightly at the soles of my feet, making my clit swell and quiver with longing for the same treatment. His mouth is getting closer to me and I push my thighs wider apart so that he can reach me easily. He murmurs as his lips run right up to the top of my inner thigh.

'Oh, Winter, you're delicious. I've missed you so much. I have to taste you again.'

He slides my knickers down over my thighs. His mouth is close to my lips now, his nose pressing on my mound, his teasing breath running over my entrance and blowing lightly on my bud where it emerges, eager for his touch.

The tip of Miles's tongue touches me very gently, sending electric currents of pleasure sizzling along every nerve. He teases me with the soft tip, as it comes out to lick me in feather-light movements, going from just below my clit downwards towards my entrance. I want to press myself up to meet his face, but instead I try to control my panting breaths, licking my own lips and biting them with longing. Now he's back, moving upwards.

Take me in, Miles, kiss me and suck me, please . . .!

His mouth is at my clit now and I moan loudly as, at last, his tongue comes out to touch me, making a burst of pleasure explode through me, travelling outwards from my core. He starts to work on me, putting pressure on to my bud as he licks and kisses it. I can feel his fingers now, trailing up my thighs to where my entrance is hot and slippery, waiting for him with hungry need. As he nibbles and licks my bud, his fingers play there, teasing me as he presses one tip and then another into my hole. Then, as I gasp, he pushes in three fingers, reaching deep inside me.

I cry out, thrusting my hips up to meet his fingers, my hands pressing down on his head to make his mouth harder on my clit as his tongue flicks back and forth over it, making those electric tingles flash out all over me, bringing me closer to the brink.

'Miles! That's . . . oh God! That's beautiful!' I'm gasping as I talk, bucking my hips to his mouth.

He pulls away and a moment later, his wet mouth is on mine, his tongue covered with my juices plunging deep into me, twisting around mine so that I can taste myself on him.

He's between my thighs now, his hot erection pressing against me. Miles pulls his mouth from mine and presses his fingers between my lips. They're slippery too, ripe with the taste of my desire and I suck them eagerly, wrapping my tongue around them, caressing them, while I reach down to the huge hard cock that's pressing against me. I pull it out through the gap at the front of his shorts, and wrap my fingers around the hot girth. Massaging it against my palm, I move the skin up and down, taking it over the tip of his cock and making him groan with delight. He takes his fingers from my mouth and takes them back to my sex, where his fingertips begin to rub and tickle at my clit, smoothing down to my entrance to anoint them in the honeyed wetness there and then bringing them back to toy with me again.

I play with his cock while our tongues are entwined, but I don't know how long I can wait for him now. I'm ready to come from the unbearably delicious tickling on my clit and the way he suddenly pushes his fingers into my depths. I push at the cotton shorts he's still wearing and release him entirely from them. Now I can feel his flesh, the hardness of his muscle, his firm thighs and buttocks.

'Miles . . .' I pull away from his mouth and gaze up into his dark blue eyes that are burning into mine. 'I can't wait any longer. Please . . . fuck me . . .'

'Freya,' he moans. 'I want you so much. Your beautiful body . . .' He moves so that he's between my thighs, kneeling on the edge of the bed. I'm still propped on my cushions, my hips tilted up to him. He gazes down, evidently savouring the sight of my open sex. He puts one hand on my waist as if to stabilise me, and with the other holds his cock, ready to push it into me. He has to press it downwards so that it rests at my upturned entrance. I gasp as I feel its hot velvety tip against me.

'Yes, now, please . . .' I beg.

He makes a low sound in his throat, almost like a growl, as he thrusts forward slowly, pushing his cock home with that exquisite control that enables me to feel every centimetre as I widen and stretch around that hard width, and he fills me up to my belly. He goes in as deep as he can, until I can feel his balls against me and my breath comes in short shallow pants as though his cock is forcing it out of me, he's so far inside.

We're utterly joined now, as close as it's possible to be. I'm replete with him. We stay like that for a while, gazing at each other, relishing the beautiful sensations of my body tight around his, his hard penis inside me. If we could stay like this forever, I would. Is this heaven? Is it the closest thing to bliss we can ever know?

But we can't stay like this for too long, our bodies won't let us. His cock twitches with need inside me and we begin to answer the call of the ancient rhythm as he starts to thrust in and out, while I bring my hips up to meet him, my clit pressing against his body, taking pleasure from the friction as we fuck.

We make it last as long as we can, going as slowly as our bodies will let us, until the desire we have for each other builds to an irresistible pitch. The pillows beneath me are allowing him to reach so far inside, I feel as though he's found new depths within me. As we pick up pace, he puts his hands to my waists and moves me in time with his thrusts, fucking me harder and harder. I'm moaning loudly now, my own arms thrown out, my hands clutching at the covers with the force of the delight I'm experiencing.

Miles lets go of my waist and pulls me to him with one arm, his other taking his weight as he gasps and moans.

'Oh God, I'm going to come, Freya,' he pants. 'You're making me come, sweetheart, I can't stop it.'

His words send a powerful thrill over me, and my own excitement goes up a notch. Ripples of pleasure start flowing out from my core, heading for every nerve in my body. I know I'm about to come too. It's taking me up in steps, as though I'm climbing a staircase of pleasure. My whole body is seized by it as suddenly the convulsions come, each one engulfing me in a wave of harsh pleasure. My head is thrown back, twisting as I cry each time it takes me in its clutches and shakes me in its grip. It's so powerful it's almost close to unbearable. As my orgasm shatters around me, I can feel Miles's cock throbbing inside, swelling to its maximum as it shoots out his climax.

I'm almost sobbing as the waves diminish and leave me panting and exhausted, Miles collapsed on top of me, his breath loud in my ear, his weight heavy on me.

When I can speak again, I run my hand over his broad back. He's still hard inside me. 'That was beautiful. Thank you.'

'You're beautiful.' He turns his face to mine and kisses me gently. 'Thank *you*.' He smiles. 'I'm afraid it was rather a straightforward lesson this time. But heartfelt.'

I smile back. 'You know what? I must be a rather simple character after all. Because these ones are my favourite.'

Miles rolls off me and we lie together for long, silent minutes. I listen to his heart beating in his chest and run my fingers over the warmth of his skin. His hand holds my other, occasionally lifting it to his lips so that he can kiss my fingertips.

'Miles?' I say softly. I don't know if this is the time, but I have to know the truth before we can make any real decisions about our future.

'Hmm?'

'There's something I want to ask you . . . About your other girlfriend.'

He stiffens and says, 'My other girlfriend?' in a wary voice.

'Yes – the one you told me about. The one who died.'

He turns to look at me, frowning. 'My girlfriend who died . . .'

'Yes. You told me about her in the chalet in Klosters. I asked if you were running away from a woman and you said yes, but that she was dead.'

He nods slowly. 'Oh yes. I remember. But what makes you think she was my girlfriend?'

'Wasn't she?' I ask, surprised. 'I just assumed . . .'

Miles sighs and closes his eyes for a moment. 'No. She wasn't my girlfriend. I never met her – not properly anyway.'

There's a pause while I take this in. 'You never *met* her?' I almost hold my breath waiting for his answer.

'I left the army because I failed her. She was called Emma Trent, and she was one of life's good guys. Born into a solid happy family, given a good education and everything she could want . . . and she decides to spend her life giving back what she can. Emma went to a top university, studied medicine and could have had a very comfortable life and career. But instead she went to Afghanistan to help the people there, working for nothing and risking her life for others.'

I'm very quiet, listening hard.

'She spent three years saving lives and helping the sick and wounded, and women and children. Then one day she and three other aid workers were taken prisoner by a unit of rebel fighters, probably Taliban, and shut away in a compound. Special forces were called in to mastermind their release. She was allowed to speak to us by telephone a couple of times, to act as a translator and I told her not to worry, that we would get her out of there. She trusted me. The orders came to storm the compound and release the prisoners but the whole thing was a shambles. The rebels panicked. They shot all the prisoners. They were dead before we could reach them. All we were left with at the end was a stack of dead bodies, including Emma Trent, with all her kindness and hopes and dreams and her complete belief that I would get her out.'

I bite my lip, tears in my eyes. 'I'm so sorry,' I whisper.

'Not half as sorry as I was. I couldn't stay there after that. I'd lost my nerve somehow. You have to have faith in your-self to succeed in the kind of crazy missions we're sent on, and I didn't have it after Emma died. I just saw hopeless-ness. The way people slaughter each other for no real reason. I couldn't be part of it any more. So I left.' He looks at me with a wry smile. 'I thought that looking after spoiled rich girls would be as far away from Emma Trent as I could get.'

I feel as though I deserve the stab of pain that comment provokes in me. He's right. One Emma Trent is worth ten of me. I'm possessed by a deep yearning to be more worthy of his love and to earn his admiration.

'But,' he goes on, 'I didn't realise that you'd need me just as much as she did. To survive and to get through. I didn't understand that rich girls can be unhappy, and that your challenges may be different, but they matter too. Everyone suffers in life, I suppose, and who's to judge what the degrees of suffering are?'

'You've saved my life,' I say sincerely. 'Not just that day on the mountain, or in Jacob's flat. You've given me hope and love.'

Miles turns to me so that we lie facing each other, our cheeks almost touching, our lips close, as we stare into each other's eyes. 'You've given the same to me,' he murmurs. 'Hope and love. Love and hope.'

'I think that means we have to be together,' I say softly, my heart welling up with love for him.

'You know what?' He kisses the tip of my nose. 'So do I. I think we're going to have to make it happen, Winter . . .'

I sigh happily. 'Looks like I haven't graduated yet!'

'Are you kidding? You're still a junior. We've got plenty to learn together yet.'

'As long as we're together, I'm happy to be taught by you forever.' I kiss him on the lips and we begin to touch the tips of our tongues together, opening our mouths into a deep kiss.

Suddenly I pull away and sit up, saying loudly, 'Rhino!'

'What?' Miles sits up too, laughing. 'What do you mean, rhino?'

'And Mandy!' I say, almost stuttering in my excitement. 'Of course, Mandy!'

'What are you talking about?' He looks at me bewildered.

I clutch at him and say hotly, 'It's not Jane-Elizabeth. She didn't do it. She didn't tell the press anything. It was Estella.'

Miles stares at me. 'How do you know that?'

'Because she told me herself! I expect she thought she was being very clever.' I laugh at the memory of it. 'She was talking about me finding something to do with myself and we were talking about charity work, and she said something about me helping Mandys and other fallen women – or *saving the rhino*!' I gaze at Miles, my eyes bright.

He shakes his head, still puzzled. 'It's no clearer, I'm afraid.'

'Estella must have just watched that tape of Jacob. She got her hands on it somehow. He was filmed having sex with call girls and one of them was called Mandy! She's mentioned on the tape. That's where Estella got the name from. And Jacob has a tattoo of a rhino, and the camera was on it for ages. She was letting me know that she'd seen the tape but enjoying the joke, thinking I wouldn't guess.' I blink as thoughts flood into my mind. 'I bet Jane-Elizabeth doesn't know that Estella has hacked her email and is rifling through my father's office. I've got to warn her.' I make to get out of bed, but Miles pulls me back, embracing me in his strong arms again.

'Hey,' he says, 'calm down. For one thing, it's late. And for another, we need to think this through. If you're right, then any message you send to Jane-Elizabeth will be intercepted by Estella. You'll need to take your time and think of a strategy.'

'You're right,' I say, relaxing. 'I got carried away.' I nuzzle into his shoulder. 'No one knows we're here. We're safe. We'll come up with a plan together, won't we?'

'Yes. And something tells me that we're going to be a formidable team.' He kisses me gently.

I sigh. 'I'm so happy though! So happy that it's not Jane-Elizabeth after all. I don't know how I could have suspected her.' I rub my cheek against him. Fatigue envelopes me in a kind of blissful torpor. I yawn.

'You're tired, Freya. Time to go to sleep. I'll be with you in the morning and we can make our plans.'

My eyes start to close. 'But we'll be together, won't we? You won't leave me?'

'We'll be together, Freya, I promise. I'm not going to leave you.'

Wrapped tight in his arms, I fall asleep, knowing that the nightmares won't come any more. I'm safe again, sheltered from the storm in Miles's arms.

ACKNOWLEDGEMENTS

My thanks to everyone involved in the creation of this book, particularly to Francesca, my very patient editor, to Justine for her wonderful copyediting and to Clare for proofreading the script. I thank the Hodder team for all their splendid support and hard work, especially Carolyn and Emilie. I also want to mention my agent Lizzy and her assistant Harriet, for their unfailing support and work on my behalf.

Thanks to all my readers and the many lovely messages I get over Twitter – I value your enthusiasm and encouragement very much!

You'll be captivated by the second novel in Sadie
Matthew's exhilarating, intoxicating Seasons
Quartet series, coming soon . . .

SEASON OF PASSION

Flora Hammond is trying to make her dream of being an
actress come true by studying her craft in Paris. But she cannot
escape her privileged background and the paranoia of her
wealthy father who is obsessive about his daughters' safety.
The situation is not helped by the fact that Flora's older sister,
Freya, has just run off with her bodyguard.

Drawn into the family scandal, Flora tries to make peace
between the warring factions. In the meantime, her path crosses
with that of a mysterious businessman, Andrei Dubrovski, and
there is an instant attraction between them. Even though Flora
is warned off getting involved with him, she doesn't think she
can resist. Is Freya right when she claims that their father's girlfriend Estella is engaged in a campaign against the sisters? And
where has Freya disappeared to? Does Estella have the power
to split the family apart, even to the point of breaking the bond
between Flora and her twin sister, Summer?

As Flora's obsession with Andrei grows, it's clear that where
passion is concerned, the heart has its reasons . . .

HODDER

Have you read the After Dark series by Sadie Matthews? Deeply intense and romantic, provocative and sensual, it will take you to a place where love and sex are liberated from their limits.

Read on for a taste of the first book in the series . . .

FIRE AFTER DARK

It started with a spark . . .

Everything changed when I met Dominic. My heart had just been broken, split into jagged fragments that can jigsaw together to make me look enough like a normal, happy person.

Dominic has shown me a kind of abandonment I've never known before. He takes me down a path of pure pleasure, but of pain, too – his love offers me both lightness and dark. And where he leads me, I have no choice but to follow.

Out now in ebook, paperback and audio

HODDER

CHAPTER ONE

The city takes my breath away as it stretches beyond the taxi windows, rolling past like giant scenery being unfurled by an invisible stagehand. Inside the cab, I'm cool, quiet and untouchable. Just an observer. But out there, in the hot stickiness of a July afternoon, London is moving hard and fast: traffic surges along the lanes and people throng the streets, herds of them crossing roads whenever the lights change. Bodies are everywhere, of every type, age, size and race. Millions of lives are unfolding on this one day in this one place. The scale of it all is overwhelming.

What have I done?

As we skirt a huge green space colonised by hundreds of sunbathers, I wonder if this is Hyde Park. My father told me that Hyde Park is bigger than Monaco. Imagine that. Monaco might be small, but even so. The thought makes me shiver and I realise I'm frightened. That's odd because I don't consider myself a cowardly person.

Anyone would be nervous, I tell myself firmly. But it's no surprise my confidence has been shot after everything that's happened lately. The familiar sick feeling churns in my stomach and I damp it down.

Not today. I've got too much else to think about. Besides, I've done enough thinking and crying. That's the whole reason I'm here.

'Nearly there, love,' says a voice suddenly, and I realise it's the taxi driver, his voice distorted by the intercom. I see him watching me in the rear-view mirror. 'I know a good short cut from here,' he says, 'no need to worry about all this traffic.'

'Thanks,' I say, though I expected nothing less from a London cabbie; after all, they're famous for their knowledge of the city's streets, which is why I decided to splurge on one instead of wrestling with the Underground system. My luggage isn't enormous but I didn't relish the idea of heaving it on and off trains and up escalators in the heat. I wonder if the driver is assessing me, trying to guess what on earth I'm doing going to such a prestigious address when I look so young and ordinary; just a girl in a flowery dress, red cardigan and flip-flops, with sunglasses perched in hair that's tied in a messy ponytail, strands escaping everywhere.

'First time in London, is it?' he asks, smiling at me via the mirror.

'Yes, that's right,' I say. That isn't strictly true. I came as a girl at Christmas once with my parents and I remember a noisy blur of enormous shops, brightly lit windows, and a Santa whose nylon trousers crackled as I sat on his knee, and whose polyester white beard scratched me softly on the cheek. But I don't feel like getting into a big discussion with the driver, and anyway the city is as good as foreign to me. It's my first time alone here, after all.

'On your own, are you?' he asks and I feel a little uncomfortable, even though he's only being friendly.

'No, I'm staying with my aunt,' I reply, lying again.

He nods, satisfied. We're pulling away from the park now, darting with practised agility between buses and cars, swooping past cyclists, taking corners quickly and flying through amber traffic lights. Then we're off the busy main roads and in narrow streets lined by high brick-and-stone mansions with tall windows, glossy front doors, shining black iron railings, and window boxes spilling with bright blooms. I can sense money everywhere, not just in the expensive cars parked at the roadsides, but in the perfectly kept buildings, the clean pavements, the half-glimpsed maids closing curtains against the sunshine.

'She's doing all right, your aunt,' jokes the driver as we turn into a small street, and then again into one even smaller. 'It costs a penny or two to live around here.'

I laugh but don't reply, not knowing what to say. On one side of the street is a mews converted into minute but no doubt eye-wateringly pricy houses, and on the other a large mansion of flats, filling up most of the block and going up six storeys at least. I can tell from its Art Deco look that it was built in the 1930s; the outside is grey, dominated by a large glass-and-walnut door. The driver pulls up in front of it and says, 'Here we are then. Randolph Gardens.'

I look out at all the stone and asphalt. 'Where are the gardens?' I say wonderingly. The only greenery visible is the hanging baskets of red and purple geraniums on either side of the front door.

'There would have been some here years ago, I expect,' he replies. 'See the mews? That was stables at one time. I bet there were a couple of big houses round here once. They'll have been demolished or bombed in the war, maybe.' He glances at his meter. 'Twelve pounds seventy, please, love.'

I fumble for my purse and hand over fifteen pounds, saying, 'Keep the change,' and hoping I've tipped the right amount. The driver doesn't faint with surprise, so I guess it must be all right. He waits while I get myself and my luggage out of the cab and on to the pavement and shut the door behind me. Then he does an expert three-point turn in the tight little street and roars off back into the action.

I look up. So here I am. My new home. For a while, at least.

The white-haired porter inside looks up at me enquiringly as I puff through the door and up to his desk with my large bag.

'I'm here to stay in Celia Reilly's flat,' I explain, resisting the urge to wipe away the perspiration on my forehead. 'She said the key would be here for me.'

'Name?' he says gruffly.

'Beth. I mean, Elizabeth. Elizabeth Villiers.'

'Let me see . . .' He snuffles into his moustache as he looks through a file on his desk. 'Ah, yes. Here we are. Miss E. Villiers. To occupy 514 in Miss Reilly's absence.' He fixes me with a beady but not unfriendly gaze. 'Flat-sitting, are you?'

'Yes. Well. Cat-sitting, really.' I smile at him but he doesn't return it.

'Oh yes. She does have a cat. Can't think why a creature like that would want to live its life inside but there we are. Here are the keys.' He pushes an envelope across the desk towards me. 'If you could just sign the book for me.'

I sign obediently and he tells me a few of the building regulations as he directs me towards the lift. He offers to take my luggage up for me later but I say I'll do it myself. At least that way I'll have everything I need. A moment later I'm inside the small elevator, contemplating my heated, red-faced reflection as the lift ascends slowly to the fifth floor. I don't look anywhere near as polished as the surroundings, but my heart-shaped face and round blue eyes will never be like the high-cheek-boned, elegant features I most admire. And my fly-away dark-blonde shoulder-length hair will never be the naturally thick, lustrous tresses I've always craved. My hair takes work and usually I can't be bothered, just pulling it back into a messy ponytail.

'Not exactly a Mayfair lady,' I say out loud. As I stare at myself, I can see the effect of everything that has happened lately. I'm thinner around the face, and there's a sadness in my eyes that never seems to go away. I look a bit smaller, somehow, as though I've bowed a little under the weight of my misery. 'Be strong,' I whisper to myself, trying to find my old spark in my dull gaze. That's why I've come, after all. Not because I'm trying to escape – although that must be part of it – but because I want to rediscover the old me, the one who had spirit and courage and a curiosity in the world.

Unless that Beth has been completely destroyed.

I don't want to think like that but it's hard not to.

Number 514 is halfway down a quiet, carpeted hallway. The keys fit smoothly into the lock and a moment later I'm stepping inside the flat. My first impression is surprise as a small chirrup greets me, followed by a high squeaky miaow, soft warm fur brushing over my legs, and a body snaking between my calves, nearly tripping me up.

'Hello, hello!' I exclaim, looking down into a small black whiskered face with a halo of dark fur, squashed up like a cushion that's been sat on. 'You must be De Havilland.'

He miaows again, showing me sharp white teeth and a little pink tongue.

I try to look about while the cat purrs frantically, rubbing himself hard against my legs, evidently pleased to see me. I'm inside a hall and I can see already that Celia has stayed true to the building's 1930s aesthetic. The floor is tiled black and white, with a white cashmere rug in the middle. A jet-black console table sits beneath a large Art Deco mirror flanked by geometric chrome lights. On the console is a huge white silver-rimmed china bowl with vases on either side. Everything is elegant and quietly beautiful.

I haven't expected anything else. My father has been irritatingly vague about his godmother's flat, which he saw on the few occasions he visited London, but he's always given me the impression that it is as glamorous as Celia herself. She started as a model in her teens and was very successful, making a lot of money, but later she gave it up and became a fashion journalist. She married once and divorced, and then again and was widowed. She never had children, which is perhaps why she's managed to stay so young and vibrant, and she's been a lackadaisical godmother to my father, swooping in and out of his life as it took her fancy. Sometimes he heard nothing from her for years, then she'd appear out of the blue loaded with gifts, always elegant and dressed in the height of fashion, smothering him with kisses and trying to make up for her neglect. I remember meeting her on a few occasions, when I was a shy, knock-kneed girl in shorts and a T-shirt, hair all over the place, who could never imagine being as polished and sophisticated as this woman in front of me, with her cropped silver hair, amazing clothes and splendid jewellery.

What am I saying? Even now, I can't imagine being like her. Not for a moment.

And yet, here I am, in her apartment which is all mine for five weeks.

The phone call came without warning. I hadn't paid attention until my father got off the phone, looking bemused and said to me, 'Do you fancy a spell in London, Beth? Celia's going away, she needs someone to look after her cat and she thought you might appreciate the chance to stay in her flat.'

'Her flat?' I'd echoed, looking up from my book. 'Me?'

'Yes. It's somewhere rather posh, I think. Mayfair, Belgravia, somewhere like that. I've not been there for years.' He shot a look at my mother, with his eyebrows raised. 'Celia's off on a retreat in the woods of Montana for five weeks. Apparently she needs to be spiritually renewed. As you do.'

'Well, it keeps her young,' my mother replied, wiping down the kitchen table. 'It's not every seventy-two-year-old who could even think of it.' She stood up and stared at the scrubbed wood a little wistfully. 'I think it sounds rather nice, I'd love to do something like that.'

She had a look on her face as if contemplating other paths she might have taken, other lives she might have lived. My father obviously wanted to say something jeering but stopped when he saw her expression. I was pleased about that: she'd given up her career when she married him, and devoted herself to looking after me and my brothers. She was entitled to her dreams, I guess.

My father turned to me. 'So, what do you think, Beth? Are you interested?'

Mum looked at me and I saw it in her eyes at once. She wanted me to go. She knew it was the best thing possible under the circumstances. 'You should do it,' she said quietly. 'It'll be a new leaf for you after what's happened.'

I almost shuddered. I couldn't bear it to be spoken of. My face flushed with mortification. 'Don't,' I whispered as tears filled my eyes. The wound was still so open and raw.

My parents exchanged looks and then my father said gruffly, 'Perhaps your mother's right. You could do with getting out and about.'

I'd hardly been out of the house for over a month. I couldn't bear the idea of seeing them together. Adam and Hannah. The thought of it made my stomach swoop sickeningly towards my feet, and my head buzz as though I was going to faint.

'Maybe,' I said in a small voice. 'I'll think about it.'

We didn't decide that evening. I was finding it hard enough just to get up in the morning, let alone take a big decision like that. My confidence in myself was so shot, I wasn't sure that I could make the right choice about what to have for lunch let alone whether I should accept Celia's offer. After all, I'd chosen Adam, and trusted him and look how that had turned out. The next day my mother called Celia and talked through some of the practical aspects, and that evening I called her myself. Just listening to her strong voice, full of enthusiasm and confidence, made me feel better.

'You'll be doing me a favour, Beth,' she said firmly, 'but I think you'll enjoy yourself too. It's time you got out of that dead-end place and saw something of the world.'

Celia was an independent woman, living her life on her own terms and if she believed I could do it, then surely I could. So I said yes. Even though, as the time to leave home came closer, I wilted and began to wonder if I could pull out somehow, I knew I had to do it. If I could pack my bags and go alone to one of the biggest cities in the world, then maybe there was hope for me. I loved the little Norfolk town where I'd grown up, but if all I could do was huddle at home, unable to face the world because of what Adam had done, then I ought to give up and sign out right now. And what did I have to keep me there? There was my part-time job in a local cafe that I'd been doing since I was fifteen, only stopping when I went off to university and then picking it up again when I got back, still wondering what I was going to do with my life. My parents? Hardly. They didn't want me living in my old room and moping about. They dreamed of more for me than that.

The truth was that I'd come back because of Adam. My university friends were off travelling before they started exciting new jobs or moved to other countries. I'd listened to all the adventures waiting for them, knowing that my future was waiting for me back home. Adam was the centre of my world, the only man I'd ever loved, and there had been no question of doing anything but being with him. Adam worked, as he had since school, for his father's building company that he expected one day to own himself, and he was happy enough to contemplate living for the rest of his life in the same place he'd grown up. I didn't know if that was for me, but I did know that I loved Adam and I could put my own desires to travel and explore on hold for a while so that we could be together.

Except that now I didn't have any choice.

De Havilland yowls at my ankles and gives one a gentle nip to remind me that he's there.

'Sorry, puss,' I say apologetically, and put my bag down. 'Are you hungry?'

The cat stays twined around my legs as I try and find the kitchen, opening the door to a coat cupboard and another to a loo before discovering a small galley kitchen, with the cat's bowls neatly placed under the window at the far end. They're licked completely clean and De Havilland is obviously eager for his next meal. On the small white dining table at the other end, just big enough for two, I see some packets of cat biscuits and a sheaf of paper. On top is a note written in large scrawling handwriting.

Darling, hello!

You made it. Good. Here is De Havilland's food. Feed him twice a day, just fill the little bowl with his biscuits as if you were putting out cocktail snacks, lucky De H. He'll need nice clean water to go with it. All other instructions in the useful little pack below, but really, darling, there are no rules. Enjoy yourself.

See you in five weeks,

C xx

Beneath are typed pages with all the necessary information about the cat's litter tray, the workings of the appliances, where to find the boiler and the first aid kit, and who to talk to if I have any problems. The porter downstairs looks like my first port of call. My porter of call. Hey, if I'm making jokes, even weak ones, then maybe this trip is working already.

De Havilland is miaowing in a constant rolling squeak, his little pink tongue quivering as he stares up at me with his dark yellow eyes.

'Dinner coming up,' I say.

When De Havilland is happily crunching away, his water bowl refreshed, I look around the rest of the flat, admiring the black-and-white bathroom with its chrome and Bakelite fittings, and taking in the gorgeous bedroom: the silver four-poster bed with a snowy cover piled high with white cushions, and the ornate chinoiserie wallpaper where brightly plumaged parrots observe each other through blossomed cherry tree branches. A vast silver gilt mirror hangs over the fireplace and an antique mirrored dressing table stands by the window, next to a purple velvet button-back armchair.

'It's beautiful,' I say out loud. Maybe here I'll absorb some of Celia's chic and acquire some style myself.

As I walk through the hallway into the sitting room I realise that it's better than I dreamed it could be. I imagined a smart place that reflected the life of a well-off, independent woman but this is something else, like no home I've ever seen before. The sitting room is a large room decorated in cool calm colours of pale green and stone, with accents of black, white and silver. The era of the thirties is wonderfully evoked in the shapes of the furniture, the low armchairs with large curving arms, the long sofa piled with white cushions, the clean line of a swooping chrome reading lamp and the sharp edges of a modern coffee table in jet-black lacquer. The far wall is dominated by a vast built-in white bookcase filled with volumes and ornaments including wonderful pieces of jade and Chinese sculpture. The long wall that faces the window is painted in that serene pale green broken up by panels of silver lacquer etched with delicate willows, the shiny surfaces acting almost like mirrors. Between the panels are wall lights with shades of frosted white glass and on the parquet floor is a huge antique zebra-skin rug.

I'm enchanted at this delightful evocation of an age of elegance. I love everything I see from the crystal vases made to hold the thick dark stems and ivory trumpets of lilies to the matching Chinese ginger pots on either side of the shining chrome fireplace, above which is a huge and important-looking piece of modern art that, on closer inspection, I see is a Patrick

Heron: great slashes of colour – scarlet, burnt orange, umber and vermillion – creating wonderful hectic drama in that oasis of cool grassy green and white.

I stare around, open-mouthed. I had no idea people actually created rooms like this to live in, full of beautiful things and immaculately kept. It's not like home, which is comforting and lovely but always full of mess and piles of things we've discarded.

My eye is drawn to the window that stretches across the length of the room. There are old-style venetian blinds that normally look old-fashioned, but are just right here. Apart from that, the windows are bare, which surprises me as they look directly out towards another block of flats. I go over and look out. Yes, hardly any distance away is another identical mansion block.

How strange. They're so close! Why have they built them like this?

I peer out, trying to get my bearings. Then I begin to understand. The building has been constructed in a U shape around a large garden. Is this the garden of Randolph Gardens? I can see it below me and to the left, a large green square full of bright flower beds, bordered by plants and trees in the full flush of summer. There are gravel paths, a tennis court, benches and a fountain as well as a plain stretch of grass where a few people are sitting, enjoying the last of the day's heat. The building stretches around three sides of the garden so that most of the inhabitants get a garden view. But the U shape has a small narrow corridor that connects the garden sides of the U to the one that fronts the road, and the single column of flats on each side of it face directly into each other. There are seven altogether and Celia's is on the fifth floor, looking straight into its opposite number, closer than they would be if they were divided by a street.

Was the flat cheaper because of this? I think idly, looking over at the window opposite. No wonder there are all these pale colours and the reflecting silver panels: the flat definitely has its light quota reduced being close to the others. *But then, it's all about location, right? It's still Mayfair.*

The last of the sunshine has vanished from this side of the building and the room has sunk into a warm darkness. I go towards one of the lamps to turn it on, and my eye is caught by a glowing golden square through the window. It's the flat opposite, where the lights are on and the interior is brightly illuminated like the screen in a small cinema or the stage in the theatre. I can see across quite clearly, and I stop short, drawing in my breath. There is a man in the room that is exactly across from this one. That's not so strange, maybe, but the fact that he is naked to the waist, wearing only a pair of dark trousers, grabs my attention. I realise I'm standing stock still as I notice that he is talking on a telephone while he walks languidly about his sitting room, unwittingly displaying an impressive torso. Although I can't make out his features all that clearly, I can see that he is good looking too, with thick black hair and a classically symmetrical face with strong dark brows. I can see that he has broad shoulders, muscled arms, a well-defined chest and abs, and that he is tanned as though just back from somewhere hot.

I stare, feeling awkward. Does this man know I can see into his apartment like this while he walks about half naked? But I guess that as mine is in shadow, he has no way of knowing there's anyone home to observe him.